I0649068

Roses from San Gabriel

a novel

by Jose Sevilla Ho

ABOUT THE AUTHOR

Jose Sevilla Ho was born in the Philippines in 1961. He went to study film directing at the Moscow Film Institute and lived in Russia for seven years. He has since worked as a university lecturer in the Philippines, Hong Kong, and Singapore, teaching film theory and screenwriting. He now lives in the United States with his wife and daughter. This is his first novel.

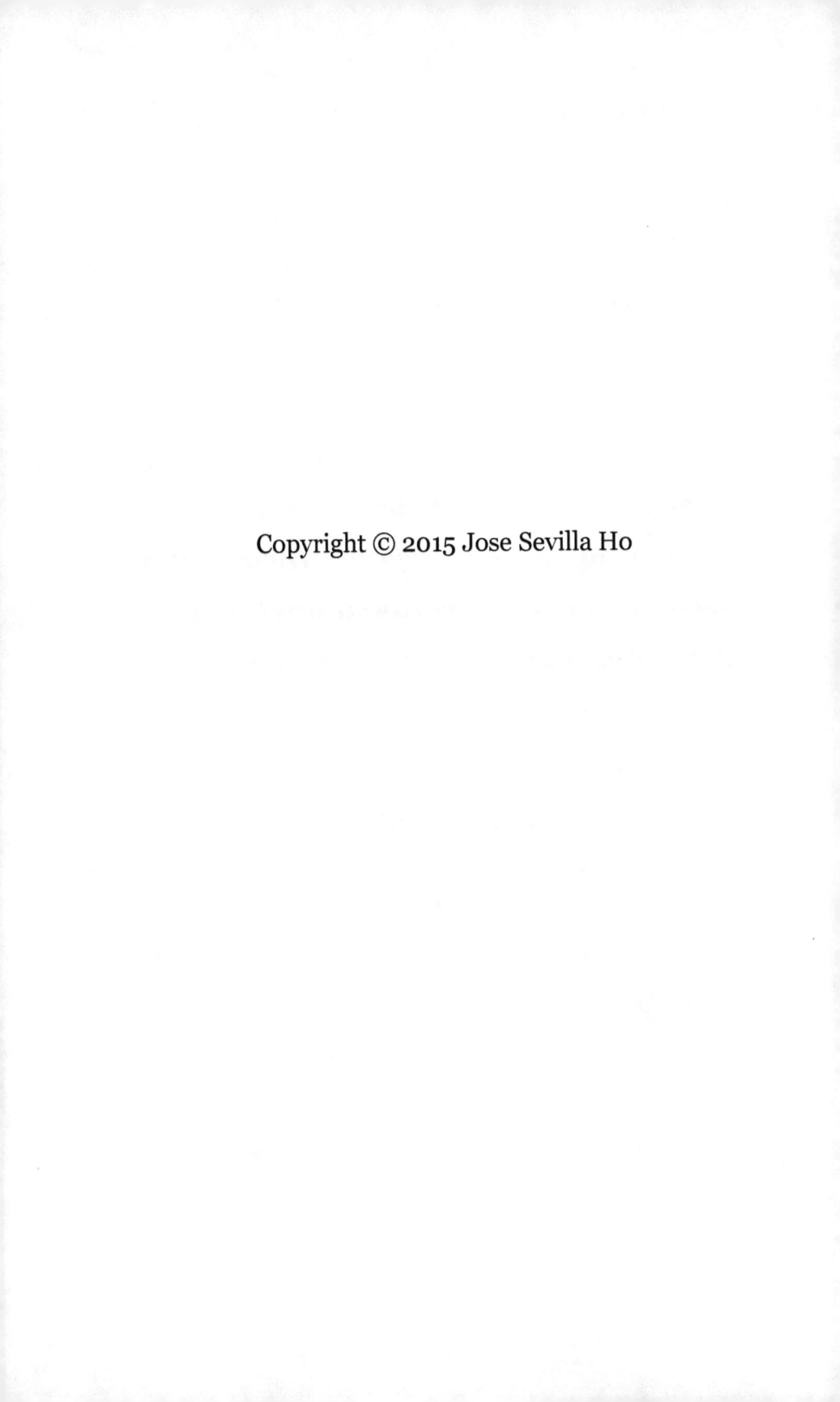
Copyright © 2015 Jose Sevilla Ho

"Like in the wilderness on some high tree, all the birds living with their mates assemble in the evening and at dawn disperse, so are the separations of the world."

Gautama Buddha

To my wife Marie Frail,

and my daughter Nadia

PROLOGUE

Three years before their mother Rosanna died, she found someone who loved her more than their father. That day in July she got up at dawn. She had slept through the roar of the monsoon storm, a downpour like it would flood the world. In her dream a sunbeam entered the bedroom to wake her up. When she opened her eyes, the light was shining between the curtains. The rain had stopped.

The streets were empty and the car's wheels splashed through the puddles. Birds were beginning to sing as they sped through the city towards the pier. Rosanna opened the window. The engine seemed to be making too much noise as they crawled through the narrow space between the houses. They passed the plaza and reached the docks. The car came to a halt. Rosanna stepped out on the slippery ground, black with grease. There was a gentle sea breeze as she joined the trickle of pedestrians making their way towards the gate.

She stopped. The chauffeur was following her, carrying her bag. She reached out for it. 'Just put it down.'

She spoke curtly to him. She was afraid he sensed the trembling in her heart, her fear about what she had set out to do. She grabbed the small overnight bag and walked through the gate. Her long black hair was tied in a single braid, which reached down almost to the small of her back. She was a young woman with small shoulders, a soft oval face with oriental eyes, and dark Hispanic features.

The chauffeur was still following her, tall, stooping to keep his head somewhat level with hers, his expression dumb and inquiring.

Rosanna stopped walking. 'I'll be all right,' she said to him. 'Just go back.'

He made an effort to comply. He stepped away from the people streaming towards the ferries, but a flush of hesitation made him stay where he was, waiting for more instructions.

'I'll walk to Fort Road from here,' Rosanna said. 'Sara's house is just around the corner.'

He nodded his head.

'I'll stay with them a few days,' Rosanna tried to explain. 'I'll come back myself.'

He stood waiting.

'Just *go*.'

The chauffeur finally turned and left.

Rosanna was relieved. She had lied easily. But as she climbed the gangway she remembered how they had passed Sara's house on Fort Road, the chauffeur had slowed down, expecting her to get off. But she had told him to drive on.

It was all a lie. She had never intended to go to Sara's house so early in the morning. Her real intention was to catch the ferry for San Gabriel.

That was the reason for the lie. The reason for travelling to San Gabriel was less simple, and its secret made her embarrassed. It made her aware that of all the decent people making the trip this day, she alone was here on a furtive mission of love.

At last she was on the deck, laying her bag down against the railing. Passengers had already taken their places on the long benches laid out below the portholes. She looked out over the sea. The scent of roses reached her, so light it seemed to come from her dreams. The water was glassy. The first crates of flowers were arriving on small boats gliding in from San Gabriel.

At a command from the bridge, the gangway was rolled away and stowed. Hectoring shouts went back and forth among the workmen on the quay, then, with a tremor from deep below their feet, the vessel shook into life. Rosanna watched the multicoloured whorls and dimples in the water as the gap widened between them and the quay.

The ferry gave a shudder and then they were floating out to sea. Birds flew shrieking above them. Rosanna glanced back. The sun was rising over Puerto Reina. Gold glinted on the edges of the town that used to be the last port in the most remote dominion of Spain. Before then it was known only to traders from Malacca. Now it lay sleeping, safe in its recess of a far, uncharted ocean. *I loved you since I saw you on the terrace with the sunbeam in your hair.*

Rosanna fingered the note. It had come with the roses she received long ago from San Gabriel. *Love so brittle it shatters in your hands.*

She felt sad. The mystery that had kept her spellbound for a time was now over. What happened that it ended as soon as it had begun? Would she ever know?

Towards dusk the ferry entered the strait of San Gabriel. The water was very clear and a huge shadow that used to be mistaken for the wreck of a sunken ship could be seen below them. Rosanna remembered seeing it from before, on her first trip to the island. But looking at it now, she felt as if she was seeing a part of her life that could no longer be salvaged.

San Gabriel came into view. There were gasps of awe among the passengers. The sight of the beautiful old town awakened in Rosanna an old enchantment. The terrace over the bay peered out like something from a dream.

As they coasted into port, Rosanna got a whiff of the old scents: the flowering of flame trees mingling with the earth's warm breath through the foliage; last light falling as dusk gathered over the harbour. She closed her eyes for a moment and realised that something had drawn her with fatal force into the past.

The ferry quickly emptied. Rosanna found her way across the wharf to the road that curved back into town. Kerosene lamps glowed in the shops and houses. The purple tinge in the sky was fading.

She reached the avenue of old acacias and knew she was back in the only place where she could plumb the mystery that had once made her happy but now left her strangely bereft. She studied the florist's address on the gold-embossed card. She found the place and went in, sliding the card across the countertop. 'Did you send this?' she asked.

The attendant looked at it and nodded. 'The order came from there,' he said, pointing across the road.

Rosanna went back into walked past a noisy café. The smoky rowdiness that came from inside reminded her of years ago when she and her friends had just arrived, anxious to explore the town.

The street ended in a cul-de-sac and she found herself in front of a house with a balcony on the second floor. Rosanna was nervous. Then she remembered. *A rose is for awakening the secret senses.*

She knocked on the door. A latch was pulled back. Rosanna felt her knees weaken. She looked around. Would she now meet the man who had loved her secretly all these years?

The door opened.

Would he still love her?

A face peered out.

Rosanna straightened up.

An old woman was staring out at her.

Was she the man's mother? His wife?

'Yes?'

Rosanna faltered. 'Someone's been sending me roses...'

'Go to the florist.'

'I just did.' Rosanna looked into the room. Dark drapes were drawn over the windows. Separated by a wooden screen, under a red Chinese lantern, was a table covered with dark velvet, worn out in places where cards were shuffled and laid out. A distant memory came to her from the time when she and Sara had chanced upon the fortune-teller's shop and had dared each other to go in.

'And?' the old woman demanded.

Rosanna smiled. 'You're a fortune-teller?'

The woman's face hardened. 'I am.'

Rosanna moved closer. 'Perhaps, I'd like...a reading.'

The woman's face relaxed. She stepped away from the door. 'Come inside.'

She led the way to the table behind the screen. The room was dark. The only light came from dim lamps in the corners. Last light lingered in the sky outside. In the room it was a cool and timeless night.

Rosanna sat down. It was difficult to discern, but she sensed a large space beyond the wooden screen. The old woman slowly gathered up the cards. Then sat down wearily and faced Rosanna. She was heavy and moving about seemed to cause her strain. Behind the thick glasses, her eyes were small and intent. She squinted at the cards like they were distant objects. Their meaning was vital if she could only get them in focus.

Rosanna found it hard to imagine the link between this woman and the roses she had been receiving.

The old woman gave her a smile. 'What aspect of your life is of interest?'

'Love, I suppose,' answered Rosanna after a momentary pause.

The woman closed her eyes and nodded. 'Ah, yes.' She tapped the table with the cards and put them aside.

'Secret love,' Rosanna said, leaning forward.

'Oh?' The woman looked at her more closely.

'A man's been sending me roses,' the young woman explained. 'He sends beautiful notes, but never signs them.'

The fortune-teller nodded, gave her a small smile. She picked up a jug and poured Rosanna a glass of water.

She took a sip, then continued. In the old woman's odd acceptance, the small, encouraging smiles, in the room that seemed forever dark, Rosanna found it possible to disclose everything that had been causing her torment and shame.

'It began a year after I got married,' she said.

'Do you love your husband?'

Rosanna was taken aback. 'Well...'

The old woman continued in an even voice, 'Your marriage is dead. Full of regret.'

Rosanna tried to find the words to form a reply. But all she felt was the cold and sullen void that had made her plot for days, then lie to everyone to come here.

'Yes,' she said, surprised that it made her feel good to admit it to someone. 'I realised long ago. I had made a great mistake.'

The old woman watched her with her undisturbed gaze. Rosanna felt there was no need to be ashamed and wanted to tell the old woman more. 'But in all those years that the roses came, I felt there was something to live for.'

'Do you love this man?' said the fortune-teller. 'Even though you still don't know him?'

'Perhaps,' the young woman replied.

'Why?'

Rosanna sat for a while in the darkness. Then she said, 'Because, now that the roses have stopped coming, I'm afraid.'

'Afraid of what?'

Rosanna answered softly. 'Afraid something in me will die.'

The fortune-teller sat lost in thought for some time. Rosanna felt embarrassed, wondering if she had confessed too much. Her hand curled anxiously on her chest.

Then at last, as if returning from somewhere far away, the old woman shifted in her seat and sighed. She turned around and pulled herself closer to the table, flipping thoughtfully through the cards.

She looked up and there was a sad look in her eyes. 'Ah,' she said. 'So you are the one.'

Rosanna waited.

'Long ago, a young man came to see me.'

Rosanna sat forward. 'When?'

The fortune-teller strained to remember, glancing first at the lamp above her, then at the cards. She smiled. 'Some six years ago.'

'I was here six years ago,' said Rosanna.

The old woman fixed her gaze on the shadows. 'Yes. It may have been around the time. He arrived one afternoon, looking very troubled. He demanded to know what would happen in his life...'

Her face had taken on a wistful languor, and she gazed at the darkness behind Rosanna, as if the past could be glimpsed there. 'He said he was in love with a girl. He believed she loved him, too. But she had made some hasty choices. And they were leaving San Gabriel to go on their separate ways. They might never see each other again.'

Rosanna felt a foreboding as she listened.

'He was sick with love,' the fortune-teller said. 'One could almost sense he would die of it.'

Rosanna bit her lip.

11

'So I told him there are many ways to keep love alive,' the old woman continued. She explained how they had come to an arrangement. 'I would send roses to the girl he loved,' she said. 'He could pay me from wherever fate took him. I only needed to know where the roses had to be sent.'

Rosanna sat looking at her hands. 'Who was he?'

The old woman shook her head. 'He never said his name. And I never asked. It wasn't my business to know.' She slumped in her chair. 'And anyway, I would have forgotten. Everything's fading away now.'

The old woman shuffled her cards listlessly, but had nothing more to tell. 'Come back when you've rested,' she said with a kind note in her voice.

Rosanna got up to leave. At the door, she turned to the old woman. 'Did you do a reading for the young man?'

She gave it some thought. 'Yes. He left quickly after it. It seemed the cards had given him hope.'

'What did the cards say?'

The old woman walked to the door, opened it and stared out into the dark, quiet street. 'They said no matter what happened, he would come back to this place of love. The girl would, too. But it wasn't certain they would meet.'

Rosanna passed the café again on her way back to her hotel. It was late and the streets were deserted. She reached the hotel and thought of going in. She was tired, but something in the breeze teased her out into the night. She turned around and made her way across the avenue towards the ornate terrace over the bay. The sea roared from below. She placed her hand on the stone railing and felt the cool spray.

Her footsteps echoed on the stone. She was alone. Out on the mouth of the bay she could see the cliffs where a hundred years before, pearl divers were said to have found the wreck of the *San Gabriel*, the flagship captained by Vasco da Gama when he set out to find a route to India. How the ship strayed so far into the Pacific and ran aground on the shoals of the island, no one knew.

Rosanna made her way down to the promenade and headed back for the hotel. The thunder of the waves against the rocks stayed with her as she entered her quiet hotel room. The sea was still rumbling in her ears as she got ready for bed.

As she unpacked her bag, a scent escaped that reminded her of home. She sat down, thinking of her husband. *He's been away enough*, she thought. *Now it's my turn*. There was only that dim image of the time when his passion had excited her, when she believed they had love enough to be happy.

They had long begun to sleep apart. Rosanna had taken the room by the stairs on the ground floor. But on those nights she still sneaked up to her husband's room and found him gone, she sat crying on his bed because she realised love had become an empty room.

six years before it had been different. Rosanna had come to San Gabriel to defy her family. Everyone: her aunt, her feckless, indifferent father and the new wife he had brought home. She had made the trip with only one thought. When they returned to the city she would marry Leon Gil, the man she had been meeting secretly outside her music teacher's house and who had begged her many times to marry him.

Two of her friends came along, Sara and Juan Rodrigo. They had dreamed of making the trip long before, and with Leon Gil they became accomplices in Rosanna's final mutiny.

Now the thought of it made her smile.

The first place they had gone to was the famous rose market on the slope of the hill.

'My mother once said there were roses in San Gabriel with purple petals and only one thorn,' Rosanna said.

Juan Rodrigo laughed. 'I didn't know there were still people who believed in roses with no thorns.'

'But there *is* a special rose in San Gabriel,' Juan Rodrigo said. Then he told her about the pendant found on the body of a mysterious woman who had drowned in the bay. 'She was said to have jumped to her death from the terrace,' Juan Rodrigo said. Visions of her were reported near the rocks on moonlit nights when the sea was calm. 'Those who saw her said she was beautiful.'

Juan Rodrigo's fixation with the story seemed strange.

Two days before their departure, an untimely wind began to blow through the island. It knocked down stalls in the bazaar, shattered windows in the shops. Its sudden arrival was ominous, and Sara was afraid to return home.

'Maybe we should wait,' she said.

On their last night the wind whistled through the town. It shattered a mirror in Juan Rodrigo's room and left terrible gashes on his hand. Leon had to take him to the hospital but in the end Juan Rodrigo was fine. He and Sara came to see off their friends at the pier. 'Just nature making sure our visit was unforgettable,' Sara laughed. The ferry steamed out into the bay. Rosanna remembered Juan Rodrigo waving to them with a bandage over his hand.

She looked out of the window at the wharf where they had all said goodbye. The streets were empty and Rosanna thought she could still hear the wind. She turned off the light. Sitting on the bed, she removed the clasp from her hair, shook her head gently and lay down to sleep. *We swam in the bay. Your long black hair spread around you like a shadow that darkened the sea.*

Rosanna walked the streets lined with hundred-year-old acacias, thinking of the man who had sent her the roses. Why had he brought her back to San Gabriel a second time? She wondered if perhaps he lived in one of the quiet houses she had walked past, harbouring the secret that was also hers. Rosanna crossed into a small alley, her heart beating fast. She wondered if this was the last time she would ever feel expectancy like this, seeking a dim figure, nameless and invisible but for the tender words on scented paper still fresh when she opened them.

Rosanna heard laughter. She was back on the promenade.

Sara was laughing. The four of them had come running down to the terrace. It was past midnight but the promenade was bright from the full moon. The avenue above them was still full of revellers just on their way to the bazaar. Sara pretended to climb over the railing to jump onto the rocks below. She and Juan Rodrigo had made them all laugh.

At the bazaar they had found an old man selling pearls. Some of the trinkets he was peddling were said to have been salvaged from the wreck of the *San Gabriel*. Among the ivory, porcelain and old silver, there was a pendant in the shape of a rose. The old man held it up to let the light shine through its amethyst core.

'Was this found in the bay?' Rosanna asked.

The old man was surprised. 'Those who found it called her the amethyst rose.'

He smiled. 'It was nearly thirty years ago now. Yes. A sad rose. But very beautiful.'

Rosanna agreed. She remembered Juan Rodrigo's story about the woman who had last worn it. Yet when she saw the jewel she felt a rush of desire to have it. But the bazaar was closing. Dawn was about to break. She tried to persuade Leon to buy it for her.

'Every place has a story like that,' he scoffed.

'But not every story is so enchanting,' Juan Rodrigo said behind Rosanna. 'Or every girl.'

Rosanna ignored him.

The four of them walked away.

'He's just saving money for his old age,' Juan Rodrigo teased Rosanna.

'He's right,' she laughed. 'It's just a pretty trinket.'

'But it's clearly your heart's desire,' he said.

'One's heart is often wrong.'

'But what a loss when it's right, and one didn't listen.' He had his hands in his pockets, looking thoughtful.

Rosanna became serious. 'Leon's right. We can't think of those silly things now.'

They were passing a clock shop, and the noisy clocks in the window were ringing the first hour of dawn.

'It's a new day,' Juan Rodrigo had said and walked away.

She recognised the clock shop and stopped. The time pieces were quiet now. The glass cabinets were empty and covered with dust. She peered through the dirty window at the unswept floor and the cobwebs above the shelves. A sign said the shop was for sale. *All clocks tick in expectation of an hour that never comes. The minute that a thousand tickings never struck.*

Rosanna crossed the avenue and looked out over the sea. Across the strait Sulu pirates used to ambush silk-laden galleons destined for Spain. She walked past the square where birds flocked on the benches. They burst out over the trees as she passed. *Love's heartbeats perched like birds on a wire. Erupting in flight, afraid of dying.*

Rosanna had been sitting in the garden when the first roses arrived. The note spoke of a feeling she had already come to understand. *Where does it start, the hour that never comes. Where does its pining end?*

She had grown to hate the isolation of the property where her husband had taken her to live, and his long absences made it even harder to bear. She felt trapped by the road in front of their house that led nowhere, by the path through the woods that only wound back to the cemetery, rocky mounds and wooden crosses of the first few of the city's dead.

Rosanna recalled the pleasure of holding the first bouquet, the unsigned note that stirred a hidden delight. It made her smile. Over the years, many more roses followed, a secret stream that kept her heart alive. The furtive expectancy it awakened in her soul was all that protected her from the silence of Aguada when her husband was away, and the emptiness of the forest that threatened to engulf her. Only her young son helped to sustain the faith that life was still possible.

Until one day, the long wait for her husband was suddenly cut short. Leon Gil's sudden return was brightened even more when Rosanna realised there were two other people in the car with him. The unexpected guests were standing in the driveway, staring up at her in amazement.

'Rosanna! Sweetheart!' Sara was jumping up and down, happy beyond belief.

Leon stood back and smiled as Rosanna embraced her old friends. 'We just happened to be returning on the same ship,' he explained.

'Just like old times,' Sara said.

'Can you believe it?' Juan Rodrigo kissed Rosanna on the cheek.

They were all a little older, but everything was almost the same. 'We're moving back here,' Sara announced. 'The company's renting us a house on Fort Road.'

She and Juan Rodrigo had married a year before in the capital. The four friends hadn't seen each other since San Gabriel. Juan Rodrigo had gone straight to the capital to join his father's firm. Now he looked like a very successful man.

Over the next few months Rosanna would make countless trips to her friends' house on Fort Road. Sara and Juan Rodrigo frequently returned her visits. Their easy laughter on the veranda or in the garden chipped away at Rosanna's old gloom. They came to stay on weekends. There were parties when the driveway filled with cars, and they danced with the other guests as if nothing had changed in their lives.

Sara was the only one she told about the roses. Sara understood what the secret adulation meant to her friend, but she had no inkling of the yearnings Rosanna now felt. It was a hunger she struggled to control, but it broke free one day when Sara and Juan Rodrigo failed to visit.

Where does it start, the hour that never comes? Rosanna knew the desperation as she waited for her friends to call. She tried to reach them as the first rains began.

In a frenzy she had herself driven to Sara's house in the downpour. She was met by Sara's brother. He broke the awful news to her.

Juan Rodrigo had gone to San Gabriel a few weeks before. While he was there, the car he was driving skidded over a barrier and fell into the sea. Stricken with grief, Sara had been taken to her sister's house, far from the city.

Rosanna's brief dream of redemption shattered, like a mirror smashed by a freak gust of wind. She drove back to Aguada without speaking to anyone. Her husband was away and the silent rooms of her house oppressed her even more. She locked herself in her room, afraid to come out to the doomed shadows of the hallway.

She sat at the bureau and took out the notes she had been keeping since the first roses came. They made her smile. She basked in their distant ardour and allowed their enigma to save her.

She gasped for breath in the stifling room, and got up to open the window. Raindrops spattered on her hand. The downpour still blurred the garden. She pulled the window closed. *I have to get away*, she thought.

She sat down at the bureau again, touched the silver clasp on her hair, studied her straight, dark features on the mirror. She toyed with the letter opener, tested the dull blade against her skin. It was then that she felt the sudden urge to leave. I *must* go, she told herself.

Why did Juan Rodrigo go to San Gabriel? She thought she suspected the answer. But it eluded her. It frightened and excited her like the scent of those roses that had first surprised her. Why had they stopped coming?

She forced herself to sleep, but the tumult in her mind would not let her. There were bouts of tears and screaming. She was so distraught a doctor had to be called. In the temporary calm after his visit, she came to a decision. She would leave the next day.

'After many years I saw the young man again.' The fortune-teller removed her glasses to rub her eyes. 'He was back in San Gabriel by himself. He had gotten married and seemed content. But he still loved the girl. The one he loved all those years. He still couldn't forget her.'

'What did he want?' asked Rosanna.

'He wanted to send her roses. One last time, then no more.'

'Why?' asked Rosanna.

'The old woman shrugged. 'He asked me to send this message.' She got up to open a cabinet. 'I was to send it with the roses and a box.'

'What kind of box?' Rosanna turned to face her.

The old woman didn't answer. She parted the drapes and peeked outside for a long time. 'Then I heard about the accident on the hill. Just before the rains. A car drove over the railing.'

Before the rains Rosanna still thought happiness was possible.

'I'm glad you came,' the fortune-teller said. She handed Rosanna a small velvet box. 'I couldn't trust this to strangers.'

Rosanna studied the box. 'The man gave this to you before he left?'

The old woman nodded. 'When I heard about the accident, I wondered. If he would ever come.'

Rosanna said goodbye. On the street she read the note on the box.

The day ends with a last brightness
on the fringe of night.
To vanish in the waning fire
Of the sun that fed its lustre.

In the afternoon she was finally able to reach Sara at her sister's house. Sara's voice was hoarse from crying. 'We're just preparing everything,' she said weakly. '*Everything.*' There was a great emptiness to her voice. Behind her Rosanna could hear officious, intrusive voices, busy with the arrangements of death.

Rosanna told Sara she was in San Gabriel.

'Oh?' There was a happy note in Sara's voice.

Rosanna smiled. 'I was just remembering,' she said. 'Six years ago when we all came here.'

'Yes.'

'Like it didn't happen to us somehow. But to other people who were so happy.'

Sara attempted a laugh. 'Strange how Juan Rodrigo hurt his hand.'

'You think he hurt his own hand?'

'I don't know. The landlady said she found him lying on his bed, bleeding. Just lying there, waiting.'

Rosanna remembered. Juan Rodrigo had broken away from them at the terrace. That evening after dinner they had gone to look at the moon. That was when Rosanna told her friends she would marry Leon Gil. 'We'll have a secret ceremony in the city,' she had said. 'There'll just be the four of us.'

The wind was already whistling above them, driving the waves against the rocks. Sara looked at her without a word. Juan Rodrigo said goodnight and walked away. Rosanna followed him up the steps.

'What's wrong?' she said after him. 'I thought you'd be happy for me.'

'You said yesterday your heart is often wrong,' he said.

'This time it's not,' answered Rosanna.

'That man doesn't love you.'

'He does. He's asked me many times to marry him. *Begged* me.'

'That's no proof.'

'What more proof is needed?'

'That he'll at least give you what you want.'

'He will. He says we'll buy a house.'

'Is that all that matters?'

'It's very important.'

Juan Rodrigo was quiet. They had reached the top of the avenue. 'It'll be a cold, passionless house,' he finally said.

Perhaps Rosanna was thinking of her own mother when she said, 'I've seen it happen. When passion dies, a lover leaves you just as easily as a heartless stranger.'

Juan Rodrigo slowed down, gazing out on the promenade.

'I hope you'll be happy,' he said.

Rosanna crossed her arms. 'I'll never go back to my father's house.'

The wind blew over some tables laid out on the promenade below. Chairs fell over, glasses smashed. A waitress cried out.

'See?' Juan Rodrigo said. 'Everything is against it.' He crossed the street and disappeared into the dark.

'Rosanna? Are you there?' Sara's voice on the phone startled her.

Rosanna cleared her throat. 'I was just thinking about what you said.'

She felt the same foreboding the wind had blown into her room all those years ago. 'Sara, tell me about the accident.'

'When Juan Rodrigo cut his hand?'

'No. The accident with the car.'

Rosanna swallowed. She pressed her ear to the phone.

'He swerved to avoid another car...' Sara's raw, tormented voice planted the incident firmly in Rosanna's mind. She pictured the scene over and over in her mind. Life had become a thousand tickings for an hour that never came.

Juan Rodrigo's car flew over the railing as the sun was setting. In a heartbeat he was in the sea. *Heartbeats erupting in flight to a better realm.*

It was all clear in Rosanna's mind now. Juan Rodrigo had died for her. She understood all the notes he had refused to sign.

It was nearly dark. Rosanna hurried down to the pier. She arrived just as the last ferry was leaving. She watched its lights drift into the gathering darkness, fighting panic and a thrust of pain. A desperate fancy remained that if she hurried, something might dispel this dreadful knowledge she had received. If she crossed back quickly from one part of her life to another, misfortune might miss her.

Then she realised there was no longer any urgency. The man who had loved her secretly was here in San Gabriel, dead, drowned in the sea where they once swam.

Rosanna walked around the beautiful town, wondering where it was that Juan Rodrigo had begun to love her. She stayed up until dawn, when the old town became deserted and hers alone.

At first light the ferry sailed. Half-way to Puerto Reina, when the island was long out of sight, Rosanna opened the box. She gasped. It was the amethyst rose, a wish she had forgotten from that night long ago in San Gabriel.

I.

They were out on one of their walks when Adia pointed to a man she said was being followed by a tongue of flame. 'That man will be dead by August,' she said.

All afternoon they had wandered along the avenues where empty mansions stood, their shattered windows covered with vines. Jorge was tired but Adia kept drawing his attention to things that enchanted him and so he wasn't in a hurry to go home.

The lawns of the abandoned Spanish buildings they passed concealed fountains that had dried out long ago, and Adia kept him rapt with tales about the sad marble statues staring out through their sharp-tipped fences. Adia basked in the serenity of the old avenue where imposing houses slowly perished behind the underbrush and the rusty gates. Old flame trees shed their fire-tinted blossoms onto the street.

She took him into a narrow alley where the clatter of horses' hooves jolted hem out of the afternoon's dreamy haze.

'*Whoa.*' The coachmen gently coaxed their flighty animals through the passage. Jorge looked up at the great wood-spoked wheels and the beasts passing before them. They pressed up against the sides to let them pass, afraid of being trampled or splashed by the foam from the horses' mouths.

They were the last remaining cabriolets of Puerto Reina, brightly painted like ice- cream carts. They caused too much chaos in the busy roads, weaving in and out of traffic, and so were banished to the side streets, where they clomped in the narrow laneways between the houses.

Roaming in that air of wasted grandeur that hung about the quiet town gave Jorge the feeling that he had come too late into the world and had missed something. He was eight years old, with large front teeth that peeked out between his lips and forced them into a readiness to smile. He had big, round dreamer's eyes that an inner delight or curiosity gave a gleam. On top of his head sat the sharp, scraggly hair, a fiendish source of annoyance that he had learned to ignore.

Adia had taken care of him as far back as he could remember. He sensed her presence as he wandered through the empty rooms of their house, puzzled in particular by one room near the stairs with pictures of a pretty girl. Adia told him he was born in that room. He remembered being drawn to it since he was able to walk, fascinated by the dark drapes in the windows, so rich there was a sweet smell that wafted in when you parted them.

In that room was a drawer where Adia showed him pieces of a broken mirror. 'This belonged to your mother,' she told him.

He found this very strange, for he had always wondered if Adia was his mother. She was tall and slim with short white hair. She was brisk and domineering, though at times the boy noticed a delicacy and a curious trace of elegance. Adia had large brown eyes and high cheekbones. When they waited to cross the street she would tilt her head to one side, feet together like a proper lady. And when she did the heavy chores at home she was fastidious. She would wipe the table or water the plants, wearing her serene expression, humming softly to herself. Her friendly face was slender and when her hair fell over her eyes she flicked it away with a youthful gesture.

Jorge would stand at the doorway to watch her on quiet mornings when she sat gazing at the sunlight dappled on the floor.

'Wonderful,' she would sigh. She would turn to him with the light shining in her eyes. 'What are you snickering about over there?' and get up to ruffle his hair.

'You're too young to know how wonderful peace time can be.' She said it in a singing voice, pinching his cheek. He knew she was embarrassed to be caught unawares.

He didn't know why she was raising him and his brother. He had heard that she once had children of her own but she abandoned them before the war. The chauffeur had told him that Adia had done many things a little boy shouldn't know about. He even hinted that Adia had 'been friends' with far too many men, but the maid giggled and nudged him and he stopped talking.

Jorge's mother died when he was very young, and ever since he could remember there was only him, his brother Miguel and their father. Adia took care of everyone in the house, even the maid and the chauffeur, like she was the mother of them all.

34

She made sure the maid went to the market and cooked the meals on time. Even when only Jorge and his brother were at home, Adia insisted on serving the meals promptly. Most of the time their father was at work in the city or on a trip to check on their family's plantations.

The two boys preferred to eat at one corner of the table, opposite to where their father sat when he was at home. They ate without looking up or talking, except when Miguel had just come back from town or the village and had something to show his brother.

'Psst!' he'd say. 'Guess what's inside.'

He would hold up a box or similar container, opening it just enough so Jorge could peek in. Something blue shone briefly and he put the box away, flicking it out of Jorge's grasp as though he had timed the whole act.

'For one look you give me your dessert and *all* your money.'

Their house was half an hour from the city, and Jorge seldom went there except with Adia, so he had little use for money. But there were Christmas parties when their uncles or their father's friends would visit and give them envelopes with cash. Miguel knew his

35

brother put those envelopes safely away for purposes he hadn't yet conceived.

Adia's desserts were another matter. Jorge lived for their lusciousness and their sugary explosion in his mouth. Miguel didn't lack persistence, however. When his brother showed no interest in whatever he was peddling, he would start to make irritating noises with his tongue. *Blblblbleh...*

The younger boy would take his plate to sit in the music room and eat in peace among the cobwebs. There was a large grand piano in the middle of the room that once belonged to his mother. But after she died their father locked the lid and no one was able to play it again.

It was like a huge, silent animal with a forbidden secret. Leaning against its curved ebony legs comforted him, and if he swept away the dust he could lie on top and daydream for hours.

It was there she knew to find him when their father unexpectedly came home. Poking her head through the door she would call out sweetly, 'Dinner, Jorge dear! Your father is waiting.'

The two boys were uneasy around their father. Miguel often urged him to run away. On the field behind the house he would whisper, 'Let's go now. No one will miss us. Let's not go back to that awful house!'

Jorge refused and always tried to pull his brother back with him. But one day Miguel broke violently away.

'I'll go without you then,' he shouted as he disappeared into the gathering dusk. 'You'll be alone in that empty house!'

Jorge ran home terrified, unable to hold back his tears, and was already bawling when he burst into the kitchen, running into Adia's apron that smelled of wood smoke and aniseed.

After a long absence their father came home to sell the car. Jorge and Miguel hovered around the doorway to the living room.

'Eh!' Finally, he called them in. 'Your aunt wants you to write more letters,' he said to Miguel. 'Here's the book you asked for.' He dropped a small package on the table and Miguel pounced on it.

'Wow!' Miguel mauled the wrapping until it was just brown tatters on the floor. Then he turned a grinning face towards Jorge, with a look the younger boy already knew how to read. *Your dessert and all your money. Just one look.*

'You,' his father said to him. 'Your aunt says stop picking your nose with paper clips.'

Jorge looked around, baffled at how the news got to his aunt.

His father was holding out something. 'Your uncle gave this.'

Jorge unwrapped it. It was a policeman's whistle, still new and shiny.

'Blow it outside,' said his father before he could put it in his mouth.

The next day, Jorge waited until he was sure his father was gone, and walked to the far edge of the field. He looked around him at people going about their business, not knowing how their peace was going to be shattered. Jorge took a deep breath.

He put the whistle in his mouth and blew with all his strength. He felt the air bursting in his ears. The sound was shrill and authoritative. He was pleased. It felt like everything came to a halt. Even the birds seemed to have fallen silent. Jorge looked around him in the stillness.

A cabriolet had stopped in the middle of the road.

'Hey!' shouted the driver. He pointed his finger at Jorge. 'I thought they had a traffic policeman out here, too. Careful with that thing.'

It was Nicanor, the old man who drove Adia and him to town in the afternoons.
'I was going as slow as I could,' he said with a laugh. His carriage was empty and he waved the boy over. 'Want to hop on?'

Jorge shook his head. He could see the smoke coming out of the kitchen and knew Adia would be readying lunch.

He went back to the house feeling it was free and all his. The rooms and their empty beds lay unclaimed, like the closets where he could rummage all afternoon. Adia didn't seem to mind the piles he often left outside his mother's cabinet. She seemed pleased he was so curious, and would put the things away singing to herself.

There was a room on the second floor that he was afraid to enter. It was full of statues, some small enough to put in his pocket, others so massive they frightened him. Made of hollow plaster, they were much lighter than they appeared, but the undisturbed dust of many years made them look like immemorial prisoners in the murky room, cobwebs hanging from the crooks of their arms and in the spaces between them. They were so old the plaster showed through the paint, and when Jorge touched them the powdered pigments came off on his hands.

Adia told him they were the saints to which his great-grandmother used to pray. He could sometimes sense her presence when he walked in the room. A breeze would sometimes blow through the room and make a hand move. It was a while before Jorge stopped being startled by the angel behind the closet, whose broken hand dangled, lifelike, from its plaster stump.

'They say she was crazy,' Miguel said, strolling over to the blue-robed female figure whose head nearly touched the ceiling. Jorge found it the most frightening one of all.

'Who?' Jorge asked.
'Doña Juana. Our great-grandmother,' Miguel answered. 'Tried to walk across the river once.' Miguel stood scratching his chin at the doorway, and by the time he and Jorge got downstairs he had thought up a game.

It took them several days to carry all the statues down to the yard, struggling with the weight of the larger ones. They hid them in the shed until Jorge and his brother had thought up a fitting scheme for their destruction.

Miguel walked around the assembled statuary one last time, making vicious accusations and giving them a chance to plead for mercy. But there were no pleas from the frozen figures and so their fates were sealed.

They dragged them to the back and, with elaborate ceremony and vicious cries, took a shovel and beheaded them all. They threw the heads and severed bodies into the pond where Miguel used to raise his frogs.

'Down you!' Miguel used a plank to beat the head of a female saint that kept floating up.

When that game was over, Adia shook her head and resolved Jorge needed something to occupy his mind.

That was when she decided to show him snow. She led him to his mother's room and from deep within the bureau she produced a water-filled glass bubble Jorge had never seen before. There was a little house in the centre surrounded by trees. The windows were lit up by a hidden a bulb. Adia shook it to stir the white particles in the water. Jorge was mesmerised by the white swirl as it scattered and fell gently around the trees.

'That's snow,' Adia said. 'It's pure and white and beautiful. Someday maybe you'll see it.'

She told him his grandfather bought the toy for Rosanna when the fair first came to Puerto Reina. Jorge was enchanted by it. From that moment on he could barely resist stealing into his mother's room to gaze at the snow. He later discovered that Miguel did the same, though he pretended Jorge's childish fixation was something he had long outgrown.

Adia spoke of how their mother used to hold Miguel when he was just a baby, shaking the toy and holding it before his spellbound eyes. Now Jorge would pass the room and see his brother hunched over the bureau, stirring the snow, and he wondered if Miguel remembered being held in their mother's arms.

The snow-filled dome was the first of Adia's revelations that encouraged him to find out more. Perhaps it was the reason he spent so much time rummaging about the house. In some of the rooms were riddles waiting for him to find and unravel. And Adia helped him.

'But we need a place to start.' She held a finger to her cheek and pondered.

They began by trying to find pieces of the broken mirror in his mother's room. It wasn't an easy task.

'Why do we have to?' Jorge asked.

Adia couldn't fully explain. She told him it was related to things that had happened long ago, and the deep memories that still lay hidden somewhere in the house, in the secret parts of its rooms.

They struggled to find all the fragments of the mirror. Adia promised that if they succeeded he might see his mother's face. Once in a back room he picked up a small shard from under the bed. He saw an eye staring out at him as if peering from another room.

His search often took him to the driveway, looking in the dirt and gravel under the car. His patience paid off one day when he found a large piece of the mirror just after his father had driven out. He was convinced the car must harbour some more of the shards, and was disheartened to learn his father was selling the vehicle.

An elderly couple with a dog bought their car. They came to the house very excited one Sunday morning. They piled inside and the old man kept trying the horn. The chauffeur opened the gate and the boys watched them drive out, the engine laboured and nearly stalling. They heard the metal crunch as he the old man shifted gears. He gunned the motor and made it roar. His wife laughed, the dog barked, then they sped away.

Miguel and Jorge rarely went up to the second floor where their father had his room, but sometimes they passed his open door and saw him, sitting by the window or pacing, deep in thought. Often he was fiddling with the things on his desk, rubbing his eyes and not making a sound. They often wondered what he thought about.

'I think he cries when he's alone,' said Miguel. It was one of those unbelievable things he said with a grin.

'Maybe he misses mother,' Jorge said.

'Maybe he's thinking of selling the house!' Miguel's eyes sometimes had a mad gleam. 'We'll be given away as servants!'

'Shut your mouth!' Jorge ran away from him. But all the same their interest in the contents of their father's desk deepened. It was the one place in the house that was out of bounds to Jorge's snooping.

Because of what Miguel said, Jorge agreed their father required close observation. They noticed how he changed when his friends came to play cards. He was a different man in the smoky room with his jolly card mates, carefree and jocular, accepting a cigar from his friends and laughing a their jokes. But when his friends were gone and the cigar haze had vanished, he passed through a veil and became his distant, unhappy self again.

Once when Miguel saw him leaving the house before supper, he and Jorge followed him to the village about ten minutes away. At the corner he hailed a taxi and drove off.

'I wonder if that's the reason he sold the car,' Miguel mused. 'So no one will know where he goes.'

There was no way for them to follow him in a taxi. Night had fallen. The boys were about to go home when Jorge heard a clomping in the darkness. 'Whoa, girl!'

'Nicanor!' Miguel cried out.

'Yeesss...?' the coachman answered.

'Are you going to town?'

'I will if you will,' Nicanor said, clicking his tongue to steady the horse.

'We have no money,' said Miguel.

Nicanor seemed to mull it over. His face was in darkness.

'We got left behind,' said Miguel in a pleading voice. 'Our father's gone.'

'Well,' Nicanor finally said, swaying as his horse shifted from side to side, 'remember something tasty for my horse.'

'I will. I promise!' said Miguel.

Nicanor laughed. 'All right, then. Just to the railroad then you can catch a bus.'

'Thanks, old man!' Miguel hoisted himself up on the carriage and his brother followed.

The boys found their way to the Hotel Oriente where the taxis stopped. The bulbs over its entrance cast a red glow on the street. The idle drivers stood around with red on their faces, like devils in a comic book Jorge had read.

The pavement was crowded with people. He had never seen the city so lively at night.

'This way!' said Miguel and he started to run.

'Where?'

'I think I saw him.'

Their father's trail led them to the noisy nightclubs of *Calle* Luna. Jorge and his brother nervously set out to discover what not only their father but all grownups did when they left the house. Food being roasted on the roadside sent delicious aromas into the air. Loud music was coming out of the open bars.

The two boys stopped to peek through the window of a cabaret. There were women dancing on a stage.

'Zapata girls!' Miguel grinned at his brother. 'They can play castanets under their skirts.' He pretended to know all the mysteries that were baffling to Jorge, who struggled not to lose him in the dazzling maze.

Miguel and his brother looked more like outrageous misfits in the city than they did in Aguada. Like the other village children, they dressed with no regard for colour, shape or style, slapping on any garments that would fit them. Miguel's red-striped shirt was at odds with the brown pants he had nearly outgrown, the cuffs hanging loose above his ankles. Jorge trailed him in his loose yellow shirt and rumpled pants, which looked like they'd been stolen off a neighbour's backyard.

The two youths were drawn by the sweet coloured lights, but found the darkness behind the doorways barred to them. 'Hey you!' The men at the door would shout and chase them away. An old doorman tried to scare them off with a nightstick. Then there was a vicious midget who threatened to punch Miguel. The brothers laughed at him because he was not much bigger than them. Miguel gave a tap to the bulge behind his neck and they ran away. Jorge saw the midget running behind them holding a long knife that flashed under a street lamp.

'Help!' Miguel began to shout. 'Help!'

'Help!' There was another voice shouting behind them. 'Quick! *Help the two girls!'* The midget laughed. His voice was all around them, big and amazingly loud for such a little creature.

They didn't stop running until they reached another part of the city that had no street lights. It was strangely quiet. The noise of *Calle* Luna seemed very far away. The sky was clear above them and they slowed to a walk. They passed the old theatre. Its arched entrance and windows were boarded up. On the pillar were shreds of posters from films they had never seen. Across the street was an empty lot. The spear-tipped fence that surrounded it looked like the one at their house.

'This is Paseo Gardenia,' said Miguel. 'That's where our house used to stand.' Thrusting his hands in his pockets, he walked kicking the pebbles in his path. He studied the light falling on the debris scattered on the vacant lot.

'I've been here many times,' said Miguel. 'This is where our mother used to live.'

'What do you mean?' Jorge asked.

Miguel didn't answer and crossed to the other side. 'We better get back.'

Jorge followed him, getting angry, but afraid to be left behind. 'What do you mean? Tell me!'

Miguel started walking faster.

'Tell me!' Jorge shouted. His voice carried across the empty city block. Miguel was getting farther away.

Finally, Jorge dashed after him, his fury rising. He knew his brother would never tell. He got out of breath trying to chase him.

It was Miguel who came up with the idea that their father had been waylaid. They believed he was probably being held somewhere against his will and needed their help. This planted the suspicion that the man who came back to the house at night and slept in their father's bed was an impostor. He must have wanted something very important to go through such an elaborate charade. Did he want money? Or jewels their father bought long ago? Or perhaps some important papers.

Their instincts seemed more and more correct as they watched their father at the other end of the table, eating his food without saying a word.
'He's afraid to speak,' whispered Miguel. 'because we'll know he doesn't have our father's voice.'

That was probably why the man seemed to know nothing about them or their mother. But he succeeded in fooling everyone, their uncles and their aunts. It was just their intuition but they had to find a way to expose him. They had to go to the police and convince them that the man wasn't their real father, but had done something bad to him and taken his place.

Their memories were still fresh of the man who used to laugh and play with them, who let Jorge run into his arms when he came back from town. But this stranger had somehow replaced him, and, more important than getting rid of him, they wanted to know how to rescue their real father.

Miguel offered to go out every day to learn what had happened. He came back and gave Jorge daily accounts because Jorge was too lazy and too timid to leave the house. One day Miguel said that he had seen their father with a woman. She lived in *Calle* Luna behind a club called *Sweet Dreams*.

'Maybe she's drugged him,' said Miguel. He clenched his fists and said through gritted teeth, 'We'll make the witch *pay!*'

The idea of liberating their father obsessed them for a long time and Jorge didn't know if Miguel ever forgot about it. He only remembered his brother coming home one day, tired and disheartened. 'Maybe it's time we gave up,' he said, punching his other hand. That must have been the time they both began to grow up. When they accepted that their father had changed. The man they had once known was gone and would never come back.

Once they were summoned to the front of the house by the sound of brass and snare drums. It was a funeral procession, a column of mourners all in black, moving slowly like a dark vision in the noonday sun. They were walking behind a glass-sided hearse, drawn by an imposing black horse draped in purple. The sad horn wailed over the bereaved as they struggled along the rocky road to the solemn cadence of the snare drums.

'My God,' sighed Adia beside Jorge. 'It reminds me of your mother.' It seemed as if she was about to cry.

'You stood by yourself outside the door, watching the hearse pull away.' She was looking down at him curiously. 'Your eyes were so serious. I wondered if you understood.'

After that he often came to the corner to watch the funeral processions. The sorrowful parades drew many onlookers from the village, fascinated by the spectacle of people even less fortunate than they, moving in the shock of adversity, locked into the mysterious guidance of a dark, purple-draped animal. The horse stepped lightly, almost jauntily, as it pulled the fragile hearse of glass. Jorge watched the coffin inside, hermetic and out of reach.

But in truth the black, velvet-covered horse frightened him. The sound of its hooves sometimes echoed in his dreams. Its grim, malevolent pride lurked in nightmares that made him cry out at night, drawing Adia to his side.

She tried her best to comfort him, but at night he gave vent to his greatest weakness: he was a cry-baby. And that was when Adia struggled to muster the best of her tales to distract him.

She told him about the time when vampires roamed the city. She said their skin was shiny and they smelled of snakes. She seemed to believe that the best cure for sadness was terror. The tale did not comfort Jorge though it distracted him enough so Adia could turn off the light and leave the room.

But Jorge's tears, like his fears, were plentiful. Once, probably because she was at a loss, or thought it was all that would console him, Adia did a very strange thing.

Jorge cried out in the middle of the night and after some minutes, she walked in and handed him something. It was hot to the touch and Jorge held it to his face. It was a milk bottle. Adia had left before he could ask what he was meant to do with it.

He put it in his mouth. Perhaps it was the warmth of the milk or the thought that Adia had gone to such trouble, but he found, to Adia's horror, that the remedy was to his liking. The hot sweet milk stifled the flood of sorrow and he lay down to sleep.

It became Jorge's secret pleasure and source of his deepest shame. He lived for the moments when he could take furtive sips of the sweet milk that Adia dutifully made and placed on his bedside.

Perhaps he grew up faster than anyone had expected, but he was not weaned off the habit. He grew up with a secret, like everyone else around him.

All the while he kept collecting the pieces of the mirror that Adia told him to find. After a long time he was ready to put the pieces together. In a darkened upstairs room, Adia told him to close his eyes. After a while she said, 'Now take a deep breath and look.'

Jorge opened his eyes. He was alone. He looked into the broken mirror. Behind him he could see an open door. Through it he could see a hallway. He took the mirror and went out. He kept walking until behind him he could see the whole house, just as it had been before he was born. The rooms filled with voices he had never heard before. A pretty girl ran laughing across the hall. Jorge stopped and turned around with a start. He tried to find the source of the noises and walked down the hallway opening doors. But fragments of the mirror were still missing. There were places in the house he couldn't see, parts of the story he didn't know. Miguel wasn't aware of Jorge's quest. He left the house every day as soon as he could, coming back only by nightfall, his clothes dirty and sometimes with a cut on his face.

A boy came to the house to help with the chores. Jorge recognised him from when he and Adia had first seen him on one of their walks. He had come with the travelling performers who stopped at the plaza one market day.

Wearing a bright fez, the boy had fluttered his eyes as he moved his hands and body in a sinuous Javanese dance, at the end of which he took off the fez and begged the crowd for money. Adia dropped in some change and started talking to him.

His wide eyes inspired pity, and Jorge could tell Adia was moved by his story. Before joining the itinerant performers he had tried selling water and cigarettes to passengers on the North-bound buses that converged outside Puerto Reina. He clung expertly to the bar above the running board and jumped off just before reaching the next town. He knew their names by heart, all the way to the tip of the island—*Guimbal, Sara, Dueñas, Pavia, San Joaquin*—and he had seen them all in the sun and rain.

He and his mother had arrived in the city with no money. They lived in a shed made from empty cartons they pulled out of rubbish heaps. They had fled their home after his father was murdered in some dispute over land. Adia told Jorge it often happened in the dark interior.

The rains broke up the wandering entertainers, but Adia found the boy again. He was living in the slums outside the city that had grown around a mountain of trash. His mother had given up and gone in search of a better fortune in other towns. The boy confessed that he had tried eating lizard eggs.

Adia insisted that he come back to the house with her. And so Jorge saw the boy again. His wide smiling eyes and strong teeth gave him a look of openness. But when he sat alone in the back of the house a dark expression settled on his face that bothered Jorge. It made him think of the gloomy abandoned buildings in the centre of the city. Miguel took one look at the boy and said, 'He looks like a gargoyle.'

The chauffeur agreed. And so, even though the boy insisted his name was Mamun, from that time and for always he would be known in their house as Goyle.

They learned that Goyle had also boxed for money. He was once part of an attraction thought up by a roving snake-charmer. The itinerant boxing boys were very popular in the country towns and earned the snake-charmer a lot of money. Goyle wasn't a skilful fighter. He had been hit more times than he could clout back, but the stoical resolve of his face made the crowds think he was invincible. He was a good sprinter and could climb trees as fast as any lemur.

'Hmm.' The chauffeur scratched his chin and watched with a glint in his eyes. 'Imagine how useful this boy could be.'

Gold teeth showed between his lips and Jorge remembered Adia telling him that the chauffeur had once been a gangster on the docks before Jorge's father decided to hire him. But for some time now, he had been a chauffeur without a car to drive. Perhaps it was pride in the more respectable profession Jorge's father had given him that made him start driving a taxi again. He continued to live with them, bringing the taxi back to the house in case Jorge's father needed a ride.

He parked it in the driveway in place of the old car, but it was thought of as the chauffeur's taxi, and Adia and Jorge still waited at the corner for Nicanor if they wanted to go into town. What criminal instincts Goyle awakened in the chauffeur's mind were short-lived. By nature, Goyle was no felon, and the erstwhile gangster had to be content with watching him wrestle stray dogs or Jorge for everyone's amusement.

In the far-flung town where he was born, the nuns who ran the new Catholic schools forced the native girls to wear skirts and blouses, while the boys still wore loincloths to class. Goyle ran away from the missionaries after a year of wearing shoes. His grandfather had been one of the first natives from the interior to become a constabulary recruit. Goyle's most cherished possession was a picture of his grandfather wearing a pistol and a Sebastopol hat, a constabulary regulation shirt over his loincloth.

Goyle nurtured a dream to follow his ancestor into the armed forces and be an honoured warrior among his people. Doing chores alone in the yard he showed an intractable preference for the liberty of loincloths.

Later that year, the maid, toothless and embarrassed, told Adia she was leaving the household to get married. That was when Melba came. She was barely taller than Jorge, round-faced, with a dumbfounded expression. She was twelve, but her small body was that of a ten-year-old. She had anxious little eyes and a mouth so small Jorge wondered how she ate.

After a few days helping around the house it was clear Melba was crazy. One morning Adia caught her trying to rub off the varnish from the old furniture. Then she knelt down to pry the bone-inlay out of the banisters.

'She's not a thief,' Adia said. 'Just not very smart.'

One day Jorge saw her trying repeatedly to sweep away a spot of sunlight on the floor.

'You can't sweep that off,' he laughed at her. 'No matter how you try.'

'Why not?' she answered, bending down with the dustpan. She turned her back on him and busied herself with the broom. Then she walked away.

Jorge looked and the spot of sunlight was gone. Melba smiled at him from the doorway. 'It's goblin's gold,' she said.

He began to watch her. At dusk that day he saw her open the cabinet in the hallway. She shook the dustpan into it and carefully closed the door.
'All her people are quite mad,' Adia said.

Jorge learned that Melba's family was from the north. They worked as porters bearing goods over the mountain range near their home. From an early age Melba had lugged heavy loads balanced on her head, as all her kin trekked up and down the slopes with sacks of grain or hemp. Perhaps all that weight had squeezed the joy out of her, leaving only the pained, confused expression, so that even when she laughed she looked about to cry.

'He's watching the house...'

Jorge was lying on the landing when Melba stepped over him.

'Who?'

'He's out in the field,' she said, turning her head to listen. 'I saw him from the kitchen.'

Jorge sat up frightened. He had watched the day dim into dusk through the window, and now it was dark. He hadn't noticed when his father had come out of his room to leave the house. There was still no sign of Miguel. Faint smells of cooking were floating through the dark house.

'I can smell him,' Melba said. She went down the stairs.

'Wait for me!'

He found her standing at the edge of the yard, looking towards the empty field. He stood beside her. There was a noise and she turned with a gasp.

'Let's go back inside!' He tried to pull her away from the fence.

'Don't be scared,' she said. 'Mad dogs are nearly blind.'

Her small eyes scanned the darkness. 'And anyway, it's about to die.'

'How do you know?'

'I can smell it. It's sick and hasn't eaten for days.' She went inside and she left Jorge watching the motionless field. From that time he wondered what it was that Melba had really brought into their lives.

He often thought that everyone was wrong and Melba was right. That dreams didn't only come out at night and leave by morning. They were always *there*. And though he joined Adia and the chauffeur in laughing at Melba, many times he could swear there was something glowing in the hallway cabinet when she opened it at dusk.

Once Melba chanced upon him in his mother's room. It was raining outside.

'What are you doing here all alone in the shadows?' She looked around at the old lamps, the bureau, the pictures on the wall.

'The faces are blurred,' she said. 'Are all these people dead?' She sat down beside him on the bed.

'That woman in black looks scary.' She hunched her shoulders as if she were cold. 'You like sitting here, don't you?'

Jorge shrugged.

'I heard you were born in this room.'

Looking over his head she noticed something. 'What's that?'

He turned to look. 'It's my mother's mirror.'

Adia had put it back in its old place by the bureau.

'No,' said Melba. 'I mean *that*.' She was pointing at something reflected in the mirror. She got up and picked it up. She showed it to him. It was a dusty old dagger. 'Were you playing with this?'

'No. I've never seen it before.'

'It's all right,' she said, putting it in the drawer. 'I won't tell.'

She stood in the middle of the room. 'It's a beautiful mirror. Shame it's broken.'

'I'm putting it back together,' Jorge told her. 'There are pieces scattered everywhere.'

'Oh? I might be able to help you.'

She was walking to the door when she stopped. 'Did you hear that?'

'Hear what?'

'A voice. Crying.'

'What voice?'

Melba listened. Her face seemed to grow sad. 'You shouldn't keep sitting here on your own,' she said and left the room.

Her behaviour confounded him all the more. He followed her to the hiding places where she tried to be alone. It was her search for better concealment that led her to Jorge's appalling secret.

One day she caught him at the back of the house, sipping sweet milk from the baby bottle.

'What a disgraceful thing for such a big boy!' she cried out, holding the bottle up over his head. Jorge punched her in the stomach and scratched her face.

'Ow!' In revenge she flung the milk bottle over the fence.

'I'll *kill* you!' Jorge ran out to retrieve it. His gaze was so fixed on the creamy liquid dripping on the dirt that he didn't hear the scratching of claws, the panting lunge and suddenly a growl that froze him in his tracks. The milk bottle was in the jaws of the rabid dog. Its crazed yellow eyes glowered as Jorge pondered what to do. Already, the hot milk was escaping through punctures made by its fangs, mingling with the foamy drool on its mouth.

For a moment Jorge considered lunging at it to grab the precious bottle back. Then, a hail of stones thrown by Melba rained down on the dog. It scuttled back yelping to the field with the forbidden milk bottle.

Melba ran up to Jorge, happy to see him whole. She seemed unaware that in her own harrowing way she had weaned him.

'Come here,' Melba called him to the hallway one day. Weeks had passed and he had found it in his heart to forgive her. She led him to the cabinet under the stairs and opened the door. 'Look what I found.'

He was surprised at the breath of cool air from inside. His eye caught something shining at the bottom. 'Is this what you've been looking for?' Melba got down on her knees and dug into the cabinet.

'There,' she said finally. 'I think that's all the pieces you need.'

She was holding up fragments of a mirror. Jorge was so delighted he nearly kissed her. It was a great find. Finally he could finish the task Adia had given him.

He didn't know if it was part of Adia's plan, but as he put the pieces back together, an image began to form in his mind. It was a memory from before he was born. A recollection that belonged to the spirit of the house, that glued together the debris of its forgotten life hiding in the dusty rooms. It was an image of his mother crying by the window and throwing something that smashed the mirror.

That strange vivid vision made him want to learn more. So that when he had finally hunted down the last fragments of his mother's story, he would understand why she did what she had done. And what had happened to make their house so empty by the time he was born.

Jorge didn't know when the city buses stopped coming to the house. For a while Nicanor and a few other cabriolets were the only ride into town, and it was getting harder and harder to get back. Once they were at the market when a rainstorm began. Adia tried to flag down a taxi. But when she explained that she and Jorge lived beyond St Mathew's cemetery, the drivers shook their heads, 'Why that's a place beyond the grave. I'm not ready to go there.'

The one who took them that day laughed loudly at his own joke. Adia said sternly, 'Well, the boy and I are from that place. We like to come back once in a while.' Her eyes shone when she said this, and she must have somehow frightened the man. He drove without turning his head, his eyes darting to the mirror to take nervous peeks at them sitting in the back. He dropped them off at the gate in the pouring rain, snatching the fare from Adia's hand and driving off so fast he nearly skidded into a ditch. Adia laughed.

Past the cemetery the road turned rocky and curved up towards an enormous tamarind tree. In its ample, creaking shade, the city buses stopped. There they waited to venture further into the interior or back into town. The drivers and bus conductors dozed in their vehicles, buzzed by flies, or under the shed nailed up against the tree. They took turns napping precariously on narrow wooden benches. On these same benches they counted their money, played cards or ate their meals, sold by women moving quietly through the heat, lugging pots of hot food and plates.

At the corner, where people sometimes came to watch fights or funeral processions, Adia and Jorge would wait for Nicanor. His sagging cabriolet swayed from side to side, seeming to do a happy dance as Nicanor swung towards them. They knew he only came their way because he could find no better fares in the city.

'We and Nicanor keep each other alive,' Adia said.

Nicanor pulled up making clicking noises with his mouth to make the horse stop. Climbing on board was a tricky business. If Adia or Jorge sat down too abruptly, it made the carriage pitch sharply to the rear, pulling on the harness painfully so the horse protested with an angry neigh.

'Whoa!' Nicanor would cry, then *Tsk, tsk, tsk* again, clicking his tongue to calm the beast.

'Everyday I find it harder to feed her,' he lamented. He was skinny and appeared in need of better nutrition himself. But his eyes lit up when he could coax the horse into a canter on an empty street. *Whoa! Tsk, tsk, tsk. Whoa girl! Tsk, tsk, tsk.*

'See?' he turned them. 'still some of the old racehorse in her.'

'And some of the old jockey in you,' replied Adia.

'Oh,' Nicanor smiled shyly. 'Oh, oh.'

'How old is your horse?' Jorge asked.

'Her?' Nicanor frowned. He couldn't seem to remember.

'It looks a hundred years old.'

'Ssh!' Adia said.

It was all skin and bones and frothing at the mouth. Nicanor looked determined to keep her alive. He rarely used his whip, though he kept its end dangling by the horse's ear, and the animal appeared to know when to speed up or to slow down, just from the clicking noises its master made. It made Nicanor sound like the bats that came out ticking at night.

At that time there was a very popular show on TV called 'The Coachman's Tales.' Its main character was a carriage driver like Nicanor. Every week there was a different story, and Jorge asked Nicanor to tell them a tale as they drove to town.

He basked in the boy's misconceived admiration, and happily told them accounts where he was always the hero who managed to save a pretty girl who had flagged him down to plead for help. In his most outlandish tale, his horse found it in her old bones to gallop and leap across a broken bridge to deliver a beautiful woman from her tormentor.

'That old *thing*?' Jorge asked.

'Sure!' Nicanor said whole-heartedly. 'She's not one to show off. But, boy, the things *she* can do.'

His eyes gleamed when the boy proved willing to believe him.

'My,' said Adia beside Jorge.

Nicanor was happy. In the child's mind he found license to indulge his old dreamer's heart.

Then one day, Nicanor failed to appear at the corner. Adia and Jorge had to wait till the chauffeur came home. He told them all about the fracas in town the night before.

Nicanor had used his whip on a policeman who was trying to break up a fight between Nicanor and his wife. The coachman was very drunk and was hauled off to jail.

'Poor man,' Adia said. 'The things hunger will drive a man to do.'

'You're right,' the chauffeur said to Adia. 'It was hunger.'

They waited for him to elaborate. He took a drag on his cigarette and exhaled. 'He came out to harness the horse. It wouldn't move. Nicanor got ready to give it a lashing. Then one push and the beast falls down dead.'

'*Poof!*' He spread his hands and let his gaze rise slowly to the ceiling. 'One moment it's standing there. Legs locked like it was sleeping. Then...' He shook his head, as if at a mystery he couldn't explain.

'I suppose that's the end of poor Nicanor,' Adia said.

The chauffeur shrugged. 'He loved that horse more than his wife,' he said by way of commiseration. 'But what can you do for a man who's caught between a nag and his horse?' He laughed at his own joke. Adia and Jorge were sad to lose the cheap fare to the city. But they were sadder to lose the friendship of old Nicanor.

It wasn't long before a new breed of vehicles started to ply the old bus routes. They were noisy and painted more brightly than any of the cabriolets, with chrome plating and multicoloured tassels flying from the roof and side mirrors. The brash new vehicles were reconditioned American jeeps salvaged from the war. Passengers sat on two long planks bolted length-wise to the sides. Children were charged half-fare if they sat on someone's lap, full-fare to sit by themselves. It became childhood's first rite of passage not to be cradled on a parent's lap but accorded the rights of a full-paying passenger on the long seat.

Jorge fought off all of Adia's attempts to make him sit on her lap when they first boarded those jeeps. He clung ferociously to the bar over the middle aisle, fending off all of Adia's efforts to grab him, while casting a look of contempt at a boy travelling half-fare, head lolling against his mother's chin.

But even full-paying adults gazed with deference at those daring few who jumped onto the jeeps' rear running board and gripped the handles all the way into town. Miguel and Jorge soon devoted themselves to perfecting this bold behaviour. But the drivers became wise to this brigand's mode of travel and tore around the corners to keep joyriders from clambering aboard.

When Jorge and Miguel managed to get a free ride into town in the early evening, they always headed for *Calle* Luna to watch the neon signs. Many others gathered at the corner of the plaza to do the same thing.

The glittering signs were the first to appear in Puerto Reina and people stared up at them, as if baffled by the flowering incandescence of dreams.

Some argued about how they were made, others boasted that they had seen better. A man who had been to the capital said he had seen signs that jumped and spun over the buildings like a giant Ferris wheel. Children mingled with dreamers and madmen, and all stood gaping as if the bright apparitions on the rooftops were a munificent promise that had formed in the sky.

Flights of fancy were emboldened under the neon signs. As if the extravagant assurance of light made anything possible. There was a turbaned traveller who called himself the snake man. He said he was selling a glowing spider that spun webs of light, found only in the witches' town of Capiz.

It was there that Jorge and his brother first encountered the astounding ventriloquist who could make rocks speak. He made the crowd hear voices from behind, above and below them. People lifted their feet to see if their shoes really were talking to them. They looked under their armpits for sources of the uncanny sounds. They heard the people next to them make strange and embarrassing admissions. Fights broke out between strangers who found themselves suddenly insulting each other for no reason. It was a bewildering thing. The deaf-mutes begging at the corner spoke up for the first time in their lives. The unhearing beggars looked at themselves to see what was making the crowd laugh and point at them.

It only stopped when the ventriloquist held up his hand and said the performance was over. He took out a small sackcloth bag from his pocket. His audience was again astonished when he refused to take their money.

'I only ask one thing in payment,' he said, walking around in front of the throng. He held up the sackcloth bag. 'This is what enables my skills to continue.'

His listeners nodded, thinking they understood.

The ventriloquist moved into the crowd. 'I ask each of you to speak into this bag.'

People obliged, smiling, amused by the funny claim.

'And your voices will be heard in the next town. Even long after you are gone, your voices will live on,' the man continued. 'And when I'm lonely up in the hills where I live, I need only put his bag to my ear and hear you, you and all the voices of the hundreds of people I have met.'

Each time someone spoke into it, he closed the sackcloth pouch tightly, as if afraid to let something escape.

No one knew when he said goodbye, or when exactly he managed to slip away. There was just a voice that seemed to come from nowhere and spoke to them all.

It said, '*Just remember. Only one voice allows us all to speak.*'

Then the street went back to its ordinary life.

Not far from the corner where the long disused tramlines crossed, there was an old shop with a giant seashell over the entrance. Its name was barely readable in the eroded marble. *Lamarre Jewellers.*

It was run by a man Adia called the Frenchman, about whom she had told them many stories. His dark eyebrows curled over his eyes as he pored over a watch spring. He was sitting in a chair that creaked every time he moved. Now and then he raised his head to squint through the grimy window on the front, which turned passers-by into foggy apparitions from another time. He peered down at Miguel and Jorge for several moments when they came in, as if they were creatures that had come out of nowhere.

The dusty shop was full of ornate, metallic boxes that filled the air with a multitude of clicks and ticks in various, contrasting rhythms. The two boys went down the narrow room surrounded by the hurried, relentless cacophony of time. They picked up clocks and put them down again, shaking the dust off their hands.

'Where's the old market?' asked Miguel.

'The old market...?' The Frenchman seemed relieved one of them had spoken. He looked confused. 'Isn't...your mother coming?'

Jorge wondered what his brother would say.

'No. She's not coming,' Miguel said. He looked at Jorge and shrugged.

'Oh,' the Frenchman said. 'I thought you boys got off the tram.'

'There's no tram anymore,' Miguel said.

'Of course,' smiled the Frenchman. He got back to his watch spring. 'I seldom go out," he said. 'I'm trapped here.'

'Why?' asked Miguel.

'I can't stand the silence outside. It suffocates me.'

Miguel exchanged glances with his brother. 'Someone told me the old market is behind your shop,' he said to the Frenchman.

'Why, yes.' His chair creaked as he got up. He led them to a door in the back and opened it. The boys shielded their eyes in the sudden brightness.

They followed the Frenchman out into the empty lot in the blinding bright sun, and saw the thick pillars of Puerto Reina's old market. The stalls were empty now, the walls blackened by a fire that destroyed the district long ago.

The railroad tracks that led from the market to the docks were still there, snaking through clumps of grass. Just where they ended there were three railcars with their doors open, their cargo being unloaded. From a fourth car they could hear the sounds of big animals raging against their confinement. The rampage of the beasts made the heavy railcar rock from side to side.

Jorge walked around a little frightened. On the ground were large rolls of canvas and tent poles of various lengths. They saw only one tent standing that day, but two more were being raised at the edge of the lot.

'It's the *Feria Nacional*,' said the Frenchman, rubbing his hands in excitement. There was a smile behind his beard and his eyes twinkled.

'They come every year,' he said, 'no matter the weather.' His leaned down to speak to Jorge. 'You should come with your brother tomorrow night.' He opened his eyes wide. 'You'll see lots of creatures you never thought existed.'

He straightened up and seemed to Jorge tall enough to reach the rooftops. 'They come just once a year. It makes everything bearable till the next time.'

Jorge had no idea what he meant, but the sounds from the closed railcar intrigued him so he couldn't sleep until they could come again.

They returned on a cloudless night to find an ephemeral city of tents. There were pits and trenches between the tents and Miguel kept warning his brother to be careful of snakes. They entered one tent and saw their first goblins. There were no seats inside, just a rope dividing the audience from the stage. On the stage there was a large glass cube on a table.

The audience was made to wait until midnight. Then assistants finally carried in a box where they said the goblins were kept. There were locks and latches to be undone. The showman passed a candle flame several times over the lid. He wore a shiny black suit buttoned tightly at his middle. He had large, effeminate eyes and a wide mouth that often broke into a smile. It always filled the crowd with anticipation because his smile seemed to promise many things.

A hush came down in the tent as the lights were dimmed. In the darkness whispers went back and forth. *Where are they?*

Are they really there?

'Ssh!' The showman held a finger to his lips. 'They think it's daytime and we must not let them know we're here.'

The audience surged forward and there were murmurs of disbelief.

My God. It's real.

Through gaps between bodies Jorge glimpsed shadows moving into the glass cube. The showman laughed softly. 'They think they're still by themselves in their little earth mounds. Where no one can see.'

The rope was tightened to keep the stage from being swamped. Jorge craned his neck to see.

'They're playing with light,' laughed the showman again as three small figures pranced around a bright spot being beamed from above. 'They think it's something you can pick up and hold.'

He said that goblins saved up the light to warm their homes deep in the earth, and could answer queries about the dead. He asked for questions from the audience and a woman called out, 'Is my husband there?'

'Is my grandmother happy?'

'Where did Carlos hide the key to the box?'

The shadowy figures laboured around the luminous spot, and Jorge and Miguel strained to see as the showman sometimes got in the way. He spoke with the goblins in an inaudible language and came back with answers from beyond the grave. The audience never stopped shifting on their feet, squirming to get a better view of the stage.

In the hot air of the tent messages went back and forth between the living and the dead. It was an arduous task for the showman and in the end his face was shiny with sweat. Until the audience finally fell silent, disheartened and sad.

At last, the beam of light was extinguished, and darkness fell in the tent. When the lights came back on, the figures in the glass cube had disappeared. But a pool of water had formed in the middle of the glass square.

'Tears from the other world,' the showman said. He scooped it up, then with a flick of his girlish hands it became a sparkling bracelet that he dangled before the audience. He offered it to anyone who would take it.

No one moved. He stood near the entrance holding it up until people began to leave. 'No?' he said. 'No takers?'

The crowd shied away from him like he was cursed.

The Feria's lights were still in full blaze by the time Jorge and his brother left. They stood on the street corner for a while, watching the glow over the rooftops. It seemed the noisy life in the tents would go on till dawn.

Miguel was excited, giggling about the things they'd seen. 'It's always like this for them,' he said. 'Bright and fantastic.'

They found it hard to tear themselves away from the radiant sight of the fair and move on into the quiet night. They caught a late bus trawling the empty streets in front of the closed bars. On the long, dark drive to Aguada, Miguel kept talking about the fair. His chest heaved as though he were angry. 'They have their own ship,' he said to his brother. 'They sail to all the islands. All year round.'
He seemed lost in thought for a while, then in the darkness Jorge heard him say, 'One day I'll go to the docks. Jump on the first ship that will take me.'
Jorge knew his brother spent most of his time at the pier now, talking to the sailors. They told him about all the places they'd been.

The street lamps shone on Miguel's face as he stared out the window. His curly hair fell over his eyes and Jorge could see the glint that appeared in them when he spoke about far-off places. Jorge was puzzled by his brother's pent-up anger, his breathing becoming short whenever he talked about going away.

'Better than to go back to that miserable house!' Miguel punched his fist into his other hand. Jorge watched him at those moments and couldn't understand. Miguel was four years older than him, with pale skin and those high cheekbones that Adia said would break many hearts. His full, girlish lips looked petulant, which gave him his capricious charm.

The bus stopped at the cemetery and they had to walk the rest of the way. They finally reached their house and went in as quietly as they could. They tiptoed through the hall to reach their rooms and Jorge felt the cold, mysterious breeze blowing through the house again.

Jorge knew somehow that the money they spent in the house came from sugar planted in San Gabriel. It was his uncle who later explained to him how the planters there lived always on the brink of ruin. They fought battles with workers and each other to ward off penury. There was a planter who used to come to their house, an old relative from San Gabriel. He was always looking up at the sky or studying the foliage, his face gloomy, afraid of disaster. His shoulders stooped from the constant expectation of calamity, and his ravaged face bore proof of past and possible misfortune. He noticed something in the leaves of the hedge in the back that made him fret. He squatted down to speak to Jorge. 'You know what locusts can do, son?'

'I've eaten locusts,' Jorge said. 'They're tasty, like shrimps.'

'Sure, sure, ' the man nodded. 'But did you know locusts could eat you?'

'Really?'

'Your crops, your home. Your family, your *life*.'

Jorge hadn't known. He was glad he had eaten so many now.

'What do they do with the house paint?' he wondered.

'The house paint?'

'When locusts eat your house, do they eat the house paint, too? And does the paint stay in your stomach when you eat the locusts?'

'No, no.' The man shook his head and laughed. 'I didn't mean that.'

He got up and started pacing on the gravel near the gate. Jorge heard him ask Adia what time his father would be back. Adia mumbled an answer and the man put his hat on and left. He was one of a number of people who came to the house erratically. Their arrival at the door was always startling, coming in from the road where no one seemed to have any reason to come.

Rust was eating the thick iron bars of the fence. Adia said Jorge's grandfather had built it from steel he salvaged from elsewhere. He got workmen from the village to dig a trench around the property, then finally put down the fence when he decided he would never go back to live in the city. The sliding windows on the second floor had panes made from Capiz shells. They gave a view of the bell tower in the next town, whose chimes echoed in the rooms at dusk or in the morning. Birds liked to roost on the railing around the roof. Miguel and his brother pelted them with stones to see them scatter in flight.

Jorge and his brother played near the village until dark. Adia would be lighting her stove when they came back. Sometimes Jorge would come into the house and hear the buzzing in the dark. The smell told him it was a grain fly.

He hated the buzzing but couldn't kill it. Its squashed body would infect the house for days with its smell of calamity. Adia said it was the revenge of the helpless, and they let the nasty insects fly around in the darkness rather than suffer its reeking penalty.

Miguel didn't like to show it, but Jorge could sense he was a little frightened of Adia.

'It must be true what everybody says,' he told Jorge. 'She *is* a witch.'

Sailors at the pier had told him about the sorcerers of Capiz. 'You know what they call grain flies there?' he asked his brother.

'What?'

'They call them witches' pets.' He gripped Jorge by the shoulders. 'How come she knows all these things? About our mother. About *us*?'

Jorge pushed him away and went into the kitchen. The warmth from Adia's stove made him feel it wasn't true. He believed Adia knew the reason for everything. Even the chauffeur believed she could read people's minds. She'd been around so long, she had raised so many people, just like she was raising him and his brother.

At the back of the property was a shrivelled tree that Adia still watered and called the sacred tree. She said one day she woke up to find the top branches in bloom. New leaves had sprouted overnight. By the end of that year Jorge was born, his mother's second child, and the last of their line.

Melba did her work assiduously, in the kitchen with Adia, except when Miguel made her cry. Then she would disappear and no one could find her. Since the time Jorge discovered her secret he always knew where to find her.

She would be sitting in the crawl space under the roof, looking at something shining brightly in the corner.

'What's that?' Jorge asked her.

She didn't look up but she motioned for him to be quiet. She said, 'It's all the light I'm putting away.'

When the afternoon was cool Adia never failed to go for her walks with Jorge. They would start at the plaza and wander down to Fort Road, all the way to the docks. Between Fort Road and the church of Santo Domingo they passed a place called *Madame Fung*'s, with its large Chinese characters carved in black and gold hanging between tall vermilion columns made of wood.

Drying laundry flew over shells of old villas facing the sea, hung out by squatting families who had taken over the abandoned properties. Their sun-darkened children ran half-naked on the deserted pathway along the water, once meant only for the rich residents of the luxurious neighbourhood.

A short distance away was the famous Navy Club. It was a two-storey mansion with a large paved courtyard dotted with palms and frangipanis. An American flag hung in shreds from one of its arched windows. A striped green- and-white canopy sagged over double doors which opened to a wide marble stairway. The U.S. Navy had built it for its officers when their squadrons were first stationed in Puerto Reina. After the war the Americans left, but the Navy Club remained. It became a lavish meeting place for Puerto Reina's wealthy planters, who were once the only locals admitted into the establishment.

Adia took Jorge up the stairs to the ballroom, which was the biggest room he had ever seen. On the far side were tall windows looking out on the courtyard and beyond that they could glimpse the sea. All the furniture had been pushed to one side. The large round tables were bare and covered with dust. Chairs were stacked on them up-side down.

The long bar along the inner wall had a heavy brass rail that still looked shiny. Tattered curtains flew on the sides of the shuttered windows. Jorge and Adia walked towards a dais like the stage on the plaza. The curved wooden banister on its side was smooth and polished like the pews in a cathedral.

'What performers they had here.' said Adia softly, gazing up on the stage. The smell of dust hung all around them, and when Adia stomped her foot, a dusty puff rose around her legs.

'We used to dance here,' she said with a laugh. Jorge was startled. Adia's voice echoed in the cavernous space. Her laughter lingered like a happy strain in the air. She stood with her feet together, her head turned towards the stage. Then with her eyes closed and half-smiling, she swirled in front of Jorge with a grace that struck the boy. The light in her eyes made him think of her as a young woman, smiling at her partner in the ballroom crowded with dancers.

But she turned to one side and suddenly stood still. Above them the black ceiling fans hung like dark wings in the silence. They dangled from squeaking joints that swung in the slight breeze, looking like they were about to come crashing to the floor.

Jorge wondered what was going to happen.

Moments passed in silence. It seemed nothing would ever happen here again.

Adia motioned for him to follow her. Downstairs in the courtyard she darted in one direction and stopped. She held her hand to her face as if something confused or saddened her.

'What are you looking for?' he asked her.

'It's here somewhere,' she said, her eyes still dazzled by something in the surroundings. He wondered if it was the sweetness from the frangipani trees.

'You just can't see it,' Adia said.

Jorge looked around. 'What can't I see?'

Adia's eyes were fixed on something behind him and she smiled. 'You can't now. But you will.'

As they were leaving, she turned to him once more and said, 'As you get older you'll begin to see the past.'

They didn't talk until they got to the old bus station, just pillars and rubble now. Adia gave a squeal of pleasure and bent down to a crevice behind the wall. Jorge saw that she had retrieved something from the pile of debris there. She dusted it off . It was part of a doll.

'A doll for Rosanna,' Adia said, holding it in both hands. 'A doll any little girl would have loved.'

Hearing Adia say his mother's name puzzled Jorge. He wondered if after all Miguel was right. Perhaps, Adia was mad.

When Jorge told his brother about it that night Miguel laughed. 'That old woman is turning you into a puff-brain,' he said. 'Just like her.'

He liked the word he had just invented, and kept repeating it *puff-brain, puff-brain, puff-brain,* chuckling to himself until he went off to sleep. It was another insult he had added to the many his brother couldn't answer. Jorge hadn't yet thought up a good retort to *whistle-bottom,* which his brother dreamt up one night in front of the TV, after a meal of peas, when Jorge couldn't control the excitement of gasses in his stomach.

Melba told him not to mind his brother's taunts. She promised him one day she would show him the veil she had passed to make her sadness go away. By that time they had realised that it wasn't madness that afflicted Melba's people. It was melancholy. It was a crippling contagion that infested those living in faraway towns on the edge of empty seas. The disease could be fatal, Adia said. That was why so many of Melba's people flocked to the city, dazzled by the lights.

They walked for miles without rest, hoping to lose the heaviness in their hearts. They were among the people Jorge and his brother saw standing on street corners staring up at the flickering neon lights, hoping perhaps to cure their illness. But the infection in their breath tainted others with their hopelessness. Soon their growing numbers threatened the city and no one knew what to do.

One day Jorge fell ill. Adia feared the worst. She thought he had succumbed to Melba's disease. In the night he was weak and hot with fever and they carried him to his mother's room. He struggled with them because he was afraid. He didn't want to sleep in that room, where the smell of roses kept drifting in.

He faded in and out of dreams under the heavy sheets, sweating and crying from the pain in his head and chest. He was fleetingly aware of Melba coming in. She rubbed his chest and slipped something under the sheets. When she left, Jorge felt something hot burning against his skin. He took a look and saw something shining next to his body under the sheets. He fell asleep.

He dreamed that he floated in the darkness for a long, long time. When he woke up he saw the sun shining in a circle on the floor. Melba came in. She felt his forehead, his neck, then his chest. She smiled and hugged him.

'See?' she said. 'The light made you well.'

One day an important guest came to their house. He sat in the living room with their father. Miguel told him the visitor was their uncle, Ruben Zandro, their mother's brother. He was an influential senator in the capital.

Adia refused to come to the dining room to serve the guest. But she kept stealing glances through the doorway at the senator. When he was gone, Adia went quietly to her room. Jorge found her crying on the bed, her hands shaking. 'It's a miracle what he's become,' she sobbed. 'They were such pitiful children. I was so sorry for them all.'

Jorge didn't understand. He went out to find Miguel.

The next day they rode into town to see the carnival one last time. But it was too late. The tents had been dismantled and the fairground was empty. The brothers looked at the holes left by the tent poles, the tufts of grass on the dry earth. Jorge felt sad. It was such desolation from the music and the noise of the week before.

They hopped on a passing jeep and got off at the pier. They used to go there and watch ocean liners stopping over on their way to other places. It enthralled them to hear the names of the cities the ships were bound for, names that for them were merely magical sounds. The ocean liners appeared briefly on their shores like vessels on uncanny journeys and quickly vanished again. The massive visitors shrank on the horizon to disappear like dissipating dreams.

Now, the ship bearing the *Feria Nacional* was sailing away, taking their cheer and their enchantments with them. Jorge and Miguel watched it getting smaller and smaller, until the ship that carried a movable colony of miracles was just a grey speck on the waves. It took a long time for it to disappear.

Then, without saying a word, Miguel walked towards the watchtower that looked out over the pier. He started to climb. Jorge followed. The boys got to the ledge that blocked off the top of the tower. 'Help me up,' Miguel said.

Jorge gave his bottom a push and watched his brother pull himself up to the very top.

'Can you see anything?' Jorge shouted up to him.

'Sure,' Miguel shouted back.

Jorge could see him getting into position, walking around on the ledge. 'What can you see?'

'I see islands! Lots of them,' answered Miguel.

'How many?'

'I don't know. Too many to count.'

'Help me up.'

'I'm going to the farthest one!' Miguel suddenly shouted. He laughed, then shouted again. 'I'm going to all of them!'

II.

That was the year Miguel first disappeared. He had just turned fifteen and grown tired of waiting. When Jorge came home from the village that day Adia was waiting at the gate for him. 'Where's your brother?' she asked.

He shrugged, sure Miguel was just in the city and would soon come back.

'He didn't sleep here last night,' Adia said.

'No?'

They went to Miguel's room and found his maps, pencils, and a compass. 'He'll be back,' Jorge said. 'He won't go anywhere without these.'

Adia took a deep breath. 'I hope so.'

But days passed and Miguel didn't appear.

Those first few nights Jorge was afraid to face his father. He felt guilty for not stopping Miguel. He climbed the tree at the back and tried to hide. From where he positioned himself, their house looked like it was leaning to one side. All around it there was just the darkness. What business did it have being there? Jorge wondered if Miguel was right to leave. If he shouldn't just run away, too, and perhaps try to find his brother.

He went to his room thinking of Miguel, wondering what adventures he was having now. He was sure Miguel wouldn't even tell him. If he ever saw his brother again.

Puff brain..Jorge woke up in the darkness. He blinked a few times and looked around the room. Nothing stirred. He thought he had heard Miguel's voice, standing over him, taunting him awake.

He went out into the hall. It was deathly quiet. In the living room he saw where his father had sat on the couch, his book and his pack of cigarettes. Looking out the window at the dark field, he remembered Adia's warning: *There are snakes in that field.*

He wondered if Miguel and he would ever play there together again. He felt cold. There was creak from the large, carved furniture in the shadows. Adia said they were made from antique wood, older than his father. Wood that had seen people live and die. He climbed the stairs to his father's room. He wanted to knock, but changed his mind, and walked back to his own room. He felt the slight chill in the air again.

It was Miguel who first noticed that sometimes there was a breeze that blew through their house. It was blowing from the time their mother Rosanna was a girl, seeping everywhere even when all the doors and windows were shut, chilling everyone to the bone. It was perhaps the only story Miguel remembered their mother telling him.

'There it is again,' she used to say. She told him how the only time her whole family came together was when they were huddled in the living room, lighting candles and lamps against the inexplicable breeze from nowhere.

One late afternoon, a bent old woman arrived. She rapped on the door so softly no one heard. When Jorge came out she said hello to him and he gave a start. 'Ah!'

He called Adia.

Adia knew immediately that the old woman was from the interior. She was so thin the skin hung from her bones like old leather. Though she looked very old, there was not a white hair on the woman's head. Her long hair was strikingly black. She had several missing teeth, which gave her mouth a twisted shape. Her lined face had a curious pallor, and her sunken eyes were bloodshot and anxious. Adia gave her a drink of water.

'The buses to the north are all gone,' the old woman said. She had a small, heavy box with her, and Adia's expression changed when she saw it. She began speaking to the woman in a familiar way, as if she had known for some time she would come.

'You can come in,' Adia said, and the old woman started to wipe her feet. 'But you have to leave the box outside.'

The old woman stopped wiping her feet. She stared into the house behind Adia, trying to see into the shadows inside. Her eyes looked so tired it seemed they had never known sleep.

'All right, then,' she said in a high singing voice that very old people had. 'As you say.'

The woman picked up her box and left. Jorge watched her walk to the tamarind tree where the buses usually parked. She held out her hand, as if to flag down a vehicle. It was late Sunday afternoon. The road was empty for miles in both directions. There would be no more buses till the next day.

Adia and Jorge came out later and she was still on the roadside, looking from side to side, wondering why no buses had appeared.

'There won't be anything passing till tomorrow,' Adia called out to her. 'You can spend the night in the house, if you just leave the box outside.'

She shook her head and sat down near her box, her tired eyes staring out into the distance. Adia went back to the house while Jorge stayed behind. He asked the woman what she had in the box. Her face brightened up a little.

'Why I can let you look inside,' she said in that high voice. 'As long as you bring me something I want.'

'Like what?'

She looked down on the ground, thinking. When she looked up she had a smile on her face. 'A key. An old one. Bring me any key.' She called out after him. 'One nobody uses anymore.'

Jorge ran home to think about the strange request. By nightfall he had forgotten. They came out the next day and the woman was still there. Some jeeps had already driven by, but the old woman refused to move, sitting with her arms crossed over her knees, staring into space.

'She hasn't left yet, poor soul,' Adia said. 'I wonder what she's waiting for.'

Jorge was afraid to tell her that he knew. Adia scanned the skies and looked worried. 'I hope she won't be here when it starts to rain. She'll catch her death of cold.'

It was late in the day that Jorge finally remembered his promise to their persistent visitor. He went into the house to look for keys. He found several old ones in different rooms. The search took him a long time. It was getting dark.

He chose three keys. He took them to the old woman and she snatched them away, giving them a quick wipe on her skirt. She seemed very pleased, chuckling to herself in what sounded like a dry croak. Then she picked up the box and started to walk away.

'Wait,' Jorge said.

She stopped and turned around.

'You promised to show me what was in the box.'

She seemed impatient to go, looking up at the darkening sky. She looked at him uncertainly. 'Are you sure?'

'Yes.'

She put down the box and motioned for him to come closer. 'All right, then, brave little man.' She squatted down on the ground and opened the box and quickly shut it again. Jorge started to protest that she had not opened it long enough.

Then he realised that something *had* jumped out of the box. It was leaping back and forth above their heads in the branches of the tamarind tree. He tried to get a better glimpse of it. But it kept jumping around.

'Well,' the old woman said. 'That's our bargain. Now I must go.'

She had already picked up the box and was walking away. 'I've got the keys to three rooms where no one goes,' she laughed.

When it hung still for a moment, Jorge got a good look at the thing that had jumped out of the box. It was a white spider with legs like glass. The web it spun on the branches throbbed with some kind of light.

The woman laughed again and gave a wave. 'I hope you'll learn to live with what you asked for.'

She walked down the road and disappeared.

The white spider jumped from branch to branch, weaving threads that grew brighter in the gathering dusk.

One day after the rains, Miguel suddenly reappeared. He stood in the hall outside Jorge's room still with mud on his shoes. Jorge was happy to see him. He watched him closely as Miguel came in and sat down on the bed, looking very tired. He kept rubbing the palm and fingers of one hand, as if trying to erase something.

'This is the farthest place in the world,' he said, looking gloomily at his hand. 'We were born in the smallest, farthest place on earth. You know sailors can't even find us on the map? We'll never go anywhere.'

'What do you mean?'

'All you see here are people passing through.'

Jorge could tell he had been at the pier. 'No one ever comes here except by accident,' said Miguel. 'I met a girl. She was so pretty. She and her family were going to Australia.'

'Where's Australia?'

'I don't know. But it's not like here. It's a *big* place. With lots of parks and nice things to do. Not just old buildings and mad people.'

He propped himself up on the bed and said, like he was speaking to someone Jorge couldn't see: 'I'm going to Australia.'

'When?'

'I don't know. Some day.'

He sat staring at the wall for a long time and Jorge wondered what he was thinking. He didn't tell Jorge where he'd disappeared to. But his brother guessed that something happened to make him sadder than before.

One day Jorge heard him throwing stones at the roof. Adia shouted for him to stop. Out of his window Jorge saw his brother kicking a can around the yard. He watched as Miguel picked up a large stone and hurled it towards the house, shouting, 'Away, you stupid birds!'

Jorge heard the crash on the roof and the sudden outbreak as birds flew away to escape. He saw them arc over the field as Miguel laughed and jumped, running around the yard flapping his arms like wings, shouting, 'Away! Away, away!'

Jorge was in the dining room waiting for lunch when he heard Melba scream. He ran out to see the shed on fire. The chauffeur was trying to put it out with buckets of water, sand and gravel that he was scooping up from the driveway. Everyone helped and finally the flame was put out.

'That boy,' Adia shook her head. 'What are we going to do with him?'

They stood looking at the wet ground around the shed.

'I heard someone hanged himself from the tamarind tree the other night,' Melba said to Jorge.

The disclosure bothered him. 'The tamarind tree?'

Melba nodded. 'They've removed him now.'

He went to have a look. There was nothing in the tree when he got there. He was relieved. He clearly remembered the old woman standing under it with her box. As he walked away he saw children pointing at the tree behind him.

Then he saw it swinging over the branches. The white spider was spinning its web of light. He shuddered to recall the old woman's words as she walked away. He tried to erase them from his mind. *I hope you'll learn to live with what you asked for.*

When he got home he found Miguel was slumped on the couch, reading a book. Adia put a drink on the table beside him, then put her hand against his cheek.

'It's just a slight fever,' she said. 'Drink some more. It'll go away.'

Miguel let out a stricken sigh. His eyes looked swollen and his forehead glistened with sweat. Jorge moved closer and saw the rash on his neck. Miguel groaned in pain. Something on his shirt caught Jorge's eye. He leaned in to see it better.

'What's this?' said Jorge, as he removed a glowing silken thread from his brother's chest.

The chauffeur was sent away for a doctor.

The old man arrived and shook hands warmly with their father, who was pacing around in Miguel's room. The old doctor seemed to recognise Miguel, too. 'Ah, how you've grown,' he said, brushing his hand against Miguel's forehead. He looked at Jorge with curiosity.

Jorge left the room.

'He's a good doctor,' Adia said to Jorge in the hall. She told him the doctor had been called to the house many times before, once to give his mother an injection of morphine. Everyone huddled at Miguel's door until it was quite late. Jorge got sleepy waiting to hear what was wrong. He walked into his mother's room, sat on the bed and began to doze. Opposite him was the patched-up mirror Adia had hung back on the wall. Jorge looked at its fractured surface. In the half-light he thought he saw a reflection from a long time ago. He envisioned his mother passing the doorway laughing with her friends. He could hear their voices, their laughter fading as they climbed the stairs.

Sometimes, their mother's brothers came to the house. Ruben, the senator, rarely visited because of his work in the capital. His older brother Augusto lived in the city, however, and would sometimes bring his unruly children. He had three daughters, and three sons who often ended up fighting with Goyle, Jorge or Miguel.

The girls liked to play with Jorge's hair, brushing their palms against the back of his head to see how sharp it was. 'Like barbed wire,' the eldest one laughed, rubbing her palms with a wince. Carla, the second girl, rubbed a piece of plastic on the back of a chair, then pressed it down on Jorge's head. They made him sit while the three of them stood around him clamping down on the plastic, Christine, the eldest, repeatedly asking, 'Is it down yet? Not sticking up anymore?'

He yielded to their attentions in the belief it would save him from further humiliations in the world. Miguel had thought up the name *Porcupine-head* for Jorge's hair, which seemed to have a life of its own, springing upright after every pass of the comb. Even after he'd massaged water, pomade, baby oil, and finally spit on it. Going to town was a torment since he became aware of the problem. He walked on the street conscious of people looking at him. *Porcupine-head*, their eyes would say.

Suddenly there was a crash in the kitchen and the girls shouted, 'Nicolas!'

Nicolas was the oldest of Jorge's cousins and wherever he went with his brothers they were followed by a crash.

There was a shout from Melba. Then from Adia. And from their exclamations Jorge could follow the progress of the brothers through the house. Then from behind the shed came the chauffeur's voice, 'Jesus Christ!'

There was a long silence.

After a while there came from somewhere in the house the first tinkles of the piano. *Ting , ting, ting*.

Quiet and gentle at first, like the first sighting of a storm. The stillness that followed was tense. Then the other noises came all in rush, sudden and inexorable, the boys shouting, something falling down, and the massive cacophony of the huge, tormented instrument in the music room. Trills and glides on the keys like Jorge had never heard before. One dominant sound pervaded the shrill staccato of the higher notes. It was an ominous crescendo of destruction. *BOING. BOING. BAM! BAAAANG. BOING!*

It stopped only when they heard Adia's voice in a high-pitched scream. 'Put down that crowbar. *My God*. The *piano!*'

Their cousins were hastily taken away and did not come back for a while.

On the anniversary of Jorge's mother's death everyone came, even their Uncle Ruben. That was the day Jorge and his brother heard their uncles arguing in the back of the house. They came upon Ruben and his brother Augusto hissing at each other with clenched fists, and voices they struggled to control.

Miguel and Jorge had known for some time that their Uncle Augusto was some kind of smuggler. Over the years he had become one of the city's most notorious men. He was short and stocky, with a large forehead and thick eyebrows that jutted over his eyes in a permanent scowl.

Miguel and Jorge and Augusto's six children were all afraid of him. They watched warily as Augusto moved around with his gruff clumsiness. Jorge had heard that when their uncles were boys, Augusto had saved Ruben from drowning. They were playing on the field by the river when Ruben somehow fell in. Augusto had jumped in and dragged his brother back to the riverbank.

Unlike Augusto, Ruben was tall, like Jorge's grandfather, and had a thoughtful air about him. He had eyes that Jorge thought were gentle. He was soft-spoken and calm, although the boys had heard that he could be vehement and relentless in a court room.

Jorge and his brother were curious about why their uncles were arguing. When they found them,

Augusto was reminding Ruben of all the favours he had done for him. 'I saved you when your life once,' he said angrily. 'Now look at you. So important you can't remember those who once helped you!' Augusto was red-faced with anger. 'I nearly drowned, too. Don't you forget that! All that matters is what people do for *you*!'

Ruben tried to calm his brother down. His hands imploring, he stooped to appease the other. 'The law is the law, Augusto, 'he said. 'I can't just wish it away if I want.'

'You're supposed to be a powerful man, Ruben. You're saying you're just as helpless as me?'

'In this case, yes. I can't change the judge's decision. He's decided what his conscience tells him is right. That's what I'm powerless against.'

'Doesn't *your* conscience tell you to repay your damned debts?'

'It does. And I will pay my debts. In any way but this! Augusto, you committed a crime. No one in the world can save you from punishment. '

'Your friends steal thousands more than I do. They're guilty of much bigger crimes. Are they ever punished? The hell they are! Everyone loves to punish

111

the small fry. The big fish just swim away! You're just a hypocrite. You make me sorry to be your brother!'

It was worse than any fight Jorge and Miguel had ever had. And Jorge wondered if Miguel would one day ask a favour of him like this. And would he, the younger, refuse?

'So let them catch me,' continued Augusto, his breathing slower now. 'Leave my family to starve. If I die in prison, can they come to their uncle for food? No!' Augusto's chest heaved with every breath, but his tone was defeated. His shoulders slumped, his spiteful eyes were sad. And when he turned his back on Ruben, the boys could see his face was full of regret. He broke the twig he had picked up and crushed it in one hand.

'Don't ever think I'm not grateful for any of the things you've done for me, Augusto.' Ruben said behind him. 'But you must understand. My feelings have no bearing on my duties.'

Augusto turned to face him. 'Never mind,' he said hoarsely. 'I guess it's foolish to expect gratitude. It means nothing. It's the most worthless thing!'

The boys walked away quietly from the sad scene. Jorge would always remember the weary tilt to

Ruben's body as he faced the condemnation of his brother.

Nearly two years passed before Augusto and his family visited again. Jorge heard the taxi pull up, unload and drive away. He peered out and saw his cousins. Boxes and hastily packed suitcases were scattered on the road around them.

They had clearly left their house in a hurry. Cecilia, the youngest girl, and Octavio, her brother about the same age, were crying. Augusto and his wife were having a hushed, agitated conversation away from their children, Augusto gesturing frantically while his wife cursed and stomped her foot.

Finally, Augusto strode to the front door and knocked. He called Adia and soon she and Melba were carrying suitcases into the house. Miguel and Jorge watched as the displaced family was ushered in and their things taken to the vacant rooms.

Augusto's wife directed everything with her shrill voice, but her children squabbled about certain rooms or certain beds. Raucous disputes flared up and had to be resolved by their mother with slaps or vicious blows to the head.

At last, the boxes were cleared from the hallway and, for the first time since Jorge was born, the rooms of their house were all filled.

At play in the yard, the children revealed what they knew of their situation. Christine seemed the only one aware that their father was in trouble with the law again. They couldn't go back to their house for fear the police or one of his enemies might be waiting. They'd had to abandon everything to get away this time.

'Drop your gun or drop your pants!' said Christine, holding both her hands like an imaginary pistol. She touched her forehead in a mock-weary gesture. 'Drop your *life*. And at a moment's notice. The old bandit's rigmarole. Hmm.' She pretended to stifle a yawn with a dainty motion of her wrist. She was growing up to be quite a precious miss, with her long hair in tight braids and short skirts fluttering high above her knees. Jorge was aware that his brother found her pretty.

'If only she didn't have such skinny legs,' Miguel snickered, mimicking the dainty motion of Christine's wrists. 'Oh, oh, oh. Aarrghh!'

In the evening Augusto and his wife went out for a drive. Their children maintained some restraint until Adia began preparing dinner. Christine hugged her sister Cecilia, who was rubbing her eyes, ready to cry again. Octavio was stationed at the front window looking out for passing cars in case it was their parents coming back. But finally, when Adia had already fed everyone, and there was no sign of Augusto and his wife, their children began jumping all over the house again, on the chairs, on the bed of Jorge's mother, on the dusty, battered piano.

Everything suddenly came to a stop when they heard a door opening upstairs. They froze in anticipation.

Then, '*Uncle Leon!*' whispered Octavio across the room.

Jorge had completely forgotten that his father was still with them.

It was the happiest time he and Miguel remembered, when the house was filled with their cousins' voices, and games went on at all hours in the hall or in the yard. They had fun frightening each other in the empty rooms upstairs and waiting for the eerie breezes in the hall.

Just as Jorge and Miguel were getting used to a house bursting with people, and having a family of

sorts, Augusto decided to uproot his restive brood
again. They stole out at dawn like a band of thieves,
taking everything they had brought with them.

Jorge and his brother looked in the messy,
vacated rooms, searching for their cousins, worried
something bad might have happened.
They found Adia serenely fanning the coals in the
kitchen, humming to herself.

'Where'd everybody go?' Jorge asked her.

'Why, back to their own house,' she said. 'Thank
God.'

It would be many years before they heard
anything else about Uncle Augusto. Jorge was already
a student, about to leave for university when they
heard that Augusto had died in a hail of bullets as he
tried to ram through one of several police blockades
set up in the city to catch him. The funeral was highly
publicised because of Ruben's position. He came to
Puerto Reina for the burial and was photographed
touching Augusto's coffin with his face broken up in
tears. The picture appeared in all the papers, and Jorge
would always wonder if at that moment Ruben was
thinking of the last insult his brother had made about
his ingratitude.

Miguel and Jorge realised that the worst onslaught of their cousins was nothing compared to the agony of being by themselves in their father's presence again. As before, they retreated into the kitchen, Adia's domain, where she not only gave them things to taste but teased their minds with her endless tales. The warmth of the coals in her clay stove made them feel safe from the unsettling breezes of the house.

The air in the kitchen was pungent with spices, and in its aromatic cloud Adia conjured up images which enchanted the boys. Miguel would become an adventurer and Jorge, a writer, because of the servant woman with the vivid imagination and astounding memory.

She told them about a people called the Waqwaqs who sailed in great boats from somewhere across the Pacific to settle in the uninhabited archipelago. She talked about the revolt against Spain as though she had seen it herself, when the Spaniards left in defeated warships, to be replaced by happy, whistling, drunk Americans. After the Americans, there quickly followed the war, which Adia also talked about, leaving out bits that seemed to cause her pain.

117

'There was dancing,' she said. 'Even when bombs were falling.'

Melba and the chauffeur smirked and furtively made 'windmill' gestures at their temples. Goyle listened with his mouth agape, his eyes catching the glint from Adia's coals.

The chauffeur sat on his haunches near the doorway, always alert for a summons from Jorge's father and the possibility of an errand to run at any hour. He was a wiry man with thinning hair and a scar over his right eye. His wide mouth often showed disdain and his small eyes took in everything, looking you up and down. When Adia argued with him he muttered things under his breath that she found threatening.

He was friendly with many of the unsavoury characters that loitered around the old Hotel Oriente in the city. Adia objected to them coming to the house, even if only to chat at with the chauffeur at the gate. Adia protested it wasn't a good influence on boys like Miguel and Jorge, and threatened to tell their father about it. But the chauffeur boasted that he knew things about the boys' father that gave him power over everyone in the house. Adia avoided him like the grain flies she was afraid to kill, lest their stench of calamity spread in the house.

'What really happened to Tata Isio?' Melba asked once. 'Did the Japanese really chop off his hands before killing him?'

She and the chauffeur often asked Adia about people from the war. Some of them were legends whose fame lived on in peacetime. Adia said she knew most of them from the Japanese internment camp. She spoke of their last words, their grotesque ends.

There was a man who laughed uncontrollably because of damage to his nerves. They shot him in the leg and he laughed. They crushed his hand with hammers and he laughed. They put a noose around his neck and he seemed to find it hilarious. They could hear his giggling through the bag they placed over his head until they kicked the chair over.

'There was a Japanese soldier who couldn't stop crying,' said Adia, starting another tale. 'An injury had torn his tear ducts and his face was always wet with tears.' She said. 'Even when he danced with the girls he was crying.'

She told them of how Rosanna's mother left when Rosanna was young. Rosanna once found a gold coin among her mother's things. It was a coin from Spanish times called a *cruzado*, and it was the only thing she had of her mother. Rosanna kept it like an amulet until she got sick, when she felt it had brought her nothing, as it had brought her mother no good fortune. Adia always wept when she told this story. And there were tears in Jorge's eyes by the time she finished it.

Miguel would pinch his brother's face and laugh. 'Look, goblin's tears!' Those were the only times Jorge got angry enough to fight Miguel. Melba and the chauffeur would hold the pans and knives out of the boys' reach, and Adia would cross her arms and vow not to tell any more stories until they stopped.

They always stopped because they couldn't resist hearing more about their mother. The tale they liked most was about the roses from San Gabriel. Whatever had made their mother return to that distant town, it would always haunt their lives.

Rosanna had been longing for release from the marriage she had thought would save her. But the liberation came not in the form of divorce or death, which she had even begun to long for. It came instead, in the unlikely person of Cheng Ho, the friendly village postman.

'Roses,' he called out from the doorway one morning. 'Roses for Rosanna Zandro.'

That he had used her maiden name told Rosanna that the sender was someone from her past. Cheng Ho confirmed this when he produced the bouquet, saying, 'Roses from San Gabriel.'

A wave of pleasure rose through Rosanna as the fragrance of the famed blossoms began to suffuse the room. The enigma of the flowers would take her back to the island of her untroubled youth. Her husband came back from one of his trips to find a letter that said there was a man in her life after all who truly loved her. Perhaps she had written it with no inkling of what awaited her in San Gabriel.

So Rosanna did return after her trip and tried once more to salvage her marriage.

'But nothing was the same again,' Adia said, wiping her eye.

Slowly, as Adia told these stories, Jorge began to understand.

For even when Rosanna's second child was about to be born, her husband could not shake off the mistrust left by her letter of farewell. 'I won't answer for your mishaps, Rosanna,' he said when she first told him about the child. He knew only that they had long slept apart, and couldn't remember the nights when he still loved her and she longed for him. The child was born, but faith was never restored between them again.

One day, deeply troubled, Jorge confided to Adia. 'Miguel keeps saying I'm not really his brother.'

'What does it matter?' Adia consoled him. 'I'll love you whatever.'

Years later, Jorge would learn that Adia had consumed great quantities of opium in her youth, which may have affected her mind. But Jorge had grown up with her stories. He felt that only she could help him understand what that had happened before he was born. He would also begin to sense that in order to unravel his family's secret, Adia would have to reveal her own.

III.

Rosanna wrote to her friend Sara about her husband's long absences, and told of the times she climbed the stairs in the dark to reach his door, even when she knew the bed would be empty.

She watched the moonlight slant through the window across the silent room. The pale light looked forlorn on the pillow where they used to lay their heads. She gazed out the window and wondered what Leon saw there at night. If he sensed the same wretchedness in the shadows of their garden that she did. If he felt, as she did, that the tall hedge that shielded their house from the road was a prison they could not escape.

Since that time long ago when they began to sleep apart, Rosanna awoke in the mornings with a despondency tinged with guilt. She wondered if her husband upstairs felt the same fleeting wish that things could be as they once were. Now she lay her hand on her husband's unused pillow on the nights when he wasn't home, and felt the silence press down on her. She rested her head on her hands and cried. Her chest heaved and her sobs seemed to fill the room until she found it hard to breathe. It was always like that now. She cried as if some violent blow had winded her, and she gasped for air.

At first she only cried in her own room. Later she wept in hidden corners of the house, as the servants tiptoed around her, never daring to come near or ask the reason for her tears. In her heart, Rosanna knew they understood. The knowledge blew around the house. Her marriage was dead. And before the breathlessness became a crushing pain in her breast, she rushed back to her room. There was no way to dispel the certainty that shamed her, it hovered like chilly gusts over the hall.

In the half-light of her room, screened by curtains her stepmother Conchita had chosen, she poured out her feelings in letters to Sara she thought she could never send. They were folded, instead, into the diary she kept in her bureau.

In one of the drawers was a picture taken at her wedding. She had brought it in from the living room because seeing it there every day with its frozen gaiety sickened her. Looking at it now, she saw how the colours had faded, the smiling faces of that happy day had dulled into a toneless blur. The images that remained clear, did so thanks only to her own memories.

Rosanna recalled the formal ceremony and the sensation of the stiff lace collar of the wedding dress her father had bought for her. Jose Zandro and his wife Conchita embraced her after the service, as if all enmity had ceased with her marriage to Leon.

Acuzena Ruiz had stood in the back of the gathering, glowing with triumph at Rosanna finding her man. 'At last, my beauty,' she beamed. 'You'll be so happy.'

Her father and Conchita invited them to live with them for the first year. Rosanna agreed. Leon was to take up a position in the shipping company owned by Rosanna's grandfather. The job would send him to the other islands for long stretches of time. At first Rosanna asked to join him. But she had inherited her father's frail constitution and Leon insisted that his rugged destinations would not suit her.

Jose Zandro grew tired of life by the small village, so he and Conchita moved away. Rosanna ended up taking possession of the house in Aguada. She could remember when it was an unused lot by the river, which their father would take them to visit on weekends. Rosanna and her brothers played in the fields around it, catching frogs on the riverbank and taking them back in bags to the city. Once, Conchita met them at the gate, and cried out as something leapt out of the children's bag onto her chest.

Now Rosanna wandered through the spacious rooms of the house, read books by the pond in the garden, savoured the quiet in the music room where the piano was once locked by Conchita. Rosanna busied herself with the house, tending the orchids in her garden, having the furniture arranged the way she liked. She was mistress of the space where her life as a step daughter had been so curtailed. Now and then she found a few moments to retreat into the music room and play the piano. Though the pieces were merely mechanical exercises now, something about the halting effort it had taken to learn them brought back the rosy anticipations of her youth.

She wrote letters to Sara, finally forcing herself to send some of them, and bought books to read in the afternoons. She liked reading into the dusk so she wouldn't notice how another day had slipped from her, its last golden glint receding from the window sill like a hurried lover pulling away.

She buried her head in a paperback romance when the rains came, losing herself in fantasy until the sun came out again. One day she raised her head in the veranda, and looked around her blankly at the wet leaves sparkling in the sun. The rain had stopped. She tried to remember what it was that had made her stop reading and look up. Her gaze fell on her wrist and she thought: yes. *Time.*

She was wondering where all the time had gone. What had happened to all that bare, unused vastness that she had no idea how to fill? She went through the rooms of her well-kept house in panic, trying to find any signs time may have left in its passing.

Her first son had already been born, and time had begun to define itself in the little encroachments he made on the world.

Rosanna noticed a tiredness around her eyes when she looked in the mirror. It wasn't from the nights she spent without any sleep. It was something else. She found that her secret tears had left a ghost of their sorrow.

She loved her son. He was a perfect, happy child. The love in his eyes was the old adulation she had always craved. But there were times when something told her there should be more. She quarrelled with her husband when he was home. She blamed him for his long absences, his zeal for his work. She despised him for not having the spine to refuse her father's offer, for not insisting on building his own house for her. Instead he had acceded to inheriting this old relic that had been rebuilt on a secluded road she had grown weary of.

A broken look had settled on her chiselled features. The thin, dark eyebrows arched over the charming eyes with a subtle provocation. Her small mouth and elegant nose retained their appeal, but like everything about her, they seemed imbued with panic. She didn't know what was wrong. She struggled to stop the seepage that she knew was draining her life. Her house was clean and safe, so clean it had nothing to fight the darkness that suddenly swamped her. It flowed in like the insidious rush of the river that flooded Aguada in the monsoon months.

Her son had long begun to walk. And when she saw him standing at her door, it was as if she saw him on the edge of some abyss looking down at her. She reached out to him, and it seemed only his small hands could save her. She began to live for him, and every act of learning became a reward for her soul. The first steps at climbing the stairs, the first rapture as he stumbled then broke into a run. The early utterances that began to know the name of things. Then words strung together in ways that startled her.

The things he said gave Rosanna her awed discovery that a little human being was starting to make his own sense of the world. She realised, humbled, that in her child's mind there was now a vast, nocturnal universe where clouds had meaningful shapes and the people and animals (cows and goats led by young boys from the pasture) passing in front of their house walked into dreams that crowded his mind. Dreams that he told her about in the morning, and made her understand that in her child, time was becoming things, becoming feelings and desires that one day would bear fruit she couldn't conceive of.

Sara wrote to her one day in triumph. She and Juan Rodrigo had gotten married in the capital. His job was a great success. *We're thinking of moving back to Puerto Reina now*, she wrote.

Rosanna replied that now she wanted nothing more than a second child. Her son needed a companion to wander in the fields around Aguada, as she and her brothers had.

She talked to her husband about having that second child. He smiled in agreement, but his distracted assent was an affront to her. She failed to infuse him with the passion she felt, but still she climbed the stairs at night to join him in his room. She came away listless and down-hearted, isolated from the man she struggled to keep loving her. Reaching the dark hall at the bottom of the stairs she felt a great distance from him, from everyone, as if she had wound up alone on the farthest destination of her grandfather's ships.

She couldn't face the possibility that Leon had stopped loving her. She told herself things could still change. She continued buying the romances peddled by the bookseller in the market and was aghast to find one day that she had become a mere spectator to imagined experiences she once believed she herself would have.

Rosanna had grown up on the fringes of her father's love, stepping aside for her stepmother's children in the house where she was born. Rosanna's mother had left them in great disgrace when Rosanna was very young. A group of people from the ill-famed house of *Madame Fung*'s showed up one day at Jose Zandro's house. They clutched notes they said were proof of his wife's gambling debts. Their arrival in the quiet cul-de-sac of Paseo Gardenia brought with it the whiff of shame.

Jose Zandro's marriage to his street-hardened pretty wife had never been easy. From the moment he brought her to the house, his mother and sister Emilia had done nothing but wish an end to the union. Now Jose Zandro's wife Claudia had brought about the outcome they had been praying for. It was all they needed to cast her out of their respectable house.

'Look what you bring into our lives, you vile woman!' Emilia screamed at Claudia. Jose struggled to keep the two women apart.

'Get out!' Emilia shouted over his shoulder. 'Go back to the slime you came from!' The fight carried on into the street where they threw out Claudia's bags. They closed the gate behind her and threatened to have her thrown in prison if she ever tried to come back.

Claudia finally left to save her children from more anguish. She promised herself she would come and take them back. But it would be a long time before she could even think of trying.

Jose Zandro was slow to get over his wife's betrayal. But during this time he started taking his children to the land he had bought by the Aguada river. They chased butterflies over the fields and he was relieved that in time they stopped asking about their mother. He promised them one day he would sell the house in Paseo Gardenia and build a new one by the river. Jose could tell by their happiness that they, like him, had banished their mother to the farthest edges of their minds.

He remarried. His new wife Conchita Aguilar brought a sternness into their lives that ended the anxious but unfettered interlude after their mother's departure. When Conchita first came to live with them, Rosanna ran around the house until she was breathless, asking her father when they could go to Aguada again. Conchita was the one who answered for him. 'You can play in the yard,' she said. 'There's no need for pointless wandering.'

Sometime after her seventeenth birthday Rosanna began to show an interest in playing the piano. Her father had bought the Steinway Grand for her mother Claudia, shipped in at scandalous cost from England. Since Claudia left, it had stood idle in the music room. Though he did not relish a reminder, Jose was glad his daughter had inherited a love of music.

Jose and Claudia had fallen in love at the piano. She was a shop assistant at *Lamarre*, a jewellery shop in the city owned by a Frenchman who was rumoured to smuggle his goods into the country with the help of an old slave raider from Sulu. Jose Zandro was the darling of the crowd that frequented the Navy Club on those hot nights sweetened by frangipani-scented breezes.

When the orchestra took its break he would saunter up to the stage and play a tune on the keyboard. Tall and languid with delicate artist's hands, he was adored by the young women who came in silky gowns to dance the Charleston or the cha-cha. On afternoons when her work at the jewellery shop was finished, Claudia would meet Jose at the stone benches outside the Santo Domingo church. From there they often walked across the square to the ballroom of the Navy Club, where they would sit and watch the sea. Jose would pull her up towards the piano and pick out notes that echoed in the cavernous room, still quiet before the frivolities of the coming night. They both loved the ivory keys where their fingers would touch and then entwine, while their bodies grew hot, first from the humid air, then from their lips touching.

And so Rosanna one day asked her stepmother if she could learn to play the piano. It gladdened Conchita because she saw it as a way to occupy at least one of her husband's idle children. But Rosanna saw it merely as a means to escape the house and her stepmother's stern supervision. When Conchita made her one condition, Rosanna had to keep from jumping for joy.

'You'll have to practise somewhere else,' she said, folding her arms. 'I'll find you a teacher with an instrument you can use on weekdays.'

Conchita was a quiet, serious woman who was annoyed by unnecessary noise. 'Besides,' she cleared her throat, 'I gather your father doesn't appreciate the sound of the instrument as he once did in his youth. We don't want to subject the poor man to needless torment.'

She smiled at Rosanna with malice.

So a teacher was found just at the end of Paseo Gardenia, near the cinema. Her name was Acuzena Ruiz. She was half-Spanish, with stiff coiffed hair and a sensuous, wide mouth. She saw piano-teaching as a chance to plant radical ideas in the heads of girls who came wanting to learn how to play *a polonaise or perhaps a minuet for Mama's friends.*

'*Crescendo* means when something grows larger and larger and you can't stop it blowing up in your face,' she would say, her chest heaving, her hands busy playing a mass of bass notes peppered with the high keys.

Booorm. Doom-doom. She assaulted the length of the keyboard with her hands. Her brightly painted nails would click against the ivory. *SHAROOOM.* She made the notes thunder before releasing the pedal and letting the clamour fall into a soft whisper.

'Like *that*,' she would say in a small, airy voice, emitting an erotic-sounding sigh before turning to the young lady. 'Yes. *Crescendo.*'

She smiled. 'Some of us are lucky to get it all the time. Some of us have to fake it all our lives.'

Most of her students quit after the first lesson.

Coming into her house with music sheets always gave Rosanna a feeling of liberation. Acuzena touched her cheek before they sat down. 'So pretty,' she said. 'You could get by with a much smaller instrument, I'm sure. But let's try Mathew & Sons.' And when after a year of lessons, Leon Gil came into Rosanna's life, Acuzena seemed more thrilled than her. 'Don't tell him to wait for you at the corner,' she said. 'Tell him to come to my house.'

What would have been forbidden behaviour in her own home was encouraged in Acuzena's house. It was on the street corner in view of the teacher's front window that Leon Gil first accosted Rosanna with a letter and a box of chocolates. He had watched her looking at the pastry shop display and noted the sweets in front of which she had lingered. When it turned out he had given her the wrong chocolates—she had wanted *mocha-toffee*—Acuzena gladly relieved her of them, licking her fingers and wiping them on her skirt before starting again on Schubert.

Acuzena encouraged Rosanna to take a lover. And when she found out Leon had a job she was delighted, almost as if she were embarking on an adventure herself. 'You'd be wasting these lessons if you weren't going to have at least one affair,' she said. Years later, Rosanna would meet the music teacher again. With her old Spanish features, she had become one of those relics that walked through the city, drawing stares and children's taunts, an eccentric survivor of a vanished world.

She and Rosanna found each other browsing among romances in the same market stall. "My sweet!" Acuzena jumped when she saw Rosanna. "I can't believe my eyes!"

They went round and round the market stalls, talking.

'I have children now,' Rosanna told her. The teacher smiled.

'Wasn't I right?' Acuzena said as they parted, tilting her head. 'I knew you would always be lucky.'

Rosanna had shrugged. They would never meet again.

Sara wrote to Rosanna. *I found my mirror from Borneo. I was worried I'd lost it. Do you remember the night we got it in San Gabriel?*

The town was crowded when they went that year. Sara and Rosanna had to spend the first few nights in the Catholic girls' dormitory, while Leon and Juan Rodrigo found lodgings above a popular café. The two young women had to agree to be in their rooms before the dormitory gates shut at ten o' clock. Well before the time they agreed to meet.

At midnight on the first night, Rosanna and Sara lay awake in their rooms, waiting for the signal that would summon them. A flickering disc of light appeared in the shadows above Rosanna's bed. She got up and went to get Sara.

The two couples went to the bazaar. Rosanna asked Juan Rodrigo how he had shone the light into her room. He smiled but wouldn't explain. In the morning Rosanna found two roses in the dormitory's empty vase. One stem had the thorns picked off except one. *One for Sara, one for me*, she thought, refusing to acknowledge the dizziness that spread from her head to her heart. Like she refused to tell Sara about the excitement of waiting for the tremulous disc of light that would enter her room and call her out into the night.

At the bazaar she and Sara bought mirrors from a Bornean merchant, a matching pair that he said was cut from the same glass.

More letters arrived from Sara. She and Rosanna wrote to each other so much it seemed fated they would meet again. Sara knew intimately about Leon's travels and his frequent trips to the capital.

One day the car pulled up into the yard, the chauffeur blowing the horn. Leon climbed out of the back, dazed from the long sea travel.

'Rosanna! My God!' Sara leapt out of the car, followed by Juan Rodrigo. 'I had to go and ferret him out of his hiding place,' Sara said to Rosanna as their bags were being unloaded. 'I threatened to enter the nunnery unless he married me. We know he'd do anything to keep from adding any more nuns to the world.'

She and Rosanna laughed. Juan Rodrigo came up and hugged her. He had become a successful man. His company was renting one of the lavish villas on Fort Road for him. Rosanna would go there often, sometimes taking her son. She would sit on the terrace facing the sea all afternoon talking with Sara. Sometimes she thought secretly of the roses that came for her all the way across the strait from San Gabriel. Sara doted on Miguel. She played games with him on the beach or the porch, like she would with a child of her own. When she and Juan Rodrigo came to Aguada, she brought toys for Miguel.

When her friends came, Rosanna was like a young girl again, happy and light on her feet, whispering intimacies to Sara. One day she showed her friend a note that came with the roses she had just received. 'A secret lover,' Sara whispered. 'You sneaky thing!'

Miguel remembered the flowers arriving for his mother, which she took to her room and placed in a vase.

Sara and her husband sometimes arrived with other friends that Rosanna knew. They would sit around the dining table and talk all night, the way Leon and his friends came together for a game of cards. There were larger and larger gatherings, when Miguel's uncles would arrive with their friends. On occasion city politicians came with Ruben. Leon's shipping partners came with their new cars. The yard would be so full of the latest machines from Italy and America that when it was time to leave, the chauffeur had to act like a traffic policeman, directing the vehicles out onto the road.

The servants were always preparing the house for some party. Tables would be rented and laid out in the garden, lights would be shone from the upper widows so a dance could be held in the front yard. Once Imelda Gomez, back from a successful performance in Mexico, came as a guest of Ruben's. She sang a few songs accompanied by Rosanna on the piano.

When the house was quiet, Miguel saw his mother sitting by her window, smelling a rose and reading a note that had come with it. That was the time Miguel had discovered tadpoles in the pond. He and the chauffeur would scoop them up in their hands and release them into a jar.

He watched the jar on the windowsill every day. The little black spigots swimming in the water grew little tails that gradually formed into legs. He was amazed to find that those black balls transformed into small frogs, so perfectly formed. Miguel was enchanted by the magic that turned those floating black orbs into creatures he loved.

Once his jarful of frogs fell over and smashed on the floor. He chased the leaping animals through the house until his pockets were bulging. He showed them off to Sara when she came over. She got down on her knees at the pond with him and tried to scoop out more tadpoles. Juan Rodrigo watched them smiling. Miguel remembered him as a dark man with soft eyes. Sometimes he saw him standing in the hall, gazing through the open door at the fresh flowers in his mother's vase.

One afternoon Rosanna found Juan Rodrigo standing alone in the veranda. 'We were building a house for one of our company's clients,' he said. 'We dug a pit in the centre of the lot. At the bottom we found a flower bed full of fresh flowers. Beautiful yellow flowers.'

'How strange,' Rosanna said.

There was an ashen look on Juan Rodrigo's face. 'It reminded me of a dream I had.'

'What kind of dream?'

'There were people living under the ground. They had everything there, mountains, trees, streams.

They worked on the fields just like normal people, played music, tended their gardens. But all in the ground under our feet.'

'Ghastly dream,' said Rosanna, sitting down by the veranda's blue glazed-plaster banisters.

'I found it a comforting one.' He turned to her and smiled.

Rosanna remembered his friendship from even before she knew Sara. There was a twinkle in his eye that always hinted at some unexplored possibility. Despite his success now, she couldn't help feeling that he thought he had failed at something. They turned to watch as pigeons flew by above them.

'Like the ones that fly over San Gabriel,' he laughed.

'All this time, still flying. It must take a long time to get somewhere better,' Rosanna said with a smile.

'Yes.'

She went inside.

In San Gabriel they had walked through the square together. Birds on the telephone wire erupted as they passed.

'Lucky creatures,' Juan Rodrigo had said.

'Why?'

'They're free from everything that weighs us down.'

'Don't sound so dissatisfied.'

'It must be something to be such happy, enamoured creatures. Not to feel trapped.'

'You don't understand,' Rosanna had said. 'They fly here and there because there's so little food everywhere.'

'From where we are, anyone just passing by looks like they're going somewhere better.'

She watched the birds disappearing into the fading light. 'Maybe,' she had said.

Even during the merry gatherings in her house, there were times when Rosanna thought the lethargy would defeat her. She would sit in a corner while the party was underway and try to fight off the dizziness. Then she would return to her guests, telling herself all was well and nothing could go wrong. It was a hectic, rowdy time and no one suspected or understood her frenzied hunger for the revelry to continue: the noise and the light staved off the darkness that was always there. Lurking in the corners of the house, waiting to engulf her.

In time even Leon saw that Rosanna was wearing herself down needlessly. He ordered the servants to stop preparations for a party she had planned. It gave rise to the biggest fight they had ever had. Rosanna shut her door and cried. She picked up the vase and hurled it at the mirror on the wall. Someone rapped on her door and she shouted for them to go away. Her moment of lucidity came only when the door swung open and she saw her son standing there.

'What happened?' Miguel asked, looking at the silver shards scattered on the floor.

And so the parties dwindled and then came to a stop. Not until the hiatus came did anyone realise how sick Rosanna was. The pain in her chest kept her in bed for days. A doctor was called. He had to come back several times, but when Rosanna felt well enough she insisted on going to the city herself. 'I'm not quite bed-ridden yet,' she snapped when her husband tried to stop her.

Miguel saw her having a quiet fight with his father when he was about to go on a trip again. Miguel walked into her room and she put her arms around him. Her face was hot and Miguel could tell her breathing was tired and weak, not like the times when she laughed out loud and danced in the upper rooms with her friends.

After a time even Sara stopped coming to the house. After weeks with no word from her, Rosanna got worried. She waited on the veranda one day, willing Sara to come.

Miguel came out to her and sasked, 'Did you fight with your friends?'

'Who?' she turned to him.

'Your friends. The man and the woman.'

'Oh Sara,' Rosanna smiled. 'And Juan Rodrigo? No, silly. Of course I didn't fight with them.'

'How come they don't come here anymore?'

It seemed Rosanna made up her mind then.

The next day she went to Fort Road. It was dark when she got home and Miguel sensed she was forcing herself not to cry. He watched her go quietly to her room. Later through the crack of her door he saw her reading something at her bureau. He knew they were notes someone had sent her with roses. He saw her wiping her eyes.

'What's wrong?' He came in and stood behind her. She held his head and pressed it to her breast. He

146

could hear her heartbeat, heavy and warm. There were tears in her voice when she said, 'Something's happened to mummy's friend.'

'What happened?' said Miguel. 'What?' In his child's heart he believed that if he knew he could comfort mummy. But she didn't answer.

The monsoon downpours had begun, pounding tumult from the heavens that was said to unloose gloomy ghosts from the swamps. One night in the rainstorm Rosanna woke up screaming, saying a man had entered her room. She was cold with sweat, her whole body shaking. A doctor was called again. He came and injected Rosanna with morphine. He ordered her to rest for several days. She was feverish and restless, obsessed with Sara and Juan Rodrigo, and the news she had heard on Fort Road. In the haze of her sedation, she made her decision. She would return to San Gabriel.

She made preparations to go. An old woman had joined the household, so her son wouldn't be left alone. Early the next morning she left, creeping up to her husband's room at daybreak to leave the letter she had stayed up all night to write. The rain had thankfully stopped.

Rosanna's last trip to San Gabriel did not take long, but it seemed to age her. She came back sadder than before. There were times after her return when she spent all day in her room, sitting in the dimness so her son could hardly see her face. She went for long walks alone by the river.

Juan Rodrigo's car was never retrieved from the sea. And before his body was found there were rumours he was still alive. Sara said she woke up once in the middle of the night and saw him standing in her doorway. Perhaps that was why Rosanna began to sleep with her window open even in the rain, the saturnine scents blowing in from her garden perfusing her dreams.

Finally, Juan Rodrigo's body was recovered and there could no longer be any doubt. He was buried on a day when the red blossoms of acacias littered the roadside, and floated in puddles left by the storm. The procession to the cemetery was slow and forlorn, the starched black lace of Rosanna's collar rubbed painfully against her skin. The mourners struggled to walk on the muddy road.

Some relatives had sent pink gladioli and they stood to one side during the service. Rosanna held

Sara's arm as they stood. They were half-way through service when a car arrived and two men brought out a white rose wreath. Only then did Rosanna break down and cry. She lost all sense of time.

The following year, Rosanna's second child was born. The child she had long wished for came at a time of her greatest anguish. She knew most of her life was now in the past. As her health grew worse she spent more time thinking of all that had happened. One day as she waited for dusk in her garden she remembered the dazzling moment when she had seen the conjurer of time.

Their last night in San Gabriel was the night of the fair. The tent was hot and crowded when they arrived. 'I can take it in my hands and shape it into anything,' the conjurer onstage was saying. He was holding something Rosanna couldn't see. 'As time turns into something real, it changes everything around us.'

He held up his hands, clasped around something. 'It replaces the world we knew just a moment ago so it's gone forever.'

The audience fell silent.

'The secret is in this invisible substance in my hands.' The conjurer spread his hands as though setting something free. The audience held its breath. 'Can you see it? Can you see how it's changed everything?'

His listeners smiled. Some old people sadly shook their heads.

'Time is everywhere,' said the conjurer. 'Becoming things. Things we *desire.*'

He reached into a box and lay a dying dove on the table. He raised his hand as a turquoise spot formed around it on the cloth. 'See?' he said. 'It's not blood seeping out of its body. It's time.'

As the crowd was leaving that night Rosanna could hear the conjurer's voice, whispering but still audible even outside the tent. 'Don't let time seep out!' he said.

On the morning of their departure, Sara and Juan Rodrigo were swimming in the bay. They called to Rosanna as she looked out from the steps. They were like happy children in the water, waving to her. Leon Gil had left the day before to begin a new job in the city. Rosanna felt an empty foreboding in her heart. She had made a decision she knew would change everything. When Sara asked her to stay on with them in San Gabriel she was tempted to agree. Part of her felt it might delay the moment that gave her such misgivings. But in the end she decided she had to go ahead.

'Come join us!' Sara ran up, breathless and dripping seawater. Rosanna considered for only a moment. She grabbed her bag and changed in a boathouse. She undid her hair and let it tumble to the small of her back. She waded in and let the cold, clean water envelope her as Juan Rodrigo watched. He wore an expression like on the first night when she asked him how he had shone the light into her room.

Years later she woke up to see a light flickering over her bed. It danced in the shadows until she was forced to get up. She went out into the living room and looked for it. Still baffled and half dreaming she went out into the garden, then walked barefoot across the road. She opened her eyes on the edge of the river, its cool comforting sheen just inches below her feet. The next day she woke up and wasn't sure it had really happened.

We swam in the bay. Your hair spread around you and darkened the sea. That was the last note she

found in her bureau. Juan Rodrigo must have written
it just before he went out to end his life. Perhaps he sat
by the window as he wrote it, looking out to sea.
Rosanna had promised herself she would burn
everything. The pain in her chest was becoming harder
and harder to bear. She woke up one night gasping for
air. She got up and without bothering to put any
clothes on walked out into the garden, struggling to
breathe as freely as she had once before.

She was found the next day, face down and
naked in the pond, her long hair spread out and
blackening the water as Juan Rodrigo had described in
his last letter.

IV.

The house used to stand in the centre of the city. It was held together by enormous beams salvaged from galleons discarded from the Manila Acapulco trade. They had the sheen of a hundred years of voyages, stretching out over the rooms, dark remnants of the gigantic Malayan timber from which they had been cut.

Jorge's grandfather Jose Zandro and his sister Emilia, for whom the house had been built, loved it like a living relative, and couldn't bear seeing it destroyed. So when the war came to Puerto Reina, they had it dismantled and moved from its original location to save it from the advancing Japanese army.

Jose Zandro owned a patch of land near an abandoned orchard outside the city. The house was transported there in twelve trucks, months before the city's evacuation. As the first bombing raids pounded Puerto Reina, Emilia oversaw a feat of cunning and love as nearly a hundred unemployed masons and carpenters put the house back together exactly as it had stood on Paseo Gardenia. Their refuge by the Aguada river proved impossible to find, and the family was able to survive and save the precious house, while half the city was razed to the ground.

The old orchard was wildly overgrown but one could still make out the rows of trees whose fruit was once picked by workers hired from the village. Jorge and Miguel grew up on the edge of that forsaken Eden where the little bounty that appeared on the trees was quickly stolen by village children, who crawled through the rusty barbed wire fence, braving nests of snakes in the brush. At dusk, the orchard seemed to quiver with the noise of distant fruit pickers, and Adia said she sometimes stood there and glimpsed a wandering tongue of flame.

The tallest trees by the river were kapok trees. Jorge and Miguel liked to pick up their cotton pods from the ground, breaking them open to reach the white flecks of cotton and the sweet black seeds inside. The women gathering firewood on the riverbank collected them, too, using the cotton to stuff pillows at home. Sometimes the pods would break still hanging from the branch. Birds pecked to get at its seeds and dug out the cotton. The wind often scattered the white tufts in the air and for a moment the place would be transported in their weightless, wispy dance, like the perfect world in the snow-dome, the house resting untroubled in the dream-like flurry of snow.

One Sunday, Adia took Jorge with her to the city. They arrived just as people were coming out of mass. It was nearly dusk.

'It's a wonderful time of day,' Adia said with a burst of excitement. 'When I was young I couldn't wait to come out of church and see if my friends were at the Navy Club.'

She hurried towards the old club and they surprised a group of vagrants searching through the garbage heaps on the quiet street. Adia waved to them, laughing.

'No need to stop on my account,' she said cheerily. She blew kisses at them as she walked by.

They reached the door under the torn canopy and entered the club. The air was musty as they climbed the stairs to the ballroom. Jorge studied the brass fixtures on the bar, covered with grime. The dusk gathering outside mingled with a more permanent shadow that hung over the room. Jorge looked up at the dusty chandeliers when suddenly Adia stopped and stared at the pock-marked floor.

'I can still hear the laughter,' she said to Jorge with eyes shining. 'We laughed and danced here until dawn!'

She turned to look to the swinging doors behind the bar. They were moving, as if someone had just passed. 'Anyone there?' Adia called out. She moved forward and called out again, 'Mercedes? Are you hiding from me?'

There was no answer from the large, empty room.

Adia walked towards the swinging doors and pushed past. Jorge followed. They walked through the murky corridor in the back of the ballroom, passing doors that were ajar or nailed shut, the glass fanlights above them shattered. At the end they reached the cluttered, dusty storeroom. There, shadowy figures were rummaging around in the dimness.

They froze in panic when Adia suddenly pushed the door open. There was light enough to see three filthy children and an old couple, inching away from the pile of things they had gathered on the floor.

'You rascals!' Adia said. She turned to Jorge and laughed. 'Pretending they don't know me.'

She slapped her leg and beamed at the vagrants. 'So glad you could come. *Bienvenido!* What a shindig we're going to have!'

The derelicts relaxed. They knew she was no threat. One of the children made a windmill gesture at his temple and the others smiled.

At that moment Jorge wished he was more like Miguel, who managed to avoid Adia's excursions and wander off on his own, befriending the sailors at the pier. He was learning their gruff ways, spitting and swearing. He told Jorge he had started helping to haul sacks of sugar onto small sail craft on the quay. One day he showed Jorge a tattoo on his shoulder. *Zabaj*, it said.

'Did it hurt?' Jorge asked.

Miguel made a contemptuous sound and said, 'Only if you're a little flower!'

But Jorge knew the walks with Adia were still better than sitting at home. They kept him from sleeping too much or having to see his father.

Their father had taken to disappearing for weeks at a time. He never told anyone where he'd been. Only the chauffeur had any idea, and what little he knew, he revealed piecemeal, in a way that overstated his own importance in the matter.

Their father had started leaving money under the breadbox for Adia to use in running the household. When the money ran low, she became anxious for Jorge's father to show up. It was said his business was not doing badly, and he had succeeded in cornering the local market for tuna and mackerel. How much money he left under the breadbox gave Adia a fair indication of how his venture was going. But there were times when Adia found only a tin or two of mackerel where the money should have been.

'My Lord,' Adia scratched her head.

Their father's reticence about his undertakings was a cause for concern. So distracted were they with worry that they hardly noticed when a new presence appeared in the house. She had come late one night when everyone was asleep. The chauffeur's taxi rumbled into the driveway, the front door opened with a woman's giggle, then Jorge heard loud footsteps on the floor of his father's room.

She began to appear frequently from then on, always when the house was dark and quiet. Early one morning Jorge glimpsed her legs through the high slit of her skirt, as she hurried down the stairs from his father's room. He saw the reddish tinge of her hair and thought she looked like a stage actress. They all wanted to know who she was.

The chauffeur admitted that he often drove Jorge's father to *Calle* Luna and picked him up from there. So they came to think of her simply as the woman from *Calle* Luna. With time her manner became less furtive, and her presence became an open, inescapable intrusion, like the grain flies they all hated but could not kill.

'What a stench it will leave,' Adia said again.

Jorge heard the woman laughing one night and was surprised at how raucous she sounded. Her laughter boomed through the door of his father's room like a man's.

It was a Sunday morning when they finally got to meet her. Their uncle Augusto was expected to come for a visit and it seemed Jorge's father had decided to come clean. Jorge and Miguel were at the table for breakfast when the woman came down in the clothes she had been wearing the night before.

'Why, hello.' She wore a fixed smile and had rather fierce eyes that put them on guard. 'My, what handsome boys,' she cooed huskily and tried to pinch Miguel on the cheek. Miguel turned his face away so violently the sausage in his mouth fell to the floor.

The woman then went over to Jorge and stood with a pause. It seemed she briefly considered ruffling his hair. Her eyes scanned the edges of his scraggly head like it was an animal she wasn't certain was safe to pet. She decided to pinch his cheeks instead, and Jorge found her fingertips rough and bumpy, like a worker's hands. Her hair was dyed red to make her look like a Spanish woman, but on the back of her head Miguel could see she was going bald.

Their father made no introductions. He sat in his usual place to eat his breakfast, while the woman went to the living room to drink her coffee while she smoked. But their uneasy acquaintance had begun. Before the end of the week the boys would learn that the woman could be shrill and vicious when things didn't go her way.

Higher up the slit of her skirts, the boys snickered to see her muscled thighs. They considered it revenge to glimpse the hem of her underskirt and find it looked like their tablecloth.

'Her voice sounds like a train whistle,' said Miguel. *'Peet!Peeet!'*

They observed her for more defects over the days and were thrilled when they found more. There were many, many more. On some nights she stayed over and had Melba do her laundry. Jorge and Miguel waited for the quiet moment at dusk when they could throw stones at her clothes drying on the lines.

Jorge took to wearing her garments before Melba took them up to press. He got many laughs by putting them on in the kitchen, tightening the pantyhose with her white belt, and tying the black brassiere in knots around his neck.

One night he had made several turns around the table to enthusiastic applause when the laughter suddenly stopped. Jorge knew he had been caught. Like a trapped animal wanting to know its fate, he turned around for a peek.

'That brassiere is imported from Italy,' the woman shouted from the top of the stairs. 'But it's not too good for stringing you up from the rafters, you little dwarf!'

'Little Porcupine,' said Miguel as the woman and their father descended. He pretended he had found none of Jorge's antics funny at all.

'Yes!' the woman laughed. She turned to Jorge's father behind her, 'How'd you get a son with a toilet brush for a head?'

Everyone laughed. But what hurt the most was something she added in a slightly lower voice, but not so low that Jorge couldn't hear. 'Sweetie, maybe you're right he isn't really yours.'

The more their father brought the woman home, the more they retreated to the kitchen and the backyard, Adia's part of the house. Jorge sometimes went with her to the market and saw what work it took to feed the household on the money his father left under the breadbox.

The chauffeur told him that Adia was one of those fallen ladies forced to work hard for their living rather late in life. Jorge thought about this, and he wondered about the terror that welled up in her eyes some nights when the rain was pounding. 'Poor souls,' she moaned in the dark hall one night, thinking there was no one there. A thunderstorm was wreaking havoc and she stood in the back doorway looking out into the rain. Jorge was startled. He wondered if she was aware of him when she spoke again in a tortured voice he had never heard before. She uttered a curse as she stared out at the darkness racked by lightning.

It rained so furiously in May that a dike broke upriver, and the first flood of the season came. They heard of people trying desperately to patch up the defences, and how some of them died in the effort. In the muddy water that flowed in from the riverbank they saw rubber slippers, a pair of pants, a hat.

Jorge's cousins Nicolas and Octavio showed up unexpectedly. Adia brought out buckets and asked them to help bail the floodwater out of the house. They scraped the mud from the walls and furniture legs, the stairs, and lastly, the floor. After it was all finished Adia thanked them and told them they could stay for supper. They seemed anxious to leave, however.

'Their father's probably got them on the run again,' said Adia, sadly shaking her head.

A long while passed before the cousins started sneaking back to the house for short visits. They were just as tense as before, watchful as hunted rabbits. Even when they sat down for a meal they were always on guard, ready to drop whatever they were doing to pack up and take flight.

They found release in playing cruel, twisted games, and took inordinate pleasure in tormenting Melba. 'There she is!'

Melba screamed at the mere sight of them. At first she tried to defend herself, but, given the cousins' flair for fighting, she soon found it a better tactic to run.

They would catch Melba and tie her up, then carry her triumphantly out to the field. There they would play a much loved game of making her plead for her life, before lowering her head-first into a dried-out well. They would release the rope slowly, relishing every moment. There was a beatific look on their faces when Melba finally screamed, her voice coming up from the deep cavity like a cry from hell.

'What a strange language her people speak,' the cousins would laugh. 'Agh! Agh! Arrrgh!!!! How do they understand each other?'

Later Jorge would climb into the crawl space under the roof in the far wing and find her, sitting quietly, watching the strange glow from the corner that seemed to give her strength.

'I'll just wait,' she whispered. 'They'll see. I'll just wait.'

Melba's room was next to Jorge's and sometimes he could hear her sing in a clear, high voice. As the years passed, Jorge noticed that Miguel sometimes did nice things for her. Once as a joke he gave her ginger blossoms from the field and it made her very happy.

But Miguel hated the house more and more every day. One night he saw the woman from *Calle Luna* coming out with her hair wet from their mother's room. The next day he whispered to Jorge, 'Let's run away now! Let's take the money from his drawer.'

'What if he doesn't have any money?' Jorge said.

'Of course he does. What else would he spend on her? We should take it. It's for *us!*'

Their cousins must have heard something from their own parents. 'We hear your father's buying a house in America,' the oldest boy said.

Miguel was excited. 'A house in America! Wow!'

'We heard it's near Florida,' said Christine.

'Wow!' said Miguel.

'Where's that?' Jorge said.

Carla, the youngest girl, added, 'We heard your father wants to leave you.'

Everyone fell silent. Jorge saw a smile forming in the corner of Christine's lips as she gathered up her hair. He wondered if it was just another twisted game his cousins were playing.

Miguel introduced their cousins to the enticements of the plaza. They went there to idle away the afternoons in the shade of the trees or to ponder the daily dramas that played out among the hedges that reeked of urine and spilt rum.

A mother was reunited with her son on the stone benches along the flower path. He had fallen asleep in a bus and woke up in the next town. The dusty old men who slept under the stage and the shoeless boys selling newspapers and cigarettes knew all the details of the doings around the square.

One morning a man pursued his wife with a knife around the empty bandstand while she tried to fight him off with a laundry paddle. Their children ran around them with tattered clothes and bare feet, crying and dancing from the heat of the scorching pavement. The woman swung the paddle at her husband and drew a ribbon of blood. They cursed each other with expletives Miguel hadn't heard even from the sailors. People gathered to watch the scuffle, which ended only when a Constabulary patrol came and seized the fighting couple.

In all the years that Jorge and Miguel still saw their cousins, going to the plaza remained their favourite diversion, the initiation into life they couldn't get elsewhere.

One afternoon a caravan of cars arrived with sirens wailing, followed by a tray-back truck with entertainers wearing crepe paper costumes. They hopped down and ran squealing and laughing to the stage, where they set up brass instruments, microphones and cardboard backdrops.

'Looks like we're getting a visit from the mayor again,' said one of the old men stretched out on the benches. 'He must have thought up another speech.'

'The elections must be coming soon,' said another. 'They're coming more often then they used to.'

The old men rubbed their knees, glad for some distraction. It was late afternoon, and workers from the entourage were setting up bright lights around the plaza. Jorge and his cousins learned that the time before elections meant celebrities of all kinds coming to shake hands and make friends with the people. Campaigning politicians put on shows to entertain the crowds. Trinkets were given out with cans of milk, hand towels and bars of soap.

Once Jorge's Uncle Ruben made an appearance with a large, important-looking delegation. Jorge, Miguel, and their cousins climbed on trees and benches to get a better view of the stage. They kept shouting and making noises to be noticed by their uncle. Adia said the papers later reported that the senator met with many catcalls when speaking in Puerto Reina, mainly from the city's youth.

Another day, the mayor cut short his own speech to allow the constabulary commander to speak. The man crossed the stage in full military uniform and glared menacingly at the crowd. The silver studs on his collar and the insignia on his chest caught the light and seemed hypnotic.

'They're just waiting to BURY us...' His big voice hung in the hot air over the plaza. His listeners stood agape.

'CITIZENS! GUARDIANS OF THE PEACE!'

Each word he barked at the microphone was like the crack of a gun. People winced and averted their ears from the speakers clamped to the lamp posts.

'THEY'RE ALL AROUND US,' he said. 'Long ago they were bandits in the countryside. Now they're brainwashing people in our factories and schools!'

He paused and the crowd waited.

'Communists!' he shouted. 'These brigands call themselves rebels, but they're nothing but bandits and thugs!'

' Small disputes over land have grown into this full-blown insurgency, fanned by traitors. Their evil influence is growing,' cried the commander, 'IN EVERY TOWN AND CITY OF THE LAND!'

The silver studs on his collar began to take on a sinister gleam.

'They're all around us!' he pounded on the lectern, his big voice booming through the trees. 'Infecting our country like a disease!'

'Even among you here today there are those whose minds they have already polluted.'

He probed the crowd with his hard, piercing gaze.

169

'Be wary!' he said as he was about to leave the stage. 'Be strong!'

The politicians left, and the ventriloquist saw his chance to entertain the crowd. He climbed up to the podium with a monkey. 'Nothing ever changes in this place,' the monkey said. 'With enough money, any monkey can become mayor of this town.'

The crowd roared with laughter.

'Next year when you get bananas instead of hand towels you'll know I'm running for office.'

The crowd giggled and howled. The ventriloquist was going to say more, but a constabulary patrol was moving towards the stage. The trickster grabbed his monkey and vanished back into the crowd.

Jorge's cousins decided to take Melba with them to the plaza once. It was late afternoon when they arrived and the place was quiet. They sought out the ventriloquist and bribed him to make Melba 'speak'.

The man agreed, but had many questions to ask Jorge's cousins. Christine giggled as she whispered into his ear, throwing glances at Melba, who stood nearby, nervously clutching her handbag. They had told her they were going to church and she had dressed up in her best Sunday clothes.

Finally, the ventriloquist nodded that he was ready. The bystanders moved back so Melba was left standing alone in front of the bandstand. The ventriloquist had disappeared into the crowd. While Jorge's cousins looked around searching for him, they heard a voice.

'Anyone can see I have a secret...' said a girl's voice that seemed to be coming from Melba. Everyone turned to look at her.

She stepped back, baffled, putting a hand at her throat. Her eyes grew wild with fear as the voice continued. It seemed to be coming from her, but she couldn't make it stop. 'I'm in love with a boy named Miguel, and my poor heart beats only for him.'

Melba started running back and forth, trying to find the source of the voice that was baring her soul.

'My love is obvious to everyone,' the voice went on. Melba's face was wet with tears.

'It is clear even to an illiterate man from the hills who plays with people's voices...'

Melba covered her mouth but the voice would not stop. It continued: 'The only one who is blind to my suffering...'

Melba shook her head and started to run away. But the disembodied voice pursued her. 'The only one who doesn't know is the boy I love more than anything. On whom I spy from the roof everyday.'

The crowd hooted with laughter. Jorge and Miguel laughed with their cousins, holding their stomachs at the hilarious sight as Melba ran from the plaza. She fell twice, dropped her handbag, jumped back from a dog that tried to bite her. She fixed her skirt and retrieved her handbag, and finally disappeared behind the old theatre.

Despite talk of their father's business succeeding, his austerities at home increased. He went to town less frequently at night and often made do with a light supper of bread and fish. The cash he left under the breadbox dwindled ever more.

'It must be a big house he's buying in America,' said Miguel.

'He's buying a house in America?' Adia asked. 'Who told you that?'

Miguel frowned. 'Nobody.'

But to Jorge he said, 'Just think! What if he's going to take us to America!'

Then the woman from *Calle* Luna showed up with new clothes and a large new suitcase. They saw her removing the price tags and trying on different attire at the mirror in their father's room.

'Florida is warm most of the time,' they heard their father say. 'But it also gets cold.'

Miguel smashed the bottles in the shed. 'We're not going to America!' he spat. 'Not with him. Or with her!'

A few days later Miguel ran away. All their efforts to find him proved in vain. Several years would pass before they learned his fate.

For a long time Jorge would hear Melba crying late at night like she was in great pain. Her muffled sobs that he heard through the wall were Jorge's first inkling of the brutish stabs of love.

Adia continued in her struggle to feed the household. The chauffeur persuaded Goyle to stop chasing stray chickens out of the yard and start thinking of them as prey. He goaded him to make forays into the old orchard, fed him rumours of wild boar in the woods.

But Goyle was no hunter. He preferred to steal. One day he came home holding something wriggling in a sack under his arm. He promised them a meal of duck with a recipe he had learned from his grandfather.

'Ah, the constabulary recruit,' the chauffeur said. 'The service known for training many outstanding duck thieves.'

A dreadful crash came from the kitchen, and Goyle came running out with a knife, pursuing something. They stood aside and watched as Goyle ran around chasing the flurry of feathers just in front of him. He disappeared out the back.

Things clearly had to change.

The next day when Adia went to the market, she saw a sign advertising for boarders. Something fell into place in her mind. 'We have lots of spare room,' she said. 'We'll be helping somebody get a roof over their heads. And we can all help to put food on the table.'

They wandered from stall to stall, choosing among the produce. 'I know what it's like not to have a roof over one's head,' said Adia. 'We'll be helping some poor souls.'

At that she took Jorge by the wrist and strode decisively towards a sign-writer's shop. The man inside was in the middle of painting a shapely female figure. He stopped with a sheepish grin and gave Adia his full attention.

'Boarders?' he scratched his head. 'Hm. Please write down the address.'

Adia wrote it on a piece of paper.

'A lot of people come here asking about places,' the sign-writer said. 'How many are you going to take?'

'How many signs?' Adia said.

'How many *boarders*?'

'How many can we take?' Adia asked Jorge. 'One? Two? *Three*?'

Jorge shrugged. 'Maybe.'

'All right. Three,' she decided.

The man began the sign at once, laying a piece of cardboard on the counter and moving his brush a few inches above it, closing his eyes to imagine the finished sign. He put a lot of care in perfecting the curves of the '3.'

'Three boarders,' Adia said as they were leaving. 'Yes. That sounds about right.'

As soon as they got home she prepared the rooms that hadn't been used for a long time. That night she tried out new dishes, attempting to guess which ones a group of strangers might like.

'It'll be like a real house again,' she crowed happily in the kitchen. 'Talk in the living room, meals on time.'

It turned out she had been toying with the idea for some time, dropping hints to Leon when he came down for breakfast, striving to make him see the benefits of paying guests. But Leon's grunts and sleepy frown indicated his complete indifference to anything regarding the house. So Adia had assumed the decision was hers to make.

She set up a table in the veranda to prepare for the arrangements of boarder-taking.

'You sure they'll find the house?' the chauffeur said, cocking an eye.

Two days had passed and no boarders appeared.

Then, early on the third day, the much awaited first lodger arrived.

The girl was tall, dark, and slight of build. She had straight, smooth hair down to her shoulders, with full lips and a rather attractive nose. She didn't seem to bring much. All her belongings were bundled into a small canvas bag. Her eyes were alert in a quiet, guarded way, and she fidgeted while Adia talked. There was a restlessness that made it easy to see her moving readily from place to place. She looked like she'd been on a long, draining journey, and seemed glad to have a rest.

'And your family?' Adia was asking.

'Family...?' the girl said, uneasy. 'I lost touch with them long ago.'

'Oh,' said Adia. 'So in case of accidents, emergencies...'

'Don't worry.'

'All right, then,' said Adia, putting down her pen.

When things were agreed, the girl shook hands with Adia and got up to stretch her legs. She said hello to Jorge and gave him her slow, knowing smile. The girl brought her bag into the house. She looked around. 'It looks very safe here.'

'Oh, yes,' Adia assured her. 'Why, there hasn't been a case of assault or theft since...' She saw Goyle in the hallway and remembered the stolen duck. '...since I can't remember.'

'Good.' The girl peered through the front window. 'It looks far enough for the police not to bother us here..' she said with a laugh. She spoke in a soft voice, her discreet manner unvarying. 'I got tired living in the city and having them always come around to break up fights or break down doors.'

'There's never been trouble here that needed them to come,' said Adia by way of reassurance. 'But it's easy enough to get them. If there's a need.'

'That's good to know,' said the girl. She seemed to like her surroundings. But her secretive manner showed nothing more.

'Shall we go to your room?' Adia said. They went up to the second landing. Adia unlocked the door and showed the girl her new room.

'Oh,' the girl went up to the window and leaned out. 'You can see the road.'

Adia left her to settle in. Jorge climbed up and lingered on the landing. He watched quietly as she unpacked her bag and began putting her things on the tables, the bed, the windowsill. She wiped the mirror on the wall and tried to rub off a stain. Finally, she noticed Jorge standing outside and smiled. 'Why, hello again.'

She motioned with her head. 'Come in.'

Jorge walked in eyeing her things scattered around the room.

'What's your name?' she asked. Jorge told her again. She turned to look at herself in the mirror.

Jorge stood at the foot of the bed. 'What's *your* name?' he asked.

'Mine?' She was combing her long, straight hair. 'It's Maya.'

'Maya?'

'Yes. You like it?'

Jorge shrugged.

'You know what it means?'

Jorge pretended to ponder, then shook his head.

She went back to arranging her things. 'It's an old Indian word,' she said. 'A language called Sanskrit.'

'Oh...' Jorge absently nodded his head.

She came forward and the slow, cagey smile formed on her lips.

'It means an illusion,' she said. 'A veil.'

She led Jorge to the door and gave him a pat on the shoulder.

'Why'd your mother call you that?' he asked her.

'She didn't,' said the girl. '*I* did.'

She shut the door.

But one lodger didn't bring the fuller life Adia had been hoping for. All it brought for a while was more worry, a puzzle with a hint of risk.

When Melba said she had caught Jorge rummaging in the new lodger's room, Adia didn't seem shocked as she should have been. She had decided it was too early to give the girl her own keys.

'Just leave everything as you found them,' she said to Jorge with a wink. 'That's all.'

Jorge hadn't intended to go into the boarder's room. As always he was on the hunt for fragments of his mother's mirror. But at dusk one day he came out into the landing. He was stopped by a voice in the gloom.

'Who are you?'

Jorge turned around. Maya came out from the other room.

'It's just me, Jorge,' he tried to snicker.

'I know.' Maya came towards him, unsmiling. 'What are you doing here all alone?'

'I was just looking for something,' Jorge shrugged.

'I didn't mean that,' said Maya, coming to a stop in front of him. 'Why do you live here without anyone, in the middle of nowhere?' She reached out to touch his shoulder. 'Why is that old woman taking care of you?'

Her eyes bore down on him. 'What is she to you?'

Jorge couldn't answer. It seemed Maya had more questions about them than they had about her. He tried to imagine what their lives looked like to someone from outside.

Adia finally had keys made for Maya. The new boarder locked her room and told Adia she'd be gone for a few days.

It was Melba who found the torn note lying on the second landing. She took it down to Adia. It said:

'...*downstairs. There's another person in the house I haven't seen. Need to be careful. Don't know what this means.*'

Adia rubbed her temples. 'I don't know what we got ourselves into,' she said.

The night Maya returned, Jorge lay awake. He kept thinking of Miguel. Then he heard voices. After a while he recognised Maya's voice. A man coughed in her room.

Jorge closed his eyes and tried to sleep. He heard another noise and went to the window. He saw Maya with two other people coming out of the back, walk quietly across the yard and disappear into the dark.

In all the time he would know her, Maya was like the night. A *veil*. An *illusion*.

The mystery was far from dispelled when a new character came into their lives.

'I think there's someone coming!' Melba called out from the front yard.

Trudging up towards them was a small man dwarfed by the bulk of bags, boxes, and bundles he was carrying on his back, around his neck and on his shoulders, much like those overburdened bullocks that appeared in the city on market day. They couldn't see his head. Only his short legs were visible as he laboured under the load of his belongings. He crossed the road and stopped at the front door.

'Boarders?' he called out. 'Looking for boarders?'

The bags came off and they saw how slight and wiry he was. His head appeared too large for his body, but this turned out to be just one of the many deceptive things about Joseph.

As soon as the arrangements were agreed with Adia, he asked to take a shower. A long time later he came out wrapped in a towel, his body bare and bony. His damp hair was flat and they were surprised. His head was small and almost perfectly round, like a melon. He had little pugnacious eyes and a wide mouth.

Joseph combed his hair with a red brush and asked if there were peeping toms around. 'I was self-conscious the whole time I was in the shower,' he said. 'I had a cousin who was a peeping tom. He lived for the sight of naked bodies.'

He sat down on the veranda rail when he saw that the chauffeur was interested.
'He thought up such crazy things to get his kicks,' Joseph continued. 'Now I always feel like he's there, watching me through the slats or a pinhole.'

The chauffeur tried to hide his smirk.

'Of course he's dead now,' Joseph concluded, 'which only makes it worse.'

Joseph, it turned out, had a great love for his hair and went to extraordinary lengths to care for it. He would get up earlier than everyone so he could wash his hair and sculpt it into shape before breakfast. Like certain small animals, he seemed to use the furry covering on his head to mask innate weaknesses.

They would later learn that he was a highly qualified engineer and a secret bookworm. He had studied yoga and after a week in the house, took to doing headstands in the garden to meditate.

Joseph and Maya had both spent their best years being students. They liked to talk, to debate, and recited from books they had read. But they brought out the worst in each other. The lodgers indeed brought new life into the house, but they also brought a lot of arguments.

Joseph liked to boast that he once spent three months in prison for painting political slogans on the walls of a government building.

'Being jailed for vandalism isn't the same as being jailed for your beliefs,' Maya scoffed.

Joseph wasn't put off. 'But they *were* my beliefs.'

'Sure, *'JOSEPH WAS HERE*." Maya crossed her arms. 'What deep conviction.'

'I didn't write *'JOSEPH WAS HERE*',' he followed her into the kitchen. 'I wrote much more sophisticated things than that.'

'I'm sure it was something riveting about drugs and rock and roll.'

'Well, even if I did just write *'JOSEPH WAS HERE*'.' Joseph made a last plea. 'It's still an act of *defiance.*'

'I'm sure adding a drawing of a penis didn't help!' snapped Maya.

'What's she talking about?' Joseph turned to Jorge.

'I don't know!' Jorge snapped at him, too. They were both annoying him.

It wasn't going to be easy having them in the same house.

But thanks to the boarders everyone in the house understood why there were suddenly large spectacles with dancers and contortionists in the plaza,

185

with over-friendly politicians shaking hands with everyone.

The old president was running for office yet again, Maya and Joseph explained. 'The first time wasn't nauseating enough,' Maya said. 'Now we'll get to go round the block all over again.'

All that would have passed them by if not for the arguments at the dinner table, which brought the outside world crashing into the peace of the house.

It was a great relief to Adia when a third boarder came, who would act as an occasional peacemaker between the other two. His name was Roberto. He was about the age of Jorge's father, but he had a happy face that made him seem much younger. With his arrival, the household seemed to find a balance. Roberto was placid where the other two were all too spiky.

They all began having supper together in the dining room and their varying dispositions brought zest to the mealtime conversations. Adia was happy to be cooking for a full house again. After their first few nights together, Roberto sat forward and said, 'Is there a ghost in the house?'

Adia raised an eyebrow. 'No.'

'I'm sure I heard something,' said Roberto, looking up at the ceiling. 'Bumps on the landing. Stairs creaking at night.'

'I *saw* something,' Maya said. 'Wandering around in the dark.'

Joseph put down his glass and gave a shudder. *'What?'*

'I saw it when I came out for a cigarette,' Maya explained.

'Upstairs?' Adia said.

'Yes.'

Roberto leaned forward. 'What did it look like?'

'Unkempt hair,' Maya narrowed her eyes, trying to remember. 'Fat. Filthy dressing gown.'

'Filthy dressing gown?' Adia began to smile. 'Torn at the back?'

'Huge rip. Just over the buttocks.' Maya giggled into her hand. 'Hairy ass.'

'Yes!' Adia snapped her fingers.

'Why, that's not a ghost!' Jorge cried. 'That's my father!'

The boarders relaxed. Then they looked confused.

'Yes,' Adia seemed embarrassed. 'I'm sorry I didn't mention it. We've forgotten all about him.'

Maya gave Jorge a pitying look and put some food on his plate. 'Maybe next time I'll go to the garden if I want to smoke.'

There was a vigour in the house that hadn't been there before. Jorge got used to his new housemates. Now he had a reason to stay home when Adia went off on her wanderings.

Joseph was glad to find the grass in the yard thick enough to do his headstands without a mat. Roberto rummaged through the shed looking for tools to fix the bathroom.

'Let's put in more locks,' Joseph egged him on. 'Then we'll feel safe with our clothes off.'

Roberto didn't share Joseph's vulnerabilities, but he obliged. He was a good handyman, and soon he was fixing parts of the house that had been thought beyond repair. Roberto liked to cook and tried to give Adia advice in the kitchen. He had trapped monitor lizards and knew various ways to skin and season them. Adia refused most of his suggestions.

Maya liked to do her laundry by the standpipe, using a wooden paddle which she brought down on the clothes with a ferocious energy she seemed to enjoy. At such times she undid her hair and walked around the yard on bare feet. Joseph got up from his headstands when she passed.

'Maya's skirts don't seem so long from this angle,' he said. She threw the paddle at him.

Soon Jorge found it hard to imagine life without the boarders. Their existence seemed complete and imperturbable, as of it had always been that way.

Jorge's father made little effort to meet the new lodgers. He and the woman from *Calle* Luna locked themselves away in the far wing of the house. There were rumours his business had failed. He rarely came out, and only at ungodly hours, drifting through the rooms still in his sleeping clothes, befuddled by his increasingly unfamiliar surroundings. Sometimes he looked as if he couldn't remember why he had come out at all.

One day, boxes of tinned mackerel were brought back from the city and carried up to his room. The following day he was standing at the top of the stairs when Jorge passed. He called to his son. Since his brother left, Jorge avoided being anywhere where his father might talk to him. He feared having to explain Miguel's departure.

'Who are those people?' his father asked. From the top of the stairs he had seen Joseph doing his headstands and Roberto hammering a leg back into a chair.

'They're boarders,' Jorge said. 'They're renting some of the empty rooms.'

The idea seemed to puzzle his father. His hair, dark and curly in his youth, had gone grey. He had taken to wearing tinted glasses, which only added to his eccentric, dissolute air. The gaze behind the coloured lenses was often indifferent or discontented. But in the rare moments when he took them off, Jorge saw that his fluttering eyes were small and pitiful.

'Who is that man?' he asked his son.

'Which man?'

'The skinny one with the little head.'

'With long hair?'

'Yes. The one like Jesus Christ.'

'That's Joseph,' Jorge told him.

'What does he do?'

'Him? Why, he's an engineer.'

190

'I mean, why does he have his face stuck in the ground all day long?'

'It's...' Jorge scratched his head. 'I can't explain.'

Just as Jorge turned to go down the stairs, his father called after him, 'He's a man, isn't he?'

'Of course he is,' answered Jorge.

'No, I mean. He's a man-man? No switching sides?'

Jorge understood. 'No,' he said. 'He likes girls. Maya, for instance.'

'Good.' His father looked very relieved. 'Tell Adia well done.' He tightened the strap of his dressing gown and shuffled back to his room.

Jorge still spent a good deal of his time in front of the mirror, trying to flatten his hair. On rare occasions he sneaked into his father's bathroom to steal some of the English pomade, whose container trumpeted its softening nutrients and attractive manly scent.

Days later, his father came to his room. He called out from the hall and Jorge got nervous. He had taken a large scoop of pomade that morning. He tried to wipe off the evidence from his head, but it was too late.

'Son?' his father opened the door. Jorge was thankful for the open cabinet that hid him from the doorway. He slid under the bed.

His father hadn't come alone. Jorge heard the woman's voice as she followed him in from the hall. They walked around the room, looked behind the cabinet. His father stood over the bed and lifted the quilt. 'Jorge?'

Jorge didn't move. He feared the strong, manly fragrance of the English pomade might give him away. His father sat down on the bed.

'He's not here,' he said in a baffled voice. 'I was sure I heard him come in.'

'Don't worry,' the woman said. 'Write him a note or something.'

Finally, he and the woman left ,and Jorge stopped holding his breath.

One night soon after, a bizarre disturbance upset the house. It happened after a week of sly, furious preparations. Jorge tried to make sense of it. Strangers were coming through the living room and trooping up and down the stairs to his father's room.

Then it all came to a stop. After a quiet few days, the upper floor erupted in chaos. It sounded as if a dance hall had suddenly come into being on the upper floor without their knowledge. And the same folks who had kept up a quiet, ceaseless traffic to the room in the far wing now showed up again. There was dancing and shouting, pounding on the floor behind the locked door of Jorge's father. People kept arriving all through the night, sneaking across the living room, men in gaudy pants and silk vests, women in sequined skirts.

'The cabaret comes to Mohamed,' the chauffeur said in admiration as they watched the tawdry stream of unknown guests.

The whole house shook with the ruckus. The boarders came down to complain. Adia promised to go talk to Jorge's father. She went and pounded on the door. But the racket from inside made her feeble calls inaudible. The boarders went back to their rooms, grumbling sleepily.

But several hours past midnight, just as abruptly as it had started, the uproar ended. Everything went quiet, and the last guests tiptoed out of the house.

Near dawn there was a knock on Jorge's door. He dragged himself out of bed. It was his father.

'Where's your brother?' he asked. The woman from *Calle* Luna was standing behind him with the suitcases on the floor.

'I'm leaving with your auntie Tessie,' his father said. So *that* was her name. His father bent down and tried to clasp his neck. He was trying to embrace his son, but the gesture came out very awkward. So unused were they to each other that Jorge turned away to avoid it. His father smiled warmly and patted him on the head.

'Be a good boy,' he said almost in a whisper. 'Tell your brother I'll write you both a letter. We'll discuss everything. When the time comes.'

He carried the suitcases outside. Jorge leaned against the doorway. He expected his father to come back and talk to him again, but he didn't. Jorge waited in the doorway a bit longer, then went back to bed. He heard the car being started, the bags being loaded into the back. He heard his father and the chauffeur talking, their voices muffled by the engine's noise. At last, the car rumbled across the yard and drove off.

It was all quiet.

Jorge drifted off to sleep. Before long there was a knock on the door again. Jorge groaned and opened his eyes. Bright sunlight filled his room. He got up to open the door.

It was Maya.

'Is this for you?' she was holding up an envelope. 'I found it on the floor. I think someone was trying to slip it in.'

She turned it over. 'Oh, it's to Adia, too.'

Everybody looked at Jorge when he came out for breakfast. Adia had been reading them the letter, which explained that Jorge's father had left. It said he hoped he could arrange to pick Jorge and his brother one day. 'And if things don't work out...'Adia sniffed a little, 'Please take care of the boys and tell them their father loves them.'

She blew her nose. Jorge saw the letter near Adia's plate, sprinkled with breadcrumbs. They all looked at him with sad faces. Joseph was shaking his head. Jorge was too sleepy to talk. He didn't really understand what had happened.

The boarders finished their breakfast and returned to their rooms. Jorge looked at their empty places with the scattered utensils and half-filled cups of coffee. Only then did he feel deserted. His eyes welled up and he began to whimper. His body shook with a sudden despair. His only thought was that perhaps he should have told his father why Miguel had run away. He thought, too late, that it might have made a difference. But he couldn't stop the howling, the grief poured out of him, his tears flowed too copiously for him to do anything but cover his eyes.

At last he made sense of the questions his father had been asking him all week.

If I were to buy a new house, would you like to go with me?

Jorge didn't know.

If I were...to get married again...would you like to come live with us?

Jorge had shaken his head. At bottom he was afraid of leaving Adia. Now he understood why his father had seemed disappointed when Jorge said no to everything he asked.

Jorge felt a hand touching his head. It was Maya. Adia was standing behind her.

'So he's gone?' Maya said softly.

'That must have been his farewell party,' she said, rolling her eyes.

Joseph came in and saw Maya looking up towards the room of Jorge's father. He did the same. 'Didn't you say he had boxes of mackerel in his room?'

'His room!' Adia suddenly remembered. 'Let's go see!'

They ran up to the far wing. Joseph knocked. He turned to them with a grin. 'Just in case...'

There was no answer.

'Let's break it down!'

Joseph and Roberto kicked the door open. They found the room empty and a mess.

'They just packed up and left,' Joseph said.

Roberto looked in the empty closet. 'What happened to all the mackerel?'

'They took it with them?' Maya said in disbelief.

Adia shrugged. 'I guess.'

They all went down to the yard, forlorn for different reasons. Maya put her arm around Jorge.

'Boy, believe me,' she said. 'You're lucky to be rid of that one.'

V.

Roberto hated being idle, and one day he
performed a miracle no one in the house dared
attempt before. The TV set had gathered dust in the
corner since breaking down nearly a year before.
Roberto pulled out the back of the set and dug into its
mysterious innards. He sent Joseph off in search of
parts and when Joseph returned they called everyone
to the living room. Everyone watched as the grimy
black screen flickered into life for the first time since
the boarders arrived. There was a round of applause.
But the household had done for so long without the
appliance, it was pushed back into the corner as a
reminder of what miracles could yet happen in their
lives.

Adia had more money to spend at the market
now because of the boarders, but she still complained.
She always served the meals with apologies, wishing
there were other ways to cook the fish and vegetables
she always served. It was just her way. But the

boarders thought she was unhappy, and tried, in various ways, to help her.

'That's prime rib,' Roberto said one day. He was smoking at the back fence. Jorge followed the line of his gaze and saw the cow grazing untended by the river. Joseph came out to join them. They all stood there watching the gentle, indifferent creature.

'There must be a hundred kilos in her,' Roberto said. Joseph got the idea and laughed.

Adia howled in protest when they told her their plan.

'Why not?' argued Joseph. 'It's getting fat on grass that's on your land.'

'It's not *our* land,' Adia said. She came out to look at the cow. 'And it's not getting fat at all.'

'Who cares?' Joseph countered. 'The land belongs to *us*. The *people*.'

'I think we'll get by without stealing,' Adia said firmly and walked away.   But that didn't stop the two men from scheming and obsessing about the cow. They walked through the dining room the next morning, murmuring. 'If it walks in, it walks in,' Joseph was saying. 'As long as we did nothing to coerce the creature. Free will, you know.'

Roberto was nodding.

'Imagine, fresh milk in the morning,' Joseph said. 'It'll be like communism came early to this place.'

They both laughed. Maya was drowsily drinking her coffee then. She looked up at them and scratched her head.

Jorge often caught Joseph and Roberto doing strange things in the back. Standing at the fence they held out tufts of grass and made all sorts of noises, intent on enticing the cow. But the animal was unmoved. It went on with its sad, weary chewing, quite out of reach. There seemed no hope of drawing it any closer. Until the day Goyle came back from the market with a broad grin on his face.

He was wearing a new shirt. He had been doing errands at the market when a shopkeeper asked his help unloading goods from a truck. When they finished, the grateful merchant pulled a shirt out from his stocks and gave it to Goyle. It was a very bright red shirt and they could see him from a mile off.

They saw him walking along the river towards the house. As he crossed the field Jorge and his two companions couldn't help noticing how the cow became agitated. First it snorted and stomped its front hoof, flicking its tail from side to side. As Goyle waved to Jorge with a big smile, the cow threw up its head with an angry groan. It started swaying.

All of a sudden it broke loose from its stake. Joseph and Roberto watched in disbelief as the cow that had been so cool to their attentions suddenly started trotting towards Goyle.

At first Goyle thought the cow was in a friendly mood and stood still to welcome it. He and the others belatedly noticed how it had lowered its head and the trot turned into a charge. Jorge and the two boarders were shouting to him, waving their hands. *Ruuuuun, Goyle! Ruuuuuuun!*

A burst of desperation propelled Goyle across the field. They helped him over the fence, just as the cow was circling back towards the river.

'It's the red shirt!' Joseph said. 'Damn. Why didn't I think of that?'

They saw that the cow, now back at its stake, still seemed intent on Goyle, with the kind of obsessed attention Joseph and Roberto were giving it days before.

'Now we know what she likes,' Roberto said.

And so the game of *El Matador* began.

One of them, Goyle, Joseph or Jorge (Roberto was too slow) would take Goyle's red shirt and wave it in the cow's face. After rousing the beast they would dash away still waving the red garment in its face. Their aim was to steer the cow into the yard, where Roberto had built a little enclosure.

The cow, incensed at being hit with sticks or pelted with pebbles, would snort and lunge at them. It clearly didn't get much nourishment from the poor grazing in the field, but its sudden, furious energy always surprised them. It thundered after Jorge or Goyle, who would run screaming towards Roberto's paddock. Joseph and Roberto sat on the back fence, trying to confuse the cow with shouts of 'Toro! Toro! Toro!'

One day Goyle got too brazen, clowning in front of the cow as he ran, dancing and hopping on one foot while twirling the red shirt in one hand.

The others were shouting at the top of their voices. 'Be-*HIND YOU!* She's right be*hind* you!'

They saw how the horn sank into Goyle's bottom. He jumped up, used his hands to cover the rip in his pants, then he had to run again. The cow lunged and they heard Goyle cry out, 'Ow! Jesus, Mary, Joseph!'

He jumped into the river for his life. Jorge was impressed he knew the names of all the saints.

One day after weeks in vain, the cow's owner turned up. He found the cow missing from its stake and flew into a rage. He roamed the fields near the river, calling late into the night. The next morning he came out of the woods holding a cutlass. 'I'm warning you!' he shook it at Roberto and Joseph standing at the fence. 'I've been sharpening her horns.'

He took the cow and led it back towards the woods. 'You want to feel a sting in your backsides,' he shouted. 'Just try it again!'

It was around this time that a man with a familiar melancholy air arrived at the house. He asked to speak to Melba. They spoke at the gate and when he left, Melba rushed crying to her room.
Adia explained to Jorge, 'Melba's mother has died.'

Later Jorge often found Melba standing quietly at the gate after supper. Her complexion had cleared somewhat, though she still wore bangs that hid her eyes. Her chores made her think less of her troubles and she had shed some of the despondency of her people.

From the gate she looked across the river towards the city.

'What're you doing here?' Jorge asked one night.

'Just thinking,' Melba sighed.

'Of what?'

She didn't answer. After while she said. 'Wouldn't it be nice to go away?'

Jorge didn't like such talk. It made him think of Miguel.. 'Where do you want to go?' he said.

Melba shifted her weight and shrugged. 'Anywhere.'

'Although, I'm going to the village tomorrow,' she said wistfully. 'I suppose that's far enough.' She went inside.

The water at the standpipe sometimes ran dry, and when it came back, the tap coughed out rust and slime. So Melba began taking the laundry to the village, where she enjoyed the company of the other women washing their clothes at the pump.

She would return at nightfall with the wrung out washing in a bucket balanced on her head. One day she didn't come home till after suppertime. Adia had been worried.

'Where have you been?' she asked as soon as Melba walked through the gate.

'I was just talking to the sisters,' said Melba as she took her bucket to the back.

'What sisters?' Adia followed her.

'The nuns,' said Melba. 'They were talking to everyone.'

'What on earth could they want?' worried Adia. 'We have nothing to give them.'

Slowly, they learned each of the boarders' stories, though Joseph remained a hard man to read. He never stopped taking good care of his hair, and for hours after his shower he hardly moved so he could preserve its sculpted shape. They never found the man behind the subterfuge and big talk.

Maya, though warmer and gentler than she had at first seemed, was always soft-spoken and discreet. She remained, like her name, elusive.

Roberto was a former shop owner who had lost his business through debts. He enjoyed a drink and his eyes lit up on those occasions when he and the others could afford to buy liquor. He was casting around for chances to start his life over, and was living off the money that his creditors didn't take. At dinner one night he revealed that his wife left him after his business failed. She had acted on the stage and was used to the good life.

They were people simply making a stop at the house on their way somewhere else. The boarders liked to linger at the table after supper and talk. Jorge was fascinated by these rambling conversations at the dinner table. Through them he began to know what life outside Aguada was like.

Joseph liked to blame everything on something he called, disgustedly, '*politics*'.

'It's all politics,' he would grumble. 'Dirty politics!' making it sound like something worse than witchcraft. From the buses no longer running up to the house, to him not being able to find work. From Roberto going out of business to Maya not wanting to talk to him. It was all down to one thing. 'Damn politics,' he would mutter as he went up to his room.

The boarders had cleaned out the cobwebs in the music room and turned it into a pleasant place to read.

'We can all use this time for learning,' Joseph said. 'Even for you,' he said to Jorge. 'Come here, little man.'

He had taken to reading to Jorge from the few books he had brought.

Adia looked at some of the covers and fervently objected. *''Rape of the Amazons'!'* she gasped. 'Keep that away from the boy!'

'It'll raise the boy's awareness,' Joseph retorted. 'What's wrong with that?'

They were to learn another of Joseph's secrets.

Once, sitting in the garden after dinner, Joseph suddenly announced, 'I've written a poem.'

Roberto and Maya shifted in their seats. Jorge didn't know what to say. After some hesitation, Joseph said, 'You want to hear it?'

'Hm?' Roberto scratched his cheek and yawned. Maya kept still.

'Sure!' Roberto answered after a long pause.

'Really?' Joseph sprang up and ran to the house. In no time at all he was back, flipping through a thick notebook. Maya groaned. She got ready to leave.

'Aha!' Joseph said. 'Just a moment, please,' he said to Maya. She sat back down.

Joseph read his poem. He recited it in a breathy voice like he was trying to put a baby to sleep. His listeners were lulled into a deeper and deeper stillness.

A long silence followed the poem's last, vanishing line, and no one realised Joseph had finished. Roberto was slumped heavily in the garden chair, his eyes fixed on a few stars. Maya sat without stirring.

'Well?' said Joseph, his voice alert. 'What do you think?'

'Think?' Roberto sat up. 'Think of what?'

'The poem, man. The one I just read.'

'Oh...'

But Joseph wouldn't let him off. 'You think I got any talent?'

Maya shifted in her seat. She cleared her throat.

'Multi-faceted is what I'd call it,' she said.

'Oh, yes?'

'Yes,' said Maya, running a hand through her hair. 'A bit of Yeats. A bit of Tennyson. Even Brecht. All nicely slapped together like a ransom note.'

Joseph took it all in. 'How about Mao?' he said pertly. 'You don't see Mao in my poetry?'

Maya conceded. 'Hendrix, maybe.'

'Oh yeah.'

'Haze. I just see haze.'

Joseph ended up throwing down the notebook and stomping out of the garden. At the front door he clenched his fists and shouted, 'No one understands me! No one knows how hard it is to create!' As he opened the door to go in, he made a last, resigned gesture. 'Ah, politics!'

Strange new things came with the boarders. In the music room with Joseph or Maya, Jorge heard tales more spellbinding than any Adia ever told.

He had begun to find Adia absurd. There were times he felt he knew her better than anyone. At other times she seemed like a baffling stranger who had no business living with them.

One morning she overreacted to a mishap at breakfast.

Joseph was bringing his coffee cup to his lips when he jumped up and gave a shout. 'Ow!' He tried to brush off the spilt coffee from his shirt.

'These damn old cups!' he complained. 'They're chipped everywhere! Don't we good people deserve better?'

He was only joking, but Adia took offence. She got up and stalked out of the room. That day she worked through the debris in the store room. She battled through the detritus of the many lives that had passed in the house and succeeded in retrieving a magnificent set of tableware made from fine bone china, complete with matching silverware. It was laid out for breakfast the next day.

'It's imported from England,' Adia boasted. 'Jorge's grandfather bought it from a man who came here from Manchester. Politicians and rich planters used to come to the house and dine on these.'

Her manner said that her lodgers now had no cause to complain. And so from that day on she insisted, still with hurt pride, that they use the expensive tableware at all times. 'After all,' she said, 'good people deserve good things.'

Joseph made a show of being appreciative. He made sure to feel the heft of the silverware each time he used it. 'Ah, the weight of silver,' he said as he sliced the fish. 'Makes food so much more a *pleasure*. With fine engraving, too. So nice to the touch.'

He saw Maya rolling her eyes. He squinted at the engraving. 'JZ to C'. Is that something in Latin?'

'Jose Zandro to Claudia,' explained Adia. 'Jorge's grandfather bought it as a gift for his wife.'

Sometimes they lit candles and felt truly grand. Adia always collected the tableware after each meal. She stored them in the glass cabinet in the hallway, where they were visible even from the front door, and could always be admired. She often stood there counting the porcelain pieces, as if their round number completed something in her soul.

'Now, they'll think we're people worth stealing from,' Roberto said.

'If Adia loses the key to that cabinet, we might have to go back to eating off the table with our hands,' Joseph added. He laughed expansively to show Adia he was only joking.

Alas, by some mishap, three cups went missing. Adia buzzed around the house in a panic. 'Oh God! Oh God!'

Everyone felt compelled to help. They turned the rooms upside down and managed to locate two cups Joseph had taken to the shower and didn't bring back.

'Don't jump to conclusions,' he said defensively. 'No one said you can't enjoy a coffee while washing your hair.'

He avoided the strange looks they were all giving him. 'I don't know where the other one is! Leave me alone!'

The search brought Jorge and Goyle to the old orchard, where they found the entrance to an abandoned shaft. They climbed down to look.

It was pitch-black below, the air hot and stuffy. Jorge said, 'We need a light. I'll get a candle from the house.' He had gone up a rung when Goyle struck a match. The flame gave them a flickering view of the dank, small chamber with a smooth earthen floor. Then Goyle let out a curse and blew out the light. In the darkness Jorge heard the rush as Goyle climbed over him and scrambled out of the shaft.

'Wait for me!' Jorge shouted. 'Goyle! Come back!'

But Goyle was gone. Jorge couldn't see anything in the blackness. He started to sweat. He didn't know how long it took him to fumble his way out of the shaft, screaming for Goyle in the dark.

He got home and confronted Goyle. 'Why'd you leave me?' he shouted. 'It was your idea to go down!'

Goyle pointed to his eyes. 'If *you* saw what *these eyes* saw, you'd have done the same thing.'

'What was it?'

'Human bones, Jorge,' answered Goyle. 'Legs, arms, ribs, a skull. No eyes. Just holes staring at me.'

Jorge wasn't sure whether to believe him.

'Anyway,' Goyle said to Adia. 'There was no sign of the cup.'

'Oh, well,' Adia sighed. 'you can't have everything.'

But from that day on they often saw her standing in the hallway counting the set of fine bone china with a wistful bend to her head. Jose Zandro's sumptuous collection looked sad without the missing member. Fragmented, forlorn.

But soon something was set to divert them again.

They had just settled down for supper one night, with silverware, candles and all, when they heard shouting outside. 'Where are the evil ones? Come out!'

Adia and the boarders went to the door and saw
the angry band standing outside, some of them
carrying torches. One or two men in the front wielded
machetes.

'My Lord,' Maya whispered. 'They look like
they're out to lynch someone.'

'Go on, Joseph,' she prodded. 'Be a man.'

Adia went out the door before anyone could
stop her.

'Ah!' shouted the wild-eyed man at the head of
the group. Adia moved towards him, indifferent to her
fate. They faced each other and she listened to his
complaints.

The boarders rushed out and gathered behind
Adia. The leader was fuming about thefts. 'Things go
missing right under our noses! No one's house is safe!'

They were all people from the village. But the
torches gave a demonic cast to their faces. The
boarders noticed that stuck inside the middle of the
group were a few women in mourning clothes. Their
faces were wet from crying. Some of the men were
clearly drunk, as baffled about what was happening as
Adia and her lodgers.

Joseph finally inched forward. 'We didn't mean to offend anyone by toying with that cow,' he snickered. 'Just little games, you know. Good for the animal. Good for everyone.'

No one paid him any attention.

'Babies have been found dead in their cribs!' the group's leader said.

Joseph and Roberto looked aghast. 'No,' Roberto shook his head. 'We'd never do such a thing!'

'Three infants died within weeks of each other,' one of the grieving women screamed. 'What else could it be?'

'Right!' said the ring leader. 'What other possibility exists?'

The boarders huddled closer together. Goyle came out of the kitchen and stood gaping at the torches.

'Who can we blame?' the second grieving woman cried.

'What could it be?' The third woman shouted heavenward. 'If not witchcraft!'

The men in the group raised their machetes.

The boarders and Adia held on to each other, backing up towards the house. Maya pulled Jorge back with her.

The group kept inching forward until their leader was standing in the yard. He said, 'We know the problem lies here with you.'

Adia swayed.

'It's here!' the leader pointed at the house, screaming.

'It's around here,' said another man in the group.

'No, it's around the back,' yet another pointed towards the field.

Others started pointing, too. 'It's near the back fence.'

Adia and the boarders watched as the group made its way around to the back of the lot.

'*There*,' the leader finally said. 'The devil's nest!'

The torch-bearing villagers ringed around something, standing with their feet wide apart as if to prevent escape. Jorge craned his neck to see, expecting a dog or a wild boar. The culprit turned out to be a mound of earth in a corner of the field.

The leader began an entreaty, 'Oh mound of spirits! Let our sufferings cease!'

A big man came forward from the rear of the group.

'We beseech you!' the leader was saying to the mound. 'Leave us in peace!'

The burly man who had come forward held up something. The light from the torches shone on his big, heavy shotgun.

At a signal from the leader everyone drew back. The burly man was left standing alone in front of the mound.

'All right, then,' said the leader of the group. 'We've spoken to the malevolent ones. We have asked them to leave. Now let them feel our wrath!'

The big man cocked the shotgun. The loud crack of steel echoed in the silence as everyone waited. The man aimed at the mound.

A tremendous explosion came from the gun. It made the crowd gasp, heaving with satisfaction at the gush of energy through the air. Jorge covered his ears.
'More!' the leader cried.
The burly man fired again.
'More! Let the little ones taste fire!'

The man let off a deafening volley that shook the ground. The flare from muzzle lit up the darkness like flashes of lightning, showing the grimace of pleasure on the faces of the villagers as they dealt out revenge for their misfortunes.

'E-*nough!*' the leader finally said, raising his hand. 'I think the message has been received.' Joseph's face showed that it clearly had. He was as pale as a bone china plate.

The crowd slowly dispersed. Jorge followed Adia and the others back into the house.

At dusk one day Melba appeared with the laundry bucket perched on her head. Jorge came out and sat on the ground as she was hanging things up to dry on the lines behind the kitchen. She was digging into the bucket for more clothing when something bounded out and leapt across the yard in one incandescent arc.

'Melba, look!' Jorge sprang to his feet. 'Oh!' Melba turned around. They watched the squiggle of light jumping on the wall. Melba leapt forward to try and catch it, but the luminous creature streaked out of her grasp. Melba picked up a broom to try and hit it.

'Don't!' Jorge cried. The flickering spark retreated to a corner under the eaves.

'Wait.' Melba ran inside and came back with an empty glass jar. Its lid had been punched with holes.

'Here,' she gave Jorge the broom. Then they blocked off all means of escape. The expression on Melba's face was intent. After dashing around for some minutes they managed to catch the flighty jitter of light.

Melba snapped the lid shut with a cry. 'There!'

She held up the jar like a prize. Her fixation changed to enchantment as they watched the skittish radiance they had trapped in the jar. The glowing spider scrambled against the sides of the container, its glassy legs already caught in the shimmering filaments it had spun.

'He's beautiful!' Jorge breathed.

Melba smiled. 'We won't let him die. We'll always keep him.'

They hid the jar in a cabinet in the hall and took it out only when no one else was around. It gave them boundless pleasure to know that the miraculous fleck of fluorescence they had captured was there, safe in their jar. They made a promise never to take it out in daylight.

It was a great moment when they could bring it out at night and sit in the dim kitchen, rapt in the spider's strange glow, the glass jar shining with a cool light.

One night as they sat watching it, Melba revealed, 'Last night I dreamt I saw my dead mother.'

'What was she doing?'

Melba shrugged. 'Nothing. She was sitting peacefully somewhere.' She looked askance at him and added: 'She was drinking from Adia's missing cup.'

After a few days Jorge found her working in the field. She had dug up the earth mound. They got down on the ground and burrowed into the hole with their hands.

'Careful of broken glass,' Melba said.

After a while she sat up. 'Oh my!'

'What is it?'

Melba dusted off something in her hand. 'It's Adia's cup!'

It was still perfectly white, whole and unscathed. Melba put it down with a puzzled look. She sat with her hand pressed against her cheek for a long time. 'Perhaps it's a sign I should leave this place.'

The day Adia had long been dreading finally came. Five nuns arrived at the house. They stood at the fence and called out to Jorge, 'Boy, come here.'

A friendly one among them leaned down and said, 'Do you have a mother and father?'

She gave him a sweet smile. 'Who's taking care of you? Would you like to go to school?'

Jorge was transfixed by their bright white habits.

Adia came out of the kitchen. The nuns explained they were from the city and had come to Aguada looking for orphans to take under their care.

Maya opened her window upstairs and saw the nuns. She came down in a hurry. 'He's being taken care of here,' she shielded Jorge from the nuns. Roberto and Joseph came out, too, smelling trouble.

'He gets more than enough looking after here, as you can see, ' Adia said. 'He'll be fine.'

The nuns smiled and left. But the sisters belonged to an order of legendary persistence. They would come to Aguada again and again.

Jorge liked to watch Joseph do his early morning callisthenics in the yard. He bent his skinny body into dramatic poses and swung his bony arms. His hair always got into his face and he swept it back tetchily. He said, 'You know Samson had to put up with the same thing.'

To join the conversation at the dinner table, Jorge resorted to telling bizarre tales. They were a mixture of his imaginings and the strange things that had happened around him. He relished the pauses he caused, the baffled attention he got from saying shocking things. But he began to betray things Melba had told him in confidence. He talked of goblins storing up the sunlight and dead people appearing in his and Melba's dreams. But when he talked of digging up the earth mound and finding Adia's missing cup, he went too far.

'Shut up!' Melba shouted across the room. 'You can't stop making things up!' she said. 'You just can't stop lying!'

She ran out of the room in tears. The boarders were confused.

'Shows one thing,' Joseph said. 'The boy's mind is ripe.'

He took his glass and sat down beside Jorge. 'Must see what we can do. Shame to let such an imagination go to waste!'

For weeks, Jorge had been aware of sly goings-on around him. He saw Roberto leave the house early one morning and when he came back Joseph helped him unload a large, unwieldy package which they carried quietly across the yard. Nothing they said during the day or at supper gave Jorge an inkling of what was going on. For the first time, the whole household seemed to be colluding against him.

One afternoon he heard a bizarre noise. It pursued him wherever he went in the house. He heard his name being said, over and over again.

First he heard Roberto's voice, saying, 'Jorge.'

Jorge wanted to answer, thinking he was being called. Then he heard a high, unnatural voice mimicking what Roberto had said, *Jorge.*

'Good, good,' Roberto cleared his throat. He was in the room next to the kitchen. The door was shut.

Jorge went down the stairs and Roberto's muffled voice followed him down the hall. He said clearly: as if trying to record his voice, 'Jorge is a good boy.'

Jorge is a good boy, said the other voice.

'A good boy,' said Roberto.

A good boy.

Jorge decided to keep an eye on all his housemates, and in particular, Roberto. That evening before supper, he saw him coming out of the room by the kitchen with a small dish of water. He looked around before quietly shutting the door.

Jorge was disheartened to find he was no longer included in the dinnertime conversations. The talk around the table fell into silence the moment he came in. He felt reduced once more to a child excluded from the world of grownups. He began to regret his outrageous lies. Perhaps Melba had been right. But when he saw Joseph and Maya exchanging glances he couldn't help thinking something was afoot.

The boarders managed to bribe the chauffeur into driving them all to the plaza. The bribe must have been barely adequate, because the chauffeur never stopped grumbling, muttering under his breath.

The plaza was crowded and noisy when they arrived. Bright lights shone from every corner of the square, and large banners flew over the stage. The outsized writing on them welcomed visitors from the capital. A small orchestra was gathering under the intense lights, tuning their instruments.

Joseph bought a newspaper.

'What's going on?' said Roberto, looking starry-eyed at the lights. People were milling excitedly around them. Huge posters of the old, wrinkly president had been tacked on the tree trunks and wrapped around the lamp posts.

'We're in time for a show!' Joseph said, scanning the newspaper. 'Some politicians have come to town.'

Hello, hello. Someone was testing the microphone on the stage.

Maya and Roberto wandered off to find out what was going to happen.

'You're a lucky boy,' Joseph said to Jorge. 'They're putting on this show for you.'

'Really?'

'Well. For all of us.'

'Why?' asked Jorge.

'Because of something called elections, my boy.'

'What's that?'

'It's a fine tradition we have,' Joseph answered. 'Every few years we choose which thief is going to milk us dry.' He looked up to the stage. 'It's the civilised way,' he said. 'One thief at a time.'

Maya and Roberto came back. 'There's wonderful news,' Roberto beamed.

'Oh?'

'They say Imelda Gomez is coming to perform.' Roberto seemed very excited.

'My, my.' Joseph rolled up the newspaper into a telescope and peeked at the stage. 'Oh, Imelda! Where are you?'

Sirens wailed as the entourage arrived. Applause swept through the crowd as the mayor came up to the microphone.

'Oh, no!' Joseph and Roberto held their heads.

'I have some news to break,' he started solemnly. 'There's been some disturbance in the capital.'

"We have received reports about an attempt on the president's life.' He waited as his message was absorbed. 'We don't know what may yet happen...'

His amplified voice reverberated from the many speakers scattered over the square. A gloomy silence fell on the crowd as his unsteady voice thundered out again. 'This only proves that THE ENEMY NEVER SLEEPS. He never misses the chance to try and TOPPLE OUR CHERISHED ORDER!'

'What is it with this man,' Joseph said. 'Can't he open his mouth unless it's bad news?'

The mayor finally left and a buzz of excitement spread through the crowd.

Finally, Imelda Gomez came out in a dress of sparkling sequins that caught the bright lights and glowed like a halo around her. She walked to the microphone and began to sing.

The crowd fell into a deep and mesmerised silence. Roberto swooned as the singer's voice wafted over them. 'She brings back such memories,' he said, his eyes shining and fixated on the stage. "Ah, my wife."

Jorge had never seen him so happy.

'See, politics is not all bad,' Joseph said, looking through the rolled up newspaper again. 'Thanks to politics we get to ogle this beautiful woman.'

'Ah, polo sticks,' Jorge threw up his hands, thinking he was mimicking Joseph.

'Smart boy.' Joseph's eyes shone. 'See? He's a really smart boy!'

Imelda Gomez warbled through number after number, entrancing her audience, while the politicians backstage began to fidget, holding copies of their speeches.

The elegant chanteuse transported the crowd so much it threatened to make them forget their sharper hungers and the real reason they were gathered in plaza that night. But soon the mellifluous performance was at an end.

'Ah,' Roberto said. 'You can't go to heaven unless you're dead.'

The crowd was beginning to disperse. There was no stopping the dissipation of interest now that the beautiful star was gone. Jorge and his companions remained standing where they were.

'You know if you listen to her closely,' Joseph was saying to Roberto, 'you realise she's actually singing out of tune.'

'She's made hundreds of records,' Roberto said, getting irate. 'You're saying no one's noticed but you?'

'People don't really hear her voice,' Joseph insisted. 'They're too dazzled by the sequins. And of course the long smooth legs.'

'There's no need for me to answer that,' Roberto waved him off, 'because you're either crazy or deaf!'

They argued as the crowd thinned out and the plaza was nearly empty. The lights on the stage were turned off.

'Oh!' Joseph seemed to remember something and walked off, to return with two cylindrical packages under his arm. He walked with a rebellious swagger that implied he was carrying dangerous contraband.

They had trouble finding the chauffeur, and when they did, he tried to drive off without them. They had to run to the middle of the road and block his path. He drove them home and made no effort to disguise his displeasure at wasting his time.

The next day after supper Joseph unwrapped his mysterious packages. He unrolled them and had to stand in a chair to hold them up. They were the huge posters of the elderly president. They were taller than Joseph.

'How'd you get those?' Roberto asked in awe.

Joseph cocked his head and refused to say. The president's ancient face gazed out on the room on either side of Joseph, the eyes larger than their dinner plates.

Maya looked disgusted. 'Our nightmare enlarged to a gigantic scale,' she said. 'The man's face is a death mask. Mark my words. It's got all our deaths written on it.'

They were puzzled by her meaning and her mood. 'Soldiers killed six men trying to get into the presidential palace two days ago,' she said. 'No details have been released about it yet.'

They wondered how she knew. She was fidgeting with her hands, troubled about something. 'Machine guns have been positioned at the bridge approaching the palace,' she said.

They'd had no idea any of this was going on, then Maya added, 'A few weeks ago the president announced that he was naming his ten -year-old grandson an army general.'

'What?' They were all horrified.

Maya gave them a smile. 'That fat little brat who can't tie his own shoelaces.'

'What's this country coming to?' Adia crossed herself.

'Exactly,' Maya said. 'Some people saw how those rows of soldiers stood in formation as the little brat strutted back and forth in his oversized uniform. With a sabre that was taller than him.'

Joseph snickered. 'I'd have liked to see that.'

Roberto seemed to feel genuine grief. He clucked his tongue and sadly shook his head. 'That's terrible. It can't be good.'

'He's sinking into a horrible little abyss, the crazy old man,' said Maya softly, staring down on the table. 'He's dragging us all with him into the darkness.'

Jorge looked at their long faces and wondered what all this meant.

'Those six men were right to try and kill the doddery old bastard,' Maya said. They sat in silence.

'Very well,' said Maya after a while, her lips pressed together in resolve. 'It had to come to this sooner or later.'

Then, as if she only now remembered Jorge, she turned to him and said, 'And it's all happening in time for Jorge's eleventh birthday.' She reached over and ruffled his hair. 'What a special little boy you are.'

It was the long, torrid month before the rainstorms of June. Jorge and all the others liked nothing more than to retire to their rooms for siesta in the afternoons. The hot dreamy hour gave them a chance to ward off thoughts of trouble for a while. The unused room by the kitchen had tall, wide windows that opened out on the veranda. It used to be Jose Zandro's study and it was the breeziest room in the house. After sampling several other locations, Jorge settled on it as the best room for his naps.

Jose Zandro's things had been pushed into a corner behind one of the tall bookcases, but Jorge had never cared to examine the objects that had belonged to his grandfather. He came in during the afternoons and merely took delight in stretching out on the old leather couch by the window. So intent was he in the pleasure of it that it was some time before he noticed the brightly-coloured creature in the shadows at the far end of the room. Even when it stirred and turned its head to him, Jorge thought he was just in the grip of a mid-afternoon dream, in which the creature peered out from behind the bookcase to study him. It inched forward on its clawed feet, strangely curious about Jorge lying there, his fingers tapping on his stomach. Jorge drowsily considered the bright variegation of its feathers as it leapt to the corner of the desk and perched there to examine him.

He was startled only slightly when it flapped its wings. The pull of sleep was too delicious to resist, however, and Jorge sank back, vaguely thinking he had heard the bird say his name. He dreamt of a rainbow floating above him like a pair of wings.

Whoosh! And he was suddenly awake. Jorge sat up with a start, trying to clear the fog in his head. He looked around the room and had an instinct that something had gone.

The wide window behind him gaped out to the vast blue sky. It gave him a dreadful feeling. Escape, it said. *Escape.*

Jorge bit his lip. He got up and hurried out of the room. He kept quiet about his encounter with the strange bird, and, from that day on went back to napping in his own room.

His birthday fell on a Sunday. Melba had found cassava in the back of the old orchard and Maya offered to cook it. She and Melba pulled out a vat from the back of the storage shed. They then decided to rearrange the jumble inside. When they moved out some of the dusty boxes, Maya looked up and gave a squeal of pleasure. There were crates of empty beer bottles stacked right up to the roof.

'We can take them back for the deposit,' Joseph came and counted. 'There'll be enough to buy a whole case.'

'Everyone's going to have fun at your party but you,' Maya said to Jorge. She surprised everyone by pulling out a sheer pink dress from her closet. Jorge found it pretty. Her long hair was wet from her bath and she stomped her foot girlishly when Roberto teased her. She seemed happy.

The party was held in the music room, dusted and wiped again and again for the occasion. Adia and Melba brought in the cake. There were eleven candles of different heights and colours. Everyone fell quiet and cleared a place at the table for Jorge.

He leaned back to fill his lungs. He blew at the flames with all his strength, and an old, familiar sound came back to his ears.

Blblblbleh....

'Puff-brain.'

All at once he missed Miguel. The smoke from the candles stung his eyes and for a moment he nearly cried.

Then, at a signal from Maya, they all cheered and shouted, 'Happy birthday, Jorge!'

They threw up their hands and released a rain of confetti into the room. Scraps of paper scattered in the air, cut and shredded from the posters of the old president Joseph had brought home.

'Time for a tune, perhaps?' Maya said to Roberto.

Roberto understood. 'Of course!'

He went to the piano and tried to pick out a tune. He made several attempts to play a melody with one finger, and finally said, 'Ah! I'm delaying the important moment.'

He went out of the room. He returned with Joseph and they placed a large gift-wrapped package on top of the piano. 'Close your eyes,' Roberto said to Jorge.

Jorge felt himself being led forward.

"Alright. Open them now."

Jorge found himself in front of the covered bulk that was the shape of a bird cage. He was worried.

"Go ahead," Roberto said with a smile. Jorge tore the wrapping while everyone waited. When he had finished, they all looked dumb-founded.

The bird cage was empty. Maya looked from Joseph to Roberto, expecting a joke.

Roberto was the last to realise what was wrong. He turned to see.

'The bird's gone,' someone said sadly.

'Oh...' They all turned to see how Jorge would react.

'It's flown away,' said Maya softly, like she was about to burst into tears.

Jorge lowered his head, fighting the urge to come clean.

'We won't let it bother us,' Roberto said, clearing his throat. 'After all, it was I who taught the thing to say the important words.'

' So...' He straightened up and, in a parrot-like voice, said loudly, 'Jorge is a good boy. A very good boy. A very, very, very good boy.'

Everyone applauded Roberto. Jorge couldn't understand why they all looked at him with such pity. He glanced at the blue sky into which the bird must have flown, and felt sad only for Roberto. But he was taking large gulps from his drink and looked happy, too.

The celebration continued late into the night. Adia brought Jorge's dinner, not willing to let him gorge on cassava and cake. The boarders chatted and laughed, and at one point tried to dance to the racket Joseph banged out on the piano, which made Melba and Adia decide to leave. Jorge lost track of the merrymaking and people starting to wander off until at last he found himself alone among the litter in the music room, opening his presents. Maya had given him a pair of shoes. Goyle came in and presented him with an enigmatic piece of metal, whispered, 'Happy birthday,' and quickly left.

Early the next morning Joseph was at his door. He was sweaty and short of breath. Jorge was still sleepy and crawled back in bed. But Joseph poked his head through the window. 'Psst!'

He motioned for Jorge to follow him outside. It was still dark. Dawn was about to break. Jorge came out and found Joseph standing by the gate.

'Look what I got you,' he said, still trying to catch his breath.

Jorge came forward as Joseph pulled something out of the shadows. He saw the shiny handlebars.

'Well,' Joseph smiled. 'You like it?'

'A bicycle? For me?'

'Try it,' Joseph said.

Jorge did. 'It's perfect!'

'Good.'

'Where did you buy it?' asked Jorge, yawning.

"Buy it? Well...' Joseph tilted his head. 'Let's just say you got it from Santa.'

'Adia says there's no such thing as Santa Claus,' said Jorge, rubbing his eyes. 'Besides, it's not Christmas.'

'I meant Santana,' said Joseph. 'Carlos, that great Mexican god.'

Maya peered out of her window upstairs and came out to join them. She studied the bicycle, biting her lip. 'Why is it pink?'

Joseph acted incredulous. 'Pink? It's not *pink*.'

'It doesn't matter,' Jorge told her. 'Can I go for a ride?'

Joseph gazed out at the road. It was getting light. 'Why not?' he said.

They went out on the roadside. Jorge got ready to push off but Joseph suddenly seized the handlebars. 'Uh-oh.'

One of the buses was coming down from the corner with its pale headlamps on, setting off on the day's first journey.

'Let me go!' Jorge struggled to move forward. But Joseph pulled the bicycle back towards the gate.

'Too early to go.' He sounded nervous. 'The road's busy.'

'There's only one bus!' Jorge protested.

Joseph stood between him and the road, like he was trying to hide Jorge.

The bus finally passed and Joseph relaxed. 'All right,' he said. 'We'll have our ride later.'

So in the afternoon Jorge took the bicycle out on the road. He went past the corner where the village idlers hooted and jeered. 'Nice little bicycle, boy! Where'd you get such a pretty thing?'

'Did you steal it from your sister?'

Jorge got to the rocky slope where the buses liked to thunder down and raise clouds of dust. He had gone up and down a few times on the incline when he felt a vehicle bearing down on him from behind. It came so close it nearly touched his rear wheel, and the loud-hailer almost made him jump.

'Stop, boy! Stop there!'

From up close he saw for the first time the flashing blue light of a patrol car. From the corner of his eye Jorge saw the village boys coming up to watch the drama that was about to unfold. The policeman eased himself out of the car, clucking his tongue. He told Jorge to get in the front seat and placed the Jorge's bicycle in the back. He climbed back in, turned on the siren and they sped off.

Jorge couldn't suppress the thrill of being inside a wailing patrol car. They hurtled through the village streets, past curious, awed bystanders. Jorge stuck his head up so other boys could see him in the grave situation of being taken somewhere with a screaming siren. He kept glancing at the black, worn out pistol in the policeman's holster.

Finally, they reached the station. At first Jorge was only frightened that he wouldn't find his way home. They went inside and the policeman sat Jorge on a stool and placed himself behind a large typewriter. The policeman tried to type with his large hands, screwed up several sheets of paper before finally producing something he liked. 'There,' he said contentedly in his raspy voice.

At last he turned his attention to Jorge. 'You know what it means to give a gift, my boy?' he began almost casually. 'A gift.' He placed his large hands on his chest. 'Something from your heart.'

Jorge nodded that he knew what a gift meant.

'To a little child you love...' the policeman continued. Jorge nodded meekly to everything he said. 'Something you buy out of the little money you make.' The policemen seemed to be building up to a great outburst. 'Which is no more than a thief makes in one night!' At the words 'thief 'and 'night' he slapped the desk hard. Jorge nearly fell from his seat.

The policeman resumed in a calmer voice. 'You know what it means to have your gift stolen?' He leaned forward to look into Jorge's frightened eyes. 'To have your daughter come crying. Saying, "Papa, someone stole my bicycle." Just the day before it was her birthday. I take her to the store and she tries one, two, three. She sits on several bicycles until she finds the one she likes. It costs more than I can afford but I buy it for her. Because I love her...'

Four large policemen walked in, laughing, and asked the policeman talking to Jorge a question.

Jorge's policeman took off his cap and rubbed his forehead. 'Work to do,' he said. 'Interrogation.'

It was a frightening word. Jorge suddenly wanted to go to the bathroom.

One of the policemen laughed again. He walked around the desk and looked at Jorge. 'So this is the little rascal.'

Jorge's policeman shrugged. 'Seems so.'

'Spirited the little bike away by himself?' the other policeman asked. He scratched his chin and scrutinised Jorge. 'Starting early, eh?'

'How'd he get past your bulldog?' another policeman asked.

'God only knows.'

A fat policeman came in sniggering. His bellowing voice carried across the room. 'The chief lost half his pay at fighting cocks again.'

The others laughed. The new arrival bent down to get a closer look at Jorge. He pointed to a WANTED poster on the wall. 'Doesn't this boy look like that one there?' he said. 'Head like a cactus.'

'Got a lot of money on his head that one, cactus or not,' said Jorge's policeman. He leaned towards Jorge. 'That could be you someday, boy.'

'Maybe we could charge him with stealing the chief's money,' someone said.

They all laughed.

Jorge started to cry.

Adia couldn't understand his blubbering when she came to the phone. She had to put Maya on. Maya showed up with Roberto and Adia after a while. She explained how the bicycle got to be in Jorge's possession. Maya described how she paid a third of her wages to a man who brought the bicycle out of the trunk of a car.

'Well, miss,' Jorge's policeman said. 'I'm afraid you wasted your money because it's stolen goods.'

Jorge was in tears all the way back to the house. Maya was seething beside him, wringing her hands like she was strangling something. She kept muttering under her breath, 'Joseph, Joseph, Jos*eph*...'

The incident led to the first of Joseph's many prolonged absences. Nearly two months passed before he came back. When he did he gave Jorge a heavy book.

'Where are you going to ride a bicycle in this place?' he said. 'Better to sit in your room and read.'

The book would become one of Jorge's favourites. It was called *The Labyrinth of Dreams*.

VI.

Over the years, more houses had appeared around the village. Even in Aguada, time was doing its work. The growing settlement was creeping towards the deserted orchard, impinging on the seclusion Jose Zandro and his family once sought, hoping to flee their old misfortunes.

In time they realised that Joseph wasn't a completely hollow man. Behind his mask there was a quiet, almost melancholic side. In the evenings Jorge often found him lying on the grass outside, hands clasped under his head, watching the stars.

'There's Orion,' he said to Jorge one night. His hand swept the brightly dotted heavens. Jorge sat down on the grass beside him.

'People have seen scorpions in the sky,' Joseph said. 'Long ago they saw a great flying horse. If you let your gaze wander, you can make out a bird. A phoenix.'

'How come they've got funny shapes like that?' Jorge asked.

'Only because we're here to see them,' answered Joseph. He sat up. 'If we weren't here to gaze up at them, they wouldn't have any shapes at all. Just a mass of disconnected things up there, twinkling for nothing.'

He glanced in the direction of the dark house and said softly, 'Like people sometimes.'

The light was on in Maya's room. Below it the kitchen light glowed warmly as Adia washed the dishes.

Jorge thought back to an argument he had heard between Maya and Adia at the back of the house.

'God help me, you're just one of those communists!' he heard Adia say.

There it was again, that ominous word he had often heard at the plaza.

'What's your way?' Maya retorted. 'Surrender and spread your legs?'

Adia snapped back at her with an anger Jorge had never seen before. Her hands were shaking. 'How dare you insult me!' she hissed. 'You have no idea what I've been through.'

Jorge didn't know what the argument was all about. But when he met Maya in the hall that night, she touched him on the shoulder and gave him a smile.

'Who are you, Jorge?' she said. Her voice sounded gentle and vaguely amused. 'Do you know?'

Jorge shrugged. 'Just a boy.'

'No,' said Maya. 'You're a unique little boy.'

She told him to come upstairs with her. In the hallway outside her room she showed him a black-and-white photograph of an old man, a fierce-looking man with short, greased hair.

'Do you know that man?' Maya said.

The picture had been taken long ago, and there was a blurring to the image of people who were dead. 'That's your great-grandfather,' Maya told him. She squatted down to talk to him. 'Don Mariano Zandro. The infamous land-grabber of San Gabriel. Do you know what that means?'

Jorge shook his head.

'That means he was a *thief.*' Maya stood up again. 'You're the last of a greedy line.' She leaned forward and pinched his cheek. "You should be my enemy, but I like you.'

It was around that time that the nuns visited them again. The sight of their white habits at the end of the road raised an alarm, and long before they reached the front door Jorge had decided he would go and hide. He crawled down the shaft as far down as he dared go, and tried not to think of the skeleton lying below him.

Jorge came out before nightfall. Thankfully, the sisters were gone by then. He returned to the house happy about outwitting the sisters. It wasn't until late the next day that everyone realised they hadn't outsmarted the nuns at all.

Before supper, Adia came to Jorge's room. 'Have you seen Melba?' There was panic in her voice.

The entire household marched to the village pump. 'Have you seen Melba?' they asked the women doing their laundry there. Most of them were hoisting the heavy buckets onto their heads before heading home.

'The nuns came in a van,' one of them told Adia. 'Melba met them at the corner. She had a little bundle with her. We thought you had sent her away.'

Adia and the others walked back to the house a stupefied.

'She was thinking of leaving us for a long time,' Jorge said. He thought of the nights he'd found her standing outside, gazing across the river.

'Poor girl,' Adia sighed. She stopped by the front door as the others went in, and stood looking silently at the empty road. Finally, she made a resigned gesture.

'Maybe it's for the best,' she said and went inside.

Before going to bed that night, Jorge crept to hallway cabinet. He took out the glass jar. The spider pranced around in the dark, impervious to everything but its glass cage and its own desire to escape. Its skittish efforts looked like happiness. It made Jorge smile.

There was no way to make others believe the things Melba had made him see. But for now, the sparkling glow of the creature made him think she was somehow still there.

One day, Roberto asked Jorge to come with him to a house in the city. Half an away hour from Aguada they reached the end of a tree-lined street behind Santo Domingo Square, where the sweet smell of mangoes hung in the hot afternoon air. The house had stained glass windows on the upper floor, large and beautiful like in a church.

'This is it,' Roberto said. They stood at the street corner where large ferns grew over the drain. The water streaming through below made a musical sound that echoed.

'Aren't we going to go in?' Jorge asked.

'No,' Roberto said. 'We'll just wait here.'

'Why?'

Roberto shrugged but didn't answer. A dog barked, a baby cried. The radio inside was turned on loud. Jorge didn't know what was special about the house, or why Roberto refused to go to the door.

A car drove past them and stopped at the house. A woman got off and went in, followed by a young girl.

'Ah!' Roberto smiled. 'Time to go.'

'Are those the people we were waiting for?'

Roberto frowned. 'We weren't waiting for anyone. Come on, I'll take you to my old shop,' he said hurriedly.

Not far from the pier they came to the place where lighters unloaded hemp and bags of tea and sugar.

'Well, there you are,' said Roberto with his hands outstretched. 'There's my emporium.' He laughed.

It was a small shopfront beside a copra yard.

Boats came in from the pier to unload the dried coconut shells, which were stacked on the yard in piles as high as a two-storey building. The smell of the sea mixed with the sweet scent of the dried kernel.

There was a Chinese sign over the little shop. The Chinese family that now ran Roberto's old business sat around on benches in the front, dwarfed by the sacks of sugar on one side and mountains of coconut shells on the copra yard.

'They loaned me money,' Roberto said. 'When I couldn't pay them back they came and took over the shop.'

They walked to the edge of the wharf. There was an empty boat rocking against the side. 'My, My,' Roberto said, with a glint in his eye.

He motioned for Jorge to come closer. Then they climbed down to the boat. Jorge watched as Roberto untied the craft and pushed it towards the back of the copra yard. He steered with an expertise Jorge hadn't suspected, and they ended up at the back of the shop. There was an opening through which they could enter without arousing the suspicions of the family out front.

It was hot and stuffy inside, the dark unpainted walls lined with stacks of merchandise. Roberto crawled under the counter and retrieved something. It was a picture of a little girl in a short pink dress.

'Thank God they didn't find this,' he said and put it in his pocket.

In the dim space that had once belonged to him, Roberto was a different man. He bristled with an inner revolt that he rarely showed. He produced a bag, and started stuffing things inside. He grabbed packets of noodles, a tin of biscuits, and a whole box of candles from the shelves. There was an indignation in his eyes as he surveyed all that had once been his.

'Everything that'll make Adia happy,' he whispered with a smile. 'And anyway, we're only taking what belongs to me.'

They got back in the boat and pushed off. Walking away from the wharf, Roberto kept looking back as if he'd left something behind. 'My life used to be so good,' he muttered. 'I had everything.'

After many months, Melba's departure still lingered in Adia's mind. She blamed the nuns and suspected them of plotting to cause more disturbance.

Jorge heard her repeatedly conferring with the boarders about a new quandary she had.

One night Jorge glimpsed them all huddled in the music room and Roberto hastily shut the door when they heard Jorge coming down the stairs. After supper he saw them gathered again in the kitchen. He saw the boarders giving Adia money. She counted it and started ticking off items from a list.

He heard Roberto say, 'Pants and shirt.'

The next day, Adia and Maya announced that they were taking Jorge to the city. They bought him things he had never asked for, half a dozen pencils, sheets of ruled paper, plastic rulers, and a roomy, colourful bag. 'You need to learn in the proper way,' Maya said. 'The music room is no place to learn.'

The school was on Fort Road, near the Santo Domingo church. Jorge walked towards the gates expecting the worst. But the nuns greeted him with benign expressions. The other children had already been taught to draw figures on the ruled pad, though some had to be trained to stop clutching the pencils in their fists like a fork. As Jorge dreamed of the adventures at the plaza he had relinquished, the other children struggled to copy the figures a nun had written on the blackboard.

So it would be from that day on, interrupted only by the constant praise of the nuns. 'Good, children! Very Good! Now let's stand up and sing a song to God!'

Adia had told the nuns about Jorge's mother and his father's recent departure. This, and his perennially frightened expression made some of the nuns ready to love him. They made a point of walking him to the corner of the plaza every afternoon to take a jeep back to Aguada. Jorge found that the world became a safer place when he was surrounded by the nuns. This all took place at a time when wild rumours were rampant in the bored, idle city. A man had been found dead behind the stage in the plaza, and it gave rise to wanton reports of a mad murderer stalking the city.

One day at the plaza one of the nuns noticed an old man following them. The sisters crossed themselves and formed a barrier around Jorge, facing the old man. He was holding a mirror.

'Shoo!' said one of the sisters.

Another raised the cross of her rosary. 'Away, Satan!'

The old man raised his mirror and the flash of the sun blinded them.

A strange voice spoke from somewhere and said horrible things about the women of the cloth. They all looked to see where the voice was coming from. As the diabolical tirade against the nuns continued, against God, against all religion...Jorge realised in shock that the sisters were all looking at him aghast.

'God is a deaf-mute,' the voice continued to say. 'Anyone can claim to speak for him.'

Jorge slowly began to understand the reason for the nuns' horror. The disembodied voice appeared to be coming from him. He suddenly recalled countless afternoons spent at the plaza, laughing his head off at the ventriloquist's antics. Jorge recognised, too late, the man holding up the mirror, but was powerless against his demonic skill.

The nuns closed ranks again. This time away from him. There was a look in their eyes as if Jorge had betrayed their best hopes. Jorge would never feel the protection of their white habits again.

But there was no escaping the nuns' regimen. All of Jorge's attempts proved futile. Countless times he thought of jumping off the vehicle as it sped towards the school. As time passed, it got harder and harder to break away.

The nuns had already managed to introduce him to ideas of punishment worse than any beating, torments greater than any he had ever known. They stood at the school gates every day with dark expressions, arms crossed as they scrutinised the children who had not come to school the day before.

All of that just served as a warning. Jorge knew now that certain infractions could bring down hellish agony. Maya seemed unwilling to free him from this strange new drudgery. She who had seemed his great friend and protector. Even Joseph seemed glad to be rid of him. He waved happily every morning as Jorge left for the bus stop.

Jorge wrenched himself away from Aguada early every morning, the woods still dark and cool, moist with dewdrops and the remnants of last night's dreams.

The nuns told the children stories of great battles of light, of clashes of angels more violent than any brawl they had ever seen. Life was shown to be full of peril. Lessons in writing the alphabet had been relaxed to accommodate fables of how certain sordid acts triggered the baffling and incurable onset of leprosy, desiccated limbs, or blindness. Such things as they did naturally on the playground were shown to bring them closer to the abyss intended for those who dared offend God. Gloom from which there was no redemption. So dark. Dark, dark, dark.

And that was not all. There were some deeds so despicable they deserved casting into a furnace far down below the earth.

'Imagine such a great fire, children,' the nuns told their rapt listeners. 'Steel and stone would melt like wax.'

The children closed their eyes to imagine such a fire.

The vision was so vivid some of the younger children burst into tears.

'*I don't want to go to hell!*' screamed a small boy sitting in the back. He writhed on the ground in agony, squealing like a pig about to be impaled.

Soon the other children were all infected with the terror of the writhing boy. They all began to cry, wailing and shrieking, sickened by the thought of all the torment that awaited them in this world.

'I hate Satan!' shrieked a red-faced girl from the top of the table, her cheeks shiny with tears. ' I *hate* him, *hate* him, *hate* him!' She stomped her foot each time she said *hate*. 'I wish he would...' She covered her mouth before she could speak the odious thought in her mind, lest she be cast into the darkness herself.

'I don't want to come to school anymore!' another cried.

They all began bawling at once.

'Leper! Leper! He pissed in his pants!' shouted Jorge from his chair, pointing down at the writhing boy.

From then on the sisters felt the need to tell more comforting stories to their anxious young wards. Perhaps it was time to tell of a redeemer. 'There, there' they said. 'The darkness and the fire are not meant for lovely children like you.'

'Because we love God?' asked a tremulous child.

'Yes! Exactly Right!'

The other children nodded their heads, finally understanding the secret of the unspoken covenant.

'Yes, it's dark, down there. But there's no need to be afraid...'

And so the children learned of a great shining savoir would come to redeem them all. They were taught to love this selfless angel who would save them from the fire.

The gloomy process continued with a few bright moments, when one of the nuns would inexplicably jump up and say with great cheer. *Heads up, children. You've all worked so hard. Now it's time to stop everything and sing a song to God! Let's thank him for making this wonderful world around us!*

The children, now familiar with the horrific price of insubordination, sprang to their feet like the sister and belted out the sacred hymns.

Sometimes they were allowed to go to Santo Domingo Square to play. It was there that Jorge described the glowing spider in its glass jar and promised to bring it to class one day. The spellbound eyes and gaping expressions emboldened him to make more outlandish claims. He told them of the goblins he saw going back and forth across the river. But it proved too much for some of them to bear.

'Fib!' cried one boy.

To Jorge's horror, another child took up the cry. 'Fibber!'

'Fibs!'

The exclamation carried back and forth across the square and Jorge realised he had found a new ordeal.

'Here comes fibs!' they would start shouting as soon as they saw him coming.

'Fibso!'

'Fibs in his ribs!'

He truly began to regret coming to school at all.

He made few friends. But there was one boy who seemed a much bigger fabulist than him. The boy was from a Chinese family, like the one guarding Robert's shop. His father's name was Raymond Pe. The boy claimed he was named after a great American poet, and even his name sounded like a fib.

'Edgar Allan Pe?' Joseph and Roberto laughed. 'Little liar.'

Jorge first noticed him because he was carrying a paper TV across the schoolyard. Jorge followed and found him in the empty auditorium. He was sitting in the back row, cradling the paper TV. He was looking intently into the paper screen. He clapped his hands occasionally and laughed.

'Oh, they'll love this!' he said, slapping his thigh.

Jorge came up behind him. 'What *are* you doing?'

The boy turned around. 'It's my sister's favourite show. See, that coachman's going to snatch the ladle from the woman and run off on his horse.'

Jorge looked at the paper screen. He saw nothing.

'I'm sending this to my sister,' said the boy. He picked up the paper TV and left.

He showed up at school with a strange collection of paper things. There was a paper roasted chicken that looked so real it made Jorge's mouth water. Edgar Allan took an imaginary bite. 'Delicious!' he said, pretending to chew. 'My mother can eat this forever.'

One day, Edgar Allan invited Jorge to his house. They had dinner at a large round table with Edgar Allan's father and two grown up brothers. There were two empty chairs at the table and Edgar and his brothers kept placing food on the untouched plates.

Later Edgar Allan took Jorge into the garage and showed him a beautiful paper car. 'It's like the car my mother loves to drive,' explained Jorge's friend. He ran his hand over the paper door. But the greatest surprise was waiting for them in the huge back lot of the house.

There, behind the stone mansion where Edgar lived, there was a whole house made of paper. It was exactly like the stone house in front, with the same high windows, the same large double doors.

'Would you like to go in?' Edgar Allan said.

They went up to the sturdy-looking doors. But when Jorge touched them, they felt delicate and weighed almost nothing at all. Jorge followed his friend inside.

Edgar Allan guided him through the paper corridor. Jorge was fascinated. The ceiling and the walls, the stairway and the chandeliers were all made of paper. In the kitchen there was a paper refrigerator, full of food like the paper chicken Edgar Allan had brought to school.

They passed a round table like the one in Edgar Allan's house, made of paper. Edgar Allan stopped Jorge when he tried to sit on one of the paper chairs.

'No one can use it till it's been set on fire,' Edgar Allan said.

Behind the stairs there was a room with rayon pillows on a paper bed, paper dolls scattered on a parchment rug. In the largest room Edgar Allan opened a paper bureau and showed Jorge wads of paper money.

Jorge stood at the door of the opulently furnished room, with all the fixtures done in paper. He was speechless with wonder. 'It's all so beautiful,' he said.

'You'd better come when we move this house to another place,' Edgar Allan said. 'Then you'll see how beautiful it can really be.'

They went out to the yard again. Jorge couldn't make sense of it all. The knob on the door nearly broke in his hand.

'Careful,' Edgar Allan said.

They stood in front of the paper edifice.

'What a stupid house,' Jorge said.

'No,' Edgar Allan shook his head, full of reverence. 'It's a very good house. It'll last forever.'

He seemed deeply convinced of it.

'It's only paper,' Jorge said.

'So?' Edgar Allan replied. 'You'll see what I mean. My father said this house will last longer than any house made of stone.'

Jorge went home. He was too tired to argue.

An old man with a white, wispy beard walked up and down the abandoned city block. He was swinging a censer of smoking incense from the end of a bronze chain. He sang something in a trembling, cat-like voice, sending the scented smoke floating up into the gaping windows of buildings that had stood empty since the war.

A crowd had already gathered on the street when Jorge and Joseph arrived. Some of the nuns were there, too. They had come to marvel at the astonishing beauty of the house made of paper. Edgar Allan's father had had it rebuilt on an empty lot in the old city centre.

It stood amidst the ruins of the deserted quarter like a vision too fleeting to succumb to decay.

The onlookers gaped at the windows with the vermilion curtains of crepe paper that gave a glimpse of the sapphire-latticed walls of the rooms inside.

'My God!' Joseph gasped.

Sister Clara, Jorge's favourite, explained to him that Edgar Allan's mother and sister had died in a car crash some years before.

Edgar Allan later arrived with his father in a long, black car. He and his grown up brothers were dressed in mourning clothes. They got out of the car and stood on the roadside nervously. Four men dressed in black tunics came out of a second car. They brought out two large drums and some musical instruments and went to stand in front of the paper house. On the curb side were torches soaking in buckets of kerosene.

'It's what they call a ghost offering,' Joseph said. They walked up and entered the paper house and walked through the red and gold-trimmed paper corridors Jorge had seen before. At their feet the beautifully patterned walls ended in the earth, dotted with tufts of weed. The empty lot had been carefully cleaned. Joseph was awed.

'Since ancient times people have always believed that fire is the way into the spirit world,' he said, awed by the elaborate, fragile structure.

They went into the room with the paper dolls, where the paper TV had now been placed. Joseph examined the appliances in the kitchen, the toaster, the plates, the paper utensils. 'Everything one could need on the other side,' he said.

'This family believes that when all this is burned, Edgar Allan's mother and sister will have the shelter and comfort they have been deprived of in death.'

They stopped in front of the paper stairway. Joseph whistled again. 'They want to go on giving them things they would have given them in life,' he said, nodding thoughtfully. 'If they could only reach them.'

Back outside, the men in tunics stood in a row in front of the paper house. Two of them had strapped on the drums and stood ready. Edgar Allan's father came forward with his sons. There was a look of hopeful anticipation on their faces.

Then, as the old man with the smoking incense came to the front of the house and kneeled, the two

drummers started pounding their drums— a slow,
enormous heartbeat as the old man bowed and prayed.
The torches were lit. The cymbals and horns blared as
the old man continued his incantation.

The crowd moved back as the torches were
brought to the sides of the house. The flames shot up.
The crowd gaped as the beautiful paper edifice was
quickly engulfed. The fire shot out and grew hotter and
hotter, lighting up the early evening sky.

Jorge watched the inferno envelope the walls
and the bare stairway inside, devouring all the fragile
gifts Edgar Allan's family wanted to send to the other
side. The cymbals and horns were so shrill they
sounded like someone crying.

The onlookers felt the heat of the flame on their
cheeks.

'You think Edgar Allan's mother and sister will
really receive all this?' Jorge asked Joseph.

Joseph shrugged. 'Who can say? All we can do
on this side is to imagine and hope.'

When it all ended, the crowd of onlookers stood
looking at the pile of embers, unable to understand.

The smoke rose up from the scorched lot into
the darkening sky. People started to leave. Jorge saw

Edgar Allan standing with his father. His face was wet with tears, but he looked triumphant. He waved to Jorge before getting into the car.

That was the year when everything changed. The nuns spoke of punishment so often that it seemed one day it had to come. A shadow fell across the schoolyard one morning as the children were climbing the stairs. It was a peaceful day, but one of the nuns stopped to look up at the sky. She crossed herself with an imploring look in her eyes.

The children were busy at their desks when they heard the first sounds of trouble. There were people shouting. As it came closer they could discern a rhythmic, angry chant. Then something was thrown and glass shattered downstairs.

Some nuns ran into the room. 'They're all around us!'

They gathered the children in a tight circle and stood away from the windows. More glass shattered. Projectiles clattered across the floor.

'Sisters! The drapes!'

They were in fact prepared. The nuns all rushed about to cover up the windows while the shouting outside continued, hoarse voices cursing and screaming. The half-darkness from the drapes gave a sense of safety for a while. Then they heard the first explosion. It rocked the building. The children screamed and covered their ears.

The nuns ran about to kneel and embrace the crying children, as a cascade of deafening detonations tore through the air. The walls shuddered with each powerful blast, while the glass broke behind the drapes and fell tinkling to the floor.

Jorge felt someone tugging on his wrist. They were all led running out of the room and herded down the stairs. The children sprinted across the schoolyard covering their heads as more explosions erupted all around them. The nuns opened a small gate in the back and ushered all of them out.

A sister pushed Jorge's head down and whispered, 'Hurry!'

Across the street in the back, Adia was waiting for him. He wondered how she had known to come.

As they hurried away from the returning mob, Jorge looked back at the shattered windows of the school, and the ugly black marks left by the blasts on the wall.

It wasn't yet the great conflagration that the nuns had taught young minds to imagine. It was just a foretaste of the convulsion that was to come.

The real tenor of the times became clear after many months. The riots that had first broken out in the capital flared out to all the other cities. Now they had reached Puerto Reina.

It seemed Maya was right long ago when she said that things could only get worse. So when she said she knew how they could all help the situation, they were only too glad to be asked. Her vigour woke them up from the lassitude of merely waiting for things to happen. They needed her drive to get them out of the mire into which they had all sunk.

Maya came back to the house one day with a group of friends. From the van that drove them, they unloaded reams of paper, two bulky machines, and several cans of paint. They carried the machines furtively to the back of the house. One of the machines was placed in Jose Zandro's old study. The other found space at one end of the dining table.

'It's a mimeograph machine,' said Joseph, wanting to seem in the know. 'A simple but effective tool against oppression.'

In time Maya had taught Adia and everyone how to crank the contraption, so that it spat sheets of printed paper out one side. Jorge got the task of collecting these. Soon they had large stacks of printed sheets lined up against the wall.

In one of the rooms, Maya and another girl were busy pounding out on typewriters the leaflets they were to print on the mimeograph machines. Jorge and his housemates all joined in the effort. They were yet uncertain quite how the simple act of cranking out the smudgy, smelly, printed pages figured in the complex chemistry of what was happening in the nation.

Many times a day a truck sped by with lines of soldiers sitting on the benches, their guns pointing up between their knees. The first sign of a slide towards chaos was the fact that the constabulary patrols in the city had been replaced by squads of army regulars. They walked down the streets with their rifles pointing out, like an invading force.

Jorge enjoyed the part where they painted large letters on banners laid out on the veranda. It was no different to writing the alphabet at school.

'I should tell all the children about this,' he said.

Maya took him aside. 'You mustn't, mustn't tell *anyone* about what we're doing,' she said, looking him in the eye. 'Or what we're about to do.'

No one in the house had ever done anything dangerous before. It sounded exciting.

The day came and Jorge was woken up at dawn. The same van that had delivered the mimeograph machines came to fetch them. The vehicle inched forward on dimmed headlights, the driver leaning forward to peer into the darkness as he drove. It was completely dark inside the van. No one spoke. Jorge couldn't tell how many people were in there with them. They stopped a few times to elude patrols. Whispers in the dark told Jorge what was going on. He gripped Maya's arm in his secret thrill.

The van dropped them off at different places in the city. The streets were dark and deserted as they agreed where to meet. Maya held Jorge tightly by the wrist as they stepped off.

'Don't you disappear from me!' she whispered.

The freedom of a city street at night was unforgettable. It made Jorge wish Miguel was there to share it with him. He watched as members of the group painted the signs on the walls with their stealthy, dogged coordination. Jorge begged to paint one slogan with letters that were nearly twice his height. He had to stand on tiptoes to get the tops right. It would always be with him, the uncommon mischief of painting words on a wall in the stillness of the night. He stepped back with satisfaction. The nuns would have been proud. Everyone was careful not to get paint on their clothes.

'Fine,' the leader of the group finally said. 'Good enough.'

They threw the leaflets they had printed onto the courtyard of a church. They scattered them on doorways of shops and threw handfuls over the walls of houses around the hospital. Jorge was surprised what fun it was to fight oppression, and wondered if any of it would work.

At any rate, change had already come without their noticing it. Weeks later they woke up to find that Goyle was gone.

Adia sent Jorge to look for him at the street corner, but no one had seen them there. In his room the things that were normally scattered on the side table were gone.

On the bed Adia found a letter addressed to her. She tore it open, and anxiously scanned the page, her lips moving. She lowered the letter with an exasperated sigh. 'It says he's gone to join the army.'

She slumped down on the bed. 'He's a growing boy,' she said with her hand on her temple. 'I couldn't go on feeding him on scraps.'

Roberto clucked his tongue. 'Another one to the slaughter.'

'What a time to join the army,' Maya said.

She kept telling them that there was more trouble to come. It was around that time that a picture of Jorge's uncle Ruben appeared in the papers. The report said he was fighting off accusations of granting favours to the leader of a smuggling ring.

'Rotten to the core,' sneered Maya. 'This whole state deserves to come crashing down.'

There were rumours that more soldiers had arrived to bolster the local garrison. Sometimes they woke up to hear gunfire at night.

Suddenly they heard that *Feria Nacional* was coming to the city. There had been no news about the company for some time. It was the only bright spark in that gloomy year. Jorge and Adia joined the hundred or so people who gathered to welcome the company as they docked at the pier. The caravan rolled out and went around the city's main thoroughfares, lined with happy, cheering well-wishers. The troupe was said to have come with new animals, and promised to have new shows and routines never seen before.

They travelled to all the islands, even those where the disturbances had been worst. Their flamboyant spectacles were all that linked the archipelago. In better times their dreams and deceptions brightened the soul of the isolated nation and made the surrounding seas a less desolate place. But now there were greater expectations of the affair.

It was said to be a special visit that year, and the city authorities were glad for the diversion. That was the only reason they allowed the group to set up on the unused land behind the municipal hall. It was within view of the plaza, where the mayor hoped to make speeches before the opening of the fair.

Adia and Jorge didn't admit to each other that they came out to meet the caravan hoping to hear news about Miguel. When the parade passed and they didn't see any sign of him, they transferred their hopes to the next day.

'Maybe there's someone who will know,' Adia said. 'We'll find out tomorrow.'

They were still making their plans when a man arrived at the house and asked to see Maya. They went to the back of the house and had a discreet conversation for a long time. Then the man left.

But soon after he was gone, a strange frenzy seemed to come over Maya. Jorge saw her in her room, hurriedly putting things away.

'Why's Maya crying?' Jorge asked Joseph.

Joseph scratched his head. 'Crying? She's not crying.'

'Her eyes are red.' Jorge told him about the man who had come to see Maya.

Joseph clucked his tongue. 'We're strange creatures,' he said. 'We know things are meant to change. Yet, we're always surprised when something suddenly ends.'

He seemed lost in his own musings when Jorge left him.

Jorge passed Maya's room again in the evening. She seemed to be getting ready to leave. She came out to the hall when she saw Jorge. She leaned down and gave him a hug.

'Remember me, Jorge,' she held him by the arms and gave him a shake. She wiped a tear from her eye. 'Remember what I tried to do. Don't you dare forget!'

Jorge was afraid of her wild eyes and her painful grip on his arms. But she suddenly calmed down. She swallowed, then went back to her room.

Roberto and Adia took Jorge to the fair. It was a beautiful day. The troubles seemed very far away as they came to the neighbourhood of tents. It stood on the bare lot that stretched out towards swamps. The sight was a serene and comforting, an unreal settlement erected only for pleasure. A few people were moving about the quiet tents, bulging with secrets they couldn't yet unveil. A greater delight was promised for all on this special occasion.

Witnesses would later say that from the day the company arrived, trucks drove back and forth without pause from the pier to the fairground. Large boxes were unloaded at dawn and had vanished from sight by morning. Later, the company's astonishing efficiency would be seen in a different light.

Jorge and his companions arrived to see a large open platform put up in the centre of the tents. There was a sign over the one nearest to the road that said 'The Madhouse.' It seemed to augur the outlandish amusement that the company had in store.

'Madhouse.' Roberto looked at the sign and shook his head. 'I didn't think they did that anymore.'

Jorge gave a tug on his wrist. 'Let's go there!'

Adia adamantly refused. She broke away from them.

'They used to have mad people chained up in cages,' Roberto said, seemingly fixated and repelled by the sign on the tent. 'Poor souls loaned out from the asylum. Deformed people, the insane, all kinds of hideousness for the paying public to gape at.'

They came closer. The tent was empty. Only the sign remained. Roberto seemed relieved. 'Seems they've come a long way from all that,' he said. 'I'm glad.'

Many times during the afternoon, there were moments when it seemed the day would be ruined by rain. The sky would suddenly turn grey. The people who had begun milling about the tents looked up worriedly. But the rain they feared never came. It hung up in the sky, a dark threat of something.

Finally, in the late afternoon, before the evening entertainment was to begin, performers gathered on the platform, and the company's famous showman came up to welcome everyone. The audience applauded him like a celebrity. As dusk gathered, more and more people poured into the fairground and gathered around the platform. Floodlights were turned on.

...the warmest welcome we have ever received....! The showman was saying on the microphone. *You make us wish we had come much sooner.*

He was standing in front of thick black curtains that hid the rear of the stage. He made several announcements that echoed over the speakers around the fairground. A group of drummers marched onstage with a clown and a monkey. The crowd responded with laughter and applause.

The fun is just beginning, said the showman. *We want to reward everyone this year.*

At a signal from the show master the drummers began pounding out a long, anticipatory roll.

'LADIES AND GENTLEMEEEEEEEN, WHAT YOU'VE ALL BEEN WAIIIIIITING FOOOOOOOOOOR...'

The crowd was tense with excitement. Then the showman brought his hand down as if chopping the air. The drum roll came to an abrupt stop.

'Open!' the showman cried into the microphone. The curtains parted behind him.

A crow cawed from somewhere.

Nothing prepared the audience for the macabre surprise that followed. The show master's voice echoed around the fairground. *'OUR BLACK DAY HAS COOOOOOOOOME!'*

With a whooping sound, a dark gale exploded from behind the curtains. A hundred crows flew shrieking over the audience, bursting over the tents in a crazed swarm. The birds made a shrill, deafening noise and flew so low they touched people's heads. The throngs were so dumbfounded they froze.

'Help! Stop them!'

A child screamed. 'They bit my eyes!'

People held up their hands to shield already bloodied faces. 'Stop them! They're attacking us!'

'Kill them!'

'Kill the beasts!'

The malevolent storm of scavengers scattered the crowd. People screamed in agony, running with their hands over their eyes. A primal darkness spread over the fairground, pursuing people as they ran blindly through the tents, or fell on the ground.

Suddenly, a shot was fired. Several volleys followed until the gunfire came in a steady stream. Crows started to drop from the air. The gunshots continued as people jumped for cover and lay cowering by the tents.

At the height of the confusion, nearly two hundred rebels threw off their disguises and came running out of the tents with their guns. The show master threw down his hat and announced over the microphone that they were taking over the city. They claimed Puerto Reina as a rebel stronghold.

Hours of tension followed. There was great relief when the rebels promised they wouldn't hurt anyone at the fairground. All the spectators were allowed to flee. But the twelve soldiers sent by the local commander to guard the fairground lay dead, the crows hungrily pecking at their bloody faces.

The army garrison was taken completely by surprise. It took many days to make sense of the bizarre events. It turned out similar incidents had taken place all over the country. It was all a concerted effort.

The freed spectators gratefully rushed home, eager to see how the drama would unfold. Witnesses later recounted how the rebels quickly moved from the fairground and surrounded the municipal hall.

The entire city government was held hostage. The rebels were seen converging on the balcony, calling through bullhorns for the city's inhabitants to join their insurrection. They fired shots into the air in triumph, then threw a challenge to the military by unfurling red flags of the communist revolution.

It was a tense moment as the city awaited what was to come. The whole country seemed locked in indecision. Then one night, the earth seemed to heave a great sigh of revulsion. The sky was brightened by massive explosions. Far away in Aguada they heard the echoes of the rumbling that they later learned was gunfire.

Jorge and his housemates huddled in front of the TV and learned how three platoons of the army's rifle division surrounded the municipal hall. The siege went on for twelve hours. The nightmare ended in a maelstrom of vengeance as the troops stormed the building, leaving the walls and floors of every chamber as red as the flags the rebels had flown.

Soldiers were mobilised everywhere, setting up checkpoints, stopping cars, barging into shops and offices, trying to stamp out the mutiny. They raided abandoned buildings, arrested whole families, dragged struggling suspects into military vans.

One day Jorge's uncle Ruben appeared on TV with a group of army generals. He was telling people to stay calm. He said the country was in good hands. In the house, they watched with more anguish than worry. But their lesser anxieties had to pass before they could face up to their larger plight.

Maya had been gone since the day before the fair. Weeks had passed after the trouble and there was no word from her. In the confusion that followed no one understood the meaning of her absence.

Time passed and they tried to get more news. But the whole country was in chaos and there was no way to learn the truth. As they heard reports of more violence, they refused to ponder the possibility that something awful had befallen her.

Her silence was unbearable. Finally, in their desperation to know, they opened the door to her room. They found a folder with pictures of Jorge's great grandfather Don Mariano Zandro, his son Jose, and the rest of his family.

'She's been up to something all along,' said Adia. In the folder they also discovered a yellowed half-page advertisement from long ago. In bold Gothic letters it announced *the engagement of Emilia Zandro, only daughter of the Hon. Don Mariano Zandro.*

'I remember that,' Adia said. 'I don't think anyone in Puerto Reina will ever forget.'

After that they were back to their awful vigil. But many more months would pass without any news.

It was nearly the end of the year when they finally learned of Maya's fate. The report of her capture was on the front page of the papers. She was shown being led away in chains, her eyes wild, her hair in disarray. She was almost unrecognizable. For a long time they refused to believe the story.

Only then did they find out her real name. Baptised Cristina Joy, she was born on Christmas day, sixteen years before Jorge.

VII.

The army's counter offensive was like an implacable whirlwind. The force of the backlash threw the nation into a spin. An orchestrated savagery seized the cities and towns. Adia and Roberto stood would hear stories of murderous assaults on innocents all over the country. Brutes in uniformed columns were said to march into villages at dawn, rousing the inhabitants with gunfire, bringing retribution to anyone they could accuse of aiding the rebels.

In time, Puerto Reina, too, became a muted, terrified hostage to the sadistic emissaries of the besieged old president.

There were squads that barged into houses looking for guns. Their martial authority replaced everything that had held life together before. Troops moved into civilian offices and put up barbed wire fences and machine gun nests. Their chains of command usurped the hierarchies of districts and towns, and turned the whole country into a divided citadel held together by abhorrence and fear.

One day there were gunshots in the back of the house. Jorge and the others ran into the kitchen to find Adia had fainted. Several weeks later that they decided to board up the windows and conceal the front door with bricks. It made the house look like an abandoned shell from outside and gave the dubious assurance that disaster would pass them by. Fear made them do strange things. It made them believe they could hide from life and shut out what was happening outside.

They peered through cracks in the windows to see the army trucks rolling by. Sometimes there were civilians in the back, pressed into a corner by a ring of soldiers. They held onto the sides as the vehicle rumbled past. The doomed look on their faces remained with everyone who saw them.

'They take them to the hills to be shot,' said Joseph. Since Maya's arrest they had been through several states of anguish. They thought of Maya's suffering and her awful fate. They thought of their part in painting anti-government slogans on building walls.

What had seemed a mere game then seemed like insane recklessness now.

They watched as the politicians on TV discussed the insurgency and condemned its leaders. But most of all they denounced not only the ones who had taken part in the uprising, but also those who pretended to be quiet citizens, yet abetted such treason. Jorge and his housemates were prey to a growing sense of doom. *They* had been *part* of the *conspiracy* that the angry new leaders swore they would hunt down, *until every traitor— man, woman, and child—* had faced the punishment they deserved.

The sight of the army patrols made them shudder. One day one of the army trucks would stop and *booted feet would march across the yard towards their door...*

They gathered at the dinner table around one candle. Adia refused to invite calamity by having too much light. In the first few weeks of the emergency, the lights were cut off and the whole country was in darkness. No broadcasts were allowed on radio or TV. All the newspapers stopped coming out. When the TV began to receive its first fuzzy images, it seemed like a victory. Soon little things like the lights and newspapers returned.

But Adia believed in not getting too used to normal life, lest it be all taken away once more. 'It's all too easy,' she said.

As they ate together they couldn't help thinking about the empty place at the table. They missed Maya and her quiet, inscrutable ways. Little by little they started talking about her. They couldn't help wondering why she did what she did.

They watched the TV every night to see how the campaign of repression was unfolding. The ailing President had conferred his authority on a group of senators. One of them was Jorge's uncle Ruben. He often appeared on TV looking haggard, with a gleam of disquiet in his eyes.

'Poor boy,' Adia said. 'He always was a fearful child.'

She often told them stories about Jorge's mother and her two brothers. She told of how a snake bit Ruben on the riverbank one day, and his brother Augusto had to carry him screaming back to the house.

Jorge and the others laughed. The story made them feel that their lives had a link to something that would endure. Something that would outlive the repression. They begged Adia to tell them more.

All the politicians they read about in the papers or saw on TV kept talking about a new life. Soldiers became very important in this life. When the cinemas were allowed to open again, the soldiers were there, eyeing everyone standing in line to buy a ticket. Even the idlers in Aguada stopped going to town for fear of the military checks.

They heard that *Feria Nacional* had been disbanded, its owners imprisoned. Fairs and large public gatherings were banned.

To Jorge's great regret, children were allowed to go to schools again. But there were some changes. They stopped singing songs to God for a while. Instead they sang endless hymns to the old president.

Jorge hated being forced to sing the national anthem over and over again until he got the chorus right. There was a boy who was tone-deaf and lazy, who infuriated the nuns by always forgetting the words or singing out of tune. It seemed a pointless exercise. Until one day, Jorge's school got a visit from the army.

They showed the children the proper way to sing the national anthem in their booming voices, their

289

boot heels tapping out a marching rhythm. They performed a few about-faces at the nuns' request and enthralled the children with their rigid postures and stiff salutes.

Finally, they made all the children stand up and sing along with them. They stood around the room with their guns cocked and at the ready. As they were reaching the climax of the anthem, the singing was disrupted by a commotion in the back. The tone-deaf boy had vomited and collapsed because he still couldn't sing the chorus and was afraid the soldiers would shoot him.

This was the time when people tried to outdo each other in great contests of fear. They talked of bloody massacres in other villages committed by wayward units of the army. There were always rumours that Aguada was going to be raided by an insubordinate detachment that was wandering about the countryside. The villagers liked to talk of a possible evacuation and claimed they kept their belongings packed at all times.

Joseph and Roberto were frightened by the rumours, but Adia seemed unmoved.

'We're safe where we are,' she said. 'Even misfortune would get lost trying to find its way here. Believe me. I've seen it once before.'

Only then did Jorge realize that Adia had become their rock. The source of their resolve. It surprised him.

'Like all storms,' Adia said, 'this repression will blow over, too. But while it's alive it fills us with terror.'

During this time, Adia's kitchen became more of a comfort for them all. Her clay bowls filled with bay leaves and cardamom were a promise of continuity. Her jars saved from before the war were reminders of peace before and after catastrophe.
Jorge and the lodgers sat there at night, huddled on the floor to hear her stories. They relied on the warmth of her stove to preserve life in the cold universe of the house.

No matter how they tried, they couldn't help dwelling on the terror outside. And as they sat in the murky rooms they felt the eerie breezes blowing through the house again, chilling them to the bone.

Joseph told them about communists being slaughtered by soldiers, headless bodies being found.

So Adia's stories saved them from themselves, kept them rapt late into the night, when, too tired to think or to worry, they got up with a yawn and drifted off to bed.

She told them stories from long ago when Puerto Reina was young. There was a beautiful girl who lived by the river. Once a secret admirer sent her a magical book. The book told the story of one life in just a page. The suitor promised the girl that when she had read the book, she would know all lives. She would know the identity of her secret admirer and also her own.

Adia's tales hypnotised them into thinking that the arduous task of surviving the repression was no effort at all. She told them of a landowner's daughter put under a spell by a wizard who hated her father. The sorcerer told her she could only escape his curse by finding his face in a deck of cards. She tried to do so, in all the gambling houses of the town, until her family was ruined. In the end she never found the sorcerer's face, but discovered traces of him in their burnt house, in her family's ruined health, and the evil room where her father hanged himself because of the disgrace she had brought him.

Roberto added some stories of his own. They were to do with the roles and adventures his former wife played on the stage. It was clear he still loved her and spoke of her with a glow in his eyes.

Then Adia told them of the time when Puerto Reina was a rich city and was known as the Queen City of the South seas. Visitors came from as far away as Shanghai or Istanbul. Sugar was transported from San Gabriel for loading onto ships bound for America. Paseo Gardenia was a ring of lights where dockworkers spent their money in the noisy bars. Rich jewellers used to walk on the promenade at the end of Fort Road, looking for idle ladies to lure into their shops.

That was before fights broke out between the unions that had formed on the docks. The disputes became more violent, with both sides using gangsters and prison convicts to settle scores. Full gunfights erupted in the city, warehouses on the pier were set alight. It drove the commerce away from Puerto Reina, and the city's decline began. The war just dealt the final blow.

All this time, Joseph boasted of having a secret weapon hidden somewhere in the house. Adia thought he endangered them all by having it. Joseph enjoyed the show of risky behaviour, however, and talked endlessly about the time he had spent in jail.

'Three months is a long time to spend mopping floors,' Roberto said.

Joseph ignored him. 'You have to stand up to the big men sometimes,' he said.

After much bragging and cryptic talk, Joseph finally revealed his secret to Jorge. He crawled under his bed to retrieve it, and he pulled Jorge away from the window before showing him what it was. It was a slingshot made from a guava branch.

'Strongest wood in the world,' Joseph said. 'Turns any pebble into a lethal projectile.'

He dipped into his pocket to show Jorge a handful of large, black pellets.

'I also have the option of shooting with poisoned balls, ' he said smugly, expecting Jorge to be awed. 'If the soldier boys ever go after me.'

'But does it work?' Jorge asked.

Joseph made a disdainful sound. 'Ask Goliath that, my boy. Did it work?' He tapped his chest. 'Faith guides the little man.'

Despite news that military brutalities were worsening all over the country, Joseph braved a trip to the city. He came back with books from the library hidden under a basket of dried fish. He said, 'They can check for weapons all they want. But the greatest weapon is on these pages. Knowledge, my boy!'

He had borrowed *The Woolwich Manual of Fortification* and with Roberto's help began to build a fortified structure in the yard. They cannibalised the abandoned mill down the road for bricks and steel rods. The project took up most of the year. But they ran out of sand and cement before they could finish the job, and Adia later turned the unfinished structure into an outhouse.

Joseph found a puppy near the village. He took it and raised it to be a guard dog.

'Let's call him Hannibal,' he said. He fed it with leftovers. As Hannibal grew, Joseph spent hours in the back training him to attack a discarded pillow tied to the banisters.

'*Fight, fight, fight!*' Joseph shouted until he was hoarse.

But Roberto noticed that Hannibal preferred to go after mice. He scratched his head. 'How can you trust something that doesn't know whether he's cat or a dog?'

One day, a wall of the failed fortification in the yard toppled over and crushed Hannibal, and the dog became part of the outhouse.

Joseph continued piling up books from furtive trips to the library. He felt he was doing his part in resisting the repression.

'There's no such thing as too much knowledge,' he told Jorge as they surveyed the growing stacks in his room. 'Who knows, maybe one day I'll be remembered for saving this bit of human culture from annihilation.'

One day, the City Librarian, who was the sister of a Constabulary officer, showed up at the house demanding all her books. She threatened to have Joseph arrested and shot. The chance for martyrdom seemed untimely for Joseph and he tried to give away all the books, even offering them to the women who gathered firewood in the back.

'It burns real easy,' he tried desperately to convince them. But they all refused.

It was a comfort even when Adia spoke to them about the war. Talk of distant horrors seemed proof that life would go on. It was like watching a shadow play that used to be staged now and then at the plaza, adumbral fictions that enthralled crowds, and had something deep and dark to teach them all.

Adia told them of the things she had seen during that terrible time, and they began to understand many things about her. It explained why she couldn't bear to have people speak in whispers behind her. She said it reminded her of the way captives in the prison camps talked about people the Japanese soldiers had just killed and buried, the women they had dragged away. Adia confessed she never closed her eyes without hearing those voices, crying in agony, begging to be saved.

'Even if you survive, you will always remember,' she said. 'There's a dark pit always waiting for you somewhere. Where you can drown in your horrors all over again.'

One of the strangest things Adia told them was of seeing a march of corpses in broad daylight. They passed through thirteen towns, herded by Japanese guards whom they couldn't seem to escape even in death. They beat them with rifle butts and stabbed them with bayonets, but the barbarous blows made no difference to the corpses, who marched with their lifeless gaze fixed on the road ahead, moving, it seemed, from this world to the next. The grim, ragged column stretched out for miles, taking three days to pass, as people in the villages gathered on the roadside to offer succour or mutter silent prayers.

When the procession was gone, there were drops of blood in the dust. And that was how the onlookers knew that the column had been real and not an apparition. In the stillness that fell, a soft breeze blew the dust away, and it was as if the column of the dead had never passed.

Adia said the most unbearable thing was to look in the soldiers' eyes.

'Just that darkness in their gaze,' she said. 'They seemed like men. But in their eyes you could see nothing.'

They had long stopped waiting for the emergency to end. The ever-present threat in their lives had become a permanent thing. The time of carefree living became like a memory of olden times, painfully sweet now, forever out of reach.

Yet even the bleak spirit that befell them could not stop the work of time. Jorge and the other children of the emergency grew, their limbs extending, gaining strength.

Finally, one day, great panic seized the house. They had just settled down for the night when they heard the gate open. Roberto ran down and peeked through the window.

'My God,' he whispered. 'There's a soldier in the yard!'

'*Sssh!*' They all froze behind him.

Joseph and Adia pushed forward for a peek. The soldier was walking around the yard with his gun.

'Good Lord,' Joseph whispered. 'He's seen us. He's coming this way!'

Roberto shook himself from a daze and seemed to lose control. He began unlocking the door. 'Best to find out what he wants.'

Joseph tried to restrain him. 'Are you out of your mind?'

The soldier was at the door. He was removing the bricks at the threshold. Then he knocked.

Joseph and Roberto looked at each other. The soldier outside seemed to be whistling.

Roberto finally made an impatient sound and said, 'Well, come what may!'

He threw the door open.

Jorge's eyes were closed when he heard all his companions cry out.

'It's you! You gave us such a fright!'

Roberto and Joseph were laughing. Jorge opened his eyes to see the soldier standing by the door with his helmet off. He was laughing, too.

It was Goyle. They all came forward to greet him. Goyle put down his rifle and embraced everyone. He waited until Roberto had locked the door again and they had moved into the dark dining room. Then he rubbed his head and said sheepishly, 'I've deserted.'

They were too sleepy to take it in, but they were happy to be reunited.

Adia came forward for a closer look at Goyle. But she suddenly stopped. 'You look different...'

He tried to avoid her frank gaze.

Suddenly Adia screamed, 'My God! You have killed!'

Goyle shook his head and tried to laugh. She slapped him across the face.

'You can't deny it!' she shrieked. 'I can see it in your eyes. You have taken a life!'

She embraced him and cried, 'What have they done to those kind, gentle eyes?'

Goyle told them of the vicious initiations in the army, the cruel tasks, and the mindless drills. Slaps for breakfast, slaps for lunch, kicks for goodnight in the barracks.

But a long time had passed and things had changed. The army units in Puerto Reina had begun to pull out and were replaced by Constabulary patrols. The authorities kept up routine military operations, but it was clear the worst had passed.

Still, they had to hide Goyle when the Constabulary paid a visit to Aguada and knocked on all the houses. They helped him slip out through the back while the detachment poked around the yard. Their leader found the shaft in the old orchard asked about the skeleton lying there, but no one knew what to say.

From that moment, Goyle knew he could no longer stay. He imperilled everyone in the house with the penalty for his desertion. So one afternoon, he invited Jorge to the back of the old orchard to witness him set fire to his uniform. Then they buried his rifle by the mouth of the shaft. 'So you'll know where to dig it up if you ever need it,' Goyle said.

He was no longer the wide-eyed boy from the interior who performed in town squares for loose change. He was a grown man with the sinews of a soldier who had fought in battle. He never told them of all the things he had been forced to do.

And one day, in the same casual way he had joined the household years ago, Goyle packed his things into his army knapsack and disappeared. It wasn't long before even the Constabulary patrols were gone. Like a storm that had left land and blown out over the sea to die, the emergency was over.

Life slowly returned to normal. After a long time hesitating, Jorge's housemates found the courage to pull off the boards covering the windows. They turned on bright lights and came out of the house. The world was a peaceful place. Jorge saw a cotton puff floating in the air, falling gently like the flakes of snow in the water-filled dome that had belonged to his mother.

Soon Adia began her wanderings again. She took Jorge to the city to search for old friends she remembered. Only as they were reclaiming their old lives did it dawn on them: three years had passed since the troubles began. Jorge had turned fourteen. His shoulders were still narrow, but he had grown tall. The front teeth that had jutted out with mischief when he was a boy now gave him a diffident look. His expression had become cautious, and his bright smile had dimmed from all the dread he had known.

For the last time, they went to the music room. Joseph read to Jorge a book he seemed to cherish, called *Where In The World*. The cover showed creatures with round bodies and long, tubular legs, standing in a strange landscape with three moons. It told the story of a creature in a remote galaxy who had memories of once having lived on earth. He was troubled by those memories and kept wanting to go back.

'He missed the forests, the streams,' Joseph said. 'The sun shining over the sea. All the things he didn't have in that far world he now found himself in.'

After he'd finished reading, Joseph was thoughtful for a long while. 'Who knows if this is what happens to us when we die,' he turned to Jorge. 'Do we go to a far world somewhere but still remember the earth?'

Jorge didn't quite understand. He knew Joseph had never forgotten about Maya and her awful fate. He wondered if perhaps Joseph still entertained hopes of ever meeting her again.

During that time, a strange restlessness came over Joseph. Jorge often found him in the evenings pacing listlessly in the yard. He seemed beset by a new energy that had been welling up inside him. Then one night after supper, he went to his room and started packing his bags.

When Jorge came out the next morning he found Joseph sitting at the table with Adia. He was fully dressed, his hair carefully combed, looking like he had when he first arrived at the house. His two huge bags were propped up against the wall. He sat hunched forward with his arms crossed on the table, staring into space.

'I don't really know where I'll go,' he said. 'I don't know what I'll do.'

He bit his lip with uncertainty, then got up to leave.

Jorge and Adia went with him out to the gate. It was a warm, clear day.

'Do you really have to go?' Adia asked again. 'There's lots of room. No one else needs them.'

Joseph shook his head. 'I don't know why, I just know I have to go.'

He turned to Jorge and smiled. 'See? We're still in the dark. We think we know ourselves. But we don't.'

He hoisted the larger bag onto his back. 'We still say and do things whose significance we'll only realise later. If ever.'

He smiled and moved as if to give Jorge a pat on the head. Then, remembering, he held out his hand instead.

Jorge stood at the gate, watching Joseph cross the road and start to walk away. He wondered what Joseph's significance was to him. Of them all. He wondered if he would ever know.

Now their dining room seemed empty again. But for a long time he felt as if all the boarders were still there. He could still hear their voices, the noises they made in their rooms. They had made life seem permanent in the transplanted house, moved from place to place since before he was born. The vacant rooms were silent and cold, but Jorge found himself still stopping to peer into them, expecting someone to call out and invite him in.

Before it was Roberto's turn to leave, he revealed a secret to Jorge. 'I have a daughter.'

On nights they spent in the garden chairs, watching the stars, Roberto told him about the days when he was a happy tradesman with an attractive wife. 'How she loved me,' he said. 'It was such a beautiful time.'

Jorge asked why he never tried to find his wife, to woo her back. Roberto thought about it. Then, with a certain acceptance, he sighed, 'Good things happen only once, I guess. And we spend all our lives trying to recapture it... in different ways.'

A long time later he told Jorge the real reason. 'I heard she got married again. To a successful theatre director she met in the capital. They left to live in Europe during the troubles.'

His eyes brightened with hope. 'But my daughter's still here,' he said. 'I know where she lives.'

When he explained, Jorge understood all those times when Roberto took him to a house behind Santo Domingo Square. He finally knew why Roberto would just stand for hours watching the house on the street corner with the beautiful stained glass windows. That was where his daughter lived.

'When her mother was here, it wasn't possible for me to come and see her,' he said. Now it seemed he had plucked up the courage to try again.

That was how they came to be in the city the next day, standing outside a fruit seller with a bag of strawberries just shipped in that morning.

'She loves them,' Roberto said. 'It's what makes her so sweet.'

They reached the house with the stained glass windows and knocked on the door.

The girl who came out was very pretty, wearing a red dress.

'This is Verana, said Roberto, beaming at Jorge.

Jorge handed her the bag of strawberries they had brought. The girl seemed to bend her knees slightly as she graciously said, 'Thank you.'

She looked at Jorge from behind the door jamb, biting her lip. She watched him with a roguish tilt to her head, like she might stick her tongue out at him at any moment. She had long lashes and fearful, pretty eyes.

'His name is Jorge,' Roberto said to her. 'He's a very good boy.'

Her eyes widened as she took it in. Then she giggled and ran away.

The woman in the house with her was her aunt. She tried to coax the girl to come out again, but she didn't. The aunt came to the door, shaking her head with exasperation.

'Why don't you come in and speak to her?' she said.

Roberto did so and was inside the house for some time. Jorge waited on the street until he finally came out again. When he did, there was a look of relief and triumph on his face. He came out with a bounce in his step.

'Well, that's that for one day,' he said, his eyes twinkling. As they left, he walked jauntily ahead of Jorge, swinging his arms.

'I've done it,' he said with a shy smile. 'I didn't think it would be so easy. It won't be so hard the next time.'

'Why is she called Verana?' Jorge asked him.

'It means 'summer.' For the beautiful time when she was born.'

Jorge thought of the girl watching him partly hidden by the door. He smiled.

Some weeks later, Roberto invited him again to come to her school. Her aunt met them at the door of the little theatre. They went in to watch Verana perform the fandango of lights.

A group of musicians played on the stage behind her. The hall was in darkness and the audience was spellbound by the famous dance of lights. Verana floated around the stage in swaying, flowing twirls, with coloured glasses balanced on her head and her wrists. The blue, red and amber glasses each held a lighted candle that flickered as she moved. The audience gasped as Verana skipped and circled to the rhythmic, melancholy music.

There were some close calls, but the quivering candles remained on her head and her wrists. And she spread out her arms with hypnotic grace and brought the dance to an end. There was approval and relief as the dancer finished a performance of great skill and risk. The audience erupted in applause. Verana took a bow with a lighted candle still perched on her head.

309

When she came to the aisle to speak to her father, Jorge couldn't take his eyes off her miraculous wrists.

'She'll be a stage actress, just like her ,mother,' Roberto said with pride. Jorge was amused by her long lashes and her fickle, timorous gaze.

He would see her again many times, long after Roberto had finally left, walking off into the rain after a brief goodbye. By then Jorge was only glad he had come to know Verana. He would grow to love her, the girl named after the summer, the daughter Roberto could never win back. Because of her, Jorge would understand the man who had sent roses to his mother from San Gabriel, why he waited for death to free him from the torment of an irredeemable summer.

VIII.

Jorge had finished going to school with the nuns when his uncle Ruben came for a visit. Three years had passed since the end of the Repression. Ruben was at the height of his power, revered for taking charge during the crisis. It was believed he had saved the nation.

When he came to Puerto Reina, the city was still in the grip of jubilation at the end of the state of emergency. There were fiestas and parades as if they had won independence all over again. *El Tiempo* announced Ruben's arrival on its front page. After a string of meetings with city officials, he finally arrived at the house. He seemed thoughtful and subdued as he walked around the yard. The people in his entourage remained outside, keeping a respectful distance.

Ruben smiled as he came to the dead tree in the yard. 'That was still alive when we moved this house from the city,' he said to Jorge. 'For a long time you could still see the remnants of the two cottages we destroyed to make way for the house. The cottages were once Aunt Emilia's refuge.'

From the corner of his eye Ruben saw Adia standing by the back door. He watched her for some moments without saying a word. He looked puzzled and vaguely disheartened. Since the time of the Repression he had been under tremendous strain. And now, away from inspection, his exhaustion showed. He seemed to make a formidable effort to contain his feelings, but his fortitude appeared to break. He slumped against the wall and an inconsolable look came over his face. For a moment the steely senator seemed at a loss.

The fulsome attention given to his visit masked the sad reason Ruben had come. Some twenty five years had passed since he left the house in Aguada to practise law in the capital. One of his first tasks in those early years was to undertake the defence of his brother Augusto, then charged with conspiring to murder a rival in the shipping business. Ruben failed to disprove the charges, but managed to get a reduced sentence for his brother.

Years later, when Ruben was already a senator, Augusto broke the trust by escaping from prison. His lawless life became a thorn in his brother's side as Ruben rose to prominence in the government. It all came to an end in the past month, and was the real reason Ruben had come.

Augusto was killed in a shootout at a police blockade set up to capture him. It was a scandal that failed to taint Ruben's reputation only because of the eminence he had gained during the emergency.

And as Ruben came to Puerto Reina for his brother's funeral, the public scrutiny only magnified his loss. Perhaps to escape the excruciating interest, he had turned down offers to stay at the governor's mansion and decided to spend his visit in Aguada. Adia cleaned Leon's old room and made it ready for Ruben.

He was often pensive around the house, but he seemed eager to talk. He relished long afternoons spent on the veranda or walking by the river with his nephew. Jorge was troubled by the probing questions his uncle kept asking him, because they made him realise how little thinking he had done, how ill prepared he was for life after the nuns. Ruben brought up new concerns about the future, a worry that had never perturbed him before.

Like everyone, Jorge was just enjoying the new serenity that had settled over the land, though he didn't really understand what had changed. The memory of them all huddled in fear, in a house with all the windows boarded up— all that seemed very strange now.

Jorge hungrily explored the city with new, older friends he had made. His favourite was a boy named Salvador del Mundo II. He was tall, with a dark, kindly face and broad shoulders that suited his name, which meant 'saviour of the world.'
'I'm only the second saviour of the world,' he said solemnly to Jorge. He was a greedy boy who could eat half a bucket of rice with one dried fish by himself. His dream was to make so much money he wouldn't have to worry how much he ate. He needed it to fill out his long, lean frame. His arms were big from hard work since he was young, labouring on a farm and as a peon on several construction sites. His only claim to security was the fact that his father was the overseer of *El Tiempo*'s printing presses. The old man's name was Salvador del Mundo I.

'He's the first saviour of the world,' said Jorge's friend. 'I only came after him.'

'Was it his idea to save the world?' Jorge asked.

'Yes,' Salvador nodded seriously. 'If I have a son, he'll be the *third* saviour of the world.'

'Wow.'

Salvador knew the city like the back of his hand. He was five years older than Jorge and he had roamed the bowels of Puerto Reina long before Jorge even dared venture out of the house. He laughed when they passed a place on *Calle* Luna called Sweet Dreams.

'The sweetest dreams any man can have,' Salvador said, 'alas, can turn very bitter.'

With prurient erudition he explained to Jorge that Sweet Dreams was once a brothel set up for the use of the U.S. 21st Infantry Battalion when it was stationed in Puerto Reina. It was run by Lt. Col. Owen J. Sweet of the said battalion, who gave his saccharine name to the most frequented establishment in the city.

'There were girls from Singapore, Tokyo, and Shanghai,' said Salvador. 'The Yankee boys thought they had found paradise.'

He laughed. 'For a while they were right.'

He clapped his hand on his thigh. 'Then, pow! God gets angry and they're out of paradise. One bug and it's the end of sweet dreams.'

During the repression, *El Tiempo* had come out only half the time. Salvador's father used the idle time to teach his son how to run the presses. So once in a while Salvador would bring Jorge and explain in detail how the deafening, gargantuan machines worked. They roamed the city together and some of the outer towns. They swam off the pier, smoked, and Jorge had his first taste of getting drunk.

Salvador was Jorge's steadfast companion when he went to stand outside Verana's school. But Jorge always lost the nerve to speak to her, now that they had exhausted their speculations about where Roberto might be. So he and his friend stood by the hedge and watched as Verana walked across the square without knowing they were there.

'There she goes,' Salvador would nudge him.

'I know. I can *see*.'

'Look, she's about to cross the street.'

'So?'

'Aren't you going to do anything?'

'Like what?'

'Help her cross the street or something.'

'What for? She's not an old lady.'

'No. But you'll be an old man before you get to talk to her.'

'Shut up!'

The iridescent neon lights on building tops around the plaza bore the marks of fusillades fired to drive out the rebels years ago. Those vestiges of violence looked somewhat quaint now as Jorge and Salvador spent hours idling on the park benches like Jorge and his cousins used to do.

At the time of his uncle's visit, Jorge always came home for supper to find Ruben keen to talk. It was as if he had come with a purpose, to help resolve something in Jorge's life. To plant seeds in his mind.

In the long conversations they had, Jorge learned that Augusto's death was not the first misfortune to befall their family. In the days Ruben was to spend in Puerto Reina that year, quietly grieving for his brother, Jorge learned things even Adia couldn't tell him. In that time he would understand the tempests that had blown through his family's house in the years before he was born.

Jorge's grandfather Jose Zandro was a piano-playing rake who had lived in the shadow of his mother and sister. Jose was the apple of his mother's eye. While he caroused in the nightclubs of the town, his sister Emilia slaved for the family.

Emilia was a short, plain girl who had toiled away in her father's warehouse until their company was moved from San Gabriel to Puerto Reina. She was thrilled to move to the city, and she tried to be accepted by the social circle that converged on the Navy Club. But the haughty girls in the ballroom were reluctant, and their reserve was more hurting to Emilia than she had expected. Before long she was regretting her father's conspicuous arrival in the city. Don Mariano had already made his fortune and his move to Puerto Reina was of great importance to the growing port town. Tongues wagged about his daughter's rural timidity and unfortunate looks, which the bookish seriousness she affected could not make appealing.

Early in her life in the ostentatious town, Emilia fell in love with the son of a struggling Castilian shop owner. Emilia adored the handsome, artistic dandy with the pale, slender hands that had never known work, and the dreamy, floating gait which proved he did nothing but sleep and dance.

He was the perfect catch for a provincial girl who was bent on entering high society. Emilia offered to marry him and make him part of her family. So eager was Don Mariano to see his daughter married that he took out a full page ad to announce the engagement in *El Tiempo*, the city's biggest newspaper.

The penniless fop rewarded their enthusiasm by running off with a widow he had met at a dance. She was on a stopover on her way to the capital, and they continued the journey together. He took with him important papers from Don Mariano's estate, entrusted to Emilia by her father.

Emilia had to go to the man's relatives and begged them for information on how to reach her errant lover. She offered them various bribes to bring him back, threatening to kill herself out of shame. The scandal marked her for life.

Don Mariano's enemies thought the sorry affair was just what upstarts like him deserved. But it embittered his daughter. From that moment she began her exile from the town and its mean distractions. She spent her days in the confines of Paseo Gardenia, in leafy seclusion behind the church, where only the empty cabriolets passing by at night disturbed the silence of the trees.

Her father had bought land by an orchard on the banks of the Aguada river, some miles out of the city. She had two cottages built there. It was the only place Emilia went to when she tired of her own imprisonment in the house on Paseo Gardenia.

Life in the wilderness appeased her rankled soul. She began to spend all her weekends there. Puerto Reina and its memories of shame seemed like a remote country lying far away downriver, too distant to cause more hurt.

Until one day her brother brought an end to her newfound calm. He came home with a young woman he had met at the Navy Club. After months of bringing the girl to Paseo Gardenia, when he tried relentlessly to insinuate the young lady into their lives, Jose declared himself hopelessly in love.

'For the first time this month!' Emilia yawned.

He committed the inexcusable sin of bringing the young woman to Emilia's refuge by the orchard.

The girl surveyed the lush surroundings and uttered excitedly, 'What a shame we can't have guests!'

It was like Emilia's nightmare was starting all over again. Jose confided what had been on his mind: he and the girl were planning to marry.

'Before *proof* of our love comes *out*,' he smiled expressively. Emilia knew what he meant. Fearing another scandal so soon, Emilia's mother overcame all her daughter's objections and hastily arranged for a wedding.

Before the year was over Claudia had entered their lives. And so began the situation that each felt had been foisted upon them.

Six months after the wedding Augusto was born, the dreaded proof of Jose's indiscretion, and was followed a year later by Ruben.

'We tumbled into this world,' Ruben would later say to Jorge, 'Not knowing what awaited us.'

He laughed. 'Had we known we might have come slower.'

The arrival of children brightened the household. Their unknowing antics prolonged the tenuous peace in the house. For a while it seemed that things would work out.

There were cordial discussions at the dining table. The adults liked to speculate about the children's future. Augusto's thick eyebrows marked him out, in the eyes of his grandmother, to be a priest. 'His face inspires solemnity,' she said.

Emilia and her new sister-in-law both lamented the dismal quality of entertainment in the city, and agreed the Navy Club could host more well-known performers from the capital.

Claudia often invited Emilia to look out of the second floor window into the neighbour's yard. Large round tables were laid between the house and the rear wall. The noise of the happy gatherings rose up to them, mingled with the clacks of mah-jongg tiles. An afternoon spent risking money seemed a perfect way to squander time.

They started talking about holding mah-jongg afternoons of their own in the house, with the ladies Emilia hadn't seen for years. Everyone was eager to meet Jose's young wife. Word had spread about her uncommon charm.

There were often shows at the plaza, including one with a travelling singer named Imelda Gomez who astounded crowds with the first Italian and English arias anyone in the city had ever heard. It was she who made it fashionable to sing in a very high voice while wearing diaphanous dresses that made the men gasp.

Doña Juana took her feuding children and grandchildren to watch the shows, and they came home gay and chatty. But the harmony in the house would not last long.

In her every gesture, in her every thought, Claudia brought a searing pain into Emilia's life that she thought she had long ago escaped. Claudia unknowingly opened an old wound when she had the dining table moved to the side one day and said, 'See? There's enough room here for six couples to dance!'

She measured out a place in the corner where she imagined a small group of musicians could sit.

'Imagine a rigodon!' she said, clapping her hands as she hopped about the room. 'Just the thing to shake out the cobwebs of this gloomy home.'

Emilia suffered in silence. She held up her hand as if to keep out a blinding light. She told no one how it renewed her torment to see her brother's latest and final conquest, a rural girl like her, but endowed by her strange birth with one of those faces that disturb the lethargy of secluded towns. She could walk into any gathering and have all eyes turn to her.

With her acquired elegance and the sinuous curve of her body, she had easily cut a path into Puerto Reina society, deep into the spirals of its snobbery, in a way all Emilia's hard work and intelligence could never do.

The women she invited to afternoon tea were the same who laughed at Emilia's clumsiness and her impenetrable air of tragedy. Women that Emilia would have liked to talk to, but for the way their contemptuous gaze cut her down. Emilia couldn't get herself to admit it, but Claudia's presence deepened her retreat into hopelessness.

When Claudia had guests, Emilia withdrew to her room in the far wing, read her books or peered out the window. She didn't come out until dusk, when she was sure the gaiety, with its secret jeering, would be over.

Claudia good-naturedly upbraided her for her drab clothes, her habit of spitting, and her secret chewing of betel nut in her room.

'It leaves your teeth scarlet,' Claudia said, 'It's scarlet everywhere you spit.'

Claudia had not meant to be hurtful. She sincerely believed Emilia could be jolted into reclaiming some youthful charm. But Emilia was wounded.

So when Claudia suggested they rearrange the furniture in the living room, Emilia acted like she was defending sacred ground.

'The chairs are too much in the shadows,' Claudia said. 'It's nice to come out in the light.'

'Yes. Who needs the shadows if you can spread your legs anywhere with no shame!' Emilia shouted.

Claudia didn't understand the outburst. She didn't know that with all her charm and unfailing poise, she had brought fresh anguish to Emilia, who had thought herself content in her choice of a quiet, forgotten dissolution.

Then Claudia gave birth to her third child, a girl. She was a beautiful creation. Emilia and her mother Doña Juana doted on the child. They even took credit for choosing the child's name. Claudia distractedly acceded when they pressed her on their choice.

'Rosanna,' she smiled. 'Little rose.'

The girl's baptism was planned to perfection. Don Mariano gave in to entreaties from his wife and daughter to leave important business in the capital to attend the affair. All the friends that Emilia hadn't dared invite for herself came to the church, and later to the house for the reception, just to see the delightful child.

The rooms were turned upside down weeks before the event. The solemn baptismal rite was like a cleansing of the air. Serenity settled in the house after the ceremony, as if the forces ripping through the family were momentarily appeased by the girl's spell.

But Claudia was not as smitten as her in-laws thought she ought to be. As soon as her daughter no longer needed to be nursed, she went back to passing time with her friends to their houses by the sea, the teahouses on *Calle* Luna or anywhere else their idle fancy took them. She came home at dusk, rarely even asking about how everyone's day had passed.

'Like she doesn't live here at all,' whispered Emilia to her mother. She added quietly: 'A stranger she came. A stranger she shall leave.'

Her mother looked up. 'What do you mean?'

Emilia put on an innocent look.

'Nothing.' She turned around and left her mother's room.

The birth of her children hadn't made Claudia any more interested in the intimate details of other people's lives. Motherhood hadn't turned her into the wife Emilia had envisioned for her brother, the kind who gave up her own life to tend to her family and nothing else. Emilia had expected her to show at the very least a similar devotion to her brother that Emilia had shown to her father all her life, to everyone.

She felt it was she who had sacrificed youth, had given up life's bright moments. She had forfeited even love to enable this easy life everyone took for granted. The tranquillity of the house in Paseo Gardenia was thanks to her. The very running of it was the result of her daily sacrifice.

The way Claudia moved unconcerned through their lives had been at first a shock to her. Then it became a constant outrage. Emilia tried her best to endure. But when she realised that Claudia's impudence would never change, her revulsion grew. It smouldered quietly until it had turned into the most malevolent hatred she had ever known.

Emilia felt delighted when the two boys came to her for advice. She was not frugal with her embraces, although she had always been a hard, unaffectionate woman. She loved it when little Rosanna clung to her on sleepy afternoons when she lay down the girl for her nap.

Claudia had given birth to a sickly girl. But her only concession to motherly care was to make a salve she had learned to make on the plantation long ago in San Gabriel. She placed it on Rosanna's chest when the girl had her bouts of breathlessness. It worked wonders, but perhaps more from the girl's belief in her mother and her joy at being indulged. After that, it was as if everything were erased. The girl loved her mother again and believed her capable of all good things.

One day Emilia whispered to her mother, 'I could be a better mother to her children than her.'

Then on the day of Rosanna's first communion, Don Mariano came. There had been talk in the city about unrest on the old man's plantations.

He had worked his way up from being a textile merchant in San Gabriel, acquiring lands in time to profit from the sugar boom that came after the First World War. He was dogged by rumours that he was nothing but a ruthless land-grabber who maintained his own bands of thugs. It was said he had used armed force to drive small farmers from their lands to expand his holdings in San Gabriel. Then he offered generous bribes to officials of the new republic to legalise his claims.

He used a knife and fork like a workman. Once Claudia caught him licking his fingers when no one was looking. His fierce, toad-like eyes looked around him when he realised he had been observed.

Don Mariano forbade the display of religious images in any of his houses. His wife Doña Juana prayed in secret at a small altar in the corner of her room, where she daily lit candles and kneeled before a statue of the Blessed Virgin, with a black rosary dangling from her hand. It was said the devout woman sought expiation for her husband's sins.

Claudia was flattered that the great patriarch had come to visit in honour of her daughter, though Rosanna and her brothers were given their meals downstairs for the occasion, so as to leave the table for the adults in the house and some guests. Claudia usually revelled in entertaining houseguests with her wit and saucy tales. But that night, she was in a restive mood. Her reckless tongue and quick mind would get her in trouble. It was fortunate that her children were not there to witness the farce.

The lavish dinner was on its last course, the guests listening to Don Mariano enthusing about the beauty of the new threshing machines he had bought for his farms. Claudia interrupted him to talk about the workers who had died on Don Mariano's lands. 'Within sight of the crops they had planted last season,' she said, smiling at the irony, 'while a convoy of trucks were carting away three tons of harvested grain that week.'

Don Mariano stopped talking.

'Food,' Claudia continued, 'Just like this on our plates...'

Emilia sprang to her feet at her end of the table. 'Shut your mouth!' she screamed at Claudia.

The dinner was ruined. The tired, stiffly starched guests froze in embarrassment for their hosts. Don Mariano sat silent, his big hand suddenly starting to massage his chest. Among the guests were those who knew of the thousands of pesos and Mexican silver that passed every month through Don Mariano's hands. The old man's age and faltering heart had been topics of conversation in Puerto Reina for some time. The event that the city feared and his enemies secretly wished for seemed to be at hand. Would his fortune go to his embittered daughter or to his spineless son, married to this imprudent woman who had long been rumoured to nurse a secret lust for gambling?

That was the reason for her long afternoons away from her children. It was the secret reason that would separate them for good.

As Ruben went out to perform the wretched duty for which he had come to Puerto Reina, the city prepared to honour him. Adia went with him, her face powdered but still ashen. She was so grief-stricken she could hardly walk. Jorge saw her crying silently in her room, beating her chest.

He was surprised at the anguish she felt for Ruben's slain brother. Jorge promised to catch them up later, but he knew he wouldn't go. He couldn't face the thought of seeing his cousins in this situation. Jorge struggled to understand, but what little he knew of his mother's death made him unwilling to go to Augusto's funeral. It was a fear he couldn't overcome.

Instead he spent the beautiful sunny afternoon in the place where he had grown to like waiting, smelling the sweet, ripening scent of mangoes in the air outside the house with the stained-glass windows behind Santo Domingo Square. He would wait for Verana on the street corner or by the benches outside the church. When she saw him standing there she would stare blankly, uncertain if she knew him. If she turned around for a second glance as she passed, he would be happy.

He followed her in the afternoons, never coming near. He found out that she was going to dance school. Everything he learned about her was an unveiling, the paring of a mystery.

One day she came out of the dance school and saw him, then whispered something worriedly to her friend. The friend tried to distract Jorge, 'Hello...' while Verana scampered away.

Jorge ran to catch up with her. She glanced over her shoulder then broke into a run. They both sprinted across the square and skipped through traffic. Jorge jumped over flower pots and picnic tables at the plaza, stumbled on overturned bins before he caught her. Her frightened eyes darted about for something to protect her.

'Wha—?' she said breathlessly. 'What do you want?'

Jorge stood catching his breath. He tried to think. What *did* he want? He didn't know. He realised he had never thought about it. All this time he had been following her with no clear aim or even an inkling of the reason why.

'Your father Roberto,' Jorge finally stammered. 'How is he? Where has he gone?'

A disdainful look came into Verana's eyes. 'Oh,' she said with a slight smile. 'You're that boy. The *good* boy.'

Jorge pretended to catch his breath while he tried to think of something clever to say. When he did she was gone.

A week later he was standing out in the pouring rain across from the dance school when Verana came out to speak to him. A strange pride made him pretend that getting his clothes soaked in the downpour was the most natural thing.

'How's your voice?' she asked him, holding an umbrella.

Jorge cleared his throat. 'How do you mean?'
'Can you sing?'

She coughed into her hand in a way he found
dainty, tilted her head and said, 'We're practicing
duets. It's for a show we're going to have. My singing
coach wants me to find a male partner.'

She took out a small hanky and dabbed her
cheek. Jorge saw the pink strawberry patterns on the
pristine white cloth.

'Come under, ' she said, making room for him
under the umbrella. 'I wouldn't want you to catch cold.
You'll grow hoarse.'

Jorge did as she said. They walked together
back towards the dance school. They walked and a heat
seemed to surround them. It seemed to take them a
long time to cross the square. Jorge thought he caught
a whiff of strawberries as she turned to him.

'What's a boy like you doing just standing
around?' she asked scornfully.

Jorge realised she might think he was a loafer.

He was suddenly ashamed of his aimlessness.

'Well, in fact I just remembered,' he said.
'There's something I was supposed to do.'

'We can talk to the singing coach now,' Verana said. 'She'll be glad I found a partner.'

'I'll meet her later,' Jorge said, and skipped away before she could stop him. He maintained the pretence of great urgency, holding his hands over his head in a vain effort to ward off the rain as he hurried down the street and out of sight.

Augusto's funeral was highly publicised because of Ruben's presence. The senator was photographed touching his brother's coffin, his face broken up in tears. Recalling the fight his uncles had had years before, Jorge wondered if at that moment Ruben was thinking about his brother's last insult about his ingratitude.

For some reason, Ruben seemed reluctant to talk of certain things in the house, particularly in the living room or at the dining table, with Adia hovering nearby.

They would drive to places in the city to talk, to coffee houses or the opulent restaurant in Hotel Oriente. Their rambling, wistful conversations were like the mirror Jorge tried to put together as a child.

The fragments Ruben revealed to him helped him see what he might never have known.

Ruben learned only much later that their mother Claudia was the illegitimate daughter of a plantation owner in San Gabriel. His name was Amado Diez, from one of the town's richest families and a late philanderer.

His liaison with an illiterate but darkly pretty laundrywoman on his plantation exhausted his twilight passion and bore an unwanted child. The child, Claudia, grew up on the sprawling estate, hidden from Amado's legitimate children in the anonymous teeming of plantation workers. She and her mother lived in a shack on the edge of the property.

She used to wander off alone, and her mother would look for her in panic, fearing discovery by Amado's wife. She would finally find the girl in the fields, and Claudia would be taken home to be flogged.

But no amount of punishment could do anything to curb the girl's restless urges. She loved the fields, and it took her years to understand that those lands did not belong to them, that she and her mother were intruders and that one day they would be told to leave.

Her roving spirit endured, and her mother began tying her by the wrist to the steps of their shack. There were times when she went off and disappeared for days and left the girl there like a bound animal, crying, hungry and exposed.

Only then did the other workers realise the poor laundrywoman had broken through her last restraints and finally gone mad. Reports of her cruelty reached Amado.

By then the plantation owner's wife had died. All his children had grown up and left. For some time Amado had been living in the plantation house alone. One day he appeared at the shack on the edge of his estate.

The woman from the next house came and packed Claudia's clothes. The girl didn't understand what was happening. But the distant, forbidding man she had never expected was her father had come to claim her. He wanted to raise her as his own.

The girl's mother was driven off the plantation and abandoned to her fate. For years Claudia wondered what had happened to her. Amado never told her.

The uncertainty added to her turmoil as she grew to womanhood in Amado's stifling, barren house. She wanted to go to school, but Amado wouldn't hear of it. He forced her to help run the plantation, going with him to visit the workers' shacks, where Claudia used to play with the other children.

Until one day, Claudia found a way to escape. Days before the Lenten holidays, she and her friends went on a secret trip to the city. They met on the wharf at dawn and boarded a ferry to Puerto Reina. Claudia saw her first motorcars, and went on the rumbling tram across the city several times, squealing with delight.

At the end of the trip she and her friends discovered *Lamarre Jewellers* on *Calle* Luna. They didn't have any money to spend on jewellery, but they couldn't resist stopping to gaze at the gems gleaming in the glass counters. She had just turned nineteen.

She was pretty and exuberant, and the Frenchman who owned the shop took an immediate liking to her. He answered all her questions and told her more than she needed to know. Before it was time to leave he put his hand on her wrist. They had been looking for a shop assistant, he said. Someone just like her. *Lamarre* was the shop where politicians, diplomats and illustrious concubines were said to purchase their jewellery.

Claudia couldn't resist. The gems sparkled on their velvet cushions as she took a moment to think. Then and there, her heart told her to accept.

She and her friends were in a hurry to catch the ferry back to San Gabriel. But the next time she showed up at the jewellery shop, she had already brought all of her things. She didn't tell her father.

After a year at the job, there was no doubt she had done the right thing. She was living in a dormitory for unmarried ladies. After months of trial and error, she had found a way to live with mild luxury but well within her means.

She was a single woman living in the city, going to its coffee houses, attending parties, going for drives in motorcars with male friends. She was no longer a prisoner on her father's plantation. She had accomplished what had seemed so impossible just a year before.

Then Jose Zandro walked into *Lamarre*. He was looking for a watch for his mother. Claudia could sense he was rich, not just from the fine clothes but from the languid assurance he had as he strolled in and leaned over the counter to flirt with her. He came in more times than one needed to buy any piece of jewellery.

'I'm afraid that man is after more than just gemstones,' the Frenchman said one day. Claudia was flustered. She began to apologise.

'Never mind,' the Frenchman smiled. 'Love leads to wedding rings and weddings lead to diamonds.'

He winked. 'If they last that long.'

Claudia smiled.

But Jose Zandro was clearly besotted. The witty shop girl with large eyes and beautiful cheekbones enthralled him. She was shy and awkward at times, but there was a dark turbulence he sensed that excited him.

They bantered under the Frenchman's knowing gaze. He was amiable and quick to serve any customers that came in while Claudia was occupied. He didn't mind the fluttering flirtation that was quickly spilling over into affection. The seasoned trader in him knew it was good business for a jeweller to facilitate love.

The young man finally mustered the courage to invite Claudia to the Navy Club. A few days later she got off the tram before reaching her dormitory and they met. They spent the melancholy hour of dusk in the empty ballroom before the orchestra and the guests arrived. Jose picked out notes on the piano and played her a tune.

In return she regaled him with stories, some of which she made up, and some she heard from the customers at the shop. Still others she had heard from the Frenchman himself, as he tried to explain in the most circuitous way to a fresh-faced nineteen-year-old the story of how he had hidden jewels in the cuffs of his pants and crossed three oceans to get to Puerto Reina.

As Ruben's stay came to an end, he revealed that there had been another purpose to his visit, which accounted for the searching questions he kept asking Jorge when he first arrived.

'Your father asked me to make arrangements,' he said just as they were finishing supper that night.

He turned to face Jorge. 'He wants you and your brother to study in the capital. At university. He'd made plans for it long ago. I told him you can both stay with me.'

'His brother?' Adia put her hand to her lips. 'We have no idea where he is.'

'Then Jorge will go,' said Ruben. 'The offer stays if Miguel ever decides to come back.'

They finished the meal in silence. Later, as Ruben was packing for his departure, he came out to the hall and said to Jorge, 'It'll be a good thing.'

He put his arm around his nephew. 'There's more room in my house than I can ever use. And there'll always be time to talk.'

In that was the promise to tell Jorge the rest of what he had only begun to tell. Jorge's appetite for his uncle's revelations had been whetted. It was this, more than the thought of study, that made him eager to go.

'Everything should be ready by next year,' said Ruben the next morning, before getting into the car that had come for him. 'I hope you'll be ready to come by then.'

Jorge nodded.

'So soon,' Adia said when Ruben had gone. 'Why do they always give us so little time?'

Jorge couldn't stop her from packing his bags, even though his departure was still months away. She wouldn't listen to reason and worked away at the closets, grumbling and rummaging, stopping only to wipe her eyes.

She pulled out all of Jorge's clothes she could find. In the end she had them pressed and folded, packed into three bags, which she left in one of the empty rooms, with two sealed tins of biscuits she insisted Jorge was going to take.

The bags were heavy and so tightly packed it was impossible to undo Adia's premature preparations. They stood in the corner by the door all those months, a reminder of Jorge's impending journey. They were soon covered by a thick layer of dust.

Sometimes Jorge needed things that Adia had already packed. They had to get it out with much planning and effort. 'What if I don't get to go?' Jorge complained.

'Don't be simple,' Adia replied. 'Your uncle said you would, and for sure you will.'

She had such faith in his words. 'He can make *anything* happen.'

Finding a break in the repetitive rehearsals at the piano with her aunt, Verana asked Jorge to come up to her room. One of her windows was also of stained glass. It made the light fall in broken up colours across the room. The bedspread was pink, as was the flower-patterned desk.

She wanted to show him the porcelain marionettes her mother had just sent her. They were from Venice, where her mother and her new husband were staying.

'She's started performing again,' Verana smiled.

'Aren't they beautiful?' she said clutching the dolls in their dark velvet dresses. 'They're something I'll really keep.' She touched their polished ceramic heads to her face.

'Come.' She moved to show him more of her prized possessions.

In her closet, arranged like sacred objects on an altar, were the coloured glasses her mother had used long ago when she first danced the fandango of lights.

'She never broke one,' said Verana with pride. She placed them on the desk.

'That's my diary,' she said, pointing to a book on the desk with a strawberry red cover. As if remembering the need for secrecy, she dashed past him and put the diary into a drawer.

'My mother had a diary,' Jorge said.

'So does mine. Most girls do.'

'I've read my mother's diary,' Jorge said.

'You have?' Her eyes widened. 'Why?'

Jorge shrugged. 'She's dead.'

'Oh.' She leaned against the wall and looked sadly at him. 'Did you find out anything?'

'There was a man who sent her roses. Before she died.'

'Did she love him?'

'I don't know. But maybe he was the reason she died.'

She came forward and looked closely at his face. 'He wasn't...your father?'

Jorge shook his head. 'No. Not my father. But he loved her more.'

She was quiet for a while. Then she came near him, looked at him like she wanted to touch him. The room had a strawberry scent that filled his senses.

It was what lingered in his mind when he went home, remembering the hot afternoons downstairs practicing duets with Verana's aunt on the keyboard. In the heat as his eyes watched the ivory keys, he secretly reeled from the sweet, exuberant scent that hung by the piano where Verana stood.

One day Jorge was so nervous he couldn't even control his voice. They were on the third song, *Santa Lucia*, Jorge would never forget, and when they got to the chorus, he felt a deep vibration begin in his chest.

He liked the deep resonance that his voice suddenly seemed to have, but the singing coach stopped them.

'In a child's voice,' she said tapping the piano. 'You must both sing in a child's *sweet*, pure voice.'

But the warm rumble had descended into Jorge's chest forever. Suddenly, he no longer had it in him to sing, or *feel*, like a child. When Verana peeked at him from under her cap and smiled, he knew everything had changed.

Even after they parted in the afternoon, all he could think of was Verana's eyes. The long lashes tickled him deep inside. Only then did he realise that the perfume that enveloped him when he was with her did not come from some substance sprinkled on all her things. He was overcome by the discovery that the rapturous scent of strawberries that seduced him emanated from her skin.

It was one of the things that had made him want to be near her. It was the reason he had begun to follow her around. But he couldn't think of a way to tell her. To name it was to put his hands on something he did not yet feel ready to grasp. So he preferred to go on standing outside her house like Roberto once did, and told nobody about the loneliness he felt when he left her street.

The duet in the auditorium turned out not as well as the singing coach had hoped. Jorge's mouth felt dry, and he was so absorbed trying to sing in tune that he forgot to make way for Verana's parts in the chorus.

He ended up practically singing all the numbers by himself. Verana fluttered her eyes and smiled sweetly at the audience as she tried to be heard above Jorge's unvarying drone.

She cast worried glances at the voice coach watching from the front row, the stern woman's face turning stony with despair and embarrassment.

As soon as the show was over, Verana and Jorge fled the auditorium and sought refuge at the pier.

While they sat on the railing by the docks, Verana took out a picture from her purse. It was of her mother, who once performed in the same show as Imelda Gomez. It showed Verana's mother standing arm in arm with her handsome stage partner. They were both wearing glittery Spanish costumes.

'Just like me when I've become an actress,' said Verana, looking sadly at the picture. 'Or so I thought.'

She looked like she was about to cry. 'Not anymore.'

She rubbed her temples and closed her eyes. 'Oh, *Lord!*'

'Don't cry,' Jorge said. He was afraid she would blame him. He tried to think of something to distract her. He pointed to the watch tower.

'My brother climbed up there and said he was going to all the islands.'

'Then what happened?' Verana asked.

'I guess he did. He's probably on one of the islands now.'

'You don't know when he'll be back?'

Jorge shook his head. 'I don't know how many islands there are.'

When he came home that day he passed the doorway of the empty room where Adia had left his bulging bags. For the first time he was torn. He began to regret the plans his father had made for him.

It was Verana who persuaded him to explore *Madame Fung*'s, because he wouldn't have thought to go there himself. They sneaked in one afternoon when the back door gaped open in the siesta hour.

'Opium pipes!' she said as they crept through the dim rooms above the old gambling house, concealed from the stairs by clicking, stained bead curtains. Verana lowered her voice, 'My aunt told me they smoke opium here.'

They walked around the large, elaborate day beds with bone inlay in the dark wood. There were no mattresses on their long bamboo slats. Sagging, discoloured cushions lay in the corners, beside the long, polished opium pipes that after many years still had their ruinous gleam.

The oppressive smell of sweat and unwashed sheets hung in the air. Verana crinkled her nose.

'Some people came here young and never left,' she said softly, gazing at the ugly patches on the walls. 'They had to be carried out in the end, too weak to walk by themselves.'

They tiptoed to the end of the long, narrow corridor, where they could see a bulb shining behind the once-garish straw curtains.

'See?' Verana whispered. 'There's still somebody here. But they might be dying.'

On hot afternoons they sneaked into the Navy Club. They beat the dust off the chairs and then danced without music under the cracked ceiling. Verana hummed a tune half-smiling as they whirled under the broken chandeliers swaying slightly in the breeze.

They crossed the road to the abandoned villas to watch the sea. Verana sat close enough for Jorge to feel her hair tickling his arm in the gentle wind.

Walking through the plaza, Jorge tried to hold her hand. 'Go away!' she said. 'I'm hot.'

They walked in silence under the trees. Then, for some reason he couldn't fathom, Jorge stopped and said, 'I'm going to the capital at the end of the year.'

'What for?'

He watched her closely. 'To study. At university.

I'll be gone for years.' Having said it, he realised his words finally had a gravity he didn't need to feign.

'Oh, good!' Verana said, almost as if she was going to clap her hands. 'I'm glad.'

'You are?'

'Of course.'

There wasn't the least bit of change in her expression, as Jorge thought there might. He was disappointed.

They started walking again and Verana started humming to herself, her contentment untainted as she walked serenely, swaying slightly from side to side.

She got over upsets quickly, and recovered a calm that seemed unshakeable. From that moment he began to wish for a time he could see her face sad. He didn't know why.

He also didn't know that he had been spotted by someone in the plaza. As they were passing the bandstand, Verana stopped walking, and turned to him in shock. 'What did you say?'

Jorge stared at her. 'I didn't say anything.'

'You did,' Verana insisted. She put her hands on her hips, said with a laugh, 'You said you'd like to tickle my armpits.'

'I didn't say that!'

'Why, hello!' An old man got up from one of the benches and came towards them with arms outstretched.

'Tell the girl what's really on your mind,' said the ventriloquist. He walked towards Verana pursing his lips. 'Kiss, kiss, kiss. Just a kiss. Kiss, kiss, kiss, oh little miss.'

She giggled and broke away from Jorge. She went home without him.

In the evening Jorge found that a letter had arrived for him. It was from Ruben. It was several pages long, and dealt with their forthcoming arrangement. But much of it had to do with the story Ruben had promised to tell him before he left.

Jorge told Adia none of the things Ruben now revealed to him. He would always retreat to his room to pore over the pages, and unravel the story of

Claudia, the woman he had never known, but who had meant the world to his mother Rosanna and her brothers.

Liberation had seemed complete when the final preparations for the wedding were made. Again, Claudia had done the impossible. The turn of events was as impetuous as their rushed lovemaking had become. She fought hard to resist the haste, the urgency as Jose whispered breathlessly in her ear, 'Marry me,' he pleaded, 'marry me...'

Claudia let herself fall into the madness, into the helpless fate she had known as a child, to be driven away by her own father, or be taken in and loved.

It would take years of sorrow to understand that to love Jose Zandro was not to know him. To say yes to his pleas was to damn herself. She would endlessly regret agreeing to live in one house with his mother and sister; an appendage to his subservience. Every day that she put off leaving meant a growing distaste for her husband and for herself.

One day, Emilia upbraided her for showing up at the Navy Club alone late one night.

'It's unseemly,' Emilia said. 'A married woman like you. Tongues have wagged.'

Claudia laughed. Placing her hands on her hips, she said, 'Isn't one spinster enough in this house? You want me to act like one, too?'

Since the disaster during Don Mariano's visit, Claudia was aware that Emilia had been conferring with her mother. She heard them talking in the old woman's room.

Now it seemed they were tightening the snare around her. The waiter at the Navy Club whispered sheepishly that from now on she would have to pay for her meals herself. Emilia had refused to pay any bills the club had presented to her.

'Many young women think it's easy to marry into money,' said Emilia. 'That it's as easy as lying on your back.'

'Something that some of us never get to do!' Claudia replied. They were both shouting, and the subject of the exchange alarmed Emilia. She turned her head quickly from side to side, wondering if the neighbours had heard. Then she suddenly gripped Claudia at the wrists.

'If you're going to live in this house,' she hissed, 'you'll have to live by the rules.'

Emilia had done her digging. She knew about Amado Diez and the illiterate laundrywoman on his plantation. It galled her that a girl who was born in a shack, and had learned to take a bath only thanks to the good graces of her guilt-ridden father, could walk into her house and flout the rules she had lived by all her decent, struggling life.

'It's not called *living*,' said Claudia, 'when it's done by *your* kind of rules, dear.'

'Why force yourself to stay then?' said Emilia. 'I'm sure you've got any number of shacks to go back to.'

The colour drained briefly from Claudia's face. 'Any shack smells better than this *old woman*'s house!'

'You can always try begging in the streets again.' Claudia's eyes gleamed with rage. She didn't know who had been telling Emilia these things. But it was a rumour Emilia had long enjoyed repeating to her friends that one day Claudia was walking on *Calle* Luna with her fashionable friends. She was approached by a woman begging, unwashed, covered in soot.

'Claudia was going to run away,' Emilia liked to recount, 'Before she recognised the woman begging. It was her own mother!'

'I'll beg if I have to,' said Claudia quietly. 'If it means getting out of this hellish house.'

'You'll leave by yourself,' Emilia said.

'Without a doubt,' Claudia said. 'Your brother can do what he wants. You can all stay together. Spit together all you want.'

Emilia crossed her arms. 'My brother's children stay in the house.'
'What?'

'They're flesh and blood to us,' said Emilia. 'They'll be raised as the children of a decent, respected family. As for you, you can crawl into any gutter you want.'

'*My* children?' Claudia said hoarsely. 'My children will *remain* here? *Without* me? How *dare* you!'

She slapped Emilia with all her strength. Emilia fell back against the door.

Emilia stormed back into her room and slammed the door. The crash thundered through the hall. She didn't come out for a long time.

She brooded. Deep inside she was afraid her brother would fritter away the wealth meant to go to her. She had seen it all around her, landed people grown old and poor. She felt only pity and contempt for them. The thought of them made her want to spit.

The hallway that separated the rooms became an empty place where almost no one passed. Claudia never ventured into the wing where Emilia and Doña Juana had their rooms.

It was the time that Rosanna was growing up. She and her brothers played in the quiet halls of the house, and sometimes they frightened themselves going into the chilly spaces where no one went, and where Augusto claimed he could sometimes hear voices.

Emilia was a strict custodian of her own decrees. When Rosanna was old enough to go to school, Claudia wanted a pretty uniform made for her at the fashionable tailor's on *Calle* Luna. It was then that Emilia announced that not only was the tailor out of the question, but that she had decided the children would be going to a cheaper school, where the uniforms would be tailored by the nuns themselves.

Claudia tried to get her husband to intervene.

Jose delayed, dawdled, and in the end did nothing. Claudia began to feel like a fool. The last shreds of respect she had had for her husband withered away.

One day when she passed the gambling houses on *Calle* Luna, she realised she was beginning to loathe herself for not doing anything. Something about the brazen mutiny of vice in those places made her ache to rebel.

Later she decided she needed new clothes. When she asked Jose, he told her simply to go to Emilia. He revealed that his sister had always held the purse. His own father had never trusted him with money.

A silent convulsion went through Claudia. She didn't know what it meant. That was the day she gave in to an insistent urge to wander.

She found herself heading towards the entrance of *Lamarre Jewellers*. The Frenchman greeted her warmly. He knew she was married now and expected her to shop like one of the settled ladies of the city for something in his counters that struck her fancy. She had to deflate his extravagant expectations and wait for an opportune moment to explain, bashfully, the real reason she had come.

Claudia took him aside, swallowed, then said with hollow coquetry, 'I made a bet with myself whether I could charm you into hiring me again. Like the first job you gave me. Long ago. One gets wistful at the memory of such things.'

The jeweller tried to conceal his shock. He cleared his throat. 'A job.'

He told her that the only job had already gone to a young woman who came to see him just a month before. There she was at the counter, chatting with one of the clients, young, spirited, and funny.

'We were looking for a long time,' the Frenchman said. 'It was so hard to replace you.' He gave her a small smile.

Claudia smiled back. But already she had realised how quickly and foolishly one could squander the benefit of youth. The knowledge humiliated her. But her final mortification sprang from an urge she couldn't resist.

She turned to the Frenchman again and asked. She tried to make a joke of it, indeed, made it seem like some detestable caprice her idleness had made her think up.

She wondered if he could lend her some money. A frivolous amount. Marriage had its difficulties...

He pretended to consider it, and delayed his refusal for as long as he could. There was a regretful slant to his head. But his eyes said it all. The gaze had dulled from the initial sparkle when he first saw her walking in, and it told of how Claudia had failed, how the fantasy of fabulous good fortune he had momentarily indulged on her behalf was a lie.

Claudia felt a cold sweat around her neck as she hurried out of the shop. She vowed never to come this way again.

On that day she walked out of the luxurious gleam of *Lamarre Jewellers* into despondency. She walked around the city for hours, remembering the nights on her father's plantation when she lay awake because she could sense the seething of the earth around her. In the hot, hopeless silence it exhaled a sadness that made her desperate to escape.

She told herself she loved her children. But having them was not enough to quell the unsettled energies that had brought her so far from her mother's shack. Then she realised she hadn't gone very far at all. She had just given up one bleak life for another.

As she walked she recalled the only time her father Amado had read a book to her. She had sat spellbound at the images he seemed to be absorbing from the open pages. It had stopped her crying and thinking about her mother wandering alone in her madness, searching perhaps in some empty field, calling out the name of the missing daughter she could never find.

At a street corner Claudia suddenly stopped. She thought someone had called her name. She smiled. There was no one walking in the narrow street but her. But just in front of her stood the wide, welcoming doors of *Madame Fung*'s. She heard the clack of ivory tiles, laughter coming from inside.

Claudia seemed entranced as she walked in, through the smoky hall and into a room full of gaming tables. Cards, mah-jongg, dice, roulette...

She found herself sitting down amidst the noise and exhilaration that had drawn her in from the street.

Her gloom lifted from the excited tumult all around her, as bets were thrown, cards slapped down, games lost or won. Soon she joined the flux around her, placed her bets and let the game sweep her up in its frenzied pace. It all came in a heady rush and before she knew what she was doing, she had fallen completely into the snare.

The haste of the play dizzied her, but in a way she liked. The smoke, the tumbling dice, the shouts as cascades of money were scooped up from the tables gave her a feeling of riding in a whirl. In the foggy daze of this newfound feeling, she smilingly surrendered her will, yielding totally to the hazards of chance and fate.

With each cast of the die her heart leapt at her dream of liberation. Freedom for her children. A new life away from that vile house. Freedom from Emilia. Freedom from her mistake of loving Jose Zandro.

The fleeting visions of triumph rather than her niggardly gains from the game were what kept her at the table, so that time meant nothing. The throw of the dice became her only craving, and she couldn't stop herself. Before she could wake up from the spell she had done it countless times. Again and again and again.

The sun had long set outside, the evening hours flew by unnoticed until midnight had passed. But in the incandescent glare of the bulbs above the gaming tables, everything remained the same.

Except they were not. Claudia had chased after the impossible too many times. In the end she lost everything. But she had only begun her long, calamitous plunge.

She was unrepentant, Ruben's letter ended. *When later she was asked why she did what she had done, she could only say, 'It was the fall of the dice. The accursed, wonderful die.'*

Jorge finished reading the letter. He folded it and hid it at the bottom of his drawer.

Verana wrote to her mother at least once a week. Her mother wrote back erratically, from Venice or Barcelona, wherever her travels with her husband took her.

'The places sound so wonderful!' Verana said. 'I wish I could go.'

After a while, Jorge said, 'Why don't you come with me?'

Her eyes widened. 'With *you?*' She was incredulous. *'Where?'*

'When I go to the capital. To university.'

Verana made a face. 'Why would I want to go there? I want to go somewhere marvellous, like my mother describes in her letters.'

Jorge was sorry he had said it.

'Will you at least come to see me off?' he asked her partly in jest. 'It's not long before I have to leave.'

He was thinking of the war film they just saw. 'Like the crying girls waving to their soldier boyfriends. Going to war.'

'Of course not,' Verana crossed her arms. 'I'd rather sleep. Besides, you're not my boyfriend.'

They were sitting on the benches in front of the abandoned villas, facing the sea. It was a beautiful day. Such days had swallowed up the remaining time Jorge had left. He closed his eyes. The radiance was there even if his eyes were closed. The end of his year had come. He thought of his uncle waiting for him in the capital.

'You think I could dance?' Verana asked him.

'Of course you can,' he answered.

'I mean, somewhere in a big city. With lots of people watching.'

'Lots of people watch you here,' said Jorge. 'I remember how Roberto and I loved watching you dance.'

'I don't mean that,' she said screwing up her eyes. 'I meant people who know what it's all about...'

She tried to think of the word her aunt had used: 'Sophisticates.'

'Who?' Jorge said.

'Sophis—never mind. People who know what dancing is all about. People who have seen great ballerinas perform, famous musicals. Not like here.' She looked wistful, her head slanted towards the ground. 'A big, exciting place somewhere. Where people can talk about me.'

She raised her arms, stretched out like she was going to dance. 'Tell each other how wonderful I am.' Jorge looked up at her. She giggled and sat down.

He walked her back to her house.

'You'd better leave early tomorrow,' Verana said. 'They say there might be a storm.'

The day before his departure was when Adia treated him most like a child again. She waited for him at the breakfast table and made sure he ate a hearty meal. She wiped her eyes as she bundled him into the car, telling the chauffeur to leave before she started crying again. Her eyes were so red they looked almost angry.

For reasons Jorge couldn't understand she had dressed up for the occasion, and looked strange in her best Sunday clothes, standing by the desolate corner of the orchard at that early hour, waving as they pulled away.

The streets were empty as the chauffeur sped towards the pier. The houses were dark and still, and it seemed a strange, indifferent town on which he had no claim.

The pier was quiet when they arrived. There were only a few passengers getting on the one ship. Jorge got all of his things out with the chauffeur's help. He was glad Adia had decided to stay at home. She thought she couldn't take the sight of Jorge sailing away.

Jorge waited for the ship's gangway to be rolled in place. A lone figure walked towards him. Wearing clothes as ravaged as his old face, the man kept pointing to his mouth. 'Some change please, sir,' his parched voice said. 'Just for something to eat.'

Jorge had grown taller than him, but he knew the man. If only for the glint of mischief in his eyes, he couldn't mistake the ventriloquist for anyone else. He wondered if it was all a joke.

The old man rubbed his stomach, looked like he was going to faint. 'I haven't eaten for days...' he said weakly. The voice that could work miracles was fading from hunger. Jorge feared that the conjurer of voices from his childhood might now fall silent. He searched in his pockets for what bills he had and gave them all to the old man, who nearly fainted with joy.

Jorge walked to the gangway and the ventriloquist followed him, asking what he could do in return. Jorge thought a while, then said, 'There's a house behind Santo Domingo Square, with stained-glass windows, like in a church.'

The old man gave him a toothless smile. 'Yes?'

'You'll find a pretty girl living there.'

'And? What about her?'

'She's—' Jorge leaned forward. 'Ask her to say something into your pouch.'

The old man nodded sadly. 'I understand.'

He fumbled in his pockets and took out something. Jorge felt a child's glee once more to see the ventriloquist's baffling bag.

'Consider it done,' the old man said and raised his arm in a wave that was like a salute.

Jorge ran up to the deck with his bags. A strange anxiety came over him. His last sight of Puerto Rreina was of the ventriloquist walking away in his ragged clothes, setting off on a mission for Jorge's heart. Which his faltering spirit seemed eager but uncertain to fulfil.

IX.

The capital was large and forbidding, and for a
long time Jorge fought the urge to give up and leave. In
the end he would be glad. His uncle's house was in a
wealthy neighbourhood, with shady lanes that
obscured the uneasy lives lived in its elegant homes.
The waiting room off the entrance hallway was full of
the symbols of Ruben's high office; on the heavy table
lay a marble pedestal with an official seal. Over the
mantelpiece hung a brass plaque from the presidential
palace.

Walking through the high-ceilinged room,
Ruben seemed ill at ease, a frail, reluctant man
straining under his burden. He was calm and
contemplative by nature. In his quiet conversations at
night, Jorge found traces of the fearful boy Adia still
remembered.

Ruben told Jorge about the recent threats to his
life, speaking in a pensive way, like a man wishing for a
simpler time. He often talked to Jorge about his
childhood with Rosanna and their brother Augusto.

Two years had passed since Augusto was killed. Perhaps in his long discussions with Jorge, Ruben was trying to find a key to a quandary that had begun to beset him.

The state of emergency had long ended. But in the time of reckoning that followed, so much intelligence came to light that had been concealed during the crisis.

There were reports of damnable abuses of power committed at the height of the disorder. Rumours persisted that the military dispatch which triggered the mass repression had been forged by a group of young officers, and Ruben was being implicated.

It all came at a time when Ruben began to suffer from problems with his vision, and a sense of infirmity had started to assail him. During the time of Jorge's stay with Ruben, he would witness a solitary side to his uncle's life that made Jorge pity him. The languid assurance Jorge had so admired in childhood masked a hesitant side to the man who had been forced to seem so strong.

It was clear that Ruben found comfort in talking to Jorge about the past. They would sit in his study for hours after he came home from work. Jorge would pour him a drink, and over his precious brandy, night after night, Ruben unfolded the story that had now become the focus of Jorge's life.

'I still wake up sometimes thinking some trouble is about to shake up everything,' Ruben said one night as they were sitting down. He clearly remembered the scandal over his mother's gambling debts.

A group of people had arrived in Paseo Gardenia one day. Jose Zandro came out and they gathered around him to present the promissory notes his wife had signed. The debts amounted to thousands of pesos. Jose touched his forehead and seemed to sway. He checked the signatures closely, more in an attempt to deny disaster than to verify the truth.

But it was all very clear. Emilia's hands shook as she studied each note, her eyes wide, and finally she let her arms go limp by her sides as if she had lost all her strength.

'Years...' she said almost inaudibly. Jose leaned forward to hear.

'Years..' Emilia whimpered, holding her forehead and closing her eyes. 'It's going to take years to pay these off! What more shame could she bring to the family?'

Then she started sobbing and let the notes flutter to the floor. One of the men bent down to scoop them up.

'My God!' Emilia screamed. Her face was all red. Jose turned around to see her pointing a finger at him.' This is what you get for getting some slut pregnant in the Navy Club!'

Her mother rushed to her side. Together Jose and Doña Juana tried to calm Emilia down, shielding her from the visitors and guiding her back towards her room.

The visitors understood and made ready to leave. The woman in spectacles touched Doña Juana on the elbow and whispered gently, 'We'll be in touch.'

It was astounding how long Claudia had managed to hide her dilemma. Before disgrace finally overtook her she had been in a kind of dream-like state, like that of people who have partly accepted their doom. She had been trying to recapture the wonder of coming to the city for the first time, of riding the tram screaming with her friends, in that audacious year of breaking away from her father's plantation.

Even as her debts were piling up, Claudia had found ways to borrow money. She still believed she could save herself and her children with one lucky throw of the dice. Her mind was fixed on the dream of people who were said come to *Madame Fung*'s as paupers and left with unimagined fortunes.

'She never really left the gambling den,' Ruben would tell Jorge years later. He sat forward on his chair, a glint in his eyes as he stared at the wall behind his nephew.

'She chased after this vision of a new life with her children.' Ruben's expression lightened, as if he glimpsed the fleeting vision himself. 'Away from the people who crushed her soul.'

'And when the vision dissipated,' he said, 'she found it had only ruined her life.'

The people who had lent Claudia money had trusted her with vast amounts because of Don Mariano's name. Now, along with her duped creditors, Jose Zandro's family threatened to have her jailed. Her name was sullied everywhere in the city.

Claudia could only flee. So one day she got up when the house was still quiet, and went into her children's rooms to kiss them goodbye. It was still dark and Rosanna turned over, too sleepy to realise what was going on. She thought her mother had just come in to see how she was, so the girl turned over and hugged her pillow with a smile, seeing with half-shut eyes how her mother tiptoed to the door and gently shut it behind her.

Claudia hurried through the hall in the early morning hush and disappeared from their lives. For a long time they thought she would come back, chastised but eager to start afresh. They had no idea what she did to survive. There were rumours she had taken to begging for her food.

The only friends who had not turned their backs on her said that Claudia struggled during that time to pay off her debts. She wandered the city looking for work. It seemed that for a long period Claudia still believed she would one day come back and collect her children.

Jose Zandro made no effort to look for her. He was devastated by her desertion, and it only made him sink back into his lifetime of inaction, until he accepted it all as the way things must be. With time, they learned to carry on without her.

Gradually the children stopped wondering when their mother would come back. Emilia planted the idea in their minds that Claudia had gone off with another man. That she had probably found happiness away from them, and it was perhaps best to forget her.

Ruben tried to take care of Rosanna. She was the youngest and couldn't understand the trouble that had swamped their lives. Ruben noticed how his sister had begun to play secret games.

She would tear off the petals from a rose she had secretly picked from Emilia's garden, until they gathered in a ring at her feet. She showed him a strange little coin she said their mother once entrusted to her. She would keep it for years.

'Mother doesn't love us,' Rosanna whispered one day. 'She'll *never* come back.'

'Her eyes narrowed when she said 'never,' Ruben would later recall with a smile. 'It was the most serious word she'd ever used.'

Jose Zandro did his best to divert his children. He took them to the fort in the afternoons to play by the sea. Ruben spent hours on the ramparts watching the ocean. Its dark immensity awed and comforted him. It seemed the most formidable enclosure from all the evils that could come.

But the years ahead would prove him wrong. One day, the drone of planes would forebode calamity, the first sign that a hostile genie had breached the protection of the sea.

Claudia heard the same drone one night as she sat by the window of the Navy Club, where the arrival of numerous new American officers heightened the pitch of the revelry, but raised no questions about the reason for their presence. Claudia blended into the nocturnal crush around the bar, where gossip was still being exchanged about her outrageous mischiefs, and occasionally a regretful word said about her wasted charms.

Those were some of the calmer moments in Claudia's present life. A friend she had met at *Lamarre* helped her get work at a cigar factory. She came to an arrangement with the club's manager to slowly pay off her debts. That allowed her to indulge in one of the few remaining pleasures in her existence: to visit the club at ungodly hours when she knew none of Jose Zandro's respectable friends would be there.

So none of the revellers recognised her as she moved discreetly through the crowd to get back to her table by the window, where she preferred to drink alone. The sullen beauty was oblivious to the scrutiny of the young men standing in their stiff collars, staring at her from across the dance floor, and, it seemed, a world away.

The cigarette haze and the noise were like the fog of another time as Claudia looked out on the courtyard dotted with streetlamps. She wondered what could get her out of the mire she was in. If anything could possibly return her life to the way it was.

She had found a room in a small boarding house, cheaper than the dormitory she had lived in when she had just started working at *Lamarre*. All her efforts to save herself had failed. For months she had been a fugitive from her debts, a slave to her undiminished hunger for risk.

Trudging back to her quarters after a night of drinking, she stopped to look at the sky. Dawn was breaking over the quiet city. Claudia wished for something to appear on the horizon to shake up the world. To shatter the stillness that choked her and left her with no hope.

Before that day was over, something would. It was thick and dark like clouds of locusts descending on a field. More frightening than the cyclones that came churning with debris and rain from the north. It was all that and worse, because war had come.

The rumble of machines closing in from all sides and the dreadful, scorched smell in the air, all told them that an inescapable curse had fallen. Suddenly, the truth everyone had been trying to deny for so long engulfed them.

Emilia and her mother were busy packing their things while the house was being carefully dismantled. The family stayed in the quickly emptying rooms of the Hotel Oriente while the move was taking place, as the far-off sound of bombs began to draw near.

The relocation took nearly eight days, using six trucks, the men working through the night and loading the enormous beams, to cart them away before dawn. The family's belongings took up sixteen suitcases and four trunks. The piano Jose Zandro had bought for his wife was loaded separately onto one truck. The same vehicle later returned for Doña Juana's saints.

Claudia decided to join the stream of people moving out of the city. The most dreadful thing was the buzzing of planes as armoured units rolled into the main streets, firing. People prayed as they ran, maddened by fear.

Claudia dashed across the path of a truck carrying plaster saints. People crossed themselves, thinking the throng of sacred statues on the back of the truck was a sign they would be saved.

Just outside the city they were surrounded by advancing infantry, and the refugees fell on their knees to beg. Claudia was struck on the head and she fell.

A long time later she opened her eyes and heard laughter, men shouting in a language she couldn't understand.

Black smoke hung above them everywhere. Claudia was lying on the floor of a moving truck. Bodies lay on the streets where the bullets or bombs had struck them. The truck sped past burning shells of buildings that had been full of life just the day before.

On both sides of the street there were people standing. They watched motionless in the eerie silence, awaiting their fate, almost as if they were already dead.

Two hours outside the city, the truck arrived at a barracks. The beatings and the mutilations began. Her knees went weak from the stench she would never forget. She was dragged forward and Claudia felt her hair wet from the filth on the floor of the truck.

Suddenly she understood why the people she saw on the roadsides stood there like they had already died. How horrible it was to still be alive, to see all this and to *feel*.

So *this* was defeat. She quickly learned why the only solace for the vanquished was death. Claudia was among the women who were taken to the military brothel the invaders had set up in an old seminary. The women were raped continually where the crosses still hung on the walls, and chapel pews lay in burnt piles where they had been stacked vainly to form a barricade.

In that cesspit Claudia would spend the days of the war, enduring the ravages of a conquered people, turning her head towards the wall and hoping to die. Some of the women were given opium as the orgies of hatred went on.

Some took it, like Claudia, wishing to kill themselves, but fell instead into a dream that would last longer than the horror, longer than the war.

It was only at night with Jorge that Ruben could indulge the introspective mood that seemed to vanish by day. But sometimes Jorge felt his family's story like a burden.

And soon he sought refuge with his new friends at the university. They seemed unencumbered by the past. When he was with them Jorge believed other stories were possible. It gave him release he couldn't find in his uncle's house.

Jorge had found a true mentor, a professor by the name of Solomon Dominguez, who gave his lectures on a footstool he carried around because he was less than four feet tall. On this rocky pulpit he stood to rail against the life-affirming philosophies of the college.

'Happy are the deluded,' he declared from his footstool, wearing his well-pressed shirts and a tie that was about three inches long. 'Neither villains nor saints get their just desserts in this life,' he said. 'And the after-life is an ever-receding myth.

'Our brief stint at life is made possible by a tendency for rosy expectations,' he continued. 'So overwhelming are the odds against our survival that evolution, which has enabled chameleons to change colour, has enabled us to fool ourselves.'

His words were given poignant meaning by his act of getting off his footstool and hoisting it over his shoulder to go to his next class. What could make such a disadvantaged man go on?

The lecture room next to his was occupied by a woman who taught, with more emotion than understanding, English poetry. She seemed unaware of how her gushing pedantry only enhanced the delightful noonday stupor which made Elizabethan verse so much the stuff of dreams.

So fired was she with noble sentiments and love of elevated language that she seemed above noticing entire rows of her listeners napping in the back. She deferred her vengeance until she finished reading a passage, when she would call out name after name, sitting back like an Inquisitor and demanding, 'What do you think the poet meant when he said...'

Her finger went up and down the open book on her desk for the most difficult line.

'...Ah! '*Redime te captum quam queas minimo?*'

The hapless student would stare.

'*Well?*'

Often she got no more than a vacant, imploring gaze. On occasion she received an answer that drove her to despair. She would touch her forehead. 'No, no, no!'

Or she would jump up from her desk and give the class a menacing glare.

'O truant muse what shall be thy amends
For thy neglect of truth and beauty dyed?'

She pounded the desk. 'Both truth and beauty on my love depends. So dost thou, too, and therein dignified!'

She picked up the thick volume and stalked angrily back and forth in front of the class. 'Finals are in four weeks' time, forsooth, my darlings! And you shall see how much my love for you has waned!'

Some deep emotion took hold of her and she flung the book at the blackboard, sending pieces of chalk flying to the floor. 'What must I do to make you *klutzes* use your *minds*? Wake up there, *you!*'

She stomped towards a long-haired student slumped against the rear wall. 'Open your eyes, slumber puss! The harvest is reaped.'

She clapped her hands in front of his face. 'The cow is milked, and your filthy milkmaid has messed up the hay with the you-know-who!'

The class laughed nervously as the student shook himself awake. With wounded dignity, the professor walked back to her table. A small smile appearing on her face, she picked out another poem to read. She let moments pass, letting her students squirm under her damning stare. Then she began to recite.

Out of enchantment or pure apathy, her audience was completely still. Her eyes seeming to devour the page, she uttered the stanzas with such feeling, her bosom began to heave. She got to the lines:

"O for a horse with wings! Hear'st thou Pisanio?

He is at Milford-Haven: read and tell me
How far 'tis thither."

Finally, no longer able to contain herself, she burst into tears. 'It's so beautiful!'

Her whole body shook and she seemed inconsolable. 'I wish you could understand how lovely it is.'

'Such *beauty*!' she sobbed into her hands.

The bell rang and her students jumped up. 'Tis time!' one of them said. Another whispered, 'Exeunt!'

They streamed out as the professor wiped her tears.

The lecture times overlapped and Solomon Dominguez often had disputes with the poetry professor in the corridor outside.

'What a beautiful day,' he said to her one morning. 'Aren't you going to cry?'

He sidled up to Jorge. 'There's a romantic suicide waiting to happen. Every day I pray for her to have a passionate, doomed affair.'

They watched her carry her large volumes into the lecture room. 'Such sensitive souls cry out for a tragic exit.'

Jorge was among the crowd that was drawn to Solomon Dominguez's house outside the campus. They gathered under the tree across the road on Friday afternoons, waiting for the professor to see them and wave them in. It was Solomon Dominguez who made them all realise that life is full of metaphors. He said his short stature symbolised the inadequate reach of man, hence the need for knowledge and something sturdy to stand on.

'Like this,' he patted his trusty foot stool. He felt his full name Solomon Danilo Ortega Dominguez was too long for such a short man, so he insisted his students call him Sod Dom. It was shortened further, outside the campus, to Sod.

He liked to perch himself on a large cushion while his guests found space on the dusty Tadjik rugs in his living room. Sod would recline to his full length on the cushion and regale them with the outbursts he did not permit himself in the lecture hall.

There was a timeless quality to the evenings spent at Solomon's house which Jorge and his classmates felt was the best excuse to come to university. On the first night Jorge joined them he found his friends lolling drunk on the floor, talking about eternity.

'This is an endless discussion,' Solomon said. It made Jorge think of Joseph, and for an instant he missed Adia's old boarders and the strange time they shared.

Solomon had an astounding capacity to drink that was out of all proportion to his size. He had developed the amazing skill of reaching back from his cushion without looking to get one of the beer bottles lined up against the wall. But he had poor control of his bladder and had to make frequent trips to the spot behind the tree in his yard, climbing down from his cushion with a vexed sigh, 'Time to air the edifice.'

The parties went on until dawn. On the first night, Jorge kept fidgeting, wanting to leave. Solomon pointed to one of the two clocks in the room, both of which were broken. 'If you don't know when it started, how could you know when it should end?'

He laughed. 'You worry too much. Just sit down and drink.'

Jorge waited for him to say something more. But Solomon was trying to reach back for a bottle. He slipped and tumbled down to the floor.

The carousing only wound down at daybreak, when they all sat out in the garden, watching a lone star in the brightening sky.

'Solomon? Are you asleep?' one of the students asked.

'No,' he yawned, his eyes fixed sleepily on the star. 'I was just thinking. Everyone on earth is an islander,' he said. 'We all started out believing we were the only creatures in this world.'

It gave people the wrong idea to learn that Jorge's uncle was a prominent senator.
'You're so lucky,' one woman said. 'Your life must be so easy.'

Jorge kept quiet about the reality he witnessed in his uncle's house. About those nights he watched Ruben climbing the stairs, a stooped man taking careful steps.

Though Ruben didn't know Jorge's father well, sometimes he disclosed things that surprised Jorge. 'He was always a lonely man,' Ruben said. 'Cloaked in too many secrets.'

'What secrets?' Jorge asked.
Ruben revealed how when Leon was young, he had used false identity papers to get work with the government. Jorge laughed and told Ruben about the strange notion he and Miguel had as boys that Leon was an impostor who had taken the place of their real father.

Ruben laughed. 'Now I guess we'll never know his real identity.'

One day, Jorge was helping his uncle put something away in the cellar.

'Oh, look,' said Ruben. 'It's your father's old suitcase.'

He took it down. 'He used it when he came to visit me long ago. One of the clasps broke so he left it here. I'd forgotten all about it.'

When Ruben was out that day, Jorge wandered into the cellar and took out his father's old suitcase. He studied the leather, its creases and its broken clasp. In them were a record of the years of his father's life he knew nothing about. He moved his hand through the empty interior, imagining some essence left by the past.

Ruben had been seeing various doctors over the years about his eyes. But the deterioration seemed impossible to reverse. He squinted to see outside the window and took hours to read a few pages. He often sat in a chair on weekends and asked Jorge what he could see out on the street.

Jorge observed how Ruben slowly began to lose his moorings in the world, as his dwindling vision drew him deeper and deeper into the darkness within himself he could not hope to escape.

Jorge closed his eyes and tried to imagine what darkness was like. He opened his eyes to see Ruben standing in front of him.

'A letter for you,' he said. It was from Verana. *What happened to you?* Her dainty writing said. *You've sunk like a stone over there. Like I knew you would.*

Jorge was so relieved to hear from her, and suddenly longed to see her again. He started writing to her, sitting at his desk for hours at a time. He sent at least one letter a day.

Weeks later she wrote back.

One at a time, please. I can't read twenty pages all at once, especially in that awful chicken scrawl you call your handwriting.
Love, Verana

P.S. I'm sorry to hear your uncle is going blind. But it doesn't mean I have to. Please write LEGIBLY. In LARGE, CLEAR LETTERS that the naked human eye can SEE.

Her tirades did not offend him. In fact her spirit cheered him up. He wrote back and begged her to send a picture.

The peace after the Repression was a vengeful time. There was a relentless need to know the truth, to right old wrongs, to settle scores. The men held up as heroes during the crisis found themselves suddenly being maligned.

Ruben was accused of giving protection to a smuggling ring that continued its operations even during the emergency. He was inured to slander as part of the life he had chosen, but the effort to redeem his name took up more and more of his time. He often came home weary, shuffling through the hallway late at night with a harried look.

One night he sat under the rows of gilt-spined legal volumes in his study, talking to Jorge. They discussed his role during the state of emergency, and Jorge realised that those years still tormented his uncle.

Ruben rubbed his temples with a sigh and said, 'I ruined my eyes studying the law. Only to see it all crumble before me.'

As his troubles worsened, Ruben seemed to find solace in telling Jorge the rest of the family's story, remembering the ordeals he had managed to survive.

The war finally ended and reconstruction had begun. Ruben left his father's house to start a new life in the capital. Through good fortune and ingenuity, the family had survived the catastrophe.

Jose Zandro remarried, this time to a sober-minded widow with children of her own. His health had grown worse during the upheaval and after a few years, his new wife convinced him to move away to the country. That was not long before Rosanna made the impulsive decision to marry Leon Gil.

They came to live in the house Rosanna's father had left. Right up to that moment, Emilia refused to give up her half of the house. She never let anyone forget that it was her labours that had saved it from destruction.

She settled in the far wing, where Jorge's father was later to have his room. It was Emilia who was the first ghost of the house, rarely leaving the far wing, and her unyielding claim was accepted by Rosanna and her husband as their legacy. In that strange way they became a family.

Years had passed without any news about Claudia. No one knew what had happened to her. Rosanna had grown from the girl who still waited for her mother into a woman with a child of her own. But she had suffered more from her early sorrows than she cared to admit. It was not long after giving birth to her second child that Rosanna fell ill.

'She was never very strong,' Ruben would later tell Jorge. 'Then something happened that seemed to finally break her will.'

There were times Rosanna was so weak someone was needed to care for her. At those moments she remembered a salve her mother used to rub on her chest when she used to have her bouts of breathlessness as a child. She asked her husband to find the salve for her.

Leon looked everywhere. He sent the chauffeur out to other towns to search. But it seemed hopeless. Then one day Rosanna heard someone calling out from the gate. It was an old woman asking for water to drink.

There were countless wretched souls like her passing through Aguada all the time, coming in or leaving the city, blown to all corners by fate. They knocked on doors to beg for work or for something to eat. People engaged them to clean the house or go on errands, anything in exchange for a few coins.

The chauffeur came out to the gate. He asked the old woman if she knew a place to buy the salve like the one Rosanna needed. He told her what it was for. 'Yes. For shortness of breath,' the old woman replied. 'Like some children get.'

It seemed she had always been displaced. Her clothes and her skin were covered with dirt, like she had been walking for years.

'I've roamed this whole island from one end to the other,' she said. 'Everything's been destroyed. There's really nothing for anyone to go back to.' She shook her head and smiled. 'Only mad people keep searching. Hoping they can still find whatever they left behind.'

'You're very lucky in this house,' she said with a hungry glint in her eyes. 'That river looks so beautiful. It's like the war never touched this place.'

She and the chauffeur conversed some more. It had been a while since she had spoken to anyone who would listen. She told him how she had found work in an old gambling house. 'Some people come back and do little chores to pay off small debts.'

The woman explained how she slept in the kitchen where she worked, putting down her beddings when the pots had been washed and put away. The chauffeur cleared his throat and reminded her of the salve.

'But I can make it!' the old woman said. 'I used to make it all the time.'

The chauffeur got all the herbs she needed and the woman prepared the ointment in the kitchen. Rosanna applied it and she felt better. Leon was very pleased. At that time he still believed Rosanna's illness could be cured. He asked the old woman to continue treating his wife with her balm. He was so eager he offered her a place to stay. But Emilia came out of her room at that moment and the old woman hurried out of the house.

'Her face went pale,' said Ruben. 'No one could stop her from leaving.'

As his uncle spoke, Jorge realised that Ruben was about to reveal something that had perplexed him for so long.

The abuses the old woman had suffered had robbed her of all her familiar traits. Her sad fate had made her just one of the nameless unfortunates who had trudged through Aguada for years.

'The pride had vanished from her face,' Ruben finally said to Jorge. 'But Rosanna understood why the old woman could make the salve she thought only our mother knew how to make.'

Ruben starred at the wall with a gleam in his eyes, as if the improbable vision were unfolding again in his mind. 'Just before Rosanna died, she realised what an astounding thing had happened.'

Ruben leaned forward and looked intently at Jorge. 'The old woman who made the salve was Claudia, our mother. She had somehow survived. After all those years she had come back.'

When they offered her opium in the prison camp, Claudia took it, hoping to sink finally in the darkness. But she did not die. Instead she woke up in a field of flowers. The blossoms overran the prison camp, so many Claudia could have picked them for years. The strange fluorescence covered the beds of the brothel and, outside, the freshly dug graves. Their insane teeming was unstoppable, watered by pain, nourished by the opium's delirious stream. The butchery around them was perfumed by the blossoms crushed under the soldier's boots. The profusion sweetened the bombardment Claudia didn't know would ultimately mean their liberation.

Until finally, still in a daze, she joined the rush of starved, devastated souls out of the camp's shattered gates, and somehow found the strength to rejoice at finding the invaders gone. The city was empty, full of the dead.

But Claudia was aghast to find that she could escape the odious brothel, but not the horrid dream that began there. The ethereal blossoms covered the fields, stretching out nearly over the entire blackened face of the earth. Thus she joined the abandoned throngs who would wander among the ruins for months and years, no longer having a destination, just moving ceaselessly to escape the terror that had lodged deep inside.

The half-dead hordes were so hungry, they fought over locusts and bugs they caught in the grass and ate them raw. People jumped into the river to drown themselves. But soon there were too many bodies in the water that no one could come in anymore.

Night and day, there was no respite from the flowers that haunted Claudia's sleep. They were there wherever she looked. Finally she stumbled through the outskirts and found a place she recognised. The first place she went to was the corner on *Calle* Luna where she used to get off the tram to get to *Lamarre Jewellers*. She found the glass counters shattered, the roof and the columns gone.

But for the bullet holes in the walls, the Navy Club had survived. A man Claudia thought she knew from the dances at her old haunt was standing at the foot of the stairs. He was clearing a path in the debris. She came up to him. But when he looked up he just gave her a frightened, startled look. There wasn't the slightest trace of recognition. The man's face was blank and pale, his mind shattered.

Perhaps the war had wrought Claudia a kindness after all. Maybe they all thought she was dead. Everything that had gone before had vanished in the conflagration. Her disgrace was buried in the rubble. That was when she conceived the brazen idea to come home.

But she wavered. She wasn't even certain her children would be alive. If they were, Claudia wondered if they would accept her, forgive her or turn her away. She was determined. She would join the household as a servant if she must. But she knew she couldn't come as she was. Something had to change.

In tattered clothes and just one shoe she made her way to Paseo Gardenia. But when she got there, her senses were dulled by the emptiness she saw. Jose Zandro's house had disappeared. Ripped out of its foundations. As if some dry, fiery gale had blown it away.

The gate had been torn down and the grass was scorched on the yard where her children used to play. Their existence had been completely erased. Perhaps the house had been one of those devoured by flames during the bombing raids. Nothing was left.

Claudia got down on the pavement and wept. She cried for her children, for her husband Jose and their failed love. Then, gradually she picked herself up. She had nowhere else to go. So again she went to join the disconsolate flock that drifted through the abandoned city's smoking remains.

Claudia had no idea how long she spent in that limbo of wandering. But one day she found herself standing by the railroad crossing where no train had passed for years. She was engrossed in studying the geraniums growing over the tracks.

In the noonday stupor she wondered if the flowers were just part of her dream. Then something made her look up. An odd-looking vehicle was coming towards her. It was the number 14 of the Puerto Reina Bus Company, which had gone out of business long before the war. Claudia raised her hand to flag it down and the bus creaked to a stop.

She sat near the door of the empty vehicle as it took her on a long, peculiar route. It traced a path of its own through the overgrown roads until finally, they passed the cemetery. Puzzled and afraid, Claudia rang the bell to get off. She stepped out onto the road and walked some distance. When she had trudged past a large tamarind tree she stopped and gasped.

The vision that confronted her made her sway. There, in a place totally untouched by the war, stood Jose Zandro's house. By some miracle it had been saved. It looked as splendid as it had on the day Claudia left it, as if none of the horrors had happened at all.

Claudia came to the gate and called out. While still on the bus she had decided what she needed to change. She would introduce herself by a new name. Perhaps she thought it would help to hide her shame, or make it easier for her children to forgive her. So she came back into their lives, a stranger with no history, hoping her children could forget the past.

She asked to be called Adia, the nickname her mother gave her on Amado's plantation long ago. The name her mad mother used to call out over the evening fields, calling her unruly daughter to come home. It was the name that Jorge knew and grew to love her by, and her story was the missing piece he needed to know the whole of his own.

Between terms Jorge came home to Puerto Reina. Adia insisted his old room was a little boy's room and was no longer good enough for him. So Jorge ended up by himself upstairs, looking over the garden where his mother used to hold dances for her friends.

He felt like a guest in the unfilled house, sensing the chill of the quiet spaces and the rooms where the boarders once lived. The only place he still found habitable after all those years was Adia's kitchen. He spent most of his time there, helping her cook or chop vegetables. She told him that Salvador del Mundo had come to visit her, wanting to know how Jorge was.

When Adia finally left the kitchen, he was unable to resist a secret urge he'd been trying to curb. He stood up and opened the cupboard. Feeling around the tins, bowls and bags of flour, Jorge found the empty glass jar again.

It gave him a boyhood thrill to take it out, placing it on the ledge like he used to do with Melba. He sat and watched it quietly for several moments. The glowing spider was long gone, vanished back into the light. But Jorge fancied he could still sense a trace of its lost radiance.

Whatever he did, he couldn't get himself to throw the jar away. He always put it back into the cupboard in the same mood of awe he had before, going back to his room with a feeling of warmth.

He spent the days walking round in the city. One day he found himself in an alley whose walls were emblazoned with slogans. He let his gaze wander over the menacing graffiti.

DOWN WITH IMPERIALIST LACKEYS!
ARMED STRUGGLE IS THE ONLY WAY!

Jorge smiled when he realised he was confronting the seditious messages he had helped Maya and her friends paint long ago.

CONSTABULARY, BULLDOGS OF THE
STATE! BOW-WOW-WOW!

Jorge was bewildered at his childhood role in demanding the overthrow of the state, the dismantling of 'the clerico-capitalist conspiracy,' and an immediate end to schemes of 'American hegemonists.'

He was amused by his innocent connivance in the pursuit of such confounding goals. It made it all the harder for him to forget Maya and the devious, reckless path she had led them down.

During one of his visits, Adia took Jorge into his mother's room and to show him the broken mirror she had patched together for him. With her help, he had found all the pieces.

'Just like the day your mother smashed it,' Adia said.

Jorge didn't know how long her secrecy would go on. He still had no idea how to tell her about the new knowledge his uncle had given him. He looked at the mended mirror with a smile. It seemed almost like he could see the reflections whole. There were no missing pieces anymore.

It was around that time that Adia insisted Jorge come with her on a trip to the country. The journey was long and tiring, and Jorge kept wanting to go back. 'You won't regret it,' Adia tried to cajole him. 'It'll help you understand much more.'

They travelled some distance, and she perked up. 'He's so talented, this man we're going to see,' she said. 'It'll be so nice to hear him play music again.'

At last, they got off the bus and walked up a lonely country road. Adia seemed to grow apprehensive. At the end of the road there was a small house with a terrace.

'So this is where the poor man ended up,' Adia said. She turned with sad eyes and crossed over a thin stream of sewage that flowed from the back of the house. She stopped at the front steps and called out.

A woman opened the door. When Adia told her what they had come for, the woman disappeared back into the house. She returned to the terrace guiding a feeble old man. He sat down in a chair and looked out on the road. He didn't seem to recognise Adia.

She greeted him effusively, but he just stared at her. From inside the house came the tinkling of a piano.

'You have a piano,' Adia cried. 'Just as I thought.'

She ran around the veranda, trying to coax a reaction from the old man. 'Music please, maestro!'

But he just looked at her without feeling. The woman came out of the house again. She made an effort to be cordial, but she had a stern face.

'He's been like this for some time,' she said to Adia. She led her to the back of the terrace to talk.

'No memory?' Jorge heard Adia say. 'None at all?'

'He remembers nothing,' the woman said, unsmiling. 'He forgets you the moment he turns his back.'

Adia came forward and got the old man to stand. 'Surely, it can't be true,' she cooed. 'Nothing an old tune couldn't bring back,' she said jovially as she guided him back into the house. The woman followed them in. Adia sat the old man down at the piano, then leaned over to pick out a tune.

'That old rumba, maestro,' she cajoled the man. 'Certainly you remember those nights on the dance floor!'

The man brought his hand forward to rest on the keys. His eyes bulged, his lower lip protruded as he struggled to press down on the ivory. Adia and the woman waited in anticipation. All that came out was a faint, distant tune.

'That melody!' Adia clapped her hands. 'How you used to make me cry with that tune.'

The old man's head was cocked, as if listening out for something from very far away. Adia became sad. She bent her head towards the man with pity. The woman went out and lit a cigarette by the rail. She sat in the corner smoking, absorbed in her own thoughts.

Adia took the old man's hands and said softly, 'You remember the shop at the end of the tramline? The day you came in looking for a gift?'
She wiped something from her eye. 'It's all gone now. There's nothing left.'

All afternoon she tried to awaken something in him. She got up and danced a few steps in an effort to enliven him. But his unwavering stare neither changed nor showed any feeling.

Adia had told Jorge such remarkable things about the man they were coming to see. It was clear she had made the trip with much expectation. Now she looked sad and disheartened.

The other woman came in and said, 'Don't worry. It's not just you. We've been married for twenty-five years, but he looks at me like a stranger.' 'Have you considered taking him to the capital?' Adia asked.

The woman shrugged. 'It's hopeless.'

Finally, as dusk gathered, Jorge and Adia got up to leave. On the long way home, Adia was sullen and thoughtful. She tried not to let Jorge see her eyes redden with grief.

'All the way there, I was afraid he would be angry at me,' she explained. 'I was prepared he might even hit me.'

She stared in front of her as if bewildered. 'But he had completely forgotten. Everything was gone. It was worse than if he had slapped me.'

It was dark when they got home. Adia leaned wearily against the doorway. Jorge later found her in the kitchen, crying.

'Does it mean anything?' she sobbed. 'It takes so long to understand. And then it's all gone. What for?'

Jorge didn't know quite how to console her. He had no inkling why she was so sad.

Only later would he understand, when he learned that the man they had visited that day was Jose Zandro, his grandfather, the man Adia had left more than thirty years before.

Two years later they learned of Jose Zandro's death. His widow appeared at the house on Jorge's next visit. It was the woman in the country house that they visited before. She announced her husband's death as a kind of accusation, glaring at Adia from the doorway.

'I might have known,' she said. 'You suddenly coming to visit Jose after all these years. Just to see how far along he was.'

Adia's shock at the news was confounded by the woman's obvious hatred. She and Jorge watched as the visitor walked imperiously through the hall, opening doors and going into the closets. It was hard to tell what she wanted as she pulled out boxes from under the bed in Leon's old room, then came down to rake through the contents of Rosanna's bureau. She emptied the drawers and turned them over to examine the bottoms.

'You!' Adia stormed in to confront her. 'You could begin by telling me what you want. Just who on earth gave you the right to come barging in here?' The woman turned to face Adia, with her hands on her hips. 'My name is Conchita Zandro,' she said. 'I would have introduced myself much earlier. If you hadn't been so giddy the last time I saw you.'

She fished out a cigarette from her purse and lit it, blowing a puff towards the doorway. 'You might have heard about me,' she said. 'But you were no longer around when I came into Jose's life. To clear up the mess you left.' She went to stand by the window with her cigarette.

'Very well,' Adia said quietly. 'It still doesn't tell me just why the devil you're here.'

'You don't know?' Conchita cocked her head with such presumption. 'Why, I'm here to collect my husband's will.'

'What will?'

Conchita snuffed out her cigarette on the window ledge. 'Don't lie to me,' she hissed. 'I know that's the only reason you were even interested in seeing your poor, addled Jose. Quite suddenly, after years of nothing.'

Adia was dumbstruck. Neither she nor Jorge were prepared for the onslaught it seemed Conchita had long conceived.

She left that day. But early the next morning she was back.

Birds were still singing in the woods when a truck rumbled to a stop in front of the house. Workmen jumped out of it with shovels, crowbars and pickaxes. As they assembled themselves around the house with their tools, two cars drove up.

The chauffeur, now old and stooped, came out of his room in the back to watch the disturbance. He was no longer the menacing man he once was, and the thin strand of hair that he combed painstakingly across his shiny scalp was a last, touching defiance of age. Jorge went out and stood beside him.

'What do you think they're going to do?' Jorge asked.

The older man clucked his tongue. 'I've been with your family a long time,' he shook his head. 'There's no telling what will happen from one day to the next.'

They heard Adia scream. Jorge and the chauffeur ran inside to find Adia grappling with one of the workmen for control of a crowbar.

'They're punching holes in the walls!' she cried out to Jorge, who, along with the chauffeur jumped into the fray. They tried to fight off the team of labourers impatient to get on with their task.

But it wasn't long before another half-dozen men came in from outside. Adia and Jorge could only watch. The foreman came in and gave the order to start, and the workers started driving their tools through the floors and walls. Adia covered her ears.

In the middle of the confusion, Conchita came in. She stood amidst the dust rising all around them. Her eyes gleamed at Adia. 'I'm *going* to find that will,' she shouted over the noise. 'I will get *whatever* my husband left. There's no use trying to hide it. I'll destroy this house if I have to!'

Jorge went out to escape the noise and the chaos. Every time he heard a loud thump, he knew another hole was being driven in. He felt the heavy blows as if the devastation were being wrought inside him.

'We'll call the police!' Adia came running out. 'Christ! We live here!'

'Go call anyone you like,' Conchita came running out behind her. She produced some papers and waved them in Adia's face. 'This house is in my husband's name. Which means it's now mind. I can do with it what I want.'

And so Adia and Jorge stood by and let them wreak havoc. But by the end of the day, it was clear all their exertions were in vain. Whatever they were looking for was nowhere to be found.

'All right, pack up!' the foreman called out to his men. The labourers put aside their tools. It seemed no more work was going to be done that day. The truck drove off, though three of the labourers stayed behind.

It was only then that Jorge clearly saw the result of the day's madness. There were pits in the garden where he and Miguel used to play, cracks in the walls where he and his cousins once listened for strange voices they thought they heard.

The day's shadows were lengthening by the time the foreman came back. He drove his car right up to the house. The rear door opened, but no one got out. The foremen called two workmen to the car. The vehicle's trunk was opened and they pulled out a wheelchair. It was unfolded near the passenger door and the car's second occupant was helped out.

She was a shrivelled old woman, her thin legs dangling uselessly on the front of the chair. Adia came out and saw the new arrival. Her back straightened, and a hard look came into her eyes.

Jorge turned to the chauffeur inquiringly. He leaned over and whispered in Jorge's ear, 'That's Emilia, your grand-aunt.'

The crippled woman was rolled to where Conchita was standing, and Jorge heard her ask, 'No luck?'

They slowly circled the house and surveyed the damage left by the workmen everywhere.
'Can it be?' Conchita blurted out. 'He really left no *will*?' She seemed about to cry. 'How *could* he?'
'You don't know my brother, Conchita,' the crippled woman said. 'He could squander *any*thing.'
'I can't help it,' said Conchita, wiping her eyes. 'I'm sure *she* knows something.'

'She?' Emilia looked up at her. 'Who?'
Conchita pointed to where Adia was standing. '*Her.*'

Emilia motioned for her to be rolled towards Adia. When they came close enough to look in each other's face, the crippled woman's face turned pale. 'My God. You!'

She peered up at Adia for a long time. She couldn't seem to believe her eyes. Her gaze grew dull as she tried to claw through the clamour in her mind.

Finally, the old woman managed to shake herself out of her confusion. She cleared her throat. 'It's been years since I've been like this,' Emilia said, glancing down at her lifeless legs. She tried to smile. 'I've only been waiting for death.'

Emilia tried to explain to Adia how they had tried to find her. She swore they wanted to help. 'We looked for *years*,' she said. 'We *never* stopped...trying.' Her voice broke and she closed her eyes. 'Even after the war was long over.'

'But I'm so glad you survived,' Emilia said, her eyes glistening. 'You're still on your own two feet,' she said solemnly. She looked down on her withered legs curled up against the metal braces of the chair. 'While my own body is half-dead. Just waiting for the rest of me to follow.'

When it was time to leave, Emilia reached out and tightly held Adia's hands.

'It's so good to see you again, Claudia,' she smiled.

Jorge and Adia watched the excruciating process of transferring Emilia from the chair into the car. The chair was folded and placed into the trunk, and the car finally drove off.

'Claudia,' Adia repeated the name, almost in disbelief. 'No one has called me that for such a long time.'

She smiled with a strange, smouldering look in her eyes.

Jorge said it, too, for the very first time. And hearing him utter the name from the past life she had banished from her mind, Adia suddenly burst into tears. She sobbed uncontrollably, as if her mind had only grasped the full horror of all that had happened to her.

X.

On one of his visits to Puerto Reina, Jorge rediscovered *The Labyrinth of Dreams*. He retrieved the old book Joseph had given him from the dust in one of the upper rooms and began to read. The words that had made him give up after so many tentative attempts in the past now drew him in. *We each dream one part of the puzzle, and the whole they comprise is just one dream.*

Everything that had happened since Joseph left had prepared Jorge for this new understanding. He was still engrossed in its mystery when by chance he met Verana again.

It shook him out of his torpor. He had been wandering through the plaza one hot afternoon. There were preparations on the stage for a show.

The last words twirled through his mind again. *Fragmented soul trapped in the medium of yearning, pulled by visions airier and more fleeting than itself, lost in the labyrinth of dreams.*

Seeing her took his breath away. Her hair had grown down to her shoulders, and her flushed, flawless cheeks mocked him for never having found anything he could want more.

Jorge had no idea she could grow into a creature who would give him no respite. Even if she did nothing, some impression of her continued to bedevil him—the way her hair fell over her eyes, the sheen of her lips as her little tongue flicked out to lick them.

Verana stopped what she was doing and looked across the stage at him. She ran towards the front and jumped down.

'I've applied to join a troupe,' she said as they walked around.

'What did they say?' Jorge asked.

'They don't know yet. They'll decide after this performance.'

She told him the show was to be held in a week. Jorge couldn't resist telling Verana about his dissipated life in the capital with Solomon Dominguez and his friends.

417

She thought he was turning wicked. 'You used to be a sweet boy,' she said. 'Maybe that place isn't good for you.'

'There's nothing wrong with growing up,' he said.

'Still,' she stopped and looked back towards the stage. 'You seemed happier when I first met you.'

'I guess I woke up,' said Jorge with a bitter ache that Solomon Dominguez had roused. 'Everyone's a liar.'

'It's not as simple as that,' Verana said. She had her father's obstinacy, and Jorge tried to explain what he meant.

He used all the arguments he had gleaned from his evenings with Solomon and his other friends.

'Did you learn that from your stupid books?' she said.

'No. It's what I figured out myself.'

'I guess you wasted a lot of time in the capital,' she crossed her arms and turned away.

'At least I learned that the truth is important,' he followed her. 'Because life is so full of lies.'

He didn't realise that he was acting like Joseph used to do with Maya.

'That's why I love you,' Verana laughed. 'It's so easy to convince you of any nonsense.'

'In what way?' he stopped and asked.

She also stopped and looked from side to side. 'In what way is it nonsense?'

'No. In what way do you love me?'

She opened her mouth to say something, then screwed up her eyes in frustration. 'I never said.'

'You did, liar. How do you love me?'

She refused to indulge his conceit.

He chased her around the fountain but she refused to say.

'Anyway, you said it,' Jorge finally said in triumph. 'You can't take it back.'

'How you construe it is your business,' she said with a haughty twist to her head. 'After all, you're the little philosopher.'

The microphones had been turned on at the stage. Verana was being called back.

'Well,' Jorge threw up his hands and started to walk away. 'I guess that's all for today.'

'Wait.'

Jorge turned around.

'Are you coming to see me for the show?'

It was the festive week of May, when towns held contests to pick their prettiest girls for the flower parade. The procession was held after mass on Sunday, and, snaking through the side streets, wound down in the main thoroughfare.

It culminated at dusk in the plaza with the crowning of the Queen of the May Flowers for that year.

Jorge found the crowded plaza festooned with blossoms brought by the competing towns. His pride swelled when he saw Verana on the stage, plucked out of the gloom by large spotlights.

He basked in the crowd's delight as the troupe glided dreamily around the stage in bright, outlandish costumes. Listening to the soothing music played by the string ensemble under a starry sky, Jorge remembered the spectacles in the plaza that had held him spellbound as a child. He looked forward with relish to the moment when the show ended and Verana could come down from the ethereal world in which the audience now saw her.

'She should be the Queen of the May Flowers, that one,' said a woman in the audience. The show finally came to a close, and Jorge made his way backstage to find Verana. It took him a while to find her among the tired, exhilarated dancers resting after the performance. A group of them got up and started to walk away. Jorge followed.

'Verana!' he shouted through cupped hands. 'Verana! Wait!'

The noise of the excited throngs drowned out his cries. He ran after her but didn't catch up. In the group, laughing with the other performers, Verana was distant and unattainable again. He watched them get into a car and drive away.

It seemed he would always hanker for the other side of life where she was, out of his reach. At his feet he found a torn wreath of camellias from one of the performers, white against the darkness.

The plaza was a different place one day after the festival. The litter was being swept away by a few cleaners. They piled it up by the flagstone path and lit it. The smoke rose up from the mounds of leaves and debris, remnants of the efflorescent celebration of the night before. It was a beautiful afternoon. Jorge walked around the deserted plaza with a forlorn feeling for the sweet light, wasted on the dead fountain and the still flower beds.

He walked to Verana's house. He knocked on the door and waited, but no one came. All the houses on the street were still. He sat on his haunches on the roadside watching the motionless square of the street framed by the dusty trees.

He went to the corner under Verana's window. His voice echoed in the empty street as he called out her name.

'Verana...' Like it was a name by which he was calling back a beautiful day.

He made his way around to the back. Finally, he saw her. She was sitting on the back steps, her head lowered.

'You looked blue,' she said sniffing when he came near. 'I saw you.'

'Where?' said Jorge testily. 'Why didn't you come down?'

'I watched you through the stained glass windows. Your whole body was blue.' She drew breath sharply and didn't look up at him.

Jorge sat down beside her and saw her eyes were red from crying. Near her was an envelope with an opened letter. A picture was peeking out from inside. 'My mother's given birth in Spain,' she said.

'Oh really?'

'It's a boy.'

'Good!'

Verana shook her head, her eyes still swollen with sorrow. 'It's not good.'

'Why?' said Jorge. 'You should be happy.'

Verana wiped her eyes with a hanky.

'Now it'll be easier for her to forget me.' Her hoarse voice showed a cold resilience. 'Now she'll have her little brat to dote on.'

'That's silly,' Jorge tried to cajole her.

She covered her face and was quiet for a while.

Then she blurted out, 'Why did she bother having me?'

She cried again and Jorge put his arm around her and caressed her cheek. His lips touched her face and she broke away.

'Catch the ladybird!' she jumped up and ran inside. Jorge followed.

He found her upstairs standing by the door of her room. She took him by the hands and let him in.

Going to the cabinet, she took out the coloured glasses her mother used to dance the fandango of lights with. Verana had used them, too, and was always proud that, like her mother, she had never broken one.

'Maybe I'll smash them all,' she said.

She made the movements of the fandango without the glasses or the candles, moving to a music in her head. Her face grew mournful.

'I've always wanted to go up in flames,' she said. 'Explode like a fireball.'

She sat down thoughtfully by the window, looking out. 'I always hoped the candles would set me alight.'

On the second week of his visit, Jorge was awakened by Adia knocking excitedly on his door. 'A parcel's arrived,' she sang out. 'It's for you.'

Jorge was baffled as he undid the wrapping. He knew of no one who would want to send him anything. Most surprising of all, it came from a country neither of them had heard of.

'Maybe it's from your father,' Adia suggested.

Jorge opened the envelope she handed him. In it was a card. *Hello, Puff-brain.*

The box turned out to be empty, but it was shrivelled and curled inside, as if it had dried from being soaked.

'Looks like someone tried to send you something frozen,' the chauffeur laughed. Jorge found a letter at the bottom, wrapped in plastic. He tore it open. His gaze fell instantly on Miguel's large, vigorous handwriting: *I'VE SEEN REAL SNOW!*

The address puzzled them even more: *c/o MV Zabaj, docked off Greenland.*

So much time had passed. Miguel's letter told of how he had travelled all over Europe and Africa. He explained in detail how he had stowed away all those years ago on an English ship bearing hemp and sugar, working first in the cargo hold and then the kitchen, just to sail away as far from them as he could.

Miguel urged his brother to join him. *Just forget that crazy old woman and leave that monkey house behind.*

He had no idea his baby brother had already done more than that. It was a letter that had been written to a child. Miguel couldn't have conceived how his brother had changed. The boy with the dreamer's eyes had begun perhaps to truly see the world.

425

One day as they sat among the abandoned villas by the sea, Jorge contrived to hold Verana's hand. The sun had gone down and he thought of Miguel in some busy port far away.

'I wonder if we'll ever come back to this place again,' he said.

'Of course we will,' replied Verana. 'My house is just a short walk from here.'

Jorge clucked his tongue. After a pause, he said, 'I'll have to go back to the capital in a few days. When I'm there, I feel I don't really want to come back here.'

'Why?' she seemed troubled. 'What about your house?'

'They'll probably break it up and move it away again.' Jorge shrugged. 'What does it matter?'

Verana seemed annoyed with him. She turned away and quietly watched the sea. The sun's purple-orange cast was fading from the sky. They both sat as if mesmerised for a long time.

'If it matters so little,' Verana finally said. 'Then I guess it won't matter much if I'm not here when you come back.' She turned to look at him. '*If* you do come back.'

'Why?' It was his turn to be concerned. He couldn't understand her sudden change of mood.

'Just a passing whim,' Verana said. 'You're not the only one who can leave and not come back.'

'You'd go without telling me?'

She thought for a moment, as if it had never occurred to her. 'It depends.'

Jorge got up to stretch his legs. It was getting dark. They had begun a discussion he feared they would never finish.

'Anyway,' Verana tilted her head. 'It may all be a passing whim.'

The light was quickly fading. Jorge turned around and found he couldn't make out the sea anymore. Verana's face was in the shadows. He said goodbye. But in the noise of the sea he wasn't sure she heard him. She seemed surprised when he walked away.

Through Ruben's intervention, Adia had received funds from Jorge's father to repair some of the damage to the house. One afternoon Jorge saw her moving about the music room with a broom and a dust cloth. He watched as she attacked the cobwebs in the corners, stopping only to wipe the sweat from her face.

Adia ran the rag over the old Steinway grand, coughing and wheezing at the cloud of dust she raised. She opened the lid and stopped for a while. Jorge saw the awe and longing on her face as she gazed at the row of ivory keys.

Jorge had walked on to the living room when he heard the bass note radiate from the piano. Its low, gloomy resonance floated out into the hall, droning through the air like a sad bumble bee. The halting notes that followed traced a faint melody that released all the pent up sweetness in the instrument that no one had touched for years.

The enchanting tune that trickled out into the house drew Jorge back to the music room, to find Adia regaining control of the piano Jose Zandro had bought for her long ago. Jorge came in just as she ended a flourish with a high pitched dot on a black key, lowering her hands slowly to her lap as the note decayed.

She smiled shyly at him. 'It was the first piece Jose taught me,' she said. 'I had to force myself to learn it if only to prove I loved him.'
She closed the lid and rested her chin on her clasped hands. 'It's good to know Jose left me something.'

When Jorge left the room she was bent over the piano with her dust cloth, wiping the ebony surface back to a forgotten gleam.

Jorge went to meet Verana outside the dance school. They walked to the fort.

'What's in the bag?' Verana asked.

Jorge thought it was too early to tell her. He muttered, 'Something for you.'

'Oh, a present,' she said, bringing her hands together as if in applause. 'How nice!'

Jorge cleared his throat. 'No. It's not a present.'

She seemed disappointed. But by then they had already reached the fort, so Jorge gave her the package. Verana sat down on a stone bench and opened it. She found some old letters, a little black notebook, and a pressed dried rose, which she held up with wonder, lifting it gingerly between her fingers. 'How pretty!'

She gave Jorge a puzzled look.

'They're my mother's letters,' he told her. 'Her diary, and one of the roses from the man who loved her.'

She wasn't sure of his intention, and waited for him to explain.

'I wish...' Jorge shifted from one foot to the other. 'I wish you could keep them for me...'

She bit her lip and stared at him.

Jorge swallowed before he said, 'They're all that mean anything to me.'

Verana put her hands on the bundle and looked over the ramparts at the sea.

'I'm touched you asked me,' she said.

Jorge stopped moving and looked at her intently. 'But, I'm sorry.'

Jorge waited as she lifted the packet from her lap and laid it aside on the bench. 'I can't.'

Jorge felt a pain. He looked at the set of his mother's things beside her. He had offered it to her like it was his heart.

'Why not?'

'Because I never keep anything,' answered Verana with blameless candour.

'Never?'

'I don't even keep gifts from my mother anymore. Or my father.'

She admitted to having a few mementos from her friends. 'But I'm not sure I won't lose those.'

Jorge was disdainful. 'Isn't anything important to you?' he asked her with veiled anger.

'Some things are,' Verana replied.

Jorge threw up his hands. He stepped over the broken wall and walked down to the water's edge. She followed him.

'You would know what really matters,' said Jorge, 'if you lived in a house that's been moved from place to place, so you don't know where it really belongs. It's like your life is just pieces strewn everywhere, like pebbles or garbage. Look....' He pointed to the littered sand at their feet. 'Just scattered there. They don't mean anything.'

'What are you trying to say?' Verana handed him back the bundle.

'If you ever valued anything or anyone you would know what I mean,' said Jorge, turning his back on her.

He heard her draw breath sharply. 'Well, Mr. So-and-so,' she said with a quiver in her voice, 'if you must know, I've valued quite a few things and people in my life!'

'Oh?' Jorge turned around to challenge her. 'Like who?'

She let out her breath. 'I'm not telling you. I'll never tell you!'

Verana turned around and walked away. Jorge watched her back, her hair flying in the wind.

So it baffled him even more when, on mustering the courage to say goodbye, she greeted him warmly at the door, then led him upstairs past the polychrome windows. They entered her room.

Verana showed him a stack of perfumed cards, letting him read them. He sneered at the effusive dedications.

'He gets them from Denmark,' Verana said. 'He says he'd give up anything for me.'

Her face was solemn.

Jorge laughed. Verana's cheeks reddened.

'They weren't signed at first,' she told him quietly. She seemed hurt.

Verana closed her eyes. 'I remember hoping that they might be from you.'

Back at the university, Jorge threw himself into the work of finishing his course. He was glad for the distraction. The labour was interrupted only occasionally by an evening at Solomon's house.

Their parties had become more tame. The young people who had been reckless and irrepressible at the start of the course had become sober and restrained.

'We're an unmemorable people,' Solomon said in the garden one night. 'We'll leave these islands as we found them. Volcanic, storm-infested, a convenient stop for migrating birds.'

One day Jorge came back from the College Library laden down with books, and found a card waiting in the letter tray for him.

Dear Mr. Studious, it said. *If you want to see me, call this number.*

Jorge could hardly believe his eyes. Verana was in the capital with him. Only a few months remained before the end of his studies, and Ruben had helped him to get work on one of the newspapers. Jorge called the number on Verana's card.

She sounded calm and self-assured on the phone. Jorge had expected to hear a hesitant girl's voice. The full timbre of a woman's speech that he heard made him think she was someone else.

'Of course it's me, silly,' she said. 'Who else would give you such chances?'

They agreed to meet at the lobby of the Imperial Hotel by the bay. Jorge arrived in the early evening.

How she had changed. An unsuspected side to her radiance had come to the fore. She was dressed formally and was wearing jewellery he didn't know she had. Somehow, in the time since he last saw her, she had turned worldly, and seemed at ease in the crowds of the capital.

'I've been accepted into the troupe,' she said smiling.

Over dinner, Jorge was entranced by a new flair in her manner. He kept trying to find signs of the roguish, endearing girl he would always remember.

'Does that mean you'll live here now?' Jorge asked with some surprise.

'Why, yes,' she answered. 'For a while.'

A half-smile played on her face as she gazed out the window. From their table they could see the brimming twine of lights along the curve of the bay.

He found himself enamoured again. But the vagueness of what she was doing in the capital nagged him.

How did she live? Who were her friends? He wanted to know everything, but found that Verana had thrown a veil he would never be able to breach again.

They parted outside the hotel. She stood beaming at him. Then she leaned forward to embrace him, offering her cheek to be kissed.

'Remember,' she said with that unaccustomed sparkle to her voice. 'Don't vanish like a puff of smoke again. At least without telling me.'

Jorge watched her walk off, her hair blown by the breeze from the bay.

A desolate feeling came over him. Somehow, he had always thought of having her to return to in Puerto Reina.

Suddenly, he was seized by a great urgency. The next day he got up at dawn, not having slept a wink.

He went straight to the shop in the city centre where he had found the porcelain marionettes like the ones Verana's mother had sent her from Venice. He bought an expensive pair, and with the same compulsion, he made his way to a jewellers next door to ask the price of a ring.

'For your fiancée?' asked the attendant.

'Yes,' Jorge lied. 'But I think her heart is set on a ruby.'

The attendant smiled indulgently and Jorge left. He planned to telephone Verana as many times as it took to convince her to meet him. She was good-humoured but evasive. The girlish playfulness in her voice pained him for being so quickly suppressed. She said she was busy. She had other plans. She was tired from a performance.

The meeting he longed for slipped further and further from his grasp. Then one day he called late at night and a man answered.

Her landlord, he thought. *She's still living in a boarding house.* But for days, the thought of the male voice assailed him, haunting his most wretched dreams.

Even the company of Solomon Dominguez and his other friends could not calm him down. One night after drinking they went out for a walk. They'd been going around in circles on the deserted campus when Jorge suddenly asked, 'Where are we *going*?'

'Why, nowhere,' said Solomon with a casualness Jorge had already ceased to understand. 'No need to be anxious.'

'You know how I love to go nowhere,' continued Solomon. 'As long as it's in the right direction.'

When they got back to Solomon's house, Jorge confessed what had been troubling him.

'Ah, you poor fool,' said Solomon, stretching out on his cushion. He picked up a bottle and ran his finger lovingly up and down its side.

'I've never had the misfortune to fall in love,' he confessed. 'Hence this substitute for the divine reeling of the soul I've never experienced.'

'I'm going to see her,' he vowed. 'I'll find out where she's staying. I'll climb a tree. Break the windows. Sleep on her doorstep.'

He kept planning to write her a long letter. He tried to devise ways to shame her into meeting him, so he could at least give her his gifts. Grab her or mock her like he used to, make her give up this foolishness and come back to Puerto Reina with him. What would happen if she agreed, he did not know.

'I'll make her come back,' Jorge kept muttering to himself. 'I'll drag her to the ship if I have to.'

So strong was his resolve that he went to the shipping office and bought two tickets for the journey. But their meeting seemed fated not to be.

Jorge tried every ruse he could think of, but Verana resisted all his entreaties. Her manner had become more flippant and unconcerned.

After many months, he was ready to renounce her. He swore he would never think of her again. But his thoughts always returned to the wonder of her. He failed to subdue his hunger for the strawberries on her skin, the secret sweetness that seeped into his dreams.

Then one night, nearly three years later, it was she who came to him. As before, it happened with no warning. She appeared at Ruben's house during a torrential downpour. Her clothes were soaked and she had been crying. Her speech was slurred and she stumbled like she was a little drunk.

'I'll never go back to that beast!' she said as Jorge helped her into the room.

'What happened?' he asked.

'The lout's been going backstage, as we say. Every other woman in the troupe, not just me.'

Her long hair was curled, her lips bright red with lipstick. The mascara she wore made her pretty face look hard, and there was a glint of panic in her eyes.

Verana explained how she stormed out after a fight with the man she was living with. She had been walking in the rain for hours.

'He'll never see me again,' she said with her cold resolve. She crossed her arms and sank into the chair. Jorge struggled to find in the confusion of that night the Verana of years before. How she had been transformed. Yet certain expressions on her face still called up that time when he had best known her.

Poor fool! He heard Solomon saying again. *You poor fool!*

Verana sucked on a tooth and was lost in thought. She uncrossed her arms with a vexed sigh and said sadly, 'I really have nowhere to go.'

'You can stay here as long as you want,' Jorge said. 'I'll explain it to my uncle. He really will not mind.'

Verana shook her head and let out a cruel laugh. 'You don't understand.'

She walked across to the window and stared at the rain outside. After a long moment, she turned to him and revealed, 'I'm pregnant.'

Her sorrow welled up and again she sobbed. 'I'm carrying *his child*.'

She slumped down into a chair by the book case. Jorge paced back and forth as Verana buried her face in her hands.

'What about your mother?' he said.

Verana looked up, not knowing what he meant. 'What about her?'

'Surely she can help.'

She closed her eyes and kept shaking her head.

'I'll never see her again,' she moaned. She let out another disdainful laugh. 'Didn't you know? No one *ever* comes back from Spain.'

Jorge used to think nothing of telling her he looked at her picture almost every night. He thought of telling her he had been planning to buy her a ring. But now he was suddenly ashamed.

He wondered what had happened in the stretch of oblivion when she stopped writing to him and just disappeared from his life. He remembered how in that last letter Verana sent long ago, she told him about a man who had started sending her flowers.

'What's everyone going to think?' Verana said, wiping her tears. 'Just another woman with a bastard child.'

'But Verana...'

'No! I've made up my mind.' She stood up and walked towards the door.

'I'm going away from him,' she said quietly. 'From *you*. From *everyone*.'

She had whispered the last words. Jorge was suddenly afraid.

Verana pushed back her hair and looked up. 'I've met someone else. He's offered to take me away.'

'You'll go from man to man?' Jorge said. 'From place to place?' He never dreamed things could be like this.

'We're all destined to go away,' said Verana. 'To wander.'

'Where will you go?' Jorge came towards her.

She closed her eyes. 'I don't know. Who knows where fate will blow us? Any of us.'

'You'll need money.'

Jorge hurried into his room and pulled out the drawer where he locked all his money away. He stuffed what he could into an envelope and ran out to the living room.

Verana was gone.

There was no goodbye, no note to explain. There was just the rain. Jorge would never find her again. But he would keep his image of her, looking at the one picture she had given him until his vision began to blur. It was taken on a day that would remain bright forever, the sun shining down on Santo Domingo Square, the trees behind her, with a smile in those eyes that were rarely sad until now, her face as enthralling as that irretrievable time.

XI.

Jorge's stay in the capital came to an end. He told Ruben he wanted none of the jobs he had arranged for him. He sailed for Puerto Reina as soon as his papers from the university arrived.

So he returned home, just as his mother had come back from San Gabriel in the year before he was born, with a knowledge of loss. Yet Jorge couldn't help feeling the exhilaration of other homecomings, the sun rising over the sea as they neared the port.

He felt a sense of restitution when the ship finally docked, and the gangway was rolled into place with a tremendous metallic creak that echoed through the morning air. Jorge bided his time as the vessel emptied.

The mass of new arrivals streamed out of the gate. The pier was deserted again by the time he came down with his bags.

Someone gave a piercing whistle as he made his way towards the exit.

'Hey!' a man called out to him from behind the flower stalls. Jorge stopped and waited.

An old man came shuffling towards him. In the fresh lilac light, Jorge recognised the venerable man of voices from the plaza.

It was a thrill to see him again after all this time. But the world had not been kind to the man of awesome, disconcerting talents.

His face was gaunt, his skin all wizened, a man barely clinging to life. He held up his hand to shield his eyes from the rising glare of the sun, and squinted at Jorge.

'My God!' the old man laughed through his ruined teeth. He stood precariously on tired, faltering legs, so light from hunger the slightest breeze seemed enough to make him sway.

Jorge reached into his pocket and flipped the old man a coin. The ventriloquist clucked his tongue and flipped it back.

'No, no, no,' he cleared his throat and rasped, 'It's me who owes you.'

He motioned for Jorge to come near. Jorge approached as the old man fumbled despairingly in his pockets then, with a smile, held up something. It was the sorcerous old pouch Jorge would never forget.

'You asked me to do something before you left. It was oh...' The ventriloquist narrowed his eyes and looked away to think, '...a long time ago. A long, long time it seems.'

'But I haven't forgotten.' The old man's face brightened. 'A sweet-looking girl who lived in a house behind the square.'

'Yes,' said Jorge, twinged to be reminded of a wish he had erased from his mind.

'You wanted her to say something,' continued the old man, holding the strange pouch to Jorge. 'Go on. *Listen.*'

Jorge held his ear to the mouth of the pouch. He heard a babble of voices, cacophonous and indistinct. But there was one. Just laughter and a few shy words.

Jorge was overwhelmed. It wasn't just rocks or lizards that the master of voices could cause to speak. It was the voice of Jorge's heart.

In the year that followed as he tried to reclaim his home, Jorge couldn't stop himself from wandering past the dance school in Santo Domingo Square, perhaps with some hope that Verana might suddenly appear. Some mornings he saw the nuns who were still herding young children as they dragged their feet towards the school.

Going through the possessions he had accumulated in the capital, Jorge found the gift-wrapped offering he had never had the chance to give. He tore open the luxurious wrapping he remembered choosing with such care, and one of the porcelain dolls tumbled down to his feet.

That same day he took a ride to the pier with the precious figurines in their shiny silk dresses, and when he got there, he hurled them as far as he could into the sea. The ceramic figures sank into the oily eddies in the water.

It was late afternoon. The harsh sunlight had ripened into amber. He spent the quiet hours loitering around the dock, sitting on rusty bollards to watch the rickety traffic of aging, lopsided tugboats. The smell of grease and seawater mingled into the familiar intoxication of his childhood. He watched as an approaching ship blew its powerful horn.

A flock of birds flew shrieking past the tower which Jorge and his brother used to climb. He walked over to its base and ran his hand over the rough, corroded rungs. Out of boredom, he decided to climb. As he got up halfway, he heard someone shouting. He looked down to see a number of people stopping to look up at him. They seemed intrigued by what he was going to do.

Jorge clung on to the rung and observed with idle curiosity as the newly arrived ship was laboriously manoeuvred to berth. He heard someone calling his name again.

Finally, the hawsers were tied fast and the vessel came to rest. Jorge climbed down from the tower. He stood behind a cluster of well-wishers along the vessel's side. A man on deck kept shouting his name.

Jorge found it strange.

At last, the gangway's barrier was lifted and the anxious passengers came streaming down. Jorge struggled to recognise the dark man who hopped down the steps with no bags and came running towards him.

His puzzlement turned to disbelief when the stranger grabbed him by the shoulders and shouted in his ear: 'It's me, Puff-brain!'

Miguel had grown very brawny and tall, with a rough stubble on his face. He slapped Jorge on the back with a grin. 'You're still here you little flower.'

He had had a lifetime of learning from the sailors he had so revered before. He looked haggard and seemed to have aged much more than Jorge. His fanciful eyes had grown dull and world-weary. Miguel had sailed all over three oceans and said he would be waiting 'for the monsoons to change' so he could continue on to Athens, Istanbul, and Sicily.

Jorge found it hard to get accustomed to his brother as a grown man, his strong white teeth grinning at him with a lecher's glee, stark against his sun-dimmed face.

Miguel had gleaned lessons from his erratic life that gave some comfort to Jorge.

'You have to learn to trust the wind,' said Miguel. 'Go where it blows you. No matter how far you sail, there will always be stars above you.'

There was a nervous energy about Miguel as Jorge took him wandering around the city. His attention lingered on the familiar nooks only briefly, before he was impatient to move on again. He seemed perennially beset by some unseen beacon that called to him from far away.

Miguel walked with a restless expectancy, his eyes fixed on the distance ahead, like a man accustomed to scanning the horizon for more of the earth to reveal itself. Jorge could tell his brother was back only for a short time.

'Same old dusty hole,' Miguel spat. 'How can you bear to stay here?'

They walked past the old clubs of *Calle* Luna, from which they were once barred as boys. Most of them were just empty, bat-infested shells now. The brothers stood at the corner where the taxis used to stop.

Miguel's eyes shone. 'Ah, where our great quest began!'

He laughed and put his hand on Jorge's shoulder. 'So father's secret was not such a great secret after all,' he said as they walked on. 'But I would have given anything back then to learn what went on behind those curtains.'

Miguel kicked a broken bottle out of the way. 'Now I'm usually drunk when the crucial moment comes, and someone has to tell me what happened.'

Miguel gave his sneering attention to the bars' musty remains. 'Makes you wonder what they were all so cryptic about.'

Jorge took his brother to the quiet stretch between the old market and the docks. They stopped at the empty, scorched field where the *Feria Nacional* once held its fairs.

Miguel knew nothing about the terrible things that had happened in his absence. He only remembered the vivid spectacles in the Feria's warmly lit tents.

The young men continued walking. After a long time in silence, Miguel suddenly said, 'What? What did you say?'

Jorge turned to him, surprised. He shook his head. 'I didn't say anything.'

Miguel looked around with a bemused smile. 'I was sure I heard you speak.'

The street behind them was dead still between the sleepy buildings.

Miguel scratched his head. 'For a moment I thought someone might be toying with us.'

It became clear to Jorge that his brother still lived in the bewitched medium of their childhood. 'You never know where that scoundrel of a ventriloquist is lurking,' Miguel said with a laugh.

They reached the main road again and Miguel stopped to look back. He snickered like he used to. 'It's so quiet in this town,' he said. 'It's like our minds are always playing tricks on us.'

Jorge listened to his brother tell his sailors' tales. Miguel bragged about the fights he had had, lifted his shirt to show the scar on his left side from a drunken knife thrust. There were indeed women at every port, he said.

'But you count how much money you have when you go to see them.' He gave Jorge a wink. 'Then you count it again when you're done.'

They spent the evening at a new bar on Fort Road. It had Christmas lights that twinkled all year long, its tables spread out along the pavement right up to the old fountain. There was a dais in the corner where musicians performed.

That night, during a break in the show, the drunken bar owner got up onstage. There was a smattering of applause from his friends.

'You all came here on the right night,' he said through the microphone. 'Right night,' he mumbled. 'You're going get a surprise.'

There were cheers and whistles from the tables as the man raised his arm in a gesture that seemed eerily familiar. 'LADIES AND GENTLEMEEEN!'

The audience fell silent as the lone drummer on the stage beat out a protracted drum roll. 'All right, no gentlemen then.'

There was some laughter. The lights were aimed at a large fan off the stage blowing towards the audience.

The bar owner took the microphone and stood near the fan. An assistant came up and handed him a large cushion.

The drunken man screamed into the microphone. 'WHAT YOU'VE ALL BEEN WAITING FOR!'

Again, the drum roll.

'OUR DARK DAY...'

Jorge grew tense. The words set off memories from another time. Once again he heard volleys that rocked the night. He heard the deafening fusillades from when the rebels had tried to take over the city.

'THERE YOU ARE LADIES AND GENTLEMEN!' screamed the drunken man on the stage. 'IT'S SUMMER SNOW!'

With a knife he had ripped the cushion and emptied its contents in front of the whirling fan. Puffs of cotton blew everywhere.

The tipsy crowd emitted a sound of wonder, then laughed as the tables were engulfed in the tufty vortex of cotton. White wisps flew up and settled on the pavement and the guests, the glasses on the tables. They feathered the acacias along the roadside and floated about dreamily for a while.

Jorge laughed with all the others, but admitted to himself that before the joke was revealed, his heart had indulged a tantalizing wish. For an instant the thought beguiled him of Maya making a sudden appearance in his life like she had once before.

But it was not to be. The rebellion was just a distant memory now, that reckless moment that had already been swept into the ravenous pull of the past, retrieved only by the tenacious nostalgia of drunks.

Miguel and Jorge stumbled out with the last customers at dawn, still covered with tufts of cotton.

'I guess it's better than real snow,' laughed Miguel. 'It won't give you pneumonia.'

Some days later, Miguel spoke of the time he was thrown into the brig in Panama. 'There's a ritual when you first end up behind bars,' he explained. 'There was a man there. He was still a little drunk. Just slightly bigger than me.'

Jorge had lost track of the brawls and entanglements his brother had recounted in the previous nights. He asked, 'What happened this time?'

'...couldn't hurt his head no matter how I tried,' Miguel was saying. 'So I jumped on his shoulders and forced him to the ground.'

'And?'

'I pinned him down and ate his eyes.'

Jorge didn't need to hear anymore. He knew that the brother he had played with in the yard was no more. In his place was this brutal, hardened stranger.

So it surprised him to see Miguel in their mother's room one day, shaking the water-filled dome on the bureau and staring fixedly at the watery dance of white flecks. Jorge entered and Miguel turned to him with a smile. He leaned back and stretched out his arms on the chair. Then he got up.

'She used to sit there and shake that thing for hours to entertain me,' he said, looking at the bureau. He walked to the door. 'I wonder if she ever thought one of her sons would go to a place with real snow.'

It was only a few days before Miguel had to leave again. One morning he said a gruff goodbye to Jorge and was gone once more. His ship sailed out of Puerto Reina in the evening, and Jorge heard it across the distance as it blew its horn.

Later that year the Aguada River swelled again and the house was swamped. It was the worst deluge in a long time. People from the village waded through the waist-high muddy water, calling out the names of sons and daughters.

The inundation took a few days to recede, and left flood marks on the walls that seemed impossible to expunge. After many scrubbings, a trace of the waterline remained, an imprint of another disaster the house had survived.

Out in the yard, a few monstrous mud puddles held out, miniature, opaque ponds that attracted flies. Adia peevishly scratched her head. '*Ay! Ay!* What's one to do?'

She had just washed off the muck from her hands when the nuns arrived. They seemed to glide along the sludge-covered path in their spotless white habits. They appeared to be out on a special mission. The mother superior was with them, set apart by her commanding garb of grey.

Jorge was ashamed that his first impulse was to run and hide. But it had been quite a while since their last visit, and none of the sisters recognised him as the boy they once tried to drag away to their school.

They revealed that their order was in the midst of building an orphanage in the city. As they struggled to explain the purpose of their visit, it became clear to Jorge, to his growing discomfiture, that they had come to him as to someone who could grant them a favour.

'We know some day you might want to leave this house,' the mother superior said, her hands clasped to her chest. The other nuns were ranged around her, heads tilted towards Jorge in an attitude of indulgence. No longer the fearsome doves of unyielding purity who had tyrannised him as a child.

'Many people are leaving our city as we all know,' continued the mother superior, 'leaving their property to the mercy of nature...or any *vagrant* who might happen by.' She shuddered at the word *vagrant*.

The nun cleared her throat for a second time, like one about to ask a weighty favour. 'If you should ever decide to leave this humble city for good,' she said. 'We were wondering if you would consider bequeathing the house to our orphanage. To help the unfortunates who flock daily to our care.'

Jorge excused himself and walked off to think. He was secretly aghast at the burden suddenly placed on his shoulders. It seemed not so long ago that he remembered waking up in the empty, forbidding house with many rooms he dared not go, not knowing what secrets they harboured or what purposes they served. Now he was being asked to decide its fate.

Jorge was assailed by a listless indecision, and he retreated towards the back fence, as far away from the nuns as possible. All the while they stood and watched him closely, alert for any signs of what he might be thinking.

That drowsy detachment had caught up with him again. The half-waking state in which he had stumbled through his days in the capital. As if his life for the past five years had all been a long, fitful sleep. Now he was jolted awake.

There was his father to consult about the decision. There was Miguel. And of course there was Adia. Jorge found he still needed them all to shield him from the naked choices of the world.

As he mulled over the dilemma, the sisters were stirred into action, fearing perhaps that Jorge's silence might mean a refusal.

'There's someone we brought along who's been wanting to see you,' the mother superior was saying. A nun in the back squeezed past the others to stand before Jorge. He saw her sad face and he understood why, after all these years, the nuns had come.

The mother superior stood aside and said, 'You perhaps remember Sister Melba.'

Jorge was stupefied to see her. She was grinning at him through her tears. She turned away for a moment to wipe her eyes. When she looked at him again he saw that under her nun's cap, her face was bright and happy. He had never seen her looking so content.

Melba strode up to him and gave him a hug. She struggled to make him bend down so she could kiss his cheek. 'How big you've grown!'

Jorge, smiling back, answered, 'So have you.'

A quizzical look came over Melba's face, as if trying to remember something. Then she took Jorge by the hand and coolly led him into the house. They marched briskly down the hall and entered the kitchen. There, Melba reached into the cupboard and brought out something. It was the empty glass jar in which they had once kept the glowing spider. Jorge watched as Melba strode out into the yard. She stopped at the edge of the gravel path and smashed the jar.

Again, Jorge felt that he had been shaken awake.

'Sometimes we have to look elsewhere to find the light,' Sister Melba said. The other nuns had observed her actions with shock and mounting dread. Then, while Melba walked back to join her fellow sisters, Jorge touched with his shoe the fragments of the broken jar. Then he understood that for the second time in his life, Melba had weaned him.

Jorge bid the nuns goodbye and promised he would consider their request. They left waving and hopeful.

Melba's unexpected appearance left Jorge with many things to ponder. For days after the visit, he kept coming out to where she had smashed the jar. For some reason the act remained in his mind. It took him a long time to understand its meaning.

Then one afternoon, it finally came to him. He went out again and crushed the last slivers of the glass into the gravel. They glittered briefly in the sun and Jorge knew.

Melba's act made him see how his life had been a prolonged attachment to places and things, long after they had ceased to sustain him. So it was with many things, which he gave up only with great reluctance, as if grasping for a permanence he had never known.

That was perhaps why, unlike Miguel or his father, he stayed put in a bare house with its haunted memories, years after everyone else had left. Returning to it even when the disastrous surges of the Aguada River had made it impossible to live in. It was at that moment that Jorge made up his mind to abandon the house he was born in.

He had found work months before at the editorial offices of *El Tiempo*, and the Chief Editor offered him the use of quarters above the paper's printing presses. The accommodations were just across the road from the plaza, and Jorge could come down late at night or early in the morning for his walks. At midnight the streets were as quiet as in the time when the town had just been built on the swamps.

He liked to stroll, whistling to himself in the privacy of that hour, peering at the elaborate vine-covered buildings that had fascinated him as a child. He tried to discern the ghostly essence that fled from their niches at night and left the feeling that something was constantly being missed, something that always absconded into the shadows with its booty of time.

Jorge moved all his possessions to the rooms provided by *El Tiempo*. From then on he began coming to the house in Aguada only on Sundays when he had nothing to do. Often Adia would be away at church for mass.

Once he arrived at the house just as it began to rain. He walked through the rooms looking out of the windows, enjoying the soothing fullness that the drizzle gave to the silence. *Goblin's tears*. He heard the voice clearly in his head.

He passed his mother's room, with its spectral scent of roses in the air. The room was the only place that the floods did not invade, and things remained oddly dry. Jorge often came in and stood in front of the broken mirror Adia had restored. It was she who had glued it back together like the fragments of memories he had been too young to record, as he lay in the crib in his mother's room, staring with his infant's eyes at the hazy visions he still couldn't understand. That room was a place where he felt everything was just about to happen, and to see everything he only had to close his eyes.

Once in his room above the presses, Jorge woke up. It was the middle of the night and he couldn't get back to sleep. So he got up and found his way down to the plaza. There was a lot of noise, like some unseen congregation were spread out in the blackness around him. Jorge walked through the dark, deserted promenade. Voices coming from the shadows filled the night with a merry hubbub. There was laughter over the empty benches, giggling and shouts behind the trees. There was such a din Jorge wondered why no one in the sleeping street was roused. Finally, around daybreak it all stopped.

In the same abrupt way he had awakened, Jorge understood that something had come to an end. The dawn broke with such a lonely silence that he suddenly knew that the ventriloquist was dead.

With a bitter heart Jorge climbed the dim stairwell back to his room, and briefly he heard the clamour again, passing above his head like a spinning disk that banked and then disappeared. *A voice. There's always a voice. Always always always. There's a voice. Trying to say something Always. Always always. Hear that voice. Try to hear what it says.*

Adia had just discovered, with a delighted cry, the clumps of mushrooms growing along the boundaries of the house when Ruben came for a visit. He noticed the craters left by the mud pools and said the house looked worse than he remembered. Adia vented her outrage about the last flood, wondering if she'd ever see the last of it.

'Don't wish for the impossible,' chuckled Ruben. 'It's no more than our lot. Didn't they say our first ancestors crawled out of the sea?' He turned to Jorge and added, 'Maybe the oceans are calling us back.'

They walked together on the gravel path. Ruben turned his gaze towards the field in the back. 'Could it be,' he said quietly, 'there's really nowhere left to go?'

His troubles had only worsened since Jorge left the capital. The national papers reported almost daily on charges that Ruben had profited from the smuggling of perfume, cigarettes and firearms into the country over many years.

For all his worries, Ruben seemed determined to appear calm. He was casual about the flood marks that so dismayed Adia. He sat in the dining room with them and recounted worse calamities from the river. 'I remember eating my lunch with Augusto and Rosanna on the piano top while the music room flooded all around us,' Ruben laughed. He cast his glassy gaze towards the hall.

'Jorge,' his uncle said it at the end of the meal. It hung like an ending to the evening's good spirits. Jorge recognised that quiet, secretive voice his uncle used when he had urgent, disturbing news to break.

Jorge leaned forward to listen.

Ruben unclasped his hands and leaned back in his chair. Looking intently at Jorge, he said, 'I'm sorry to tell you, but your father has died.'

The years had prepared Jorge for this moment. He had contemplated it at various times, with indifference, or sometimes with regret.

Ruben was laying envelopes on the table from his open attaché case. '...papers are in my office in the capital,' he was saying. None of it made much sense to him at the time, but Jorge welcomed the particulars his uncle offered because the mesh of arrangements helped him contain the cold barrenness he felt inside.

They moved to the living room to discuss the matter point by point. Jorge wanted it finished, to be done, the door to be finally closed. Ruben took out another envelope from his pocket. 'You'll have to settle it with your brother,' he told Jorge. 'But, of course, your father left the house to both of you.'

With a wry air, Ruben spread out his hands to indicate the flood-stained living room. 'So you have an inheritance after all.'

Jorge did not laugh because he was afraid his calm would shatter. But he thought with a chill about the nuns who had come months before. Were they prompted by some prophetic intuition?

Ruben stayed up late with Jorge, having a few drinks from a bottle of whiskey he had brought. Finally, yawning and stretching, he came over and placed a hand on Jorge's shoulder.

He then walked to the foot of the stairs and stopped. 'It happened as he slept,' he revealed. 'It was very peaceful.'

When he was gone, Jorge stayed up the rest of the night looking through the papers his uncle had given him. Then almost at daybreak, he went out to the front and stood where his father's car used to stand, as if the empty driveway were somehow a reminder of the space his father had left.

He came back into the house feeling sorry that his father had made no attempt to make himself mean something to Miguel or him. But he felt a sense of relief all the same, thinking he finally had a claim, no matter how absurd, to this battered, dreary house that had been moved from place to place.

'This house was left to me,' he said softly. This motley, dimly Gothic assemblage of timber was his home, cradle of an instinct in him that always craved a return.

In the last envelope Ruben had given him, Jorge found a faded colour photograph. It was taken long ago, when he and Miguel were small boys. Their father was holding both their hands as they smiled for the camera, their car on one side with the doors open, and the sea a cobalt blue behind them.

Both he and his brother were very young, and neither of them had a memory of the day when the picture was taken. Jorge was startled to see it, as if some trickster had slipped it into their lives. That forgotten photograph seemed an improbable fiction now. It told of a time beyond recollection when their father had been happy and had taken his sons to the sea, when he had enjoyed their sunny antics and worked unremembered acts of love.

Jorge found himself outside Santo Domingo church late one afternoon. He glimpsed the gilded tracery behind the altar at the end of the wide rows of empty pews, where now and then a sly vagrant crept in to sleep. He decided to go inside. The air smelled of candles and jasmine bouquets from the morning service. He felt peaceful in the airy, stained glass calm, and ended up staying longer than he had planned. The light outside the doors slowly grew dim.

'Is there something troubling you?' a woman's voice gently addressed him. 'You need someone to talk to?'

Jorge turned and saw the white habit in the aisle. The nun was smiling kindly down at him.

'Sister Melba!' Jorge's voice echoed in the empty space.

'Don't be silly,' Melba replied. 'I'll always be Melba to you. Move over.' She slid into the pew beside him.

They talked for a long time, like they used to in the front yard before Melba left their house. Jorge told her about the things that had been on his mind for a long time.

'There are questions I could only ask someone like you,' he said.

'Oh? Like what?'

'Like...' he was reluctant to tell her.

'Go on.'

'Well, for one. Is there really—you know.' Jorge pointed upwards. 'Up *there.*'

Melba raised her gaze to the vaulted ceiling. 'Hm. That's the kind of thing we better discuss outside.'

She took Jorge by the wrist and led him out.

Dusk had gathered over the square. Red streaks glowed in the sky's dimming lavender. Finally, he asked her what he wanted to know. 'Are you happy?'

Melba screwed up her face. 'Well...I admit, I pray and I pray. But sometimes I still wonder. Is there *really* anyone listening?'

'I thought so,' Jorge said. For some reason he remembered the night long ago when his father left. There was no one listening then. There was just the quiet night with no answer.

He said goodbye to Melba. But as Jorge walked away, she called after him. He looked back and waited.

'All the same,' Melba said, coming closer. 'There are times when I'm happy and I feel the need to thank something.'

'For what?'

Melba spread her hands and smiled. 'For everything.'

Jorge left the square and walked towards the corner. He glanced up at the last shimmer in the sky and remembered the jittery dot of light he and Melba kept in a jar when they were younger. Jorge would never meet her again, but he would remember how she was that day.

She looked happy.

XII.

Jorge was reunited with his friend Salvador del Mundo II, who had become one of the reporters in *El Tiempo*'s hot and sleepy newsroom, while his father, the elder, primogenitive saviour of the world, Salvador I, maintained his watchful eye over the paper's presses.

'I think up the words,' Jorge's friend said. 'My father makes sure they are reproduced and brought to the people.'

'He's like Moses, I guess. I'm like...' Salvador groped for an analogy, but feared that the thought was taking him down a blasphemous path. He swallowed. 'I'm just me, your humble friend Salvie.'

He had given himself a moniker that he thought sounded quite American, which he deemed more suited to his title of reporter, rather than the old-fashioned, and frankly staid, *periodista*.

Jorge liked working at *El Tiempo*. It was his task to send out reporters on their daily assignments. They were hardy, itinerant people, some in their early twenties, others well into their fifties, accustomed to travelling to every corner of the archipelago, sailing on

471

the ships now owned by Don Mariano Zandro's old competitors. As members of the press they received a discount, and sometimes took their wives and children to travel for free.

It was part of Jorge's job to plan the layout of the Sunday magazine. In the back pages he tried to fit in wedding announcements with sale coupons and invitations to government auctions. There were warnings about infectious diseases or nefarious individuals, bulletins about missing persons, and, finally, three pages of obituaries.

That was how he learned of Emilia Zandro's fate. She had died quietly in a pauper's hospital. In her last years she had joined many charities and tried to have monuments built.

It showed how much time had passed and how the family had fallen from when Emilia's father, Don Mariano, had taken out a half page to announce his daughter's engagement. Emilia's obituary was the size of a postage stamp, which was squeezed between a paid birthday greeting and a formal invitation to pre-qualify and bid for pipes and brass faucets, forfeited by a local bank for bad loans.

One of the most memorable stories the paper printed since Jorge started was about the disappearance of cabriolets from Puerto Reina's roads. The article described how the horses that had clomped through the city years ago had all died, their colourful carriages chopped up and burned. It was a story that made Jorge notice the silence in the inner lanes for the first time.

He realised one day how the air was strangely still as he walked in the narrow passage between the houses of the old district. The breeze carried none of the echoes that had made the walls whisper when he was a child. He had started wearing immaculate white shirts with starched collars. The Japanese pomade he used left a lingering sweet scent, and he wasn't aware that the children who loitered in Aguada were frightened of him.

One Sunday the Society section of the magazine contained a picture of a stout Chinese businessman cheerfully handing over a large donation to a hospice in the city. Jorge was happy to see Edgar Allan in all his rotund prosperity, recalling the round-faced boy who had cried at the street corner where his father had set fire to a magnificent house of paper. It underscored how the city he had known as a child had disappeared, as if some relentless, unseen conflagration had consumed it so completely no trace was left.

Jorge had become one of the grown men that he and Miguel used to eye with suspicion whenever they passed them on the street. The sound of his heels clacking on the pavement conveyed the urgency of his gait. He always had a folded handkerchief in his pocket with his embroidered initials that he liked to finger when he wanted to appear relaxed, his hands in his pockets.

From his visits to the house in Aguada, he had already taken away the snow-filled dome from his mother's bureau. It found a place in his bookshelf, where most of Joseph's abandoned books had long been moved.

Sometimes Adia came to see him in the newsroom, bringing something she had cooked. On occasion Jorge would take her to one of the restaurants that had opened along Fort Road, to dine while watching the small boats gliding back and forth from San Gabriel.

One day, Adia appeared at the *El Tiempo* office. She came to his desk and put down a heavy leather case she had brought from Aguada.

'It was in Maya's old room,' she said smiling.

Jorge opened the case. It was a typewriter. On its keys Maya had thumped out her fierce denunciations of the state. Jorge put his hand on the lever, pulled it with a whirring sound, watched it move the hefty drum smoothly to one side, before springing back with a ping. He smiled.

The resilient mechanism seemed somehow imbued with Maya's insurgent spirit. Jorge got up and embraced Adia with gratitude. She was so embarrassed before the roomful of reporters, Jorge couldn't stop her from leaving.

He caught up with her in the hallway.

'There were other things I came to give you.' She took out some envelopes from her bag and gave it to him. 'These arrived yesterday from your uncle Ruben.'

They contained some of his father's papers. Jorge riffled through the contents of two envelopes, and in the second one he found a short note folded around a beautiful pendant. Jorge dropped it into his palm.

Adia seemed shaken. 'My God,' she whispered. 'It's the amethyst *rose*.'

Jorge fingered the ornament that his mother had brought back from San Gabriel before she died. Then he unfolded the note, surprised that his hands were beginning to shake. It was addressed to Jorge and his brother, written long ago, on some night of regret or guilt, when perhaps their father had gotten his first intimation of death. In one line it gave a shattering glimpse into their lives:

I loved your mother, but her heart was in another place.

For the third night, Jorge lay sleepless in the tiresome darkness of his room, toying with the amethyst rose. He stared bleary-eyed at the light rooted to the ceiling from the streetlamp across the plaza. He thought of those anxious early years, when the night was just the fringe of the yet unseen life that awaited him.

Jorge gently closed his fingers on his mother's pendant, with only an inkling of what it meant. He felt there was some shadow in the gloom he needed to chase away.

The persistent impulse brought him to his desk. There in one drawer he kept the sheaf of jottings he had amassed over the years. At first it had been no different to writing a shopping list. He told Salvador how he had been writing down things about his family, to keep from forgetting. But the heap of pages in his drawer had grown.

Jorge kept looking at his scribbled sheets, like an entomologist with his assortment of rare moths, trying to divine how their diverse peculiarities revealed the hidden purpose of the world. But that night he made a Herculean effort and found a vision buried in them that had been hounding him for years.

Then and there, he took pen and paper and tried to put it all in order. He had many false starts.

After many years they found out...
After a long time they learned...
Finally, I learned...

None of them was good enough. He picked up the pendant, intuiting that if there was any way to move forward, it would be through that enchanting, tragic rose.

So the next day, before Adia could leave Aguada for mass, Jorge was at the door. She came out in her Sunday clothes, the talc on her face not quite rubbed in.

'Oh! You're coming with me?' She was pleasantly surprised.

Jorge held up the amethyst rose. 'Tell me.'

Adia stepped back. 'Tell you what?'

Jorge bore down on her, insistent. 'Tell me everything.'

'What do you want to know?'

'This was found on my mother's bedside,' Jorge said. 'That much you told me long ago.'

'And?' Adia crossed her arms and leaned against the wall.

'What about the rest?' Jorge demanded. 'How did it all happen?'

Adia sighed and looked at the bright day outside. She had always known this day would come. 'Let's go then.'

They sat in the living room. And there, she told him all about the roses from San Gabriel. The telling did not finish until midnight of that day. In the end, she told her grandson everything she had not dared disclose before.

Jorge went back to his quarters early the next Monday. He managed to go to work, his mind in a daze. But that night he slept with a smile on his face. Everything was finally clear. At last he had found a way to begin.

The next evening he pulled out Maya's typewriter from its place in the closet. Then he tapped out the line that would release his own deluge of telling:

Three years before their mother Rosanna died, she found someone who loved her more than their father. That day in July she got up at dawn...

Two days later, Adia was at his door.

'It's been following me,' she said with a haunted look.

'Who has?'

'Nobody.'

Jorge opened the door and let her in. She sat down by the desk. She waited until Jorge had settled before speaking.

'The tongue of flame,' she said.

'What?'

'It hounds people who are not long for this world.'

Jorge started to laugh.

'I look out at night,' Adia went on, 'and it's outside my window, floating in the air. Then this morning I woke up before dawn. I couldn't sleep. I opened the window and there it was. On top of the old tree, like a crown of butterflies. Tongues of flame, waiting just for me.'

Jorge got up and went to his closet. He pulled out some clothes and put them in a bag. 'Is my old room still clean enough to use?' he asked.

Adia looked up. 'Why?'

'I'm going back with you for a few days.'

Adia blushed. 'Don't be dramatic. I'm not the first old woman to start seeing things.'

'Even so.'

At the house Adia showed him a mark on the wall where she said a tongue of flame had burnt through. Jorge looked closely, and there it was, scorched into the wall, the indelible shadow of a butterfly.

He woke up in the middle of the night to hear Adia calling. He found her shivering in bed. 'I'm so cold,' she whimpered. 'That breeze just keeps seeping in.'

Jorge closed the window and lay a second blanket on her. He lay a hand on her shoulder before he left the room.

'Please make sure to shut the door,' she pleaded weakly. 'Someone keeps waking me up with their damn knocking.'

The next day, Adia swore she was fine. She insisted Jorge go back to town. Some weeks passed when nothing happened to cause alarm. But one night, he woke up from a deep sleep.

A bubbling sound forced him to come out of bed. He searched for several moments before he recognised the source of the strange noise. He turned on the lamp and saw the snow-filled dome on the shelf.

The white flecks were swirling frenziedly in the water, as though someone had been shaking it. Jorge was transfixed by the storm of imaginary snowflakes. Just as the flurry started to settle down, the eerie tempest began all over again. It rocked the dome with such violence it nearly fell to the floor.

In time, it quietened down and a last forlorn speck floated down to rest. Baffled and weary, Jorge turned off the lamp and went back to bed. He was awakened by a knock just before daybreak. The chauffeur stood there leaning against the wall. He had come to say that Adia had died in her sleep.

Looking back, Jorge should have known that Adia's strange disquiet had something to do with her last revelations to him. For she had told him her own story, the most important story she would ever tell. The strain of shedding the burden of many years was more than she could bear. As if the sudden freedom made her feel so light, there were no more fetters to hold her down.

Jorge didn't know that as he sat down for another sleepless night at his desk, agog with all that Adia had told him, in her own room in Aguada, Adia was lying down to rest. She pictured the fields on her father's plantation where she used to play as a child. As a sleepy fog came down upon her, she thought she heard a voice calling her name.

It was the voice of her mother, long dead, as she searched all over the fields long ago, calling for her errant daughter to come home. Finally, from an urge she had had for a long time, Adia threw off the sheets

482

in her chilly room and answered her mother's distant call.

'I'm coming,' she said feebly that night, shivering, weak with a sadness she couldn't fathom. 'I'm coming now!'

Adia had carried her secret, unable to disclose it until the right time had come. She bore the weight of a story so oppressive it seemed the earth itself wanted to tell it through her. In the end, she had passed on the knowledge to Jorge, the child whose birth she had foretold, whose mind she began to nurture from the time he uttered his first word. So he could grow up to receive her revelation, the last of his—and Adia's – line.

Ruben promised he would be there in a few days, and Jorge agreed to meet him at the house. Ruben arrived on an overcast day, and Jorge saw what it meant for a man of his uncle's standing to fall from grace. This time he came without his entourage or his bodyguards, driven in a borrowed car. He looked pitiful and weak as he came out of the vehicle, helped by his driver. His eyes looked small and vulnerable behind the thick glasses he had begun to wear.

The unhurried service took most of the morning, as cool gusts threatening rain blew through Santo Domingo church. Then, as the sky grew sullen, the mourners boarded their vehicles for the procession to St. Matthews. The faint echo of thunder pursued them from far away.

The sombre convoy travelled down the rutted road beyond the disused railway crossing. It reached the corner with the tamarind tree, then turned into the cemetery's driveway, following the route taken by the horse-drawn hearse for Rosanna years before.

Adia had survived her daughter by many years. Enough time to pass on the light of her mind to the boy she had raised. Adia had spent the years she had left trying to feed the fruit of her imaginings to her two grandsons, who had no inkling who she was. The failed mother who had tried to redeem herself too late was to be buried a few paces from the daughter she had abandoned.

Through the glass, Jorge studied Adia's face one last time. Her white, bobbed hair that she had always tied back with one of her tortoise-shell combs. The large brown eyes were closed on her kind, wide face, the mouth which till the end had retained a hint of its fullness in youth. Jorge began to shake. The woman who had raised him had vanished, and he didn't know where to look for her. He hurried off into the woods before the last rites.

Her tales were there, so alive, as if he had lived through them himself. Everything was so clear. Jorge could hear the cabriolets rumbling in the narrow streets so loudly Adia said they frightened her when she had first come to Puerto Reina.

Jorge walked back for the rites. He heard the rumble of thunder again as dark clouds massed above. At the crossing of two paths, he passed an old woman alone. She was standing near one of the crosses with a box at her feet. She gave a start when she saw Jorge. Her bright eyes followed him and her face lit up with recognition. A half smile formed on her face as Jorge stopped a few paces away.

'Thank you for the keys, my boy,' she said softly.

Jorge walked away from her, aware of the darkness gathering in the sky. She said after him, laughing, 'It's opened so many doors!'

With a chill, Jorge recalled Adia saying how she kept getting woken up by someone knocking on her door. He stopped and turned just in time to see the woman pick up her box and walk off into the woods.

Jorge shuddered as a much earlier memory came to him.

He recalled with horror that one of the three keys he had given to the peculiar woman from the interior was the key to Adia's door. He ran back through the trees but there was no sign of anyone there. All he saw was an old untended grave.

Many nights later Jorge lay awake thinking about the woman and the keys. He wondered if he could undo what he had done. In the end, he accepted that whatever followed had its seeds planted in those days long ago. Perhaps it was the price for knowing the uncanny wanderer's adamant secret. The price for glimpsing the mysteries that had brought the strange woman to their door.

Ruben asked Jorge to visit Adia with him before he returned to the capital. It was a quiet day after the rain.

They walked to Adia's mound. Adia's stone already looked fixed, absorbed into the greenery like a permanent part of the land. Ruben got down on one knee and fingered the letters on the marble.

'All her stories are now secrets of the earth,' he said. He and Jorge placed the flowers they had brought. Ruben stood up and the two men picked their way carefully on the wet stones of the path. Jorge found his uncle guiding him towards Rosanna's grave. Ruben stopped suddenly and touched Jorge's arm.

Jorge looked to where he was pointing. There were fresh flower's on Rosanna's stone. They stopped for a while and stood in silence. The scent of the roses mingled with the tang of wet moss.

Jorge followed Ruben around the chapel. Under the drenched trees, they saw a middle-aged woman on the path. She was the only other person in the cemetery that day.

She stopped abruptly when she saw them. Then, studying Ruben, she shook her head in disbelief. She rushed forward to touch him.

'Why it *is* you!' she said. 'How strange!'

Ruben peered at her with his tormented eyes. Slowly he shook off his doubt and replied, 'Why Sara! Yes. It has been so many years.'

'My husband Juan Rodrigo is buried here,' she pointed to a mound with a white cross. There were fresh roses on it like on Rosanna's grave.

'I visit them at the same time,' Sara smiled. 'I loved them both.'

Ruben looked up at the hazy sky.

'Oh!' Sara remembered. 'Perhaps I was meant to see you here today.'

She reached into her bag. 'I've been bringing this here for years, hoping to find someone of Rosanna's family.' Sara took out an object wrapped in cloth. 'I found this among my things one day. It was Rosanna's. Perhaps I should give it to you.'

She handed it to Ruben. He unwrapped it and found a hand mirror. He briefly examined it before passing it on to Jorge.

Jorge noticed that it had the same bone-inlay pattern as the mirror in his mother's room.

'We bought it in San Gabriel together,' Sara explained. 'A long time ago.'

She smiled. 'We were young. We did everything together. She and I believed that if we looked in our mirrors on a quiet night, we might see each other.'

They said their goodbyes.

Jorge and Ruben returned to the house. They walked around to the back and found the old chauffeur sitting on his haunches, crying. There was a half-eaten drumstick in his hand. He ate between sobs, sniffled, bit a large chunk out of the chicken, cried, chewed, then cried again.

Jorge walked upstairs, opening doors, running his hand on the banister as he came down to rejoin Ruben in the yard. His uncle was holding a faded picture of Adia he had found. 'She was my mother and I never knew what she thought,' he said. 'I'll never understand why she did the things she did.'

A light drizzle had begun to fall. Ruben drew himself up and took a deep breath. 'Let's go to the pier.'

He called the driver and had him bring a large bag from the car.

Jorge followed Ruben as he went through the rooms looking for the things that had belonged to Adia. They gathered up her little crucifix, a prayer book, a framed picture Adia had kept from Rosanna's First Communion. Then the two men silently went to Rosanna's room and collected what things of Jorge's mother they found there.

They got in the car and drove off.

When they reached Fort Road Jorge could clearly make out the villas facing the sea. Turning towards the window, Ruben cleared his throat. 'Sometimes your life feels like a sail hanging uselessly in the air,' he said, gazing out of occasional gaps in the rain-marbled window. 'Then the wind starts to blow and your sail fills out. You find yourself pulled relentlessly in some direction. As if some beacon were calling you somewhere.'

Ruben turned his head so his opaque gaze was fixed in front of him again. 'The force of the gusts won't stop,' he continued. 'Until suddenly you realise you've gone on a journey you had no intention of making. And it's brought you to a place you never thought you'd reach.'

Ruben was thoughtful for a moment. 'For better or worse, that's how I got to be where I am,' he said with an incredulous expression, as if startled by his own fate.

They had reached the pier.

Jorge and his uncle took out the bag and stood on the slippery, rain-soaked ground of the wharf. 'Lead me to the water's edge,' said Ruben.

Jorge slung the bag over his shoulder and they walked past the tower that he and Miguel used to climb.

'An old priest once told me that death is like a voyage to a very far coast,' said Ruben, walking beside Jorge. 'Many seas will have to be crossed. We will be forced to jettison everything we have come to hold dear. Even their memory will fade. Each sea crossed will add to the emptiness you feel.'

The two of them reached the wharf's edge and stopped.

'But in the end,' Ruben tried to catch his breath, 'you will swim in a great ocean, and everything will be washed away.'

In the distance they could see a group of islands.

'There's San Gabriel. The largest one.' Ruben pointed towards the islands on the hazy, dismal horizon. 'If you go past the headland you can see the wreck of the *San Gabriel*. My brother and I used to go with the fishermen to look at it for hours. It was like a gigantic shadow, far, far below. I wonder if Augusto will ever forget.'

It seemed for a moment that he had forgotten Augusto was long dead. Jorge looked in the bag and realised Ruben had also brought some of Augusto's things. They were there, mixed with Adia's and Rosanna's possessions.

'Can you see the headland?' asked Ruben. 'It's so strange that the ship sank there.'

Jorge knew that his uncle could barely see anything now, and all he could perceive were the things still lodged firmly in his memory.

'When you lose something, there's a chance you could go somewhere and still find it,' Ruben said, turning his back on Jorge now, looking seaward, rocking on the balls of his feet. His mind seemed to wander, a blind man picking his way through his bleak tangle of memories. 'But death is what forces us to hope that the farthest place can be reached,' Ruben said quietly. 'That someone lost can be touched again.'

He inched closer to the edge, and Jorge began to worry. Ruben seemed transfixed by something on the sea's distant rim.

'We know nothing about that far off place we're all going to,' he said. 'We have no inkling what it means, if anything.'

He turned around and Jorge was surprised to see the serene look on his face. 'Yet we are secretly drawn to it from the first moment of our lives.'

With that, Ruben reached down into the bag at his feet and started throwing things into the sea. They made little splashes in the oily surface of the water. After a while, Jorge started doing the same. They both plunged into the bag and threw out everything. Adia's crucifix and prayer book, Rosanna's Communion picture, her diary and hand mirror, and last, the amethyst rose from San Gabriel. Ruben threw out Augusto's books and Adia's combs.

'Goodbye, Augusto,' he said. 'Goodbye, Rosanna, my baby.'

And finally, in voices that both broke, they said, 'Goodbye, Adia.'

Jorge's friendship with Salvador del Mundo grew. But after some years, Salvador suffered a setback. His father lost his hand in an accident at the presses. After a long, vain struggle to get compensation, Salvador grew disillusioned. He was one of the first to try and leave the country. 'Maybe I can better save the world somewhere else,' he said.

Secretly he had been in the process of trying to find work abroad. So at the end of that year, Salvador quit his job at *El Tiempo* and sold all his possessions. He had taken the last steps towards emigration.

'I read that the first settlers on this archipelago were sea-farers,' said Salvador on his last meeting with Jorge. 'Some of them from as far away as Polynesia or Madagascar. People who, like us now, were blown by the seas, in search of better lives.'

Thus Jorge's friend left Puerto Reina. But he didn't sail away like people once did. Salvador and his family were one of the first to leave the city using the new airport, a simple runway with both ends tapering off into rice fields.

Salvador embraced Jorge at the gate, his sons wondering what could make their big, strong protector melt into tears. The fat, silver DC-10 into which Salvador's brood of little redeemers filed was Jorge's first sight of a departing plane carrying someone he loved. He wondered how it felt to see one's home seem so small from above the clouds.

In less than a year, Jorge himself would leave Puerto Reina. He would return only once, for a brief visit after many years. Jorge and his wife would search for the house in Aguada. They passed the spot several times before Jorge realised he was on the same river bank he had known as a child.

But the house was gone. Torn down and carted away again, perhaps to the orphanage, as Jorge had agreed with the nuns. The road to Aguada was straight and paved, and the tamarind tree had been cut down. They drove by one evening and there was no leaping dot of light that spun glowing webs to brighten the night for a boy who longed only for the darkness to end.

Jorge walked past the shell of a building where squatting families hung their bright-coloured clothes to dry. Bats roosted in the eaves above the delicate alcoves of the windows. They flew out at dusk, called out by the opening of flowers, erupting into the roseate light like the birds Juan Rodrigo watched with Rosanna long ago.

Only Jorge knew that the shattered façade belonged to what was once the Navy Club, the pride of the city, where young American officers danced in the summer heat with the beautiful daughters of sugar planters, smitten and jubilant while the city's splendour lasted.

But Puerto Reina was gone. All that remained was a lingering pang that made Jorge remember that forgotten port city of the East where he was born, the farthest outpost of an empire, last remnant of that grandiose, distant dream of Spain.

Only once did he ever see Adia again, in a dream, one cold, windy night in the dark northern country where he had gone to live. He saw her in a place where he also saw his mother. They were walking by the sea.

His mother stopped and bent down at the water's edge. She and Adia were smiling. The water was very clear. The sun's reflected glints played on their faces as they picked up Adia's crucifix from the sand, where the sea had washed it in. Rosanna's hand mirror and Adia's prayer book were there. All the things Ruben and Jorge had thrown into the sea all those years ago, scattered on the shore.

The two women began to walk away, towards the darkening horizon, and Jorge followed. As they waded deeper into the water, the sea surged and they were engulfed by waves. The briny, acrid lash of the tide stung Jorge's eyes. The pain in the dream was so real and searing, he woke up trembling, and found his face wet with tears.

END

www.ingramcontent.com/pod-product-compliance
Lightning Source LLC
Chambersburg PA
CBHW060211030726
47499CB00004B/1005